Sutter's Cross

W. DALE CRAMER

SUTTER'S CROSS

Minneapolis, Minnesota

Sutter's Cross

Cover design by Chris Gilbert, UDG Design Works

Published by Bethany House Publishers
A Ministry of Bethany Fellowship International
11400 Hampshire Avenue South
Bloomington, Minnesota 55438

Printed in the United States of America

ISBN 0-7394-3230-3

For the girl with the chestnut hair, and eyes
whose color, after all these years,
I still cannot name.

ACKNOWLEDGMENTS

First, last, and always, I thank God for showing me the keys.

There are several people without whom this book might never have been written or certainly wouldn't have turned out as well as it did:

My wife, Pam, who gave me the chance, and the courage, to try.

Lori Patrick—dear Barnabas, literary sounding board and theological watchdog, midwife to this work.

Terry Hadaway, who has always believed in me, and who taught me that writing is first communication and then art.

Larry McDonald, whose blue-jeans faith and servant's heart have taught me what it means to be the arms of God.

Janet Kobobel Grant—steadfast advocate, clear-eyed editor, trusted friend.

Luke Hinrichs, that rarest of finds: an editor who thinks like I do.

Elise Skidmore (who really is a force of nature) and her happy band of coconspirators in Section 6, who encouraged me when I needed it most.

Jay Knight, who generously shared his encyclopedic knowledge of real estate development.

Dr. Scott Baker, Becky Baker, and Dusty McDaniel, who gave me invaluable technical advice. Any glaring medical errors are my own.

Lori's friend Wendell, who was so generous with his time and priceless advice.

Gary and Paulette Hill, Patty Ivers, Bobbie Winkelman, Howard and Ann Cramer, and all the others who read early drafts and offered advice, criticism, and encouragement.

The people of MCC—my friends, my family.

And last but not least, Ty and Dusty, who may have sacrificed more than anyone else for this work.

W. DALE CRAMER lives in Georgia with his wife and two sons. This is his first novel.

Chapter One

"The first time I ever saw Harley, he was wearing my pants. I knew they were mine—they were the ones with the ink stain on the back pocket."

Jake Mahaffey

Jake started keeping a journal at the age of thirty-two precisely because of what happened that day at the picnic. Somehow it seemed important. It all began at the annual fried chicken and potato salad affair held by Sutter's Cross Community Church at the old pavilion down by the Elder River. Jake was standing by the tea table talking to Orde Wingo and filling a plastic cup from a jug marked Sweet Tea, when Orde spotted what appeared to be a homeless person in the buffet line. He peered over his glasses, nudged Jake, and pointed with his eyes.

"Friend of yours?"

Jake followed Orde's stare to the lanky intruder standing with his back to them, waiting in line with a paper plate in his hand.

"Nope, never seen him before. I would have figured him for one of your kinfolks if he didn't have so much hair," he said, and glanced sidelong at Orde's new toupee, the latest attempt to cover what had been the target of jokes for years; kids called him "Orde the Gourd" behind his back. "He's probably just a hiker passing through."

"I don't think so," Orde said. "I mean, *look* at him."

He had a point. The man stood out like a horsefly in a punch bowl. He came out of nowhere and showed up at the buffet table with a wild mop of dark hair, a week's growth of whiskers on his face, ill-fitting clothes, and without a trace of khaki. His boots were old and scuffed and muddy. They were work boots, definitely not L.L. Bean.

"Last time I saw something like that, it was living under an expressway bridge down in Atlanta," Orde muttered.

"I'll go talk to him," Jake said. He was something of an outsider himself, having moved into the valley only ten years before, after marrying Lori. He figured he'd better do something before Orde did.

"Well, if you're going to tell him to hit the bricks, do it quietly, Jake. We don't want a scene."

Jake shook his head. "I don't think we should run him off. If he's hungry, I say let him eat. There's plenty of food, and he's not bothering anybody." He sipped his tea and stared at the ink stain. "I just want to know why he's wearing my pants."

He was ten feet away before he heard Orde's startled reaction: "Your *what*?"

Jake took a paper plate and fell in line behind his jeans. He expected to encounter a wave of body odor but he didn't; all he smelled was fried chicken.

"Excuse me," he said. "I'm Jake Mahaffey. I don't believe we've met."

The stranger turned. His hair, flecked with leaf matter and infringing on his face, had the same dull chaotic quality Jake had seen in his retriever's coat right before it died. The man's face was a twisted geography of misfortune and abuse: a faint purple-and-yellow bruise tinged the left jaw from ear to chin, and a dry but unsutured cut zigged like a black lightning bolt across his cheekbone. Oddest of all, his face looked warped, reminding Jake of an old pine board. He held his chin way over to the right, Popeye style, which made him appear belligerent. Or stupid. Or both.

But he held Jake for a moment with calm gray eyes, long enough for Jake to see something. His eyes smiled a little at the corners but they didn't laugh—definitely not the eyes of a dull mind. Already, in those first few seconds, Jake had begun to sense a quiet, transcendent awareness.

A stillness.

The stranger fumbled the plate to his left hand so he could shake with his right. The beginnings of a smile parted his lips for a second, then he winced and the smile went away. The sinewy strength of his hand told Jake he wasn't a bum or an accountant, but someone acquainted with hard work. He still hadn't spoken, and Jake was beginning to wonder if he could.

"Do you have a name?" Jake asked gently. He half expected the man to answer in sign language.

The stranger looked at his plate, then his gaze wandered away beyond the rocks, down to the river. The pavilion stood on a low rocky promontory that jutted out into a horseshoe bend where the Elder River ran slow and deep and green, undercutting the steep ridge on the far side and gathering itself for a thundering leap over the falls half a mile downstream. Children loved to pick their way down to the little stretch of beach on the point and play in the numbing cold water while their mothers sat on the rocks hugging their knees, fretting, ever conscious of the current with the falls so near, where the river plummeted two hundred feet into a rocky gorge. The man stared for nearly a minute at the deepest part of the pool down near the falls, as if he'd entirely forgotten the question. Then his features lifted slightly.

"Harley," he finally announced, turning back to Jake and pronouncing the name with a nod and an air of satisfaction. Tumbling from the side of his mouth as it did, his deep voice sounded like a third-rate Elvis impersonation.

"Nice to meet you, Harley. You live around here?"

He hesitated, then nodded slowly, eyes drifting downward. Without another word he picked up his plastic fork and his napkin, turned away, and wandered off toward an empty table.

Built in the 1920s, the pavilion's great polished pine logs had been hand-fitted and pegged together in intricate joints so tight a piece of paper wouldn't fit between them. Even someone lacking Jake's appreciation of the finer points of carpentry could see—or *feel*—the unity, the monolithic solidity of the structure. The floor was a mosaic of granite slabs cut from a local quarry. A magnificent stone fireplace buttressed one end of the building, a fireplace big enough to barbecue a whole hog, which it had done on many occasions. Despite its age, the pavilion was so well designed that it required no maintenance apart from the occasional replacement of a few cedar shakes on the roof. The building was wide enough to accommodate four picnic tables jammed end to end the short way across the floor, and at times like this, when the crowd didn't fill half of the tables, people congregated near the end with the fireplace. Harley went directly to an empty table just clear of the crowd and sat with his back to them.

Jake felt the need for reinforcements, but Lori was sitting at a packed table listening to Nell Prudhomme, nodding politely, and he couldn't get her attention. Even if he had, it wouldn't have mattered; once Nell locked on, she wouldn't let go until it thundered. Lori was too polite to excuse herself in the middle of a sentence, and Nell ended every sentence with "and, ah..."

He filled his plate and made his way to Harley's table, stoking his resolve. Harley didn't say anything when Jake sat down across from him. Instead, he glanced over his shoulder at the crowd, then flashed the merest suggestion of a wry smile, as if he had been expecting somebody to come question him and he was faintly amused by it.

Jake inspected a chicken leg, hesitating, then made his move.

"You're wearing my pants." He said it mostly to the chicken leg.

Dark eyebrows furrowed for a moment while Harley worried a deviled egg down to clear the way for words to form in his twisted maw.

"I paid for 'em," he finally drawled.

He was serious.

Jake wasn't sure *how* he knew, but he knew what Harley meant. Two days earlier he had cut a blown-down red oak into firewood lengths and left it there, intending to come back later to split and stack it. When he came home the next afternoon the wood was all split and neatly stacked in the woodshed, nearly a cord of it. He had no idea who had done it until now.

"And the box said Goodwill," Harley added.

Jake hadn't seen the jeans for a couple of weeks, but he figured they had gotten lost in the Laundry Triangle. Shirts had been known to disappear for as long as three months before turning up again in the closet. He would have a word with Lori later about consigning his best old Saturday jeans to the Goodwill box in the garage without his consent or at least an opportunity to say good-bye. He recognized the T-shirt, too. Though he was a little concerned about a stranger rummaging around in his garage, it didn't really matter. Harley could *have* the clothes as far as Jake was concerned, but he had to know why a man would steal a pair of jeans.

"It's all right," he said, "but why did you take them?"

Harley tilted his head and stared, as if to question Jake's sanity. "I was cold," he said.

"But where were *your* pants?" Jake was flipping through mental images, picturing a strange man arriving at his house—six miles from the nearest town and twenty from the next—without his pants.

"Long story," Harley said, and tried to smile again.

So much for resolve.

Jake watched him eat. He was eating potato salad, a whole big plateful of it, taking small bites and chewing deliberately. Apart from a few deviled eggs, there was nothing else on his plate. Jake decided to take a different tack.

"You like potato salad?"

Harley winced and shuddered, contorting his bent face as he shook his head.

The man was nuts. Jake gave up and settled into his dinner. He thought maybe Harley would open up on his own if he was patient, but after a while it became clear that he had no such intention. Harley seemed perfectly content to sit here taking dainty bites of potato salad and shuddering in silence. Reluctantly Jake decided to make a gesture.

"Look, if you need help, maybe we could do something for you. You know, if you need clothes, a bus ticket..."

Harley wasn't listening. Fork frozen halfway to his mouth, head turned, neck craned, he stared across the chattering heads toward where Lori sat, as if he had heard his name called and wasn't sure who had done it.

Jake followed the direction of his gaze but saw nothing out of the ordinary. Everybody was eating, laughing, talking—not one face showing the slightest concern.

Harley dropped his fork, swung his legs out from under the picnic table, stood up, and took one long stride toward the next row of tables before his arms sprang up and his body followed. A size eleven work boot smashed down on a crowded tabletop, and Penny Thorson, seated on the other side, caught the contents of a blue plastic teacup full in her petrified face. A basket of dinner rolls pinwheeled through the air behind Harley as he vaulted to the next row. He leaped from the second row of tables, landed short of the third, and skidded up behind Miss Agnes Dewberry, who was bent curiously low over her plate. His momentum carried him crashing into Miss Agnes's back, where in one swift motion he braced a leg under the bench, wrapped his arms about her rib cage, then heaved her backward, up and clear of her seat.

Dunbar Thornton was sitting next to Miss Agnes when Harley snatched her up. Dun was a soft-spoken man in his early fifties, humane and gentle. But when he saw the seventy-three-year-old widow jerked up like a rag doll by a berserk hobo, Dun went animal. Harley double-clutched Miss Agnes twice in a deathly bear hug before Dun lunged from the bench and smashed a fist into his jaw.

People screamed and scuttled out of the way. Others cowered in their seats, gaping, paralyzed by indecision. Still others rushed into the fray. Jake fought his way through in time to see Lori scrambling across the tabletop, scattering plates and cups in a clearly insane move to get between the two deranged men.

When Dun hit him, Harley dropped Miss Agnes as quickly as he had grabbed her. Hands caught her before she fell to the stones; other hands swept a table clear and laid her out on it while a separate mob tackled Harley aside, pinning him to the floor. Lori ended up kneeling beside Harley. She cradled his head in her lap, shielding him.

Dunbar Thornton bucked against the two men who restrained him, his face tight with rage.

Lori's voice rose above the din. "She was CHOKING!"

The clamor of voices died. Lori brushed a shock of red hair back from her face and, just like that, composed herself.

"Nobody saw," she said. "She was sitting right in front of me, and even I didn't see. She was laughing, and then she bent over. I couldn't see her face. When he grabbed her up she was blue. *This* came out of her." She held out her fist toward Dunbar Thornton and opened it to reveal a half-chewed chunk of fried chicken the size of her thumb.

Dun's face sagged as understanding rolled over him. He turned then and went to see about Miss Agnes. She could be heard coughing, mumbling. She would be okay.

As soon as Dun turned away, Lori's eyes found Jake. She was still breathing hard, but he could see anger and fear subsiding from her flushed face, replaced by something else—a question, burning so bright he could feel it.

How did he know?

Harley made no attempt to get up. He lay pale and sweating with his head in Lori's lap, his eyes closed, brow deeply furrowed, a trickle of dark blood running into his ear from the cut on his cheek. A shiver ran down him.

"His jaw's broken," Lori said, "and from the looks of it, I'd say it was broken before Dun hit him. He needs to go to the hospital."

Jake wondered how he could have missed it. A broken jaw would explain the potato salad, and maybe the hospital could learn the rest.

Web Holcombe spent that Sunday as he did every Sunday when the weather was good—soaring. Tan and trim, his five-foot-ten frame fit neatly under the polished Lexan canopy of the sleek carbon-fiber sailplane, the latest high-tech "glass slipper" from Germany. It came with a lofty price tag—more than most people's houses—but money was not a problem for Web Holcombe. Wavy salt-and-pepper hair hooded by a tennis hat, blue eyes hidden behind aviator sunglasses, his face oscillated from side to side, absorbing every nuance of earth and sky as he ghosted over the quilted farmlands at the western edge of the mountains. If another plane came within ten miles, he saw it and mentally logged its speed, altitude, and direction. He memorized every cumulus cloud, cataloguing it as a tight, growing plume, which might mark a useful thermal, or a spent bag of mist, falling apart and releasing a downdraft. Every smokestack within twenty miles told him wind direction. The whine of the wind over the canopy told him his airspeed within a knot or two without looking at his instruments. Stick and rudder fed constant input through his fingers and toes about the attitude of the craft. The pit of his stomach told him when he entered a thermal.

For Web, soaring was a metaphor for life: Understand your environment and the laws of its movement, know your limitations and your strengths, command your ship and yourself, and you can soar higher, faster, farther than the next man. Soaring stripped away pretense and reduced life to its basic elements—awareness and control.

It was his only religion.

Unlike the jagged silhouette of the brash young Rockies, the ancient Appalachians had been worn smooth by endless cycles of freeze, fracture, and thaw and were covered in a seamless forest so that the mountains stretched before the eye in gentle, rounded swells like the sleeping body of a woman under a vast green blanket. Here, Web found hours of utter serenity, where he was able to escape the endless parade of real estate agents, bankers, bureaucrats, inspectors, and contractors who crowded his workday with ringing phones and bargaining sessions—the wheeling-and-dealing, thrust-and-parry, bluff-and-call, angst-ridden game that consumes the life of a major developer. Here in his sailplane was the only place he did not wear a beeper. Basking in the silence, he seldom even turned on the NavCom. He came up here to decompress.

In his customary soaring clothes—an old T-shirt and shorts—the cooler air above four thousand feet chilled him a little, and he scratched absently at the hand-sized doughy scar on his left thigh. The nerves underneath, once burned away and mangled, had never quite grown back through the scar tissue, and sometimes a rapid temperature change caused them to itch. He scratched until he became aware of what he was doing and stopped. The scar was a souvenir of Vietnam, a memory that, once raised, led inexorably to his father. Buried nerve endings and dead fathers wouldn't be satisfied. Scratch all you want; the itch won't go away.

He shook himself and focused his thoughts on piloting. It was a fine day with tall, strong thermals, and Web stayed aloft most of the afternoon before slipping back onto the smooth turf airstrip and coasting in a graceful curve up to the hangar. Balanced precisely on its one main wheel, the sailplane remained level until it came to a complete stop, and then it slowly tilted, lowering one wing tip delicately to the grass.

After securing his plane, Web walked down past the hangar to the clubhouse in the shade of an old live oak in search of something cold to drink. A half a dozen pilots were gathered on the portico outside the clubhouse, and as Web approached he noticed a palpable gloom among them. Normally animated and talkative after a day's soaring, now they were silent, staring at their feet or off into the blue distance. Web stopped at the edge of the portico, pulled the tennis hat from his head, and wiped the back of his neck with it.

"What's everybody so happy about?"

Grant Cummings, a surgeon from Chattanooga, raised his head, nodded to Web. "I guess you haven't heard. Bob's selling the gliderport."

Web flinched. The news hit him like a baseball bat. "He's selling out? Why?"

"BMW wants to put a manufacturing plant here." Grant pointed down toward the river. "There's a fresh water source, an expressway, a railroad, and lots of cheap labor out here in the country."

"He's already made up his mind?"

"Yep. It'll be gone by the end of the year."

"But why? Bob *loves* this place."

Grant shrugged. "Sure, he loves it, but he's pushing sixty. His last medical said his eyes were borderline, which started him thinking about retirement. The Bavarian Motor Works has deep pockets. They made him an offer he couldn't turn down. Simple as that."

"Where will everybody go?"

"Most of us will go over to Sequatchie, I guess. Not much difference if you can put up with the FBO over there."

This was not an isolated occurrence. Sailplanes were becoming an endangered species due to loss of habitat; remote locations meeting the geographic requirements of a soaring operation were getting scarce. Web knew every gliderport within three hundred miles, and the Blue Ridge Gliderport was the only one within driving distance of Sutter's Cross. Sequatchie would add another hour to his travel time, each way. This was not acceptable; the trip already took nearly two hours each way.

"Where's Bob?"

"He's up giving a tow right now. He'll be back in a few minutes, but it won't do you any good to talk to him—he's already signed the contract."

"Look at it this way," Jake told Dun Thornton in the fluorescent-washed tile hallway of the emergency room, "if you hadn't hit him, he probably wouldn't be here now getting his jaw fixed. You couldn't have known what he was doing."

Both Harley and Miss Agnes were being attended to behind the curtains. Dun opened his mouth to answer, but an apple-faced young doctor appeared and turned abruptly to Jake.

"Your friend is going to have to spend the night," the doctor said. "His airway and lungs are clear, circulation's good, heart sounds okay. He appears to be malnourished, but right now we're more concerned about the extent of his injuries."

"Injuries? You mean something other than his jaw?"

The doctor scratched his head. "That's just it—we don't know yet. He has some contusions and a fractured jaw, obviously. There are some deep bruises on his legs, but we need to check for trauma to his head. When a patient presents with a malocclusion such as his and we have no history on him, no standard of reference for his mental state, we have to rule out concomitant head and neck injuries. What happened to him? Did I hear somebody say something about a fight?"

Dun ran a thumb over his bruised knuckles.

Jake chuckled, picturing tomorrow's headline in the *Gazette*: Homeless Man Injured in Church Picnic Brawl.

"No... well, there was a scuffle, but I think he was hurt before that."

"How?"

"I don't know."

The doctor made a note on the clipboard. "So you think this altercation may have exacerbated a preexisting condition."

"Uh, yeah."

"Okay. I've sent him down to radiology. I'm sure we're going to have to wire his jaw. Barring any unforeseen difficulties, he'll be here overnight and will have to eat through a straw for a few weeks. Any questions?"

Jake shook his head, shrugged.

The young doctor nodded curtly, turned to walk away, then stopped. "Oh, one other thing. He wouldn't, or couldn't, give the nurse any information about himself apart from scrawling the name Harley on the form. I'm told he's a vagrant. He has no ID, and nobody seems to know who he is. Do you?"

"Nope. I probably know less than you do. Is that a problem? I mean, you'll still treat him, right?"

Dun spoke up. "You give him whatever he needs, Doctor. I'll see that his bill is paid."

"Okay, that'll be fine. I'd still like to know who the man is, though. It would be nice to know where to find his medical records, that's all." He glanced at his watch, said "Later," and bustled away.

Scanning the crowd in the waiting room, Jake saw a handful of Miss Agnes's friends from the picnic and a few other people waiting for treatment—a four-hundred-pound man in overalls with a rattling chest cough and a haggard young couple chasing two toddlers in different directions—but no sign of Lori. A friend saw him searching and pointed to the exit.

Outside, he found Lori leaning against a brick column on the other side of the portico, hugging herself, gazing out across the parking lot, and chewing on her bottom lip.

Jake had first come to Sutter's Cross on a kayaking trip, right after he dropped out of college. He went to the river that morning proud and invincible and came away that afternoon terrified and humble. He had gotten upside-down in a wicked hydraulic that ripped him out of his kayak, sucked him under and held him, rolling and tumbling, until he passed out. Two friends managed to pull him out and resuscitate him, but he left the river feeling small and demoralized, swearing he'd never get wet again if he could help it. He never even went back for the kayak.

On the way out of town he stopped at a little roadside fruit stand, mostly because he was still too shaken to drive; he was looking for any excuse to pull over for a few minutes. And there, selling peaches on the side of the road, he found a summer strawberry of a girl with the face of an angel and eyes that seemed to know everything about him. He ate peaches until he was sick, trying to work up the nerve to talk to her, but she was too perfect. He never got beyond telling her how good the peaches were, never even asked her name. Finally, as he was leaving, she smiled and told him he'd forgotten his receipt. She picked up a little pad, scribbled on it, tore off the sheet and handed it to him. Across the top were the printed legend

Durham Farms and a phone number. Underneath was the handwritten name Lori Durham. A year later they were married.

Over the next few years Jake learned that, unlike him, Lori seldom said what she was thinking. He'd learned to read her face, her body language. She only chewed on her bottom lip, the way she was doing now, when she was hurting inside. He'd seen it often enough; they had weathered their share of storms. He saw it after her father died of a stroke, and he saw it a lot the year they spent watching her mother waste away with cancer.

She stood hugging herself, chewing on her lip and staring into space.

"I'm sorry," he mumbled, folding her into his arms. "I'm sorry. It just didn't dawn on me in the middle of all this craziness. This is the first time you've been here since..."

"It's okay," she whispered. "It's just, you know, coming back here...I try not to see her that way."

The hospital held Miss Agnes for a few hours, for observation. But when she got up and started yelling at the nurse to go find her shoes, they decided they had observed enough and released her.

Jake and Lori hung around until Harley was wired, sedated, and sleeping soundly in his room. Sometime in the wee hours he got up, dressed himself, and disappeared into the night.

Chapter Two

The town of Sutter's Cross lies on the western slope of a valley where the last long fingers of the Appalachians dip down into Georgia. It's a lovely valley, a place of cleft and crag and deep green shadows veined with crystal creeks, where cold water slips over round stones and under snags of moss-carpeted deadwood, where deer flash through groves of old-growth hemlock and trout hover in dark pools, undulating with the pulse of the hills. As with all beautiful places, the earth here has been watered by the blood of men who have fought for dominion over it—the blood of Americans and Englishmen and Frenchmen and Spaniards, and before that the Cherokee and the Creek. Always, the price of dominion was blood.

The first American settler came after the War of 1812 with a piece of paper naming him lord of the valley in payment for meritorious service in the war, but the harsh winter of 1817 exacted a greater price from Emanuel Sutter when it claimed his eldest son, his pride and joy. Sutter buried the boy in a hillside glade and then, to assuage his grief, hewed two great beams of chestnut and fitted them together, hitched an ox to the giant cross, and drew it up and dropped it into a hole at the head of the grave. Early pilgrims pushing westward through the relentless forest breathed easier when they crested the eastern gap and saw the cross gleaming in the sun on the other side of the valley. For *Sutter's Cross* was etched next to the Elder River on their simple hand-drawn maps, and they knew when they saw the cross they were on the right trail.

After the last of the Cherokee were hauled away in 1838, a town began to form in the hillside cove—a blacksmith shop and livery stable, a dry-goods store. In the clearing behind the cross the settlers built a small white church, which doubled as a schoolhouse. Homesteads sprang up in the rich bottomland around the Elder River; farmers and timbermen grappled with mule teams to feed their families.

But there was only so much bottomland. The Civil War decimated the population, the chestnut blight crippled the timber industry, and the Depression drove young men out in search of work. No railroad spur ever came up the Elder Valley, the river was never navigable by anything bigger than a six-man raft, electricity was very late in coming, and the great ribbons of pavement that carried a tide of industry and trade always seemed to go elsewhere, leaving Sutter's Cross languishing in a forgotten corner of the mountains. When Web's father, Will Holcombe, stumbled across the town on a fishing trip in 1948 he found it a veritable ghost town, a collection of peeling buildings and rusting junk in weeded lots.

But the Elder Valley captured his heart. Will Holcombe had found paradise and he knew it. He spent a week hiking the ridges, soaking up the views, often standing stock-still for hours in the cool twilight of the deep forest, listening.

He bought thousands of acres around the valley, and he bought it very cheaply too, for most of it was unworkable ridge-top land, considered worthless by the earthbound squatters in the valley. He built a cabin on the lower slopes of Laurel Ridge just north of town and made it his custom from the time his children were very small to bring his family there for the summer.

Will Holcombe continued to sell real estate in suburban Atlanta, but he also undertook projects like prevailing upon the state to pave the main road through Sutter's Cross. Later on, he convinced the county to build a municipal golf course in the valley at the foot of Laurel Ridge. Over the years he quietly spread the word among his friends in Atlanta about the hidden retreat in the cool, blue mountains where his family eluded the crippling heat of the Georgia summer. Gradually Sutter's Cross became the private playground and best-kept secret of a small clique of wealthy, commerce-weary men who went there with fly rod in hand to wade the creeks like the little boys they had always envied. And Will Holcombe, over the years, gained the respect and admiration of even the most xenophobic of native mountain folk in Sutter's Cross.

Web Holcombe grew up harvesting golden memories of barefoot summers in the mountains. Despite the fact that during his youth he lived most of the year in a suburb of Atlanta, Web came to think of Sutter's Cross as his home. Perhaps more importantly, having summered in a town where everybody worshiped his father with serflike fealty, he learned to think of Sutter's Cross as his *domain.*

But the boy who had been Web Holcombe left his sun-splashed world behind after crossing swords with his father that hateful summer—the summer after he graduated high school—and the town of Sutter's Cross was ill prepared for the man who returned two years later. The Web Holcombe who came back from Vietnam was no barefooted boy.

He laid siege to Sutter's Cross with the energy and intensity of a man driven by a ghost. In ten short years he transformed the town, almost single-handedly, from a sleepy hamlet to a thriving tourist mecca, an upscale retreat on the cutting edge of commercial viability. Some said he was a genius, a visionary. Some said he was merely ruthless.

The only time Web looked up from his creation was when he courted and married Jenny Prescott, a former Miss Georgia from the cream of Atlanta society. He brought her home to Sutter's Cross and built her a house worthy of Rhett and Scarlett. The Holcombe mansion on Laurel Ridge was officially called a "federal-style planter's house," characterized by the thirty-foot columns that flanked the front porch and the balcony directly above the front door. Web had wanted to build something more modern, but this was Jenny's domain; he bowed to her taste and proceeded to build the finest, and possibly the largest, plantation house in the state. From the wide, curving, ornately balustraded mahogany staircase to the state-of-the-art warm-water heating system underneath the marble floors, to the gold fixtures in the bathrooms, Web spared no expense.

Shortly after Web and Jenny moved into the mansion on Laurel Ridge, Eddy was born.

All through little Eddy's toddler years, the years of diapers and bottles and safety latches and endless hovering, motherly vigilance, Jenny complained that she had no life. It was true—a child, particularly one like Eddy, could be the most demanding creature on earth—so when Eddy was four years old, Jenny hired Myra Banks as a live-in maid, and Marcus came with the deal. Jenny would bear no more children, and over the next eight years Marcus Banks became the closest thing to a brother that Eddy Holcombe would ever know.

The bond between Eddy and Marcus was forged from the mystical stuff of summer: great shoulder-to-shoulder quixotic charges against impossible odds, pelting a wasp nest with rocks and beating a higgledy-piggledy retreat to the river swatting wasps off each other's backs; the smells of dust and leather that would forever conjure images of sandlot baseball heroics; the distant plaintive call of a mother's voice as bats are shouldered and boys turn toward the yellow lights of home, laughing and punching, raking sweat-cooled hair from foreheads, satisfied for today. These were the purest rays of untarnished youth, bits of joy and pain their minds would gather and sew together to keep, like an extra quilt, for when they grew old and lay dying.

By the age of twelve, Eddy and Marcus had grown similar in many ways. The two shared the same height, the same gangly preteen build, the same long baggy shorts, overlarge T-shirts, and high-top athletic shoes. But they had their differences, too. Some people said Marcus was slow. Eddy didn't seem to notice, and Marcus figured people only said it because of the awkward way he ran, with his arms flailing about. Other kids seldom mentioned his awkwardness, but they never failed to notice the way his ears stuck straight out. Kids could be cruel. Some of them made up nicknames for the black kid with the chimp ears, although they learned not to do this when Eddy was around.

School had been out for less than a week, and already Marcus was bored.

"Come on, Three, let's go *do* something." He tried again to get Eddy's head out of the video game.

He always called Eddy "Three" because the only son of Web Holcombe didn't seem big enough to wear a name like William Edward Bonner Holcombe III, and Marcus found the Roman numerals endlessly amusing, hence the nickname.

"Yo, Three!" Marcus waved his hand in front of Eddy's face, with no apparent effect. "Come on, man, let's go! I can't beat you at this game. You win, okay? Now let's *go.*"

Eddy's glare remained glued to the TV screen, his thumbs dancing on the game pad, defending the left flank of the Rebel Fleet from Empire Invaders.

Marcus reached across him and yanked the plug from the machine.

The TV screen blipped into static oblivion and still Eddy remained transfixed, his thumbs blazing away. Marcus pulled Eddy's cap off and swatted him with it.

Eddy dropped the game pad and wrestled his cap away from Marcus. He stared at it for a few seconds, then ran his thumb over the green liner underneath the bill where Marcus had inscribed a large Roman numeral III with a felt-tip marker. "Don't *mess* with my lucky hat," he said and snugged it on his head again, backwards. "Okay, so what are we gonna do?"

"Go swimming."

"Too cold. Besides, I'm pitching tonight. Coach said not to swim on game days."

"Okay, let's go down to the golf course and pull balls out of the water. We can sell them, like last time."

Eddy blew him a raspberry. "Too much hassle," he said. "Besides, that security guard's still there."

"Oh yeah... Hey, let's go four-wheeling! We can ride down to the river and see if those girls are there."

Eddy sighed. "All right. But I get to drive."

"Aw, man—"

"It's my four-wheeler."

They found Jenny in her studio, rich blond hair tied haphazardly on top of her head with a red ribbon to keep it out of the paint. She was wearing an old paint-spattered smock and nibbling absently at the wooden end of a thin brush, studying her latest work in progress.

"Mom," Eddy said, "me and Marcus are going four-wheeling."

"Uh-huh," she mumbled without taking her eyes from the painting or the brush from her teeth.

"We'll be back Tuesday."

"All right."

Marcus tugged quietly at Eddy's arm.

"We're just gonna practice sitting backwards on the handlebars and riding down the center line of the highway."

"Okay, be careful," she mumbled.

Marcus's mother was a different story. Myra Banks made them eat lunch first, then stood in the kitchen doorway with her arms folded and lectured them.

"You be back by five-thirty, you hear me? You got a game tonight. Show up late for supper and I'll dump it out—you can go to bed hungry."

They nodded, taking her blustering, vain threats for what they were. No one would ever go to bed hungry in the Holcombe house.

"Don't cross the road, and don't you go near the river! And stay away from that construction site!"

Marcus gave his mother a thumbs-up. Eddy clicked the gearshift with his left foot, thumbed the throttle, and guided the four-wheeler carefully down the brick-lined path through the flower garden with Marcus clinging to his back. A quarter of a mile into the forest he turned off the trail and jockeyed over the low bank of Pearl Creek, turning downhill, bouncing along the gentle rocky course, under the concrete bridge and on down toward the river. Technically they had not crossed the road.

The trail down to the river from the Holcombe estate might have been a path through a virgin rainforest; maple, oak, and poplar trees in vigorous early summer splendor cast a high, dense shade over a forest floor thick with succulent ferns, dotted here and there with the purple stars of spiderwort. Though the spring wildflowers were spent, rain had been plentiful and the woods still wore the magic new green of spring, unblemished as yet by the work of insects and the dusty, dulling effect of late summer drought.

But the eyes of boys adjust to such things. For Eddy and Marcus these woods were simply home, and the lushness of Eden, to their eager eyes, was only the stuff they passed on the way to where they were going.

There were no girls by the river that day. They entertained themselves for a while by throwing rocks at a turtle until the turtle wisely sought shelter on the bottom. They worked to build a dam of rocks and limbs until the river proved to them it wouldn't be contained. They looked for snakes until they began to be afraid they might find one. Finally they discovered the tree.

The dark, ancient red oak leaned out over the river, its gnarled roots undercut and exposed by the currents. The boys found they could reach the lowest limb on the landward side by pulling the four-wheeler underneath it and standing on the handlebars. When they climbed around to the two great limbs forking out over the water, Eddy saw that the limbs were exactly even with each other and, because of the leaning of the tree, nearly level—the perfect foundation for a tree house.

Marcus was skeptical. "We can't build no tree house, Three. We don't have no stuff."

Eddy grinned that little sideways grin, the one Marcus had learned to equate with trouble.

"Ain't no can't, Marcus. Come on, let's go see what we can find."

They approached the construction site from the forested side on foot, quietly, leaving the four-wheeler far behind in the woods, then bellied down side by side on a dirt pile to see if the coast was clear. The two-story house was in the middle stages of construction—inside walls exposed, wires and pipes showing here and there. There was no one in sight, no work noises, no trucks in the yard.

Marcus found a claw hammer someone had left lying on a windowsill. They filled their pockets from a fifty-pound box of twelve-penny nails and found a pile of scrap lumber in back of the house with more two-by-fours and one-by-sixes than they would ever need. For Marcus, the worst part of the whole ordeal was the trip back to the river with a pile of lumber in his lap. Ripping between the trees, he expected any moment to snag a board and get knocked off the back of the four-wheeler.

A moment of tension arose when it came time to actually drive nails; there was only one hammer.

"I'm driving the nails," Eddy said.

"No you're not. It's my hammer."

"It was my idea. Besides, you can't hit diddly. What's your batting average?"

Marcus's face clouded. Eddy's remark was unfair, even if it was true. "It's *still* my hammer, Three. Maybe I need the practice."

They tried taking turns for a while, but Marcus couldn't do it. He'd try to start a nail, holding it like a pencil and punching at it with the hammer, his tongue stuck out the side of his mouth in concentration, but if he tried to swing with any force at all he would strike a glancing blow and send the nail pinging off into space, or miss entirely and mash a fingertip, which had the same result—reflexes snatching the hand back and flinging the nail into the river. When it came Eddy's turn, Marcus watched his every move. The way he held the hammer and the nail, his grip, how much he choked up, how far he spread his fingers, where he placed his thumb, how much backswing, how many strokes to sink a twelve-penny nail. Marcus studied hard and tried to etch the moves in his mind. His fingers curled unconsciously as he watched Eddy grip the hammer and swing. He watched and he remembered, but when it came time to drive a nail his fingers felt weak and disobedient, his arm would not quite do as it was told, his timing was off, and he missed more often than not.

The platform came together slowly. It wasn't perfect. It leaned a little to one side, some of the nails were driven halfway in, bent and flattened like shiny worms beside the other nailheads, and the boards stuck out from the sides at all different lengths for want of a saw. But on the whole it was a good, wide, solid platform that rested fifteen feet above the river.

Marcus sat back against the tree trunk hugging his knees while Eddy started figuring how to build walls. Eddy crawled around the sides, thinking, probing, mumbling to himself. Near the outer edge a sprig hung down from a higher branch. Wearing his cap backwards as always, Eddy leaned out to spit off the end of the platform. When he pulled back, the twig caught the bill of his cap and flicked it spiraling down into the river. Quick as thought, Eddy planted a palm on the outermost board and vaulted into space after his cap.

"THREE!" screamed Marcus, flinging himself across the platform onto his belly in time to see Eddy plunge into waist-deep water, narrowly missing a boulder.

Eddy spluttered to his feet and bolted downstream, half wading, half running, stumbling, splashing, finally catching up with his cap in the middle of a small string of rapids. Feigning an exaggerated dignity, he stood up, squared his shoulders and solemnly snugged his cap, full of water, on his head. He crossed his arms on his chest, blew a rooster tail through the water streaming down his face, and flashed Marcus his best idiot grin.

Marcus shouted, "You a FOOL, Three!"

Eddy grinned even wider. "But I got my cap back, didn't I?"

"You *still* a fool! You can't go jumping without looking. Fool."

"Ain't no can't," Eddy said, beaming, "only don't."

"Well, *don't* go trying to kill yourself no more, okay?"

Chapter Three

Jake nearly forgot about Harley over the next few weeks, figuring he had passed on like a summer storm. For a week, the story of the incident at the church picnic flowed around town changing in hue and intensity, depending upon who told it, but after everyone had a chance at the telling, including a host of people who weren't even there, the story lost its glamour. Then, some weeks later, a young couple just in from a long hike told Jake about seeing a tall dark man doing a weird dance up on Joshua's Knee, dangerously near the edge. They had kept their distance; they thought he was crazy. A stork dance, they called it.

Soon afterward, one June evening Pug Mabry went into insulin shock while poaching deer on Chestnut Ridge up above Miss Agnes Dewberry's house. He was alone and nobody knew where he was. By rights he should have lain there and died, but instead he woke up in the hospital. Miss Agnes brought him to Holcombe Regional in the back of her old pickup truck, a fact which on its own didn't seem strange at all, except that Pug had been poaching deer *above* the escarpment, a good half a mile from Miss Agnes's house—a half mile of steep, treacherous, moss-slick rock. Jake couldn't picture Miss Agnes, at dusk, hefting Pug's two-hundred-pound frame up across her shoulders, working her way goatlike down the face, and tossing him in the back of her truck.

Miss Agnes Dewberry's husband, Wilbur, had died in his sleep three years before. She lived just up the road from Jake and Lori's place, and they saw her at church occasionally if the weather was good and she felt like driving. She had always treated them like family. After Wilbur died they gradually adopted her as their own, stopping by every now and then to make sure she was okay and to see if she needed anything. There were a lot of conveniences Miss Agnes could live without, most of which made noise of one kind or another, which is why she didn't have a phone. Jake often used that excuse to stop in and see her, but his main reason for stopping by was that his grandmother died when he was a kid and he missed her. In the summer he usually got a sackful of homegrown tomatoes out of the deal.

The long driveway from River Road up to the old clapboard house was a rutted-out dirt-and-rock washboard that tunneled its way through a dense forest of ash, beech, and tulip poplar. It looked more like a creek bed than a driveway. The house sat in the flat about halfway between the escarpment and the river, among its children: two storage sheds, a dilapidated smokehouse, and a barn with a drive-through in the middle where an old Ford pickup sat nose to nose with a tractor.

When Jake pulled up in the yard a black-and-tan coonhound crawled out from under the porch, stretched, yawned, and posted himself by the steps, pawing at an ear with his hind foot. Past the south end of the house lay a two-acre truck patch whose keeper obviously understood the earth. The lush garden radiated a deep, cool blue-green, with cornstalks already six feet high and tomatoes as big as grapefruits.

Miss Agnes sat in her cane-bottom chair on the porch holding a steel bowl between her knees, shelling peas. She wore a faded apron over a threadbare cotton print dress and kept her hair pulled back to a loose bun behind her neck, where strands of it refused to stay put and she constantly swiped them back. Her face was a leathered diary of toil and loss, yet she still had the quick, black, twinkling eyes of a mischievous schoolgirl.

"Comin' up a storm," she said, glancing skyward.

The heat of a summer day in Georgia would suck the moisture from the earth, draw it up to cooler altitudes, and make shade out of it. The steam of the flatlands, more days than not, blossomed into an afternoon shower in the foothills. Miss Agnes's hands kept on shelling while she studied the threatening sky and the swaying hardwoods.

Without another word she sat her bowl on the floor, got up, and disappeared into the house, letting the screen door slam behind her. She returned with another bowl and waved it at him.

"Well, get on up here and get to work. I ain't got all day."

Jake chuckled, but he did as she said. "Miss Agnes, I can't stay long. I just came to see if you needed anything from town." He knew he was wasting words. She'd let him know when he could leave.

She planted the bowl in his lap and filled it with pods from the bushel basket on the floor. "I reckon I could use a bag of sugar. Harley brung me two gallon of blueberries and I need to put 'em up. Oh, and some sunflower seeds. Harley chews them all the time, says it feels good to his jaw." She gave Jake a brief sidelong glance with just a hint of a smile. "You ain't got to lie to Miss Agnes, young'un. I know why you come up here—you want to know about Harley."

An eerie birdcall trailed from a tangled thicket at the edge of the woods. *Kee-ow . . . kee-ow.* Jake didn't look up from shelling.

"Yes, ma'am." He pushed his thumbs as fast as they would go, hoping she wouldn't notice she was outworking him three to one. And from the sound of it, Jake figured she was out-thinking him at about the same rate. "It's just that I got to studyin' about it," he said, realizing that the hick phrase flowed naturally from the subtle southern courtesy of adopting the speech pattern of the person you're talking to, so long as he's not a Yankee, "and I knew Pug didn't climb down that ridge, and you didn't carry him, and you can't get a truck up there. Seems, lately, every time somebody gets in trouble around here, Harley's there."

"Don't it though? Reckon why?" Black eyes danced in a brittle face. She laughed an easy laugh, worn smooth from long use. "He sure is handy. That old well pump lost prime again, and he got it a-goin'. Then he laid in a half-cord of firewood and fixed the light in the kitchen. Last couple days he's been working on that old tractor out there in the barn. He thinks he can get it running. I give him something to eat, and he didn't have no coat so I give him Wilbur's old one. Some nights he goes up on the mountain—it gets cold up there at night, even in the summer."

"Miss Agnes, you need to be careful—"

"Aww, pshhh. You needn't worry yourself about Harley." She smiled. "He's a good 'un."

It was a powerful endorsement. Nobody could fool Miss Agnes.

"Does he come around here often?"

"More'n you do." Her tone bore an unmistakable grandmotherly rebuke. "He took up here after he left the hospital with them wires in his jaw. I fed him soup till he asked me to take the wires out, then I snipped 'em with a pair of wire cutters and pulled 'em out with pliers. Mercy, you oughta see him eat now!"

The bird cried again, and Jake's head turned to listen. He had never heard such a call before. He stopped shelling and stared down toward the thicket. "What kind of bird is that?" he asked.

"Rain crow." Miss Agnes kept shelling, answering him without looking up. "They let you know when weather's coming."

A few big drops of rain splatted little mud crowns in the dust of the yard. Buster crawled back under the porch and lay down with a grunt.

"Miss Agnes, I got to tell you, I came here thinking I was going to have a hard time getting you to tell me about Harley. You wouldn't tell Pug anything, so how come you're telling me?"

"'Cause Pug's a fool. He'd go runnin' his mouth, and the next thing you know, Harley'd be gone."

"Why? I mean, what's the big secret? Is he crazy? Did he escape from an asylum? Prison? Why would he run?"

She shrugged, shook her head. "I don't know. That's the truth. He don't appear to be hiding, exactly. He just don't want nothing to do with no hospital—says he's had enough of 'em. And he ain't nervous like somebody on the run." Her hands stopped for a moment, and she gazed off through the trees, thinking. "Fact is, he's the calmest man I ever met. It's more like he just wants folks to let him alone, that's all."

"But who is he, Miss Agnes? *What* is he? There's something different about him, I can see that, but what is it?"

She shook her head and mumbled to the bowl of peas in her lap. "I don't know. I just don't know."

But she did. He could see it in her eyes. He waited, and sure enough, in a minute she perked up.

"Yes I do. I ain't sure what to make of it, but I don't doubt he believes what he says."

"What does he say?"

"He says God talks to him." She jerked a thumb back toward the ridge. "Up there."

Jake shelled a few peas, not sure how to approach the subject.

"What do *you* think?" he finally asked.

She shrugged. "I reckon he's telling the truth, as far as he knows it. He ain't making it up. That means he's either crazy as a bedbug or he's got the call, and I never seen a lunatic as calm as he is."

"You really think God lives on Chestnut Ridge?"

"I reckon He can live wherever He wants. It ain't for me to say."

"Miss Agnes, half the ax murderers on death row claim God talks to them, but you wouldn't invite them to dinner, would you?"

She cackled. "I guess that's so, only you can't live by it. Reminds me of what Wilbur said to Lenny White one time. Lenny knowed everything there was to know about anything mechanical, and he told Wilbur he'd done figured out how to build a 'lectric generator that would put out more electricity than it took to run the motor that turned the generator. Said you could just spin it one time and have free electricity the rest of your life. Wilbur told him he was a idiot. Lenny told Wilbur, 'They said that to every genius that ever lived,' and Wilbur said, 'That may be so, but they said it to a whole lot of idiots, too.'

"See, young'un, it don't matter what people say about you; it don't even matter what you say about yourself. It only matters what you *do.* You can't go around thinking everybody that claims he hears God is lyin' or crazy just because *some* of them are—unless you don't believe in God. Anyhow, Harley saved my life. And Pug's. What else you need to know?"

"He just doesn't look much like a prophet, that's all."

"What's a prophet look like? How do you know he ain't a sow's ear?"

"A what?"

"A sow's ear. Ain't you ever noticed? I know you read your Bible. Seems like every time God needs somebody for something, He picks the last man anybody'd expect. If He wants to make a silk purse, He'll start with a sow's ear every time. Like when He needed somebody to kill a warrior giant, He went and got a skinny young'un with a rock. When He got in a fire-building contest, He first wet the wood. When He needed somebody to write a bunch of chapters for His Book, He picked one of His worst enemies."

Jake couldn't help laughing at the convoluted logic. "Miss Agnes, you've got a strange way of looking at things. I'm just saying you ought to be careful, okay? You really don't know anything about this man."

"Listen young'un, there's two kinds of old widow women—the scared kind and the don't-care kind. Me, I don't care. I figure I ain't got nothing left to lose, and I'm more afraid of not living than I am of dying." She chuckled, smiling into her peas. "I sure ain't afraid of Harley."

A rain-scented breeze rolled through, cooling the air. The rain crow called again. More scattered drops drummed on the tin roof.

"You didn't know Wilbur, did you?" she asked.

He shook his head. "No, ma'am. Not real well. I met him a time or two. The only time I ever saw him in church was at his funeral."

"No," she laughed, "he didn't go to church much. He couldn't abide a necktie, and he couldn't set still without he fell asleep. He used to go all the time back when you could wear a pair of overalls, but when it got all hoity-toity and everybody started wearing ties and such, he shied away from it. But his heart was as right as anybody's, and I'll tell you how I know. Didn't have nothing to do with what he *said,* neither—you can make your mouth say anything. It's like Farrel Hilliard said at Wilbur's funeral. You was there, you remember?"

"No, can't say I do."

"It was a little thing. It was the littlest thing anybody said, and the biggest. After Farrel got done saying all the stuff he thought he was supposed to say, he said the thing he remembered best about Wilbur. He said Wilbur would 'do for folks.' Wilbur and Farrel worked together at the sawmill, back years ago. A big old pine log jumped the clamps one day, pinned Farrel up against the loader and broke his leg all up. The mill wouldn't pay him because they said it was his own fault, so Wilbur worked two shifts till Farrel got back on his feet. Had them send Farrel a check just like he'd earned it. Farrel never missed a payday. Wilbur didn't think nothin' about it; he just done it. But Farrel and his wife and them young'uns remembers it to this day. Wilbur done like that for anybody. He'd *do* for folks. I reckon there ain't nothin' tells you more about a man's heart than that."

She smiled, and the wrinkles in her face fell into their natural groove.

"No sir, Wilbur weren't no Sunday school teacher, but he never let nobody go hungry. And Harley's like that, too. He ain't always thinking about hisself. He'll *do* for folks."

Thunder grumbled across the mountains to the north. As if on cue, the rain thickened to a leaden downpour. The drumming on the tin roof grew to a roar as a beaded curtain of water draped from the eaves. Miss Agnes closed her eyes and listened to the sound.

"Gonna be good sleepin' tonight," she said.

"Miss Agnes, where's Harley now? He's not out in this rain, is he?"

She grinned. "Aw, he's fine. He's got a cot out in the barn where he sleeps sometimes, but he's gone up on the mountain today. I don't know where he goes, but he's got someplace up there where he spends the night out of the weather."

Jake was more curious than ever. Harley seemed, on the basis of Jake's own experience and the opinion of Miss Agnes, to be a good man. A strange man, but good. So why was he hiding?

"Miss Agnes, when you see Harley again, tell him I said he doesn't have to hide. He hasn't done anything wrong. His hospital bill has already been paid. If he's down on his luck, there are those of us who are willing to help out any way we can. If he needs a job or something, well, I know a lot of people in this town. I'm sure we can work something out."

Driving back down to the highway, Jake steadied a brown paper sack of tomatoes on the seat and noted that the driveway no longer looked like a creek bed. It looked like a creek.

Chapter Four

Web hated Fridays. It seemed everybody in construction piddled around all week trying to figure out the best way to cheat the weekly percentages and then ended up busting their hump to get all the work done on Friday. If they needed to pour concrete, they spent all week grading, forming, and tying steel, then had to compete with every other contractor in town to get an order for concrete filled on Friday. If a house needed an electrical inspection, the electricians would schedule it for Friday afternoon and show up to do the work on Friday morning—if they showed up at all. One of Web's contractors, a devout Catholic, while admiring a particularly grand view of the Elder Valley, had once referred to God as "The Big Contractor," whereupon Web told the man there *was* no God, but if there ever had been, He certainly couldn't have been a contractor or He would have stood around picking His nose for four days and then tried to throw the whole universe together on Friday.

Web pulled into the parking lot of his office building, a modern tinted-glass-and-aluminum structure built on a bluff high on Laurel Ridge, overlooking the town. Between the parking spaces and the building was a low mound ringed about with an army of flaming salvia, and atop the mound, a sign—a green field in a flagstone frame—bore the letters *HP* in gold, for

Holcombe Properties. Web knew his staff whispered behind his back that the letters stood for High Pressure, but he didn't mind; that was pretty much the image he wanted to convey to his employees. Web's office was in the back, affording him a panoramic view of his valley.

He breezed into his office around three o'clock, after a meeting with a county commissioner. Catherine Lowry, his horn-rimmed, middle-aged, wonderfully efficient personal secretary, lifted a stack of yellow while-you-were-out notes from her desk and jammed her reading glasses on her nose as she tailed him through the door. She launched without preamble into his messages while Web plunked his briefcase down next to his desk and took his jacket off.

"Frank called from his cell phone on the way to Atlanta. Said he twisted Dan O'Brien's arm but he won't budge. Said he'd deal with it when he gets back."

"What do you mean he won't...? No, this is too important. I never should have given it to Frank. Pull the O'Brien file for me. I'll have to handle it myself. Next?"

"Michael Downs called, from Kerner and Wright, the ones—"

"Right, the shopping center. What's his problem?"

"He says the state fire marshal is holding him up. They had some sort of verbal understanding about tying the new fire alarm system into the old one, and now they won't give him a C.O. without—"

"Without six weeks of upgrade work. Been there, done that. Call the fire marshal and set us up for lunch at Enrique's. That ought to—"

"Enrique's?" Catherine stared over the top of her glasses. "For the fire marshal?"

"Yes." Web unbuttoned his sleeves and began rolling them up. "Come on, Catherine, you've been with me for twelve years. By now you should know how to handle people. Treat a prince like a two-bit bureaucrat and—"

"A two-bit bureaucrat like a prince. Got it. I'll put him on your schedule." She shuffled the stack, adjusted her glasses, and read the next note. "Reid checked in a couple hours ago, said the bulldozer never showed."

Web rolled his eyes. "That's it for Sims Grading. Tell Reid to call Brad Taylor and have him send a dozer and a grader up to Overlook in the morning."

"Tomorrow's Saturday. They'll want a premium."

Web shrugged. "Doesn't matter to me. It's coming out of Sims' pocket."

She nodded, flipping to the last note. "And Master Edward Holcombe called, complaining that he and Marcus had captured a chipmunk, which had subsequently been denied entry into the prime residence. I told him you wouldn't appreciate him going over his mother's head and to let the chipmunk go before it bit him and gave him rabies."

Web checked his watch as he picked up the phone and started punching in a number. "I'm sure we'll be hearing from his attorneys. Right now, I've got to call the Atlanta office and make sure that idiot doesn't sell out in Gwinnett. Get me that O'Brien file."

Catherine glared, standing her ground. "You're not going to call Eddy?"

He shook his head, covered the mouthpiece. "No time. He'll want to spend an hour telling me about a new video game or something. And don't look at me like that—we've had this discussion before." Catherine started to answer him, but the phone caught his attention.

"Gina!" he said into the phone, "Web. Get me Cal Ormond." He wiggled his fingers at Catherine in dismissal.

She turned and padded back to her office, mumbling to herself.

When he finished the call Web grabbed his briefcase and rushed out. As he passed through the outer office, Catherine, who was talking to Reid on the phone, held out the O'Brien file. He took it from her on the fly, turned and held up five fingers on his way out the door. Catherine nodded and, without a hitch in what she was saying to Reid, noted Back at 5:00 on a pad.

Web wound his way down Laurel Ridge, through town and into the bottomland where the trees opened up to small farms, pastures dotted with cows, and roadsides punctuated at long intervals by great symmetrical oak trees. Showers of yellow and white honeysuckle cascaded in thick waves from the tops of barbwire fences, fighting each other for the sunlight.

He crossed the valley and started up the slope toward the gap on the other side. Not far into the woods on the other slope he turned right on Payne's Mill Road. Nobody knew it yet, but Payne's Mill Road was perfectly positioned to become the grand entrance to the most ambitious project of Web's entire career. The only remaining obstacle was Dan O'Brien's little fifty-acre patch of woods that straddled a natural sloping bottleneck on the north end of Chestnut Ridge. Yet O'Brien was proving to be a real problem.

When Web turned into the long driveway, he had already scanned the numbers in the folder and knew everything he needed to know about the man's income and expenses—what he paid for the land and how much he'd put into it since buying it. O'Brien was a small-time furniture maker and what the local people would call "an independent cuss"—big, barrel-chested, red-faced, bearded, and sometimes a little fierce when challenged.

Web parked his Mercedes next to O'Brien's truck in front of the woodshop, rapped his knuckles on the screen door, then jerked it open and strode purposefully inside. He would be firm. That was the only way to handle a man like O'Brien. Look him in the eye and tell him straight up, you want his land and you're prepared to pay twice what it's worth. Let him know you're in command and this is just how things are going to have to be.

Three minutes later the screen door banged back against its hinges, and Web Holcombe careened through the doorway, barely managing to keep his feet under him as he skidded to a stop in the gravel next to his car.

Staring at the screen door he muttered, "What comes around goes around, Dan. Remember that."

Driving back into Sutter's Cross from the east, the first thing Web saw was the billboard rising from the riverbank of the Elder next to the highway bridge. The bridge and the store next to it were both built on the site of the original bridge and trading post, which had been built by Emanuel Sutter, although the bridge was now concrete and the trading post supplanted by a convenience store with gas pumps out front and a neon Bud sign hanging in the window. The lighted billboard across the highway from the store displayed a hand-painted likeness of Jesus with his hand out and his fingers slightly curled as if beckoning travelers into the fair town of Sutter's Cross. Across the top, in flowing script, were the words *"Come unto me…,"* and beneath his outstretched hand, in the same script, the words *"and I will give you rest."* Spanning the bottom of the sign, a two-foot tall strip of white bore the legend, in lean, elegant serif lettering: Sutter's Cross Community Church.

Web glanced across at the billboard as he pulled into The Trading Post to use the pay phone in the parking lot. The painting had been there for a month. He'd seen it many times and still it made him feel uneasy, and he was never quite sure why. It wasn't the first time a picture of Jesus had made him uneasy, but this was different. The face was too angular, the beard too scraggly, and the eyes were *really* wrong. Something about the eyes, the way they opened a little too wide and seemed to reflect too much light, worked together with the unsmiling mouth and the gnarled fingers of the beckoning hand to create an image of something unsettling and insidious. On the other hand, he'd grown accustomed to the amateurish painting, and on this day he barely glanced at it; he made it a point never to waste time trying to decipher the intentions of religious zealots.

When he handed two dollars to the young gum-chewing blond girl behind the register and told her he needed quarters for the phone, her face lit up in recognition. Everybody knew Web Holcombe.

"Hey, Mr. Holcombe! How ya doin'?"

"Fine, and you?"

He took his change and turned to go, but she leaned over the counter and whispered in a conspiratorial tone, "Did ya see what they did to the sign last night?" Her eyes pointed through the window to the billboard across the road.

Web looked over his shoulder at it. "No, what?"

"Look close at his face." She was biting back a mischievous grin. "I spotted it right away and I was like, WHOA! I'm not sure if it's sacrilegious or just plain funny."

He finally saw it. Somebody had drawn a thin swastika on the forehead of the billboard Jesus. Together with the demented gleam in the eyes, the symbol brought instant recognition and snapped Web's vague feelings of uneasiness into focus: The face on the billboard was a perfect likeness of a lunatic. Web laughed out loud.

"First," he said, "I suspect Swastika Man's an art critic, not a nazi or a heretic, although I'm sure the three aren't mutually exclusive. Second, I'm inclined to agree with his assessment."

She stared, forgetting to chew her gum for a second. "Yeah," she said pensively.

The phone rang six times before anyone answered.

"Hello?"

"Benny?"

"Who wants to know?"

Web stuck a finger in his other ear as a car passed on the highway. "Web."

No response.

"Sutter's Cross," Web reminded him.

"Oh yeah. Been a while. What can I do for you?"

"I have another . . . problem. Similar to last time. You interested?"

"You got the money, I got the time. Only not right now. I'm booked this weekend."

Web took a deep breath, blew it out through pursed lips. "Okay, I'll get somebody who needs the money."

Silence. Finally the voice on the other end said, "Okay. I don't really have to leave till tonight. If you can meet me now and give me the scoop, I can probably start moving on it Monday."

Web glanced at his watch, ran his fingers through his hair. "Right now?"

"Take it or leave it, boss. It's all I got, unless of course you'd like to tell me about it over the phone."

"No. I'll meet you. Same place?"

"Works for me. Hour and a half?"

"I'll be there."

An hour and fifteen minutes later, just off the expressway north of Gainesville, a silver-blue Mercedes turned into the parking lot of a low cedar-sided building with a wraparound porch and neon beer logos in the windows. The sign out by the road said Butch's and, underneath that, Live Music Saturday Nites in stick-on letters, except the *t* was missing from Saturday. The Mercedes backed carefully into a parking spot against the side of the building, where the license plate would not be seen. Success lay in the details; Web left nothing to chance. Inside, he found an empty booth close enough to the front so he could see the entrance and most of the parking lot but far enough back to feel inconspicuous.

He nursed a scotch and water and surveyed the handful of people scattered around the bar. A young nurse in scrubs played eye games with her construction worker boyfriend across a corner table. A paunchy middle-aged man, who over the course of three drinks had removed his jacket and tie and begun to laugh and talk a little too loudly, stood at the bar trying to impress a chain-smoking middle-aged woman who sat on her barstool, leaning on an elbow, playing with a swizzle stick, snickering occasionally at his stale one-liners and wishing he'd go away. A few other people, mostly young jeans-and-tennis-shoe types, hung about the place drinking domestic beer, smoking cigarettes and making small talk.

A red Cherokee with dark tinted windows whipped into the lot and arced smoothly into a parking spot. The driver popped from the vehicle almost before it stopped and flipped a cigarette butt away as he strode across the pavement. Six feet tall, with a lean build and a quick, easy stride, dark blond hair pulled back in a ponytail, pockmarked complexion, a gold ring in one ear, and sunglasses—the narrow, plastic, chic kind—there was no mistaking Benny T. He stopped inside the door and scanned the half-lit bar. Web raised a finger when Benny looked in his direction.

He slid into the booth opposite Web, smiling broadly, and took his sunglasses off. He didn't offer to shake hands.

"So, how's business, boss?"

"Couldn't be better." Web glanced at his watch. "I need to get back, so I'll come to the point. Like I said, it's pretty much like last time. There's a piece of property I need, and the current owner is being... difficult." He slid the manila folder across the table.

The waitress appeared, smiling at Benny. He clasped his hands on top of the folder, flashed the waitress a boyish grin, and ordered a beer. His eyes did a long appraisal of her backside as she walked away. Turning back to Web, he said, "What is it this time, another shopping center?"

Web twisted his glass on the napkin. "Is there a need to know?"

"Aw, listen, boss, when are you going to lighten up? We've *got* to trust each other—we don't have any choice. We've been through a lot together." Disarmingly light and jovial, Benny T smiled constantly.

Web tried to change the subject. "I don't even know your name. What does the *T* stand for?"

"Thiberghian." He pronounced it Tibbergun. "But nobody can remember it. Benny T is easier." He tapped the folder. "So what do you want with Billy-Bob's homestead?"

"I'm building a playground."

Benny's lips pursed. "Must be some playground."

"About six thousand acres."

"Awesome! Will there be a roller coaster? I love roller coasters."

Web stifled an involuntary chuckle. "You know—and don't take this the wrong way, please—but you have a reputation for being, well... dangerous. Forgive me, but you don't seem very threatening to me."

Benny T beamed and actually dipped his shoulders, as if Web had embarrassed him with a great compliment.

"Good. You don't know what an advantage that gives me. Now you tell *me,* what's so important that you're willing to, um... solicit the services of somebody like me?"

The waitress brought Benny's beer, and Web fidgeted in silence until she left.

Web shrugged and said, "All right. It's a world-class golf course, resort hotel, convention center by the lake, winery, stables, skeet range, possibly a small ski slope. Sorry, no roller coaster."

Benny nodded at the folder. "How much of it is Billy-Bob holding?"

"Only fifty acres, give or take. But it's the door, the road frontage. The whole place is strung out along a ridge. I already own most of it, but there's no way into it except through this parcel."

"You already tried to buy it?"

Web nodded. "I talked to him this morning, made him a generous offer. He threw me out. Literally." He sipped his scotch. "It wasn't me. I did all I could. The man *chose* to make me his enemy. I generally take the Sun Tzu approach to a problem like this. Make yourself invincible and wait for your enemy's moment of vulnerability. But I'm not a patient man. I need you to produce a moment of vulnerability."

"Sun Sue. Never heard of her." Benny pulled a pack of cigarettes from his shirt pocket, thumped one, lit it, and exhaled a cloud across the table. "But I *love* working with an educated man."

Web coughed, waved a hand in front of his face. "Those things are going to kill you one day."

"Everybody dies of something. If the snakes don't get you, the alligators will."

Marcus stood in right field with his hands locked together on top of his glove, which was tented on top of his head, which was turned toward the parking lot. He was watching for Eddy's dad. He'd been watching for Eddy's dad the whole game, only now he was doing it from right field instead of the bench because it was the last inning. The coach always put him in right field in the last inning. It was a rule. Eddy wasn't talking, hadn't been talking for the whole game. This was how Marcus knew he was mad about his dad not showing up and why Marcus was watching the parking lot when he should have been watching the batter. When he heard people screaming his name, he jumped and then looked up in time to see the ball whistling down at him. Or almost at him.

His feet got tangled up when he spun around to chase the ball, and he fell hard on top of his glove, which he had almost managed to get onto his hand. Getting up, his knee pulled the glove off, then he stepped on it and left it behind in his stumbling pursuit. But the ball had bounced through a little muddy patch and gotten slimed, so when Marcus tried to heave it toward the infield it slipped from his hand and shot more or less straight up in the air. He collided with the center fielder in a race to the ball, and before either of them could get to his feet, the winning run had crossed the plate.

Marcus and Eddy's team, the Dodgers, had been up by a run until cold fate sent the ball into Marcus's territory. By the time the circus in right field was over, so was the game—and the season. Loss of the game dropped the Dodgers to second place, and Marcus knew it. He took his time gathering up his hat and glove, dusting off his uniform, tucking in his shirt, anything to keep from going to the dugout. Finally he decided to bypass it altogether and slip on out to the parking lot.

He kept his head down as he walked by the dugout, and nobody said anything at first. The dugout was too quiet for the last game of the season, the usual laughing and horseplay stifled by defeat. He thought he had gotten clean away, but then he heard his teammates hissing at him.

"Nice going, Spaz."

"How much they paying you, Dipstick?"

"Monkeyboy."

This last one was echoed by several other boys among snickers from the rest. "Monkeyboy!" It wasn't the first time he'd heard the name, and usually it came with directions, like, *Hey, Monkeyboy, don't stick your head out the car window or those ears'll suck you right out!*

He heard Eddy say, "Shut up, jerk. Just shut up," and the comments stopped. Eddy trotted out of the dugout and caught up with Marcus as he was leaving through the gate.

"Look, forget about it, Marcus. It's no big deal," Eddy said, but his voice lacked conviction. Even Eddy couldn't hide his disappointment.

Chapter Five

The sign by the bridge on the Elder River belonged to Orde Wingo. His advertising business had done well in Sutter's Cross, and he wanted to give something back, so he donated the billboard on the outskirts of town to Sutter's Cross Community Church. Semi-retired, with his company now running smoothly in the capable hands of his eldest son, Orde decided to spend some of his abundant spare time painting the sign himself. He had personally designed the broad mural of a beckoning Jesus, then bought a new set of paints and went to work on the billboard with his own two hands. It had been years since he had actually painted a sign himself, but he warmed to the task quickly, rediscovering the creative release that drew him to the sign business in the first place.

He painted a vivid color background with a purple-and-yellow sunrise breaking behind three empty crosses. While he painted he thought of the people whose hearts would be warmed by the simple elegance of the painting and how they would feel drawn to visit his church on Sunday. He envisioned new couples coming to his class because of the sign and discovering that their teacher had painted it with his own hands—how they would admire his talent, and how clearly it would demonstrate his commitment to the church. Orde could hear the words Dr. Stilwell would say from the pulpit, thanking him for this magnanimous gesture, and he practiced his own humble rebuttal as he gave all the glory to the Lord, from whom all talents flow. Dr. Stilwell would be pleased; this one billboard, standing for an entire summer like a sentinel at the eastern entrance to Sutter's Cross, might very well account for ten or twelve visitors on High Attendance Day in the fall, earning him even more admiration. Everybody knew the pastor was worried about competition from the new church on the edge of town, and Orde figured his sign would let them know just what caliber of church they were up against. Sutter's Cross Community was going to be *big*.

But he was rusty—he hadn't painted in a very long time and his skills had atrophied alarmingly. The small working drawing he had used as a guide was beautiful, a splendid representation of Christ, but he was never quite sure of the accuracy of the full-scale reproduction. He had forgotten how difficult it could be to paint something so large while standing so close to it.

When he finished, he stood back and looked at it from a distance. He knew it wasn't perfect—*something* about it was not quite right—but he couldn't put his finger on it. After a few finishing touches he pronounced it good enough and went home.

The sign loomed beside the highway bridge for more than a month, until the night somebody climbed up and drew a swastika on the forehead of Jesus. Then, finally, a good friend of Orde's called and told him the truth about how the sign had prompted a ripple of gossipy laughter from the townspeople, but he still had to patiently explain about the swastika. To Orde, it didn't look anything at all like a lunatic.

His pride was hurt, but he gathered up his paints and spent an entire Saturday reworking the billboard—painting over the swastika, then darkening the eyes and closing the eyelids just a bit to take away the sinister gleam. He must have climbed down and backed away a hundred times during the day trying to get the right perspective, until finally he accomplished what he set out to do. He brought a certain peace to the eyes so that the picture on the billboard, when he was finished, no longer resembled a madman.

Chapter Six

"Once, while helping a bunch of first graders put together a fruit basket for a lady in the hospital, Lori asked the kids if they had any ideas for adding color, to make it special so people would notice it. 'Put a turnip in it,' one of them said."

Jake Mahaffey

The things Miss Agnes told Jake about Harley didn't exactly clear up anything. Jake was usually content to mind his own business and let other people do the same, yet something about Harley drew him so that he felt compelled to go and talk to him. He couldn't explain it; he just had to know more about the man. Lori felt it too. She had sensed in Harley an extraordinary aura of serenity, as if he were the only one in the woods who owned a compass.

Jake seriously considered taking a day to hike up the mountain and look for him, but he didn't have the time. As it turned out, he didn't have to go looking. Miss Agnes brought Harley to church with her the next Sunday.

The main sanctuary at Sutter's Cross Community Church was a big, stodgy, red brick building with tall stained-glass windows and glossy white columns across the front. The old folks called it the "new building," though it had been built in the '50s, after which the original church building became an annex at the back and served as the children's church. The little rooms upstairs and around the old sanctuary had been converted into Sunday school rooms, so the original became known officially as the Education Building.

Lori and Jake happened to be out on the front portico of the main sanctuary when Miss Agnes's old pickup rumbled down Main Street and turned into the parking lot with Miss Agnes peeking over the steering wheel and Harley sitting tall in the passenger seat, so they went out to greet them.

"I was hoping I'd run into you," Miss Agnes said, slamming the truck door. "Why don't y'all take Harley to your Sunday school class? He don't need to be hanging around with a bunch of old folks like me; he needs to meet some people his own age."

"Be proud to." Jake wondered what he was getting himself into. He couldn't help feeling a certain uneasiness at the prospect of shoving a square peg into the well-rounded and well-ordered ambiance of Sutter's Cross Community Church.

Harley sauntered around the front of the truck, raking his hair back with his fingers. He was still wearing his boots, but Miss Agnes had cleaned him up a bit and put some of Wilbur's old work clothes on him—a short-sleeved plaid shirt and khaki pants. He even wore a belt. His hair, still wet from the shower and neatly parted in the middle, hung nearly to his shoulders. His face had healed. Gone were the bruises and cuts, the crookedness. He'd even trimmed his beard. He looked almost normal except for the lightning-bolt scar on his cheek. He smiled and stuck out his hand. Jake saw that he was carrying a Bible, a small old zippered one like kids carried years ago. There was no doubt where he'd gotten it; Jake knew the name Robby Dewberry would be scrawled in the front somewhere.

"Jake, Lori. Good to see you again."

It was the same Elvis voice, although much of the drawl had disappeared with the straightening of his chin. Lori gave him a big hug.

"You're looking well," she said. She reached up, ever so gently, and touched his cheek with her fingertips. He blushed. Lori always had a heart for strays.

Harley studied the stately buildings, the neatly trimmed boxwoods, the perfectly clipped lawn, the climbing roses blooming against the wall, and the crescent bed of day lilies out front in a patch of sunlight.

"Nice place," he said. "Real pretty."

"What sort of church do you usually go to, Harley?" Jake asked.

"I don't," he said. "I been to a couple weddings, but that was a long time ago. Another life. Outside of that, I don't remember ever being in a church."

Jake tried not to act surprised. "Never?"

"Not that I recall."

"Well, this ought to be an experience." Jake surveyed the crowd. A scattering of people still trickled from the parking lot, mostly young couples towing little girls in frilly dresses and boys tugging at stiff collars. Others milled around talking, heading in the general direction of the Education Building at the back of the sanctuary. All the men wore suits and ties—every one of them except Harley. Walking with him, Jake felt spotlighted.

Lori and Jake took Harley back to the Education Building and introduced him to everybody in the class. Several couples were already there, along with Orde Wingo, the teacher.

Gradually Jake realized that Harley wasn't even aware of how completely out of place he was, that it was his own misguided sense of propriety that had made him uneasy. A few people gave Harley a head-to-foot perusal when he wasn't looking, but for the most part nobody seemed to notice him. Jake began to relax.

Harley stood quietly, his hands folded in front of him, while Lori talked to some old friends. Jake overheard snatches of a conversation between Orde and one of the men in the class about a young couple who had recently had a baby and hadn't been to Sunday school for a few weeks. The young man told Orde the new mother had said she wasn't ready to leave her baby in the care of the nursery.

"You should tell her not to let that baby come between her and church or God might see fit to take it away from her," Orde said solemnly.

Jake had heard things like this all his life so he didn't think much about it at the time, but after they sat down for the assembly Harley leaned over and whispered, "Would God really kill that lady's kid?"

The question caught Jake off guard. He didn't know what to say, so he just shook his head.

Orde's lesson that morning was fairly straightforward, about the incident with the five loaves and two fishes and the feeding of the five thousand. Orde fancied himself sort of an amateur preacher, and when he got on a roll he could pontificate with the best of them. After he finished reading the passage from the Bible he started expounding on it, pacing back and forth, laying out his points in a measured, practiced style.

Jake pointed Harley to the right passage, and he sat hunched over it, tracing the words with a forefinger, engrossed. He didn't appear to be listening to Orde at all.

It was a large crowd for a Sunday school class—more than forty people—and Orde worked it like a stadium crowd. Jake was thoroughly accustomed to Orde's public speech pattern; he liked to use contrast. He would lower his voice when he was coming up on something big, so he could really drop a bomb when he got to the good part. Once he knew he had everybody's undivided attention, his pauses grew longer and his voice dropped almost to a whisper as he laid the groundwork for the explosion everybody knew would come.

Everybody but Harley.

Softer and softer Orde spoke, describing the vast crowd gathered on the grass in front of Jesus, working up to his big punch, so that by the time he got around to the part about the power of God he was practically whispering.

When he got to his big line it came out like "... and Jesus showed the *POW*er of God to the *MUL*titude!" Orde smacked his palms together when he said *POW*, booming the word out like a thunderbolt. Harley jumped as if he'd been jabbed with a cattle prod. His Bible flapped through the air like a wounded duck and flopped facedown on the floor in front of him.

He snatched up the Bible, but the little comedy had caught everyone's attention. Subdued laughter rippled through the room. Even Lori hid her face behind her hand.

Orde's carefully crafted atmosphere was shot. Harley lowered his head and sat very still, hiding behind a mop of hair, staring at the Bible in his lap.

The Sunday school teacher stuck his hands in his pockets and glared at him. One of the men had the good sense to cut the tension with a small wisecrack about how Orde should maybe crank the volume back a notch before somebody got hurt.

As soon as Orde regained his composure he started rebuilding his momentum. Jake glanced at Harley, who had opened his Bible again but to the wrong place. He started to reach over and find the passage for him again when something on the page caught Harley's eye and he began to read. Bending low, he followed the words once again with his finger. He seemed even more engrossed than before, his lips moving silently over the words. Jake watched as the look of intense concentration melted from Harley's face, replaced by a radiant smile. He gestured frantically for a pen, so Jake gave him one. He marked something in the Bible, working slowly, carefully underlining several lines of text. He reminded Jake of a little kid with a crayon. Though 1 Corinthians was visible on the upper corner, Jake couldn't see exactly what he was marking. Harley then closed the Bible and sat up straight, staring at Orde and still wearing that smile.

Orde kept pacing as he taught on. He glanced periodically at Harley's smile, which caused his faltering rhythm to all but grind to a halt. His train of thought had obviously been derailed. He put his palms together and brought his forefingers up against his lips as if he were praying, yet he looked slightly lost. Jake had seen this before, too. Orde was stalling, trying to think of a question to buy himself some time.

Finally he turned to the group and said, "What was it—" he brought his fingers back to his lips—"that Jesus was trying to say to these people through this child with his loaves and fishes?"

Silence. Like most of the others, Jake thought the question too vague to answer.

Harley shifted in his seat, looked left and right. He half raised a hand, timidly, and cleared his throat.

Orde stared at him, and his eyes narrowed. "Yes?" A hint of a smirk crept onto Orde's face.

Harley stammered, "He . . . was trying to tell them they needed to pony up . . . ?" He blushed and his voice trailed off.

Orde hesitated. "Pony up?"

"Yeah." Harley cleared his throat again and came back a little stronger. "You know—ante up? Chip in?"

"Chip in what?"

"Well, food. I mean, people were hungry, weren't they?"

Orde squinted. Jake shifted uneasily in his seat. He didn't like the way this was going.

Harley tried to explain. "What kind of people were they, these five thousand?"

"Probably Jews, mostly. And there were actually a lot more than five thousand. That was just the men," Orde said, regaining his footing.

"No, I mean what *kind* of people? Country people? City people? Rich people? Poor people?"

Orde shrugged. "A mix, I believe. Some of each."

"Did all of them travel a long ways?"

"No, probably not all of them. Some of them traveled as much as three days, but probably not all of them. What's that got to do with anything?"

"This kid—he was packing a lunch, right? So he probably lived close by. And some of the other folks were local. Some of them were rich, some probably even had, like, I don't know . . . servants or something, right? Like bearers. And some of them were country folks, like Miss Agnes. I just can't picture Miss Agnes being dumb enough to go on a trip without some groceries, that's all. I mean, it's a cinch some of these people were bogarting grub, bigtime."

Orde's brow furrowed in an effort to follow the language. "Bogarting . . ."

"Hoarding food," Jake translated.

Harley nodded and continued. "They were sitting on their stash—taking care of Number One. *Some* people were tapped out, but others had more than they needed. So Jesus gets this kid up there who's willing to give it up for the crowd and it shames them out of their—"

"You're saying this was not a miracle?"

Harley glanced at Jake, at the others, back to Orde, then shrugged. "I didn't know we were talking about miracles."

Orde took the offensive. "We're not in the habit of debunking miracles here, young man."

"Debun—"

"We believe in the inerrancy of the Word of God. If the Bible says a miracle took place, I'm not about to try and explain it away." Orde's jaw muscles flexed.

"But I never . . ." said Harley with a confused look on his face. "I just thought—"

"It's not *about* thought. It's about *belief*." Orde's words came out measured, evenly spaced and distinct.

Harley's face reddened perceptibly. A tense silence hung in the wake of Orde's thinly concealed anger so that Harley's voice, when he finally spoke, could be heard clearly, though it had dropped to a murmur.

"But ain't it a miracle if you can get five thousand people to change their whole way of looking at things and share with each other?"

Lori squirmed and opened her mouth to speak, but she closed it again without saying what was on her mind.

Orde jabbed a forefinger at the open Bible on the podium. "That's not what happened! Jesus fed five thousand people—*more* than five thousand, maybe ten or fifteen thousand—from one basket! *That's* what happened! Anything other than that is a perversion of the Word of God, and I, for one, don't want to hear it. 'As for me and my house, we will serve the Lord'!"

Harley started to say something else, but Jake elbowed him and gave him a tiny shake of the head. Taking the hint, Harley lowered his eyes and remained silent for the rest of the class.

"How come they call it a *sanctuary*?"

Harley sat between Jake and Miss Agnes and pored over every inch of the place with a look of genuine awe. Lori, being made of sterner stuff than Jake, had been drafted to work in the nursery.

"I don't know," Jake said. "I think it had something to do with a custom, way back years ago, when people could come to a church and be safe from somebody who was chasing them."

Harley nodded thoughtfully and craned his neck to see the orchestra warming up down front. The orchestra was one of the church's best-kept secrets, a genuinely talented wood and brass ensemble, comparable to some professional groups. They played a wonderful rendition of "Sheep May Safely Graze" while the congregation settled in. Jake was pretty confident Harley didn't know Bach from broom sage, but he sat forward in the pew the whole time, enthralled.

Directly in front of them, little five-year-old Heather Kendrick turned around and spotted Harley. A shy smile crossed her face, and her mouth opened in obvious awe. She tugged at her mother's sleeve.

"Let us pray," Dr. Stilwell said and launched into his prayer.

Heather's mother kept her head bowed. At first she ignored her daughter's yanking, until the child blurted out, "Look, Mommy, it's *Jesus*!" A few heads turned, someone giggled, and there were a few disapproving looks.

Martha Kendrick glanced over her shoulder at the strange man smiling at her daughter, then swept Heather up and held her in her arms until the prayer was over. Heather peered over her mother's shoulder and cautiously waved three fingers at Harley. Jake watched with growing apprehension, yet Harley had the good sense to ignore the child.

Dr. Stilwell talked about courage that morning, a message based on David and Goliath. A nice, safe sermon. Harley listened attentively at first, but after a while Jake noticed he had opened his Bible and started reading to himself. Sitting beside Harley—a living, breathing reminder of the face of the real world outside these walls and outside this sheltered town—it occurred to Jake for the first time since coming here that Dr. Stilwell, with his perfectly coifed head of gray hair, his resonant voice, his flawless delivery and limitless supply of meaningful illustrations and mildly humorous anecdotes, was exactly what this congregation wanted. Jake scanned the crowd. With Harley present for stark contrast, it came to Jake suddenly that the word these people would most likely use to describe themselves was *comfortable*—a euphemism for an embarrassment of riches. They wore comfortable clothes, had comfortable homes and comfortable portfolios; they expected their lives, their weather, even their God, to be obedient and predictable. Dr. Stilwell was comforting and comfortable. A person could come here and rest assured, no matter what.

When the service ended Jake did the best he could to hustle Harley outside before anything else could happen to him. They made it as far as the bottom of the steps in front of the church before bumping into Nell Prudhomme.

"Excuse me," she said, catching up to Harley and touching his shoulder. He turned around, stopped. "I... I don't know if you remember me, but aren't you the man who did the Heimlich on Agnes at the church picnic?" She patted her perm, waved her fingers at Miss Agnes.

Harley looked nervously from Nell to Jake, hesitating. "Um, yes ma'am. That'd be me. I didn't mean to cause a scene."

"Oh, no, don't be silly. The doctor said you saved her life." She pressed her hand to her chest. "But how'd you know she was choking? She was sitting right next to me and I didn't notice a thing, but of course I never notice anything. My late husband always said I could be—"

"It was nothing," Harley said, cutting her off. "I just heard a noise. A trick of the acoustics, I guess."

"Oh, it was *something* all right. But I've been wondering ever since—"

"Look, Mommy, I told you it was Jesus!" Heather Kendrick bolted away from her parents, dodged between the forest of grown-ups, and ran right into Harley's legs. Panic flashed across Harley's face. Jake wasn't sure whether this reaction was caused by the press of the crowd beginning to gather around Harley or something else entirely.

The Johnsons' twin boys squeezed through the crowd and popped up in front of Harley. Little Morgan Tuggle came from behind, and a ripple of laughter ran through the crowd as she hugged Harley's knee. More children pressed through and crowded around him, reaching out, tentatively at first, just to touch him. Some began tugging at his hands. It reminded Jake exactly of the way the children mobbed the guy in the Mickey Mouse outfit at Disney World. They tugged at him until, overwhelmed by this unexpected welcome, he knelt down among them.

Heather Kendrick, a very outgoing child, leaped onto Harley's knee and threw her arms around his neck as Danny Johnson put his hand on

Harley's shoulder and asked, "Are you Elijah? I saw your picture in Sunday school!"

Harley started to shake his head, but before he could say anything, Heather turned on Danny and shouted, "NO! He's *Jesus*!" Looking at Harley, she added, "Aren't you?" Then she hugged him again.

Heather's mother, with revulsion written on her face, burst through the crowd, charged in and snatched up her child, inadvertently bumping into Harley and upsetting his precarious balance. His arms flailed once and then he tumbled backward onto the sidewalk.

Clutching Heather to her chest, panting and red-faced, Martha Kendrick spun on her heel without a word and shouldered her way through the ring of gawkers.

Other parents, drawn by the commotion, found their own children in the middle of it. They looked at the raggedy man sprawled on the sidewalk and Martha spiriting her child away, and one by one they gathered their children. Jake helped them and tried to keep everybody calm. He didn't see outrage in their eyes, or even fear, just a slightly sad veil of apprehension. Better safe than sorry.

Jake and Miss Agnes finally managed to get Harley up and out of there. He wasn't hurt—not physically, anyway—but his face betrayed his confusion and humiliation. He had done nothing wrong, apart from being an incurable misfit. Nell ran after him and asked if he was okay. He nodded without looking at her.

After Miss Agnes drove Harley away, Jake went back to try to smooth things over, but by then the crowd had broken up and most of them were gone. He found Harley's Bible kicked up against the bottom step, picked it up and thumbed through it as he walked back to the nursery to look for Lori. The zipper was broken and the cover a little frayed around the edges—normal wear and tear for a book that had belonged to a boy twenty-five years ago—but the inside was in good shape. As expected, he found Robby's name in the front.

Then he remembered Harley's delight at the verse he'd found in Sunday school that morning, the way it had lit him up. Out of curiosity he flipped over to 1 Corinthians. The only thing underlined in the whole book was a short passage in the first chapter: *"But God hath chosen the foolish things of the world to confound the wise; and God hath chosen the weak things of the world to confound the things which are mighty."*

A smile crept onto Jake's face as Miss Agnes's words came back to him. *"Sow's ear."*

Chapter Seven

With an abandon known only to those young enough to believe they will live forever, Marcus and Eddy lavished precious summer days on the building of the tree house. They hauled lumber and plotted and measured and sawed and hammered until Eddy's vision congealed into a thing of beauty: a complex and multifaceted fortress suspended above the river in the stout arms of the old oak tree. The roof was covered with plastic, and there were windows on every side, though they lacked glass. Marcus was content to help where he could, carrying lumber from the supply house up to the tree house and holding boards in place while Eddy nailed. He even learned to use the handsaw Eddy stole from his father's garage, albeit somewhat clumsily. It took him forever to cut anything completely in two, and more often than not Eddy would lose patience, take it away from him, and finish the job himself. Marcus was pretty sure Eddy could build a nuclear submarine if he put his mind to it.

When he wasn't busy, Marcus kept himself occupied by laying a scrap board on the ground and driving nails into it. Blessed with a double dose of the strange proclivity boys have for mindless repetition, Marcus drove nails until he ran out of nails, then turned the boards over and drove them back the other way.

After he finished the roof, Eddy spent the better part of a day making a rope ladder. Marcus watched as he tortured the rope with his painstaking experiments, patiently testing each knot with his weight and then undoing it and starting over again when it slipped. Eddy worked his knots in studious silence the whole day while Marcus practiced hammering nails. Marcus knew without asking why Eddy insisted on such perfection. It was his dad. Marcus had seen it before. Anytime Eddy worked himself into a frenzy trying to get something just right, it was always something for his dad. Marcus knew Eddy was dreaming the entire time about the day he would bring his dad down to the river and show him what he had built.

One bright midsummer morning Marcus and Eddy came down to the tree house and found the girls there, at the base of the tree. Ashley, the tall one, wore matching pink shorts and T-shirt and sparkling white tennis shoes with the little balls sticking out the backs from her low-cut socks. Marcus couldn't imagine how anybody's tennis shoes could be that white, especially out here in the woods. Since school let out, long days spent playing in the country club pool had bronzed her skin, added natural highlights to her shoulder-length blond hair, and peppered her nose with a new band of freckles.

Eddy killed the engine, hopped casually off the four-wheeler, peeled off his helmet, hung it on the handlebar, and roughed his hair to get that matted look out of it. Marcus stayed where he was. He took off his helmet and sat tinkering with the chin strap. He liked being around the girls but he never knew what to say, so he usually said nothing.

Ashley smiled, pulled her hair back from her face. "Hi, Eddy," she said. "Is this your tree house?"

He flashed her his most dashing grin, the one he used only when girls were around. Marcus called it his "stupid grin."

"Yup. You like it?"

"Yeah, it's cool. How do you get up there?"

"You gotta use the rope ladder," Eddy said.

Ashley's cousin Brittany appeared from behind the tree. She had longer hair than Ashley and much darker, with bangs in the front. Marcus thought she was cute in a sullen sort of way, for she never smiled. Keeping her arms crossed, Brittany looked everywhere but at Eddy and Marcus. Marcus could tell from her tight-lipped scowl that she didn't want to be here. Her shorts and T-shirt were bright white, and she seemed to be taking great pains not to touch anything or to let anything touch her.

Her wandering gaze fastened on the rope ladder. "It's hanging out over the water," she said, scowling. "Ashley, I'm not getting my new shoes wet. Mom'll kill me."

Marcus knew what was coming. He slid off the four-wheeler and fished a long forked stick from its hiding place in a nearby shrub as Eddy stepped around the tree and stood on the roots where they dipped into the stream.

"There's nothing to it," Eddy said. "You just have to know how."

Marcus handed him the stick. Eddy reached out with it, hooked the ladder and drew it to the bank. He handed the stick back to Marcus, then snugged a foot on the lowest rung and reached up as high as he could to grab the ropes with both hands. He then lifted his back foot from the roots and scrambled up the swinging ladder. Once through the hole and into the tree house he leaned out the window, grinning. "Keeps out the riffraff," he said.

With Marcus's help, Ashley and Brittany caught the ladder and climbed up amid much giggling and screaming. Marcus came last.

When all were in the tree house Ashley looked over the side toward the bank. "How do you get back down?" she asked.

Eddy scratched his head. "Um, well . . . we just sort of drop off the ladder and wade across."

Brittany crossed her arms and thrust a hip sideways. "I *told* you I'm not getting my shoes wet."

Eddy shrugged. "So take them off. Throw 'em over to the bank."

She tilted her head forward, glowering at him in thin-lipped, eloquent silence. Then, suddenly distracted, she leaned a little to one side, looking past him. "Is that your swimsuit calendar?" Brittany asked.

Eddy glanced over his shoulder and nodded. "I found it."

Her thin lips twisted into a smirk. "My mom says pictures like that are degrading."

Marcus kept quiet as he watched the exchange, not quite sure what *degrading* meant or why Eddy had that trapped look on his face. All this interest in girls was new to him, kind of scary and exciting at the same time, but if Brittany could intimidate Eddy that easily, Marcus didn't want to tangle with her. He sat down on the upper platform and averted his gaze, looking at a squirrel in the next tree. Sometimes, if he tried, he could fade away. He wanted to do that now.

Ashley came to Eddy's rescue by changing the subject. "So where'd you get all the boards and stuff?"

"Oh, um, we found it laying around."

A knowing smile played on Ashley's lips. "From the new house up there?" She pointed in the direction of the construction site.

He shrugged, grinned sheepishly. "I guess so."

"They're supposed to be moving in soon. Their name's Snyder. They've got kids—three I think, a couple of little kids and a boy named Darryl, our age."

"Really? Where'd you hear that?"

"My mom knows them. She talked to Mrs. Snyder yesterday. I think she said Darryl plays baseball."

"She said he was *cute,* too," Brittany chimed in. A predatory smirk narrowed Brittany's eyes, and she focused on Marcus for the first time. "So where do *you* live, Marcus?" She said it sweetly, but her eyes gave her away.

Marcus knew where this was heading. He had played this game dozens of times before; it seemed there was a Brittany everywhere Marcus went. His eyes stayed riveted on his feet, and his head nodded toward Eddy. "With him," he mumbled.

"Oh, so you're like his brother or something?"

His voice dropped almost to a whisper. "My mom works—"

"Yes!" Eddy snapped. "He's my *brother.*"

She answered Eddy only with her thin, catlike smile.

A gust of wind gave the old oak tree a firm shove so that the boards groaned against the nails, and the structure twisted and swayed. Eddy, accustomed to the occasional pitching and yawing of the tree, bent his knees imperceptibly and stood his ground. But Brittany, caught completely off guard, went wide-eyed and let out an earsplitting screech. She braced herself in the corner by grabbing the window ledges on either side, narrowly avoiding stumbling through the open trapdoor.

"Holy smokes! Ashley, did you feel that? This thing's not safe! It's about to fall into the creek! I'm getting out of here." As soon as the swaying ceased she jerked her tennis shoes off, stuffed her socks into them, and tossed them into the woods beyond the tree trunk.

She complained bitterly at the prospect of getting her feet wet and then having to sit down in the leaves to wipe the dirt off of her shoes before putting them back on, but she didn't hesitate. Refusing to be dissuaded by Eddy or Ashley, she wouldn't stay another minute in "this deathtrap." She clambered down and dropped awkwardly from the swinging ladder into the cold stream. Feeling her way to the bank, waving her arms for balance, she nearly fell on the slippery roots along the edge of the stream, but finally she made it up onto dry ground, grumbling all the way.

Marcus went next, then Eddy. Keeping his battered tennis shoes on, Eddy dropped nimbly into the creek and took a step toward the bank but then stopped and turned back to the ladder.

"Ashley," he called, "why don't you climb down to the bottom and I'll carry you over to the bank. You can stay dry, and you won't even have to take your shoes off."

He held the rope ladder taut to keep it from swinging while she climbed down and sat on his shoulders.

Marcus saw that stupid grin again when Eddy turned toward the bank. Marcus was fading. He sat on the four-wheeler, out of Brittany's path, content to wait while Eddy flirted.

But as Eddy started to climb up onto the wet roots of the oak tree, disaster struck. Without warning, his foot slipped and he lost his balance. His legs sloshed desperately as he tried to catch himself, but his heel snagged a root and he and Ashley toppled over backward.

Ashley's scream was cut off by a very ugly splash.

Eddy flipped over and raised his head from the knee-deep water. She sat there with only her dripping head and shoulders above water, glaring at him.

And then Ashley did something Marcus didn't expect and wouldn't have believed if he hadn't been there and seen it with his own eyes: She splashed water in Eddy's face. As Eddy started to get up she grabbed his shirt, slung him into the deeper water of the pool and dove after him, laughing. They splashed and played in the river for a few minutes, until Brittany complained of the time, and then Ashley waded to the bank and climbed out, shaking water from her hands and wringing out her hair.

The stupid grin hadn't yet faded from Eddy's face, and Marcus began to fear that maybe it really *could* freeze like that.

A huge main root trailed inland from the trunk of the tree, and Brittany sat down on its great gnarled knee to put her shoes back on. Finished with her shoes, she put her hand down on the root, leaned over and studied the ground around it. "Look!" she said. "You can see it moving!" She pointed at the broken dirt up against the root.

The wind had picked up, and they could see the root straining, torturing the ground around it when the tree leaned outward. The crevice between the root and the ground slowly opened and closed with the oscillations of the old red oak.

"If this root goes, the whole tree will fall over into the creek. I *told* you it wasn't safe!"

Marcus couldn't see how Ashley and Brittany could be from the same planet, let alone the same family.

Chapter Eight

Jake stopped by Miss Agnes's place on Monday to return Harley's Bible and to talk to him about the fiasco at church. He found Miss Agnes on her knees in the flower bed, pulling weeds. She straightened up, brushed an errant strand of gray hair from her face, glanced at the Bible in Jake's hand and told him Harley was out in the barn working on the tractor.

It was a three-section barn with an open drive-through in the middle underneath the hayloft, a woodshed on one side half full of firewood, and a tool shed on the other side full of farming tools. Most of the space on the dirt floor was taken up with a harrow, plow, planter, and cultivator. The walls were hung with old rusty farm implements—crosscut saws, hay scythes, trace chains, and a hundred other things Jake couldn't identify. A workbench lined the back wall, and it too was piled with tools and parts and pieces of things Wilbur had accumulated in a lifetime of self-reliant tinkering. Miss Agnes's old truck sat in the open center bay, nose to nose with an antique Oliver tractor. The whole place smelled of hay dust and old grease.

Jake's eyes had to adjust to the deep shade in the barn when he first walked in, but he heard a faint scratching noise and followed it to the back, where he found Harley standing at the workbench. He had taken the fuel lines off the tractor and laid the parts out in a pan of mineral spirits and was scrubbing them with an old toothbrush.

"Diesel," Harley said without looking up. He turned his head and spat out a sunflower hull. The dirt floor was littered with them. "Gets all gummed up if you don't run it once in a while."

"You dropped this," Jake said. He started to set the Bible down on the workbench, but he couldn't find a clean place so he ended up just waving it at Harley and holding on to it.

"'Preciate it. You know, that was Robby's Bible, Miss Agnes's son. I need to finish reading it. Done read most of it."

"Really? When?"

Harley picked up a short piece of tubing and forced mineral spirits through it with a bulb syringe. "Miss Agnes gave it to me when I first came here. She saw me looking at it while she was cooking some chicken broth for me—I still had wires in my jaw—so she told me to keep it and read it. Wasn't much else I could do then, so I took it with me and read it, sitting up on Joshua's Knee. Been reading it ever since."

"You just sat down and read it through, like a book?"

He paused to stare at Jake for a second. "Well, yeah. It's a book, ain't it? I'm a little slow and I never been much of a reader, but I stuck with it and just kept reading from front to back. Is that the wrong way to do it?"

"No, I don't guess there is a wrong way. What did you think of it?"

He spat another sunflower hull and nibbled at the seed with his front teeth before he answered, "I think it's the truest thing I ever read. I always thought it was just a bunch of kids' stories and rules and regulations—Do this, Don't do that." He shook his head. "Ain't like that at all. There's a bunch of stuff I don't understand, and the language is a little funny, but it *rings*. You know what I mean? I understand things now, like I never did before in my whole life." He laid the piece of tubing on the bench. "Listen, Jake, I'm sorry about causing problems at church yesterday. I guess I just don't fit in."

"Hey, it's okay. It wasn't your fault."

Harley chuckled softly, staring out the back door of the barn. "They're afraid of me, but it's all right. I understand it now. I used to have a motorcycle, traveled a lot. People kept stealing parts off of it, so I bought a gun—a .357 revolver with a fancy, hand-engraved western holster. I kept it wrapped around the handlebars of the bike to scare off thieves." He stopped to spit out a hull. "First time I turned my back, somebody stole the gun. But they didn't take the belt and holster. I left it wrapped around the handlebars, empty, and after a while I noticed nobody ever touched the bike again. Finally dawned on me that most people are more afraid of the gun they can't see than the one they can." He shrugged and smiled a little. "That's how they feel about me. They're just afraid of what they don't know."

Jake had to chew on this for a minute. Harley had a strange way of cross-referencing things.

"Who *are* you, Harley? Where did you come from?"

Harley looked him in the eye. "Do you believe in God?"

Jake was caught off guard, and he hesitated. He knew from Harley's eyes that the answer to one question was somehow qualified by the answer to the other, though he couldn't guess how. Harley's eyes also told him he wasn't looking for a pat Sunday school answer.

"Yes. I do," Jake finally said.

Harley nodded, picked up a rag, and started wiping his hands as he brushed past Jake and walked out into the light, laying the rag on top of the tractor tire as he left. Out in the sunlight he turned and looked back. "You coming?"

Jake glanced at his watch. "Where?"

Harley spat a hull and glanced up at the ridge. "Let's take a hike." A grasshopper buzzed up out of the weeds, arced onto his chest and clung there, doing push-ups. He didn't move.

Jake shrugged. "All right."

"I don't know how much I can tell you," Harley said, "but I'll try. You'll need to know it one day." He shaded his eyes and squinted up toward the south end of the ridge, where Joshua's Knee stood watch over the river. "God's up there," he said. "The *real* God. The one they don't tell you about."

It was a fine afternoon for a hike. The temperature hovered in the upper seventies, and a light breeze rustled the trees. Engrossed with the land, Harley spoke very little, preferring to listen intently to the rush of wind through birch leaves, the chuckling of a brook, the businesslike thumping of a crow-sized pileated woodpecker on a dead standing tree trunk. Occasionally he would stop to admire some yellow star blooming out of a bed of emerald moss on a tangle of logs in a creek bed, or a dense drift of bluets creeping from under the ferns. He surprised Jake by knowing the names of things. Though he took a childlike pride in his newfound knowledge, he gave Miss Agnes the credit for teaching him. Sometimes he stopped for a minute or two and leaned against a tree, looking, inhaling the rich humus scent of the forest. It came to Jake then that, if nothing else, Harley had discovered the gift of delight, that curious, unselfconscious ability to pay close attention and find a simple joy in the present moment.

They seemed to be cutting a new trail, angling up across the face of the mountain. There were plenty of established trails, but Harley obviously preferred making his own.

Near the south end of the mountain, as they neared the escarpment, they picked up a trail winding along the edge of a dark jungle of rhododendron in full bloom, thousands of blossoms like wads of pale pink tissue paper against the waxy, deep green foliage. Jake followed Harley up a narrow passage through the rocks beside a tiny stream course, over boulders and through narrow hallways of granite until they emerged on top of the escarpment. By now Jake had fallen into Harley's pattern of listening and watching, and he had lost all sense of time. They followed the ridgeline under towering tulip poplars until, before Jake knew it, they emerged from the canopy of shadows onto a huge tongue of rock thrust out into space on the south end of the ridge.

Joshua's Knee.

He followed Harley out to the edge of the precipice and took in the sweeping view of the flatlands. He could see, far down to the right, the rocky promontory of Herndon Park and the pavilion in the crook of the teal river at the bottom of the steep, green-blanketed slopes. If he listened closely he could hear the roar of Cherub Falls almost directly below them, where the Elder River bunched itself behind pincers of rock, then tumbled into the chasm and turned sharply south, winding away through low, rolling country and disappearing around a distant bend. Joshua's Knee punctuated the southern tip of the mountains.

"I was somebody else when I came here," Harley said softly. He folded his legs and sat, gazing down at the river, the west wind parting his hair. "A whole other person."

Jake lowered himself onto the rock beside Harley.

Harley hugged his knees up to his chin and sat like that for a long time without saying anything. When he finally spoke, his head, resting on his knees, bobbed up and down with his words.

"I had some trouble," Harley began.

The hesitation, the sadness in his eyes, told Jake the trouble was deep and obviously not easy to talk about.

"I got a bad heart, but that ain't the worst of it. Not by a mile. I came to a place where I had nothing better to do than to pack it in and go, so I loaded a sleeping bag and some other stuff on my motorcycle, stocked up on Jack Daniel's, and rode off to see Monument Valley."

Harley was pretty sure he made it to Monument Valley, but "Jackie D kind of dominated the trip." He remembered getting kicked awake when under a road grader one morning outside Albuquerque and getting beaten up by an actual cowboy at the Branding Iron in Show Low, Arizona. He had a vivid recollection of watching a wheat-haired girl fly a kite in a grassy park in Oklahoma City, and catfishing south of Memphis with a wise old black man named T-bone who said to him, *"Keep looking, son. It'll find you."* And he talked about the rush of fragrance from a bank of honeysuckle he passed outside Birmingham.

But he couldn't remember Monument Valley.

"Shame," he said. "The only time in my life I knew where I was going, and I'm not sure if I got there."

"How did you end up here?" Jake asked.

"How does anybody end up anywhere?" He shook his head slowly. "I was tired. Tired of fighting, tired of being tired, tired of living. I was running flat-out, staying drunk, figuring on strewing myself down a highway sooner or later, and hoping it didn't hurt too bad."

He pointed to the ribbon of road far below.

"You see that hairpin curve where the road juts out over the river?"

Jake shaded his eyes, nodded. River Road bent sharply around a rocky outcropping where the mountain pointed a stubby toe at the deep pool above the falls.

"I came tooling up through there in the middle of the night, wasted. Don't know how fast I was going, but I must have been cranking pretty good. I remember I threw my head way back, killing the last of a bottle, and by the time the bottle came back down, the road got real smooth. When I looked down, there was nothing but pine tops where the road should have been."

A narrow band of white pine stood against the bluff where it pointed to the deep pool, the tops of the trees reaching almost to the height of the road. It looked to Jake like a section of guardrail was missing from the apex of the curve.

"Funny the way time changes when you think you're about to get snuffed," Harley continued. "Like time lapse. You get all these little pictures, dozens of them, like separate frames of a movie. Snapshots. I remember seeing the bottle next to me in the air, upside down, empty, just hanging there. I remember the sound of that big motor winding out, the smell of gas, and darkness in front of me. I didn't know the river was out there; all I could see out front was my own headlight pointing straight up. There's this one little picture I remember clear as day, only for a split second, there above the treetops. I'm still holding the handlebars, but it's like I'm standing, and the motorcycle's standing in front of me, straight up longways. It's like we're dancing." Harley held his fists out in front of him, remembering.

"Then I let go." He slowly opened his hands, and his eyes stared into the distance, before him the vision of the motorcycle and his life slipping away.

"I cleared the trees and landed in the river. Came up sputtering and gasping, mostly from the cold, and drug myself out on the little beach on this side. I just lay there for a while, looking up at the stars, wondering what I was going to have to do to kill myself. Weird, ain't it? I mean, I did everything I could to keep from drowning and then drug myself up on the bank wondering what it was going to take to kill myself. Man.

"After a while, I sat up and looked where the motorcycle went down. It didn't even leave an oil slick. I was so far gone it didn't matter—about the bike, I mean. I remember the only thing I said then was something like, 'Well, *that* wasn't it.' The words didn't come out straight, and when I moved my mouth it hurt so bad I almost passed out. That's when I knew my jaw was broke. I must have got tangled up with the bike when I hit the water."

It finally dawned on Jake that Harley wasn't his real name and why he'd chosen it while staring downriver that day in the pavilion.

As if he were reading Jake's mind, Harley said, "I took my shirt off, wadded it up, and held it against the cut on my cheek. It was an old uniform shirt with my name on the pocket—my real name. That name tag got right up in my eyes and sat there looking at me when I had the shirt pressed to my face, and all of a sudden I hated it. I hated that shirt. I hated my whole life and the name that went with it, so I balled that shirt up and threw it in the river. It got good to me then, and I realized I had all sorts of identification on me. There's no end to the junk you carry in your wallet that names you and labels you and numbers you. I took out my wallet and was gonna throw it in the river too, but it was chained to my jeans and I was still so drunk and dazed, I couldn't get it loose. So I just pulled my jeans off and flung them in the river—wallet, keys, money, knife and all. Then my boots. They were sitting there, and I picked them up and started to chuck them in too, but when I drew back to throw I saw this rocky knob standing up here all high and mighty against a full moon, and I flashed back to something I once saw in the city.

"Something touched off a gas leak in the hotel across the street from a high-rise I was working on. Big fire—big, fancy old hotel. And then the whole ninth floor just goes *Whoosh*! It was all over the news that night. They showed clips of a half-dozen people trapped on the tenth floor, hanging out windows and begging for help, out on the ledges, crying. One woman passed out from the smoke and fell. You could tell she was unconscious because of the way she just sort of tumbled, limp, like a rag doll. One guy couldn't take the heat anymore and jumped, pedaling his legs and screaming all the way down.

"But there was this one kid they didn't show on the news—I only know about it because I was there and I saw it. The fire must have caught him in bed, because he climbed out on the ledge in his bathrobe. Fire rolled out the window not ten seconds behind him, and he was trapped. He stood there gasping, swapping feet like he was marching. The fire had reached almost to where he was; the ledge was too hot for bare feet. Then the tail of his bathrobe caught on fire, so he whipped it off and let it drop. He stood there in his Jockeys, hopping up and down for a while, looking at the fire below him and on both sides. It all happened so fast the fire trucks weren't even there yet, and he could see he didn't have a chance. No ladder, no net, nothing. I was on the ninth floor, straight across the street, and I could see it in his face when he made up his mind. All of a sudden he got real calm. He stopped marching and planted his feet, like he just decided to ignore the burning. Then he, like, came to attention, put his hands flat against his thighs and looked straight ahead. He raised his arms, real slow, till they were straight out to the side, palms down, then bent his legs and flung himself off that ledge. He soared up and out, went into a tuck and did this beautiful front three-and-a-half with a full twist and center-punched a manhole cover in the middle of the street. If it'd been water, he wouldn't have made a ripple. I read later he was on a college diving team, in town for a meet. I swear, it was the most amazing thing I ever saw in my life. I truly admired that boy."

He picked up a pebble and sent it skittering over the rock into oblivion.

"So I spent the rest of the night hiking up here in my boxers and boots, gonna throw myself off and be done with it. I figured I'd have one more good flight, and this time I'd be sure not to hit the river. But it was a long climb, and by the time I got up here I'd lost my edge. I was still mad but not the kind of mad it takes to dive off a cliff in the dark. It ain't so easy to kill yourself when you're calm. So I sat down right here and waited for daylight. Figured I'd enjoy the flight more if I could see."

Jake leaned over and tried to see the bottom of the cliff, but the curve of the rock prevented him, and he didn't dare lean any farther. It would have been a spectacular flight.

Harley rested back on his palms and continued. "While I was sitting here waiting I started thinking about how I got here, all the things that happened to me, all the rotten cards I'd been dealt, and how everything I'd ever touched or cared about was gone. Just gone. I've worked hard all my life, and in the end I was sitting here with a busted jaw, waiting for enough light to kill myself. I knew for a fact that when I got done splattering myself at the bottom of this mountain there wouldn't be one person on earth who would care, or even notice.

"I got mad. I didn't see no point to anything. I had to yell at somebody, so I yelled at God." He chuckled. "I guess when you're sitting naked and alone, in the dark, on the edge of a cliff, it's pretty much down to just you and God. You know what I mean? I told Him I didn't much care for His world or His rules, and if He was real, if He existed at all, then where *was* He? I told Him if *He* didn't care, how could He expect *me* to? It started getting light in the east, and I screamed at God that if He was there and if He had anything to tell me, He'd better get to it, because as soon as the sun came up, I planned to meet Him in His office. I screamed at Him for all the wrong roads I'd been down, roads that ended at this cliff. I screamed till I saw colors from the pain in my jaw, and then I screamed some more. I didn't see how any God could expect me to know what roads to take when none of them are marked, and there ain't nothing you can really know for sure. Every time you think you know something, somebody'll tell you different.

"I finally gave out. When I couldn't yell anymore I flopped down on the rock, too tired to move. After a while I started listening. The birds woke up chattering, talking about breakfast and what they planned to do that day. Then the sunlight hit me, and I turned toward it. That's when I heard it. I know it sounds silly, but I heard this voice in my head from when I was a kid. I didn't even remember ever going to church, but I must have because I heard this little kid's voice in my head just as clear as if he was sitting next to me, singing 'Jesus loves me, this I know.'

"I swear it almost killed me when I heard that. I had no idea such a thing was in my head, but there it was, and it 'bout killed me. It took me back to a time when my mother was alive, when there was somebody on the earth who loved me no matter what I did. That kid's voice came ringing across all those years, and I knew it wasn't no accident. It was like God opened up the book of my own life to a page way back in the beginning and said, 'Here. This is where you start. Know this.' "

He bent over and hooked his hands behind his head, resting his elbows on his knees. Jake could barely hear him.

"I know it sounds crazy, a grown man hearing voices in his head—especially a kid singing a Sunday school song—but it was the right thing. It was exactly the right thing for me then, right that minute, and it blew me away like dust. I could feel God *breathing,* and I had nothing else to say. Nothing. I was through.

"I sat here the rest of the day, just listening and thinking. I went over everything I'd ever done, every decision I ever made that brought me to this place, and I saw that it was all my fault. Everything I ever did, I did out of pure selfishness, to please myself. My whole life was about nothing and nobody but me. I saw all kinds of places where I could have done different, but I always picked what I wanted and didn't think about nobody else. That's how I ended up here on the edge of this cliff, screaming. This is where I found out there *is* a God, and He cares. It's just that there are so many distractions it's real hard for a man to pay attention.

"That afternoon, from the dry bottom of giving up, I told God, 'Okay, I ain't done nothing but screw up. Whatever's left, you can have it. Whatever it is you want from me, you got it. I'm done with it.' I meant every word of it, too. And right then, just like that, I felt something come over me I never felt before in all my life.

"Peace. I felt as free and new and clean as a baby. Everything looked different—the sky was bluer, the leaves were greener, and the air smelled like it was fresh off God's clothesline. I wish I had better words to describe it."

"There's nothing wrong with your words," Jake said.

"All I ever had to do was let go, Jake. It's true, what the Bible says, that you got to lose your life to find it, gotta let go of the handlebars.

"I don't remember being hungry or cold or sleepy. I didn't even notice my jaw. I sat here all that day and through the night, being still. Listening. When I got up from here at dawn the next day I was a whole nuther man. What was left of me was dead and gone, washed away down the river with my name and my wallet and my motorcycle. I walked away from here seeing the world—really *seeing* the world—for the first time, and I've never seen anything like it. This place is pretty, but you ought to try looking at it through a child's eyes.

"I didn't know what to do then, or care. I haven't planned anything since then, ain't made any decisions or worried about anything. I felt free, really *free*, for the first time in my life. I figured I'd just head on out, and God would point me the way He wanted me to go.

"So I went downhill and came across your place. I could see nobody was home, and I could see cardboard boxes in the garage with *Goodwill* wrote on them. I put on the clothes, and then I found the tree all cut up." He shrugged. "Figured I'd split and stack. Pay for the clothes that way."

A small airplane cruised slowly out of the valley, flying at a level slightly lower than Joshua's Knee. The afternoon sun flashed from the tops of its yellow wings as it made a broad, lazy turn and disappeared back up the valley. Harley watched until it was gone.

"Now you know why I took your pants."

Jake smiled. "That story alone is worth a dozen pairs of pants. Besides, who am I to argue with God?"

They sat silent for a while, just looking and thinking, until Jake remembered Harley mentioning a bad heart.

"So what's wrong with your heart?"

"Long story," said Harley. "Anyway, I'm not going back to no hospital, you can mark that down."

"Is it serious?"

"I'm on borrowed time, friend. Ain't we all?" He laughed and slapped Jake on the back.

Harley's casualness and easy smile convinced Jake. He let the matter drop; the man *looked* healthy enough. He was beginning to entertain the bizarre notion that God had indeed chosen Harley for some strange purpose. "So, what is it you think God brought you here to do?"

"I ain't got a clue." He shrugged. "I figure Miss Agnes has got something to do with it. Maybe I'm supposed to protect her somehow, but I don't know. I think maybe there's trouble coming to this valley, and there's something I have to do. I don't know what it is yet, but when the time comes I'll do it, so help me God, if it's the last thing I do. Chances slip by and then you can't get them back, ever. I don't plan to be asleep this time."

Jake wondered what he meant by that, but Harley didn't elaborate. He turned his face away, rose to his feet rather abruptly, and headed back down the trail.

Chapter Nine

The impending demise of the Blue Ridge Gliderport cast a pall over Web's Sunday pilgrimages. He had always counted on soaring for stress relief, for the awful beauty of it and the rejuvenating euphoria he found at cloud base.

In his patently logical way, he discarded from the outset the notion of quitting. Soaring was far too important to him. He knew he couldn't leave Sutter's Cross, so the only remaining option was to begin casting about for a new place to establish a soaring operation. He talked to the operators of several small commercial fields in the area and even a few private airstrip owners, but none showed any interest in supporting a soaring operation. It was simply too much work for too little profit.

He would have to open his own field.

Web had no problem finding available tow pilots; all he needed was a site. He acquired topographic maps from the TVA, aerial photo mosaics from various park services, and drove long hours through the mountains on weekends looking for the perfect ridge.

One bright Monday morning in mid-June, over breakfast on the veranda, Jenny asked him what was troubling him; he'd been in a foul mood for days, and the pressure he'd felt from other pilots over the weekend only made it worse. He unloaded on her, told her about his frustrations with the gliderport situation, the difficulty meeting the requirements of a soaring operation, as well as the reluctance of fixed base operators to cooperate with him. While he ranted, Myra came to the table to pour him a fresh cup of coffee.

"Why don't you just build an airport here?" Myra spoke casually to his coffee cup as she poured.

Web opened his mouth to answer but stopped. He blinked. "In Sutter's Cross?"

"Why not? You're always talking about ridges." She shrugged. "This valley's got ridges down both sides—good, long ridges. That's what you're looking for, isn't it? And there's good open bottomland south of here. Bound to be someplace you can lay out a runway. I could loan you the money if you need it." She winked at him, burst out laughing, then headed back to the kitchen with the coffeepot.

He stared at his cup, wondering why he hadn't thought of it before. He tossed his napkin onto the plate, picked up the cordless phone and called an old friend, a retired airline pilot who owned a private strip over near Balsam, who spent his days pampering an immaculate yellow Piper Super Cub. He then called the office and told Catherine he wouldn't be in today and to rearrange his schedule accordingly.

The Super Cub hopped over the crest of Laurel Ridge, dropped into the valley directly above the town of Sutter's Cross, and then banked to the north so Web could pick out his office and his house as he roared overhead. Flying below the ridgeline, the Super Cub followed the river across the state line into North Carolina for fifty miles until the valley played out in a little cove, the headwaters of the Elder. The ridges comprising the sides of the valley seemed at times too close together for the wind to dip between them, and the slopes turned to cliffs, closing in on the plane and giving Web the impression of flying through the bowels of an inhospitable canyon. But such bottlenecks were few, and the ridges invariably opened back out to broad, tree-lined slopes with scattered farm patches in the fertile bottom near the river, mostly corn and soybean. Once, the pilot tapped Web on the shoulder and showed him a bald eagle cruising the treetops to the east. Web hadn't seen it; he was focusing on the bottomland, looking for places where a sailplane might land if it had to.

They turned about at the top of the valley and headed back south. The wind was from the west, so Web had the pilot trim the Super Cub for slow, level flight and ease in against the left-hand ridge. Near the crest they felt the unmistakable surge of lift from the air mass being forced upslope. The strength of the updraft ebbed and surged, but it was *lift,* and they could feel it for much of the trip back down the valley. The entire valley was much better suited for soaring than Web had ever suspected.

They passed by Sutter's Cross again, and the river bridge. The Elder was wider here in the southern part of the valley, but it was a shallow river, full of rocks and rapids, and when other creeks emptied into it the Elder simply gained width instead of depth. From the air Web could see every stretch of whitewater, every small turning of the river and every still pool between the rapids, but not once along the entire length of the gorge did he see a place remotely suited for a landing strip. There were plenty of flat places in the bottom of the valley; however, between the zigzagging river, the road, the power lines, and the encroachment of great paws of stone and forest, he saw nothing long enough to hold half a mile of runway.

Even so, he knew that in the southern end of the valley the ridges diverged as Myra had said, and it was on this section that he pinned his greatest hopes.

Near the middle of the eight-mile stretch between the highway bridge and the abrupt end of the eastern ridgeline at Joshua's Knee, he suddenly spotted exactly what he was looking for. Just east of the river and up a slight, tree-covered incline lay a long stretch of level land. Lying parallel to the river, bracketed on the ends by two creeks nearly a mile apart, much of the parcel appeared to have been cultivated in the past but the fields now sat fallow. Stands of trees covered parts of it, but trees could be cut; it was the lay of the land that caught Web's eye. He had the pilot turn around and make several passes over the place while he picked out landmarks. He would need reference points to fix the location on the map later.

They continued southward, scouring the rest of the valley. Web saw nothing else he liked. Turning back to the north after flying over Joshua's Knee, they buzzed over the site once more and then throttled up and headed back to Balsam.

As soon as the Super Cub landed, Web rushed back to his office and spread out the plot plans of the lower Elder Valley on his conference table. There, lying just north of Bobcat Creek, east of the Elder River, was a rectangular plot encompassing nearly the entire stretch of land he had just seen.

There was another very clear advantage to this particular location that Web had thought of almost the minute he'd spotted the place: It sat directly below the escarpment where the proposed country club would go. The added incentive of a brand-new small airstrip where patrons of the club could land their private planes would greatly enhance the value of his proposal, not to mention that the soaring operation would add another attraction to the playground. Incorporating the airstrip into his plans for Chestnut Ridge would allow him to build it with somebody else's money. It was perfect. All he had to do now was acquire the land.

Stenciled in the middle of the plot was one name.

Dewberry.

Web wasted no time. He went to see Miss Agnes Dewberry in person the very next day. The silver-blue Mercedes waddled over roots and ruts, up the washed-out driveway through the hardwoods, and into the clearing where Miss Agnes's house sat. A flock of guinea hens heralded his arrival, scurrying across the driveway as he pulled into the dirt yard. He got out, surveyed the surroundings, took his jacket off and laid it across the seat. While he loosened his tie, Buster angled toward him, slowed, dropped his head and sniffed. As soon as Web moved, the dog wheeled, bayed once and trotted back toward the house, growling over his shoulder.

The old frame house sagged here and there. Long swaths of red-and-brown rust streaked the tin roof; white paint curled and chipped from the clapboard. Across the front of the house a mixed hedge of hydrangeas and azaleas obscured much of the low porch, and a clematis spread large purple blooms across the railing. He could see the leaves of a fair-sized fig tree peeking around the corner from the south end of the house, planted up against the foundation to keep the roots warm in the winter.

The smell of fresh-baked bread met him as he walked up onto the porch and rattled the screen door with his knuckles. The inside door stood wide open. He could see all the way through the back door of the house—also open—but no one answered, and he heard nothing.

He wandered back out to the middle of the front yard and surveyed the farm. The field to the north, separated from the house by only a thin line of fir trees, lay fallow, taken over by weeds and wild grasses, populated by grasshoppers and cicadas. Looking past the south end of the house, his view was screened by a dense hedge of blackberry brambles and scrub pine back to the beginning of the vegetable garden, where cornstalks grew in high, thick rows down the near side. In the broken space between the cornstalks, he thought he caught a flash of white near the ground in the middle of the garden, so he walked toward it.

Between two rows of tomato plants neatly supported by cylinders of rusty hog wire, Web saw the figure of an old woman in a straw hat hacking weeds with a hoe. Heedless of the soft damp earth folding up around his Italian shoes, Web walked nearly up to her before she saw him.

She straightened up, leaning on the hoe, and fetched a handkerchief from a pocket in her dress to wipe sweat from her face.

"Mrs. Dewberry?"

She nodded a greeting. "Most folks call me Agnes." She swiped her face and stuffed the handkerchief in a pocket of her apron. "What can I do for you?"

"Well... Agnes, I sort of had in mind to do something for *you,* but you're a hard woman to get hold of. I couldn't find a phone number anywhere. Is it unlisted?"

She chuckled, shifted the hoe to her other side. "No sir, I don't have no phone. Used to, but it kept ringing all the time—mostly folks wanting to give me free stuff. I finally got to where I couldn't afford no more free stuff, so I had them come take the phone out. Wasn't nothing but a nuisance. Most of the folks I'd like to talk to can't be reached by phone anyway."

He remembered to take off the sunglasses—something he'd heard in a management seminar about removing artificial barriers when trying to communicate—then stood with his hands on his hips, admiring her garden.

"Nice place you got here. You tend it all by yourself?"

Her eyes narrowed. "You're Web Holcombe."

"Oh! Yes, I'm sorry, I forgot to introduce myself. Do we know each other?" He extended a hand and she shook it, surprising him with the strength and callous roughness of her hand.

She nodded, the beginning of a wry grin wrinkling her face. "I don't reckon you know me, but *everybody* knows you."

He laughed. "I guess that's true." He looked off to his right, studying the rows of corn, looking for something to anchor a bit of small talk. The cornstalks were heavily entangled in some sort of vine, which had grown to half the height of the stalks. "Why are you weeding over here among the tomatoes when it looks like the weeds are taking over your corn?" he asked.

"Them are pole beans," she said rather tersely.

So much for small talk. He made another run at his real subject.

"So, Agnes, do you work this whole place by yourself?" He already knew the answer to this and a good many other questions, but a good friend, a trial lawyer, had taught him never to ask a question unless he already knew the answer.

Her grin faded. "I ain't sellin'," she said flatly.

He stuck his hands in his pockets and watched his toe crush a clod of dirt. She had caught him off guard. "What makes you think I'm buying?"

She eyed him suspiciously. "I been here all my life," she said. "I was here when your daddy came, and I watched what he did for this valley. I knew your daddy, and I know you. I know what you do. You buy land, you fix it up, build stuff on it, and then you sell it. That's what you do. That's *all* you do. Most folks think it's a good thing that you do, and I ain't one to pass judgment on it. For the most part it don't affect me. But I'm an old woman and I don't have much of nothing you'd be interested in except for this piece of land. So I reckon if you're here to see me, you're wanting the land." She paused, gave him a slight shrug. "You'll have to wait. I ain't dead yet."

"Mrs. Dewberry, you're all alone here. And you're already behind on your taxes."

"I reckon that's *my* problem."

"Yes, ma'am, but it's a problem I can help you with. There's no way you can work this farm by yourself, and you're not getting any younger. Now, you can stay here until the county forecloses, in which case I'll buy your land on the courthouse steps for ten cents on the dollar—" he shrugged and gazed disinterestedly to the side—"or I can buy it from you now for top market price."

"I don't aim to sell."

They stared at each other for a long moment. He decided to lay all his cards on the table.

"I'm prepared to offer you eight hundred thousand dollars."

She shook her head slowly. "I ain't sellin'." She didn't blink.

He studied her for a while, his head tilted, and a small smirk narrowed his lips. "Not even for a *million* dollars," he said quietly. It wasn't a question.

"Mr. Web, do you know what I'd do with a million dollars?"

"No."

"Neither do I," she said, and her eyes flashed.

"You could build another place, a nice new place, and pay somebody to take care of it. You could live the rest of your life without having to get out here and scratch in the dirt. You could live well."

She straightened her back, drew herself up to her full five-foot-three, and centered the hoe handle in her fists in front of her chin. She looked like a fixture in the garden, as if she'd grown there, a sentry sprung from the earth itself.

"I was born here," she said. "I've lived seventy-three years on this place. I reckon there ain't but one spot on God's green earth where I could live *well,* and I'm standin' in it."

Web tried to reason with her awhile longer but eventually gave up and stalked back to his car with his fists jammed in his pockets. The old bird didn't make any sense; she wouldn't budge. He regretted the necessity of having to find another way, quite possibly one less cordial.

He was almost back to his car before he saw the pair of work-booted legs sticking out from under the Mercedes. The scrunch of his shoes on the grit of the drive announced his arrival, so he said nothing as he stood next to the feet, waiting for the man under his car to emerge. The feet twisted back and forth and the heels dug in, pulling, as the thin man squirmed out from under the car. The man drew his feet under himself and dusted off his backside as he rose to face Web. A few blades of dead grass clung to his tousled black hair. A sunflower seed hull rested in his beard.

"Hey, how are you? Is this your car?" The scruffy man wore a childlike grin.

Web nodded, sunglasses peering up at the strange face. He didn't smile.

"I'm Harley," the man said, thrusting out a hand.

"Web Holcombe." Web reluctantly shook hands, then rubbed his thumb against his fingertips.

Harley turned, spat out a hull, nodded toward the car and said, "You're leaking transmission fluid. I saw it dripping when I was coming down from the shop." His eyes indicated the barn behind the house.

Web leaned a little to one side, looking underneath the car. "How do you know it's the transmission?"

Harley's face morphed into a sheepish smile of apology as he pointed to a red stain spreading on the cuff of Web's white shirt sleeve, the residue of his handshake. "It's red. Oil's usually brown." He belatedly wiped his hands on his jeans, shrugged and said, "Sorry about that."

Web took a deep breath and started rolling up his shirt sleeves.

"You a friend of Miss Agnes?" Harley asked.

Web glanced hard toward the garden. "I'm trying to be. Not much luck, though—she's a stubborn old biddy."

"Hah! She is that."

"You live around here?" Web had never seen the man before, and he already knew Miss Agnes didn't have any family still living.

"I, uh... yeah." He pointed beyond the house. "I got a cot back there in the shed. We help each other out. Miss Agnes feeds me and lets me stay here, and I help her around the place. I've been working on the Bush Hog this morning. That thing needs a new—"

"Is she your friend?"

Harley nodded. "Yeah. I think the world of Miss Agnes."

"Will she listen to you?"

"Well, she does most of the talking, but, yeah, whenever I got something to say, she listens."

Web's face softened. He took his sunglasses off and put them in his pocket. "Then it's just possible that you and I can... help each other out. I'd like to buy this land."

Harley glanced over his shoulder toward the garden. "And she won't sell it," he said softly.

Web nodded.

"And you want me to try and talk her into it."

Web nodded again, a concerned, fatherly smile beginning on his face. "It would be in her best interests. She can't keep up the taxes on a place this size anyway, and it's worth a lot to me—this land. She could live in comfort the rest of her days. If you could convince her that it's the right thing to do, for her own good, I'd be very grateful... to you." The slight rise in his eyebrows at the end made his meaning perfectly clear.

Harley's face darkened. He stuck his thumbs in his pockets and stared at the ground for a long moment.

"It ain't gonna happen," he mumbled.

"Pardon me?"

"It ain't gonna happen," he repeated, raising his face to meet Web's stare.

"Oh, it'll happen. One way or another."

Harley shook his head. "She's lived here all her life. She'll die here."

Web stiffened. "This doesn't have to be a war. You could talk to her, get her to see reason. She's living in squalor here, and I can change that. If you could persuade her, I'd make it worth your while."

"You don't understand." A smile of sad resignation spread across

Harley's long face. "Squalor's relative. But I ain't talking about what you can do or what I can do, I'm talking about what's going to be. She's a part of this place and it's a part of her. She's not gonna leave here, ever. That's just the way it is, and it ain't right for you to hassle her about it."

Web's jaw muscles flexed, and a slight flush rolled over his face. He was getting very tired of explaining himself to people who wouldn't listen to reason. "I made an offer, if that's what you mean, and she turned it down. I'm trying to *help* her if she'll just listen. Can't you talk to her? Maybe she'll listen to you."

Harley drug a handful of sunflower seeds from his pocket and fisted them into his mouth.

"Don't see any point in it. She belongs here. Trying to buy her off the place... it just ain't right." His smile remained, but it somehow turned condescending, as if he were lecturing a schoolboy.

"*Right* according to whom?"

Harley spat a sunflower hull. "Do you believe in God?"

"No," Web said, leaning forward to be heard clearly.

Harley literally chewed on this for a few seconds and mused, "Then I guess you can do whatever you want. You can always find a way to make it *look* right."

Web had had enough of semiliterate bumpkins who refused to see reason, and this wasn't the first Bible-thumper he had run across in his dealings. He raised his voice a notch in frustration and spoke through gritted teeth.

"I'm sick and tired of people telling me there's no ethical foundation outside of some mystical storybook. I'm not trying to take anything away from Mrs. Dewberry!" He pointed his finger in Harley's face. "Yes, I want the land! But what I'm *trying* to do is give the woman enough money to live like a queen so she can quit pawing in the dirt and live out her life with some dignity and grace! Is that a crime?"

Harley spat a sunflower hull to the side and calmly uttered the words that slammed into Web like shrapnel. "No, it ain't a crime. It's just wrong."

Web flinched and took a half step back. He put his sunglasses on and, with great effort, managed to stay calm while he turned and rounded the car, fishing his keys out of his pocket. He climbed in and closed the door gently.

But when he had cranked the car and put it in gear he could hold back his rage no longer. There were no words, no counterpunch for the blow inadvertently driven home by this fool. Who was this strange man who tossed thunder without knowing it, opening wounds and conjuring a ghost he could not know existed? Web jammed his foot on the gas pedal, and the tires spun furiously in reverse as he whipped the car sideways.

The flock of guinea hens scurried to get out of his way, but not quickly enough. Two of them rolled under the middle of the car amid a chorus of cackling and screaming. Web slammed the shifter into Drive and the car lurched forward. One unfortunate hen apparently moved the wrong way in her attempt to run to daylight, because there was a distinct bump as the Mercedes sped away. The car fishtailed down the driveway, its rear wheels spitting a cloud of gravel and dust and gray feathers at Harley.

Web grew up the oldest of three Holcombe children in the small town of Fayetteville, just south of Atlanta. He wondered sometimes if just being the oldest was enough to condemn him in his father's eyes or if it was but the unfortunate birthright of any child who wore his father's name. It seemed as if he'd spent his entire youth trying in vain to please the man. He consistently made better grades than his younger sister, although Web was the one who always got the "You can do better than this" speech. His sister was the black sheep, the rowdy one who was always getting into trouble in high school, smoking in the bathroom, cutting classes, drinking at parties. Yet she remained his father's darling. Her escapades only brought her more of his attention.

His father, Will Holcombe—William Edward Bonner Holcombe Senior—owned a moderately successful real estate brokerage where Web worked after school for gas money. He would put out the signs on Friday night, take them up again on Sunday night, detail houses, plant grass, cut grass, wash windows, run errands. He did everything except sell real estate. No one actively taught him the business, but he was no ordinary teenager; by the time he graduated high school he had gleaned enough from overheard conversations to have a dim understanding of the real estate market. He began to wonder how somebody like his father could work so hard for so long in a business that dealt in units worth many thousands of dollars and still be only moderately successful.

He thought about this while he was a senior in high school, and finally hit on the answer: His father worked for a set percentage. He mediated deals to the satisfaction of both the buyer and the seller and then took a small percentage for his trouble. The only way to make more money was to do more work. Web, confident of his ability to find a shortcut, felt sure he could improve on his father's methods. After he graduated high school Web set out determined, for once, to make his father proud.

Following graduation the agents in his father's firm began to treat Web differently. They started to see him as an adult, as the future owner of the firm, and so treated him accordingly. They began teaching him, telling him what they were doing and why they were doing it.

And he listened. He read the trade papers, listened to rumors and stories around the office, studied books on real estate law, perused contracts he found unattended on desks, and pieced all the information together until he had a firm grasp of the big picture. Quietly, he developed a plan.

Armed with a handful of his father's business cards, which conveniently bore the name W. E. B. Holcombe, Web disappeared every evening in July of that summer. Every day after work he'd get in his MG and drive away, returning home well past suppertime. He told his mother he was spending the time with a girlfriend, which worried her at first, but she finally conceded that he had never looked happier. He seemed *driven,* somehow; there was a new flush in his cheeks and a gleam in his eye. Then she fretted over the source of the gleam and begged him not to get himself in trouble.

Curiosity furrowed his father's brow when, in the first week of August, Web asked for an appointment.

"You don't need an appointment, son," the elder Holcombe said.

"Yes," Web answered, "I do. I have a business proposition and I want your undivided attention."

His father agreed, and the next morning at eight o'clock sharp Web walked into his office, wearing a coat and tie, and closed the door. He sat in the leather chair facing the desk, holding a manila folder on his lap.

"Well, Mister Holcombe," his father began, clasping his hands on the desk in front of him, "what can I do for you?"

The faint look of amusement in his father's eye fueled Web's resolve. The look said, You can slick back your too-long hair if you want, and you can put on a suit and tie, but I still see a little boy at a lemonade stand.

Web was about to permanently erase that notion. He opened the folder and laid a sheet of paper on his father's desk. It was a photocopy of a map. In the center of it Web had outlined, with a yellow highlighter, an area roughly the shape of an oak leaf.

"That's the proposed site for a new reservoir in south Fayette County," Web said. "Nobody knows about it yet."

His father studied it for a moment and, without looking up, said, "Where'd you get this?"

"I'm dating this girl—her father's a county commissioner. We were having dinner at her house and he started talking shop."

His father smiled at him, the condescension still evident. "Well, son, this is interesting news. It's always good to—"

"There's more. A lot more. I went to the courthouse and got the names of everybody who owns land adjacent to where the reservoir will be. There are nine different parcels totaling almost two thousand acres, and it's all farmland. Pecan groves, grass and cows as far as you can see. I did a little research and found out the going rate for farmland in that area is twelve hundred dollars an acre, so I went to the owners and offered them fifteen."

Web took a moment to savor the melting of his father's smile, then continued. "They jumped at it—every one of them. Most of them inherited the land from their grandfathers, who bought it for like twelve dollars an acre back before the Depression, and now they're ready to cash in. To them it's retirement money, and a lot of it. I have letters of intent from all of them. Signed." He took a sheaf of papers from the folder and placed it in front of his father.

His father flipped through the papers and then stared at the folder in Web's lap. "There's more?"

Web nodded and tried to suppress a wry smile as he dropped the *real* bomb.

"The rumors have been flying around for months about how King Development is looking for a large tract for a new country club. Once I got the letters of intent I went to King and showed them the package. They want it. They've agreed to pay sixty-five hundred dollars an acre." He laid a last piece of paper on his father's desk and waited.

He knew his father had done the math even before he finished speaking. Twenty years of points, percentages, taxes, and closing costs had sharpened the man's skills to the point he could do amortization schedules in his head. His father's mind flew over the numbers, instantly subtracting the buying price from the selling price, multiplying it out and skipping directly to the bottom line: ten million dollars!

Web sat waiting for his moment of glory, the moment when his father would jump up whooping, hug him and drag him into the front office to pay homage in front of his whole little world. He would hand out cigars and bonuses like candy and tell everybody he met, "This is my beloved son, in whom I am well pleased." He would make Web a partner, and they would all live happily ever after.

But his father did none of that. He spoke quietly, patiently. "We can't do this," he said.

Web's heart stopped. His mouth opened slowly but no words would come, so he closed it again.

"It's called 'flipping,' " his father explained. "The practice is older than you are. And it's wrong. I'm sorry, son. I know you've put a lot of work into this and I ap—"

"But, Dad, it's *not* wrong! I looked it up!" Unable to sit still, Web stood up, squeezing his forehead, fighting back tears, fervently hoping he could bridge the gap between himself and his father just this once. "As long as you don't use your license, as long as we do this with private money, there's nothing illegal about it."

"I didn't say it was illegal, I said it was wrong."

"WHAT'S THE DIFFERENCE?"

"The difference, at least for me, is that I have to consider how the other guy would feel. How would *you* feel if you sold your life's work for a hundred thousand dollars and found out the next day that the guy who bought it from you turned around and sold it for a million? Wouldn't you feel cheated?"

Web leaned on his fists over his father's desk and looked him in the eye. "I'd feel like I just got an expensive education. I'd remember it. And I wouldn't begrudge him a dime of it."

His father shook his head slowly, meeting his glare. "Maybe *you* wouldn't, but I don't want to live like that."

"Like what? Rich?"

"No, son. Rich, poor—it makes no difference, morally, how much money you have. It matters what you *pay* for it."

"Riddles." Web stared openmouthed at his father. "You talk in riddles. What has buying and selling a piece of land got to do with morality?"

"Why can't you see it? Every Sunday of your life you've gone to the same church, heard the same sermons, read from the same Bible I did. How can you possibly not have absorbed the principles?" He rubbed his forehead. "Look, son, I know you don't think much of it now, but you're young. The time will come. As for me, my principles come out of my faith, and I won't betray that. Not even for ten million dollars."

Web straightened and his eyes narrowed. "Is *that* what this is about? Church? Because I'm not your little church boy, because I won't say things

I don't mean and pretend to believe something I don't, you're blowing off the biggest deal of your life? Let me tell you something, Dad. That preacher thinks a lot more like me than you. Listen to him sometime, and try to be objective for once. All he talks about is more money. And more members, because members bring more money. If he has a god at all, it's green."

"You watch your mouth, son."

"It's the TRUTH, Dad! All they're doing is hypnotizing you so they can pick your pocket."

His father sat back and raised his palms as if in surrender. "I see no point in continuing this discussion. I will *not*... do... this." He tapped the stack of papers on his desk in time to his words.

Snatching up the papers and stuffing them back into the folder, his chin quivering with rage, Web hissed through gritted teeth, "*I* will. With this folder I can get the backing of any bank I want. And when I'm finished I'll have enough money to put this shake-rag town and all the narrow-minded prigs like you behind me."

His father's eyes rested on the folder. "Not after I get through talking to your farmers."

Web blinked and collapsed into the chair, momentarily stunned by the sudden awareness that he was beaten. He had brought an offering to his father, and his father had thrashed him with it. He saw his breakout deal winging its way out the window, and there was absolutely nothing he could do about it.

Frustration reached its flashpoint. Web's chair groaned across the wood floor from the fury of his rising. He sailed the folder into the air and spun about, stalking to the door as the papers rained down around his father's head. The doorknob punched a hole in the sheetrock where he flung it back against the wall as he was leaving. He did not look back.

That evening, in a rare drunken fit of self-pitying rage, he walked into a recruiter's office. A year later he was knee-deep in a rice paddy with an M-16 in his hands when his father died of a heart attack. They had not spoken.

Chapter Ten

"Sooner or later, one way or another, every journey ends where it started."

Jake Mahaffey

Halfway between the town and the river, on a little side street behind the hospital, sat a small diner with the name Peggy's painted on the front window. It was an old-fashioned chrome-and-Formica diner where working-class people came for a hot breakfast before daylight, an unpretentious place known only to the locals, where the coffee was always fresh and the biscuits handmade, a man could wear beat-up work clothes without drawing stares, and he didn't have to pay tourist prices. Loners perched on stools at the counter, while others, in groups of two or three, sat in booths by the windows.

Jake stopped at Peggy's most mornings for a hot breakfast and coffee from a heavy white crockery cup. He always took a booth, even though he usually came in alone. He knew half the people in town—and all of the construction workers—and nearly every day at least one familiar face would walk in and join him at his table for breakfast. Jake liked the feeling of family among the regulars at Peggy's; he liked hearing the latest news, lies and rumors, and more than once he had picked up a profitable job over a western omelet.

One morning in late June he took his regular table at Peggy's. Though the little café was busier than usual and all the seats filled rather quickly,

Jake didn't see anybody he wanted to talk to until an old hiker came in, alone, wearing a battered backpack and a threadbare river hat—the shapeless, soft-brimmed cotton hat generally favored by seasoned hikers. Jake looked him over as he stood just inside the door looking for a place to sit. He wore faded navy blue pants of lightweight cotton, not the ubiquitous jeans or khaki shorts of the younger crowd. A pair of bifocals swagged from his neck, and he was shod with ordinary comfortable work boots in place of the popular mail-order-from-Maine, high-dollar, name-brand hiking boots. His hands rested on a stout walking stick, intricately carved down its length with intertwining vines, the top foot of which had been worn dark and shiny from long use. When Jake saw there were no seats left he flagged the hiker over to his table.

The man nodded and grunted something Jake took to be a thank-you as he shrugged out of his pack and slid it into the far corner of the booth. He sat down, tossed his hat on top of the pack, and roughed his gray hair with his fingers. His brown face was a reptilian web of fine wrinkles, the residue of long exposure to the weather.

Jake stuck out his hand. "Jake Mahaffey."

"Anson Zufelt," the leather face answered, and they shook hands.

"You in town for the Fourth?" Jake asked. The annual Fourth of July celebration at Sutter's Cross was a major event in the mountains. Long-term hikers often drifted into town a few days in advance.

Anson Zufelt shook his head slowly, and the wrinkles spread into what Jake thought was a curiously sad smile.

"Going home. I'm through. Came in to catch a bus—" He glanced up, interrupted by the arrival of the waitress, then proceeded to order a breakfast of admirable proportions. Jake sipped his coffee and waited until Zufelt finished ordering.

"It's the middle of the season. You been on the trail long?" Jake asked after the waitress left.

"Better part of two years."

"Wow. You been to Maine?" The Appalachian Trail, the longest marked footpath in the country, follows the spine of the Appalachians for over two thousand miles, from Springer Mountain in north Georgia all the way to Mount Katahdin in Maine. Kids, starting out all full of themselves at the southern end, when asked where they're headed would generally answer "Maine" even if they knew you were only asking where they planned to camp for the night.

Anson Zufelt shook his head. "I got as far as the Cumberland Valley in

Pennsylvania once, but I was never really geographically motivated, if you know what I mean. Got sidetracked a lot."

Jake loved stories, so he pried a few out of the grizzled hiker as he worked through a mammoth breakfast. He told Jake about fending off a black bear with a firebrand in West Virginia, about the summer night when the river came up and almost washed him off the sandbar on which he had camped, and about the night he nearly lost several toes when a winter storm caught him by surprise on a bald near Clingman's Dome. It soon became clear that, unlike most trail veterans who occasionally took a break and returned to civilization, this leather-faced man had spent the entire last two years of his life tramping around in the woods, stopping in towns only when necessary to take on supplies. Jake's curiosity slowly turned to the man himself. He was soft-spoken and reserved, and his words had that intangible quality of self-assurance that comes with a lofty education.

"If you don't mind me asking, Mr. Zufelt, what do you do for a living? I mean, I can't imagine being able to take off for two years. How do you do it?"

The leather man swallowed a mouthful of pancake before he answered.

"I was a stockbroker in Chicago. Did pretty well. After my wife got sick I retired so I could take care of her." He took a sip of his coffee. "Lung cancer. My kids are all grown, with kids of their own, and after she died I was kind of... depressed."

"Understandable. When a wife dies—"

"No, it wasn't that. After a year of... well, it was almost a relief when she died, if you know what I mean. But rambling around in an empty house without her to take care of, and the kids scattered to the winds, I started examining my own life. When the dust settled I felt bereft of purpose. I guess most people would be delighted to find themselves still in good health at fifty, unencumbered and sitting on a rather substantial nest egg. I'd bent every minute of my life to that end, but having arrived, I thought, Now what?"

Jake sipped his coffee and waited.

"I have to admit, my wife raised the kids. I never saw them do anything but sleep and graduate. I loved my kids, and I always thought I was doing the dutiful thing, being a good provider, but I just never got to know them, you know? It took my wife a year and a half to die, during which time most of our friends faded away. People mean well, but it's a rare human being who can stand that kind of proximity to their own mortality. After she died

I was alone—completely. The kids were all off making money for their own families, in different parts of the country. Funny thing about a house—the bigger it is, the quieter it gets when it's empty.

"To kill time I started reading, which made me think. And *that's* what brought on the depression. My therapist recommended exercise and a change of surroundings. So I fired my therapist, sold the house, and bought a backpack. I went to the woods to live deliberately, to front only the essential facts of life—"

"—and not, when you came to die, to discover that you had not lived." Jake couldn't resist finishing the quote for him.

The leather face curved into a knowing smile. "You're a philosopher."

Jake grinned. "Strictly amateur. I haven't read Thoreau since high school."

Zufelt pointed at Jake's hands. "So how does a philosopher end up with calluses on his hands?"

"Good question," Jake said, scratching his neck. "I was going to major in it in college, but I dropped out in my sophomore year. People told me all a philosophy major needs to know is how to say, 'Would you like fries with that?' Then there was the inherent contradiction—philosophers all tell you to figure things out for yourself, and then you spend all your time reading what other people think." He shrugged. "So I decided not to rent out my mind. My father was a carpenter, so I learned early how to work with my hands. I like the feel of hammer and saw, the smell of cut wood, and when I'm working with my hands I can think about whatever I want."

The leather man smiled and nodded. "I envy you," he said.

He leaned to one side, pulled a battered, dog-eared paperback copy of *Walden* from his back pocket and tossed it on the table.

"Somebody gave me that about a month into the trail. It didn't weigh much, so I carried it with me and read it at night by firelight. It was like a sign from God. I must have read it a dozen times until I pretty much memorized it, then I got into the habit of reading random bits. I'd pull it out at odd moments and just open it anyplace and read. I've pretty much absorbed that book over the last two years."

Jake picked up the book and leafed through it. It was torn and wrinkled from having ridden so long in a man's back pocket, the cover buckled from having been wet and the pages brown and soft from long use.

"Did you find what you were looking for?"

"I thought so." The leather man planted his elbows on the table, folded his hands together and rested his chin on his knuckles. "For a long time I thought so, but lately I've been fighting depression again. Henry and I may have come to agree that life isn't about scratching out a living, but what is it? In the end, walking up and down the hills and listening to the birds seems just as pointless. Seems like I ceased wandering aimlessly in Chicago so I could wander aimlessly in North Carolina." He paused, sat back and sighed. "Sorry. I get carried away. I rarely have anyone to talk to."

"It's all right. I don't get to have many conversations like this, myself. How come you're going home now, right in the middle of the season?"

"Well, that's kind of a long story."

Jake raised his cup, signaling for the waitress to bring more coffee.

"I can be late," Jake said. "I'm the boss. And I love a good story."

The waitress freshened their coffee, piled the spent dishes in the crook of her arm, and bustled away as Anson Zufelt began his strange story.

"People get lonely on the trail, so they find ways to communicate with each other. One of the things they do is leave little notes in the designated campsites, sometimes pinned up in the shelter, sometimes hanging from a tree limb in a sandwich bag—mostly 'to whom it may concern' stuff, because it's not likely to be a two-way conversation, since you normally don't meet the same person more than once. You only see messages from people who remain in front of you and people you've passed going the other way. They mostly talk about points of interest and unusual things they've seen, sometimes news of other travelers, like if somebody's gotten sick or broken a leg and had to go back to the world. One guy's a pretty fair poet—I've seen a lot of his stuff up and down the trail but I've never met him.

"Anyway, the last couple weeks, coming south, I started finding notes from northbound hikers who said they had run across this hermit on Chestnut Ridge. Curious stuff, as if he were some kind of shaman, a holy man or something. It's off the beaten path, but I wasn't doing anything important and, like I said, I'm easily sidetracked. So I split off and came down here to check it out. The trail swings around east of the ridge, then climbs the south end up to Joshua's Knee and runs near the crest, up above the escarpment, all the way back to this end. This is a gorgeous valley, worth a look on its own, but I didn't meet any holy man or see anything I hadn't seen before.

"So last night I made camp in a stand of white pine near a spring on this end of the ridge just above the Pyramid. You know the place?"

Jake nodded. The Pyramid was the name hikers gave to a vast, steep triangular boulder field comprising a large part of the north face, where over thousands of winters, rainwater had seeped into crevices, frozen, and shattered the monolithic granite into a million tumbled pieces. Even this inhospitable place was more or less covered by a broken canopy of trees, as scraggly pines grew between the boulders, ragged and bent, clinging desperately to whatever patch of moist soil their roots could ferret out among the rocks.

"After I made camp and had a bite to eat I climbed to the topmost boulder at the peak of the Pyramid and just sat staring down at that desolate place. There I was, at the end of yet another blind alley, and my depression turned the rocky slope into a metaphor. I felt like one of those twisted trees, scrabbling for a foothold all its life and never having much of a chance. The rocks there are littered with the mossy trunks of failed trees in various stages of decay, turning back into soil to help trap another generation in that hopeless place."

"Another man might see hope in the same process," Jake said softly.

"Maybe. But most of the time a man can only see from where he is. Anyway, the sun had dropped below the ridgeline across the valley, but there was still enough light to read so I pulled out the book, opened it at random, and this is where my eye fell:

" 'It is not worthwhile to go round the world to count the cats in Zanzibar. Yet do this even till you can do better, and you may perhaps find some "Symmes' Hole" by which to get at the inside at last.'

"I'd read it before and had given it long thought while I walked. This is exactly what I was doing—counting cats in Zanzibar for want of anything better to do. But up to that point I had held out hope for Symmes' Hole."

"Symmes' Hole?"

Anson Zufelt sipped his coffee, and his leather face smiled again, patiently. "Symmes was something of a crackpot. He's been forgotten now, and I would never have heard of him myself if I hadn't once run across a statue of him somewhere in Ohio and was curious enough to look him up. He theorized that the earth was hollow, composed of five concentric spheres, and that there was a whole race of people living inside it. He postulated that there were holes a thousand miles wide at the poles, where the oceans flowed in and out, and these alleged passages to the center of the earth became known as Symmes' Holes. It's where Jules Verne got the idea. Strange as it sounds, the theory had its proponents all the way into the twentieth century. Do you see the irony of it?"

" 'Fraid you lost me in the curve," Jake said, scratching his head.

The leather man pressed forward and spread his hands to animate his explanation. "See, it finally dawned on me, sitting on top of that rock pile, that Thoreau hung his analogy on an erroneous theory. He didn't know it then, a hundred and fifty years ago, but there *is* no Symmes' Hole. There are no answers inside, just more questions—and no way to get at them, anyway. I sat there staring at the words in the book, thinking, Here I am, looking for the opening, the way to know myself, looking for one solid foothold on knowing something, and it simply does not exist. All is argument and conjecture. There *is* no entry point.

"*That,*" said Zufelt, "is a depressing revelation. The ragged end of philosophy. In the end, there's only despair."

But the eyes in the leather face across the table held hope, not despair, Jake was sure of it. Anson Zufelt's eyes betrayed a weathered fatigue and possibly a quiet resignation to something he didn't entirely understand—but not despair. Jake waited, certain there was more to the story.

"I sat there a long time, depressed, lost and confused. Empty. Then, in that weird time between twilight and dark, I suddenly felt as if I was not alone. The hair stood up on the back of my neck, the feeling was so strong. I looked over my shoulder and there was this guy sitting on the rock with me, just sitting there a few feet behind me with his legs crossed, yoga style. He didn't look like any shaman; he looked like a hobo. Tall, skinny guy, long black hair, sort of scruffy. Neither one of us said anything. I was petrified, too scared to talk. I didn't know what he was thinking. I couldn't see his face too well in the twilight. We sat there staring at each other for a long time, then he just reached out and handed me a book, already open, with his thumb in the crease. *'Go home,'* he said. *'It's not out here.'*

"I had no idea what he meant, but I took the book and looked at the page in front of me. I could see it was a Bible, and there was a little piece underlined, but I couldn't read it. By then it was too dark. So I got a lighter out of my pocket and read it with that."

He folded his hands on the table, and his eyes dropped to study them.

"I don't remember it word for word, but it said something about being convinced that nothing, absolutely nothing, could separate us from the love of God. At any other time I would have tossed it out with a fair dollop of salt, but this was, I don't know... at that precise moment, under the circumstances... earthshaking. I turned around and he was gone. Never made a sound. He just wasn't there anymore." Anson Zufelt took a deep breath and blew it out slowly, sat back and crossed his arms.

Jake looked him in the eye. "So now you're going home."

He nodded. "I've got kids I barely know and grandchildren I've rarely seen. And I've got another book to read. I sat up all night thinking about it, and it seems to me, finally, that even the mere hope of a real, breathing, thinking, caring God is better than any other way to think. If I were to guess, I'd say God must be real, because He spoke to me up there last night. I intend to find Him again or at least be still enough to let Him find me. I'll tell you this much: I'll never forget Robert Dewberry."

Jake gently corrected him. "Robert Dewberry went missing in Vietnam twenty years ago."

"You're telling me I saw a ghost?"

"No, I'm telling you the man you saw wasn't Robert Dewberry."

"Then who was he?"

"His name is Harley."

Zufelt nodded, dug in his pack and produced Robby's Bible. He ran his hand reverently over the cover. "You know him?" he asked.

"I do."

"Then here, give him back his Bible. I'll buy another."

"You sure?"

"Yes. And tell him... tell him thank-you."

Chapter Eleven

Dan O'Brien loved his patch of land fronting the highway on the north end of Chestnut Ridge. He had no plans to farm it or subdivide it or sell the timber off of it; he just loved the place. He liked the lay of the land and the mix of trees scattered on it, the rock-strewn mountain beauty of it.

Dan got up every morning before dawn and went to work in the tidy shop up behind the house, shaping wood with table saw and radial arm, router and planer, lathe and joiner, turning raw lumber into dinette sets, hutches, beds, and dressers. Around noon he would stop work, load whatever pieces he had ready to sell into the back of his truck, grab a quick lunch at the house, then head into Sutter's Cross to consign his offerings to the retail store at the end of Main Street. He hoped someday to be able to harvest lumber from his own land, dry it in his own kiln, and produce a wide range of handcrafted furniture from it, right there in back of the house. He had visions of his children one day working with him in the family business here on his own land. It was a modest dream, but it was his.

It was that modest dream that made him toss Web Holcombe and his money out the door. This was *his* place, the home he'd personally carved out for his family. His wife loved it, the kids had been born here, and the rustic cedar ranch house he built for them looked as if it *belonged.* He didn't know, or care, what Holcombe planned to do with his land or how much he was willing to pay. He had no idea that his land lay in the middle of the future grand entrance to a playground for the rich and famous.

Dan was a creature of habit. Every evening his truck turned off the highway and followed the long twisting drive up to the house without stopping at the mailbox down by the road. He would then get out and jog down to the mailbox and back, a half mile round trip, to fetch the mail. He could have picked it up on the way in, but his work in the furniture shop was too sedentary to keep him fit, and this was his way of forcing himself to exercise every day.

It also helped him shake off the heart-crushing guilt he'd felt every day for the last week, every time he pulled into his garage. Dan had another habit that had always seemed innocuous enough, but a week ago it had led to trouble. He always stopped in at Duffy's once a week for two beers—always two, never more. There was usually an old friend around, and Dan could catch up on the latest gossip or find out what trout holes were hot this week.

But last Tuesday afternoon he went into Duffy's and didn't see anybody he recognized except Duffy, bartending as usual. Dan nursed a beer and listened to the conversation between Duffy and the auburn-haired girl at the bar.

She was sharp, in more ways than one. She was one of those rare women who, although undeniably drop-dead gorgeous, didn't seem to be aware of it. Before he knew it, Dan was drawn into the discussion. She carried her end of the conversation with a disarming, self-effacing wit and an uncommon charm. He felt a twinge of warning at first, but then he thought, *There's no harm in talking. It's a public place.* Besides, Libby had been a little distant lately, and the attention felt good.

He wasn't quite ready to leave after the second beer, so he ordered another, and another drink for the lady—just to be polite.

When she got up to leave, he decided it was time for him to go as well, and they walked out together. She told him she had enjoyed talking to him and it was a shame she wouldn't likely see him again because she was only in town for two days, on business, and would be leaving in the morning. And then, digging in her purse, she asked if he had the correct change so she could call a cab from the pay phone at the curb.

He offered her a ride instead. She declined at first but then said okay if it wasn't out of his way.

When they got to her hotel she asked if he'd like to come in for coffee.

She was very, very persuasive.

The weight of guilt tore at his heart as he jogged down the driveway, even now, a week later. He couldn't understand how it had happened; it had never happened before. He swore to himself it would never happen again, and he prayed that Libby would never find out about it.

He slowed to a walk as he rounded the curve in the last hundred yards and saw the red Cherokee sitting at the end of his driveway, the driver obscured behind dark tinted windows. A dream catcher hung from the rearview mirror, two feathers twisting slowly below it. A blue-and-white sticker on the front bumper said *Nuke the Whales.* As Dan approached, the driver's door opened, and a man with dark glasses and a ponytail stepped out smiling.

Something about this stranger set off alarms in Dan's mind. He had obviously pulled in and waited for Dan to come back down to the mailbox. Why didn't he just drive up to the house? Why would he wait at the mailbox—unless he knew Dan would be coming back down? Dan caught a glimpse of something in the man's left hand, but then he saw it was only a manila envelope. No threat. He made a mental note to stop being so paranoid.

"Dan! How ya doin', buddy?" The man was as friendly as a puppy, grinning, shaking hands as if they were old friends.

Dan wondered if he might recognize the man without the sunglasses. "Do I know you?"

"Well, ah, no. But I know *you* really, really well, and that's good enough, don't you think? So, how're the wife and kids?"

There was an ominous undercurrent in the jovial tone.

"What's this about? What do you want?"

"Oh, I just dropped by to give you your pictures." He held up the envelope, then slapped it against Dan's chest.

"What pictures? What are you talking about?" Dan opened the envelope and pulled out a sheaf of papers.

"They're not exactly pictures, actually. They're just printouts from the video, captured to computer. See, what you do is plug the camcorder into—"

"Where did you get these?" Dan thumbed through the pages, full color printouts of his adventure with the auburn-haired girl last week—pictures taken from *inside* the hotel room. His stomach slowly tied itself into a square knot.

"I told you, man, they're from the video. That's why they're a little grainy. But, hey, you can still recognize everybody, right? And if you like the book—" he pulled his glasses down on his nose and looked over them so Dan could see his twinkling eyes—"you'll *love* the movie. Marti's a terrific actress, isn't she? Expensive, but good."

Dan's knees buckled a little; his head spun. His world had suddenly become very narrow, and he couldn't get enough air. "What do you want?" he rasped.

"I want you to tell your wife you've found another place, a piece of land that's heaven on earth, and you'll die if you don't sell this place and buy it. No big deal. People change their minds all the time." He winked.

The last piece of the puzzle snicked into place in Dan's mind; he saw the plot whole, including the hand behind it, and his too-short fuse flashed away. With a roar, he flung the envelope in the laughing man's face and rushed him. He launched his huge frame across the narrow space between them with the intent of driving the smaller man off his feet, pinning him to the ground, and smashing him like the insect he was. But something happened. He didn't know how it was done—it happened so fast—but somehow his momentum was diverted in a lightning-quick flurry of movement that ended with his cheek rammed hard onto the hood of the Cherokee and his arm pinned up between his shoulder blades. His thumb and first two fingers shrieked with a pain intense enough to make Dan want to hold very, very still, lest they snap. The man bent over, still smiling, and his face drew close to Dan's ear.

"Move," the man with the ponytail said. "Find another place to live, and this little... *indiscretion* never happened, okay? Good. I knew you'd understand."

Chapter Twelve

"Sutter's Cross wears the summer like a ball gown,
the Fourth of July like a tiara."

Jake Mahaffey

Through the winter Sutter's Cross slumbers; isolated lights glint from the ridgetops on clear, brittle winter nights while retired doctors and judges read leather-bound books in front of fireplaces, safe from the winds that howl up the valley to clack dry limbs together on naked trees. But come spring the earth opens up in a gaudy peacock display, and by Memorial Day the summer people and tourists flood in. The freshly painted shops on Main Street buzz with activity from early May to late October, when the last leaf-looker has taken the camera from around his neck and gone home and the last Oktoberfest beer mug has been drained and washed and put away.

The social event of the year has always been the annual Fourth of July celebration, to be held this year at Hemlock Glen, the recreational park where the Arts League, headed by Web Holcombe himself, had constructed the new amphitheater. With its wide stage and gleaming white parabolic backdrop, the new amphitheater was perfectly situated at the apex of an imposing cul-de-sac of rock, a mini-canyon thrust out from the foot of the ridge. The seating area fanned out from the stage on shallow stone terraces, the whole of which had been recessed into the ground so as not to obstruct the view of the stage from the grass beyond the seats.

Because of the elevation of the stage and the gentle slope of parkland around it, thousands of people could recline on the grass beyond the formal seating area and enjoy a concert.

The park began filling early with blankets anchored by baskets and coolers. Church groups like the one from Sutter's Cross Community arrived early and claimed the picnic areas at the fringes. On the eastern edge of the park, the Rotary Club set up a tent awning and provided a sound system for a string of local bluegrass bands to play throughout the early part of the day. Tumlin's Pig Shack, a local favorite barbecue place, brought in a huge portable barbecue grill along with a concession wagon full of soft drinks and iced tea and set up shop between the bandstand and the baseball field.

A beach volleyball tournament kept the sand court occupied much of the morning. The annual softball game between the town police and the sheriff's department was scheduled for the afternoon, as always, but it had to wait until the sky divers finished. Men and other children stood mesmerized, heads thrown back, mouths agape, hands shading sunglass-covered eyes as bright rectangles the colors of the rainbow pirouetted to the earth, backlit by the sun against a polished blue sky. Using the baseball field as a target, the sky divers flared into a graceful running landing, trailing American flags from their backs.

The softball game, billed tongue-in-cheek as "The Annual Sudden Death Softball Championship of the Free World," was a farce. The police had never beaten the sheriff's department, but then they had never really tried. The winning team received a plaque, yet the loser had the honor of making the presentation speech, a much better prize. Police Chief TJ Nalley, a portly, cherry-faced man with a renowned wit, played a comic first base but carved himself a niche in local history with his thorough roasting of the sheriff's department in his presentation speech. Far more people gathered every year to hear his speech than ever watched the game.

When TJ finished, when the laughter and applause had died down, Sheriff Billy Thompson stepped up to the microphone. A big, broad-shouldered man in his early thirties with a shock of brown curly hair and an embarrassed smile in a shade of crimson that betrayed his fear of public speaking, he held the plaque aloft. Waving an open hand toward the escaping police chief, he leaned too close to the mike so that his words sputtered and hissed as he boomed out, "Ladies and gentlemen, TJ Nalley! The finest police chief money can buy!"

Jake and Lori showed up late in the afternoon and joined the growing throng of people from the church. Orde and Ruth Wingo and the other early arrivals had managed to secure several picnic tables near the river, in the shade of the hardwood trees. After the softball game Jake and some of the other men set up lawn chairs in the shade to talk sports and swap lies while some of the women went to the bake sale, another in a long line of fund-raising activities put on throughout the day by the Rotary Club. TJ Nalley joined the men after his speech, still wearing his overly tight softball uniform, which he filled out in true Babe Ruthian dimensions.

Orde, wearing a chef's apron, busied himself setting up the grills for the hamburgers and hot dogs, but he kept one ear cocked, listening to TJ's yarns. Orde's wife, Ruth, fussed over the tables in her characteristically meek way, straightening tablecloths, arranging dishes, putting out jars of plastic utensils, shooing away the occasional fly, all without looking up or speaking but once or twice.

"Beau was a German shorthair," TJ explained to Jake and the others. "Best pointer I ever saw until he got a taste for catfish. Wasn't worth killing after that."

"Catfish?" Jake couldn't see what catfish and dogs had to do with one another.

Orde stopped in the middle of pouring coals into a grill and grinned over his shoulder. "I love this story." He and TJ were first cousins and lifelong hunting partners.

"I didn't believe it either, at first," TJ continued. "Old Man Chitwood, down the road, must have called the house three or four times griping about my dog killing his catfish."

"Chitwood..." Jake mused. "Is that the guy whose eye points over your shoulder when he talks to you?"

"That's the one. He said he was gonna shoot the dog next time he saw him at the pond. The man's a fruitcake, so I didn't pay any attention to him. Told him he was nuts and hung up on him. But it nagged me a bit, so the next time I drove by there, I took a look up toward his catfish pond—it's in his front pasture and you can see it from the road—and I saw an old couple up there fishing. So I stopped in, you know, just to see. Anyway, I asked them how they were doing. They said they weren't catching much, but there was a bird dog just tearing 'em up.

"Tearing *what* up? I asked. Catfish, they said. Just wait and see, they said. Funniest thing they ever saw. Said the dog was up in the woods right then, burying one, but he'd be back down in a minute." TJ stopped to take a slug from a plastic Gatorade bottle and mop his face with the towel slung around his ample neck. "Sure enough, in a few minutes here comes Beau trotting down from the woods, right down to the far bank. He didn't see me sitting across the pond; he was too preoccupied. Anyhow, he pranced back and forth on the bank for a while, staring into the water the whole time. Did that for a minute or two before he finally struck a point. Prettiest point you ever saw—froze solid as a statue, head down, tail out, one foot up—looked like something out of *National Geographic,* except he was pointing at the water. He held that point for about three seconds and then busted into that pond and came out with a three-pound channel cat flopping and squirming in his mouth. Took it up in the woods and buried it, then ran back and did the whole thing all over again." TJ shook his head as if to clear it. "Strangest thing I ever saw."

Jake asked if he still had the dog.

"Oh, no, I gave him away. I was so embarrassed over having to apologize to Fruitcake Chitwood, I almost shot the mutt. But then I thought better of it. I mean, how many bona fide catfish dogs are there in the world, anyway? Only I couldn't keep him penned up—that dog could dig or climb his way out of anything. So I gave him to my brother down in Cordele. He's got his own catfish pond and he loves that dog. Put him in a concrete kennel and trained him. Now he lets him out a couple times a week and tells him 'Go get supper, Beau!' Says he could sell tickets to watch old Beau fish if he wanted to."

"But you've still got a bunch of dogs, don't you?" Jake asked.

"I do, but they're rabbit dogs. Bird dogs aren't much use around here anymore with the quail all but gone. Now I've just got the twelve beagles and two bloodhounds."

"Two of the best tracking dogs in the southeast," Orde added over his shoulder.

TJ grinned proudly. "That's the truth. Those two could track a mosquito through a hailstorm."

There was a small commotion as heads turned and people got up from their lawn chairs to greet Web and Jenny Holcombe, who had arrived from the direction of the river. Myra and the boys brought up the rear, and it was immediately apparent from Eddy's and Marcus's foot dragging and hangdog expressions that either they didn't want to be here or they were in trouble.

An electronic cricket chirp brought Web up short. Flipping open his cell phone, he turned his back and engaged in an animated conversation while Jenny kissed the air next to Lori's face. Lori had taken care of Eddy in the nursery at church when he was a baby; she and Jenny had become friends then.

"How'd you get *him* to come out?" Lori asked, nodding with a smile toward Web. "I thought he worked three hundred and sixty-six days a year."

"I have my ways, darlin'." Jenny raised an eyebrow and gave Lori a thin sidelong grin. Web paid no attention. He wandered a few steps away and seemed to be studying the cloud formations over the eastern ridge as he held the cell phone against his head with a forefinger.

"Actually, we can't stay," Jenny continued. "We're going to the concert. The Arts League always gives us front-row seats and a pass to the preconcert buffet with the conductor. He's so sweet." She scrunched her face into a devilish grin and hugged herself.

"How did you get here?" asked Jake. "You came from the direction of the river, and there hasn't been any parking left along the riverbank for hours."

"Oh, we used the VIP parking at the golf course and walked from there. We crossed on that lovely little swinging bridge over the river gorge. The boys think it's really neat."

Jake was watching Eddy and Marcus, standing some distance away, hands in pockets, kicking dejectedly at the turf. "What's wrong with the boys?" he asked. "They look like they're going to be hanged in the morning."

"They're in big trouble with Web. We went for a hike with them this morning, and they took us down to show off their tree house." She turned halfway and pointed toward the woods across the Elder a good ways upstream. "It's up there about a half mile on the other side."

Jake's brows furrowed in puzzlement. "What's wrong with a tree house?"

Jenny snickered. "Oh, there's nothing wrong with having a tree house, but they never should have shown it to Web. First of all, they're not supposed to be anywhere near the river, and this thing hangs positively *over* the river. Web wasn't happy about that. But then, when he saw the monstrosity, he started asking questions and figured out they stole all the boards and stuff from the Snyders' new house while they were building it. Some of the tools, too. You should see that thing—it's *huge*!" She puffed her cheeks out, rolled her eyes. Web had glanced around once, hearing his name mentioned, but stayed glued to his phone.

"On top of everything," Jenny went on, "it's not even on our property. It's across the line on the Snyders' land. Of course, the boys didn't know that. Web was fit to be tied. He called the Snyders and offered to pay for the stuff, but they said it wasn't necessary. They were real sweet about the whole thing, said boys'll be boys. But Web's pride was at stake, his precious pro-fes-sion-al reputation." She whispered this last with a smirk and a quick look to make sure Web couldn't hear her. "Web put the four-wheeler off limits for a month and restricted Eddy to the house for a week. Myra gave Marcus the same. It's going to put a real crimp in their summer."

"Ain't gonna help my week a whole lot, either," Myra put in. She had walked up in the middle of Jenny's explanation.

Lori giggled, shaking her head. "Boys," she said. "They're amazing, aren't they? I thought they were just mad about having to go to a concert."

"They won't be going to the concert; they couldn't sit still that long. Those boys could never survive an hour and a half of classical music, especially Strauss. We figured we'd just turn them loose here while Web and I go to the concert. Myra's going to stay and keep an eye on them."

"But, Jenny, she doesn't have to do that. Jake and I could watch out for them, and then Myra could go."

Jenny was delighted with the idea, and she was sure Web could get Myra a seat. He did, after all, practically own the place. But Myra declined, using the excuse that she wasn't dressed for it. In the end she stayed behind, arms folded, watching stoically as Jenny dragged Web by his free arm, the one not attached to his cell phone, across the park toward the amphitheater. The boys ran off to join a growing throng of kids playing tag in the lengthening shadows of the trees.

"Sure wish we could get that boy to come to church," Orde said when Web and Jenny were out of hearing range. He stared wistfully after them.

"Who?" Jake said.

"Web Holcombe," Orde answered with a slight air of consternation, as if Jake should have known. "He runs this town. That's exactly the kind of people we need if our church is going to grow. Movers and shakers. It'd be a real coup if we could get him to join."

"A *coup*?" Jake snorted. "Never heard you use *that* word before. Anyway, I'm not sure I agree with you."

"What, you don't think a man like Web could use the Lord in his life?"

Orde frowned, and Jake figured he was getting dangerously close to climbing up on his soapbox.

"No, it's not that. Of course he could. It's just, I don't know. That's not how you said it. And that kind of thinking seems sort of upside down, somehow."

Orde's face reddened. "What do you mean, upside—" He paused in midsentence and raised a hand to shade his eyes. He was staring hard across the park, to a group of college kids sailing Frisbees back and forth. "Say, Jake, isn't that your hobo friend over there?" Orde pointed. TJ's lawn chair whinnied as he got up from his seat to stare over Orde's shoulder, constabulary curiosity having gotten the better of him.

"Where?" Jake knew whom Orde meant, but he couldn't spot Harley in the crowd.

"Sitting on the ground near the guy in the red shorts with the Frisbee."

"I see him," TJ said. "The dark-haired guy with the beard, sitting there watching the belly-rubbers, right?"

Jake raised an eyebrow. "Belly-rubbers?"

"Yeah—you know, the young guys with the washboard stomachs, always standing around with a Frisbee in their hands wearing nothing but sunglasses and silk shorts." He ran a splayed hand over his ample belly and, feigning a sort of valley-girl accent, mocked, "I take care of my body and I think I deserve a woman who takes care of *her* body."

The phrase, coming from TJ's Big Bubba frame, drew a guffaw from Orde. "Sounds like you know them pretty well. I guess with all the college kids around here in the summer, the police get real familiar with them, huh?"

"Nah, they're not bad. They're just kids, never cause any real trouble. We hardly ever have to lock one of them up. It ain't a bad idea to lock up your daughters, though."

Orde pointed for Jake. "You see him? He's sitting off to the right side, watching the belly-rubber with the Frisbee-catching dog."

Jake shaded his eyes and scanned the crowd, still chuckling at TJ's mockery. As if to illustrate Orde's point, one of the young men lashed a Frisbee through the air, and a tricolor Australian shepherd rocketed after it. Keeping his eyes on the dog, the young man moved with a smooth, lanky athleticism, took a couple of steps backward, raked sun-bleached hair away from his bronze face, and unconsciously ran his fingertips up and down his rippling stomach muscles, taking care not to glance at the gaggle of girls whispering to each other on the sidelines.

Jake finally picked out Harley. He was sitting on the grass with his long arms wrapped around his knees, captivated by the dog's acrobatic prowess.

"Yeah, that's him. Wonder how he got here? I haven't seen Miss Agnes."

"He looks familiar," TJ mused. "I could swear I've seen him somewhere before, but it's hard to tell at this distance." He wore a slight frown of businesslike concentration, and Jake figured he was running Harley's picture through the police files in his head.

"He came to church that one time, but I haven't seen him since," Orde said. "Oh, and who could forget his appearance at the spring picnic down at the pavilion?"

TJ chuckled. "*He's* the one? Yeah, I heard about that. I wish he'd turn this way so I could get a better look at him."

In apparent answer to his wish, a little girl racing after a ball bumped Harley's shoulder and he looked sharply around with his face angled directly toward the three men watching him.

"Boy, he looks familiar," said TJ. "I know that face from somewhere. What'd you say his name was?"

"Harley," Jake answered grimly. "His name's Harley." He had an urge to go invite him up for a hamburger, but in light of Harley's past experiences with the church crowd he thought better of it.

Orde's wife called him, and he turned abruptly to see what she wanted. She had unwrapped the burgers and placed the platter on the little table between the grills. "I think the coals are ready," she offered timidly, leaning over one of the grills. "It's probably just about time to put the hamburgers on, don't you think? Orde?"

With a bowing and shuffling and a "Yas'm, boss!" Orde bounded, grinning, back to his position at the grill, snatched up a spatula, and started flipping burgers onto the grate. The little group had swelled to more than twenty people, and he had a lot of burgers and dogs to cook.

Jake heard Lori's voice call out, "Miss Agnes!" He turned to see his wife with an arm around Miss Agnes's shoulders, guiding her to a seat near one of the picnic tables. "I figured you were here someplace when I saw Harley. Where've you been?" Lori asked.

Miss Agnes handed her a cellophane-wrapped carrot cake and settled herself into a lawn chair. "I went to the bake sale and got that cake. Didn't want to show up empty-handed, you know. We would have come earlier, but Pug Mabry come by the house and brung Harley a new pair of hiking boots and a big bag of sunflower seeds. Them two are getting to be good buddies." She shook her head, smiling. "Harley was sure proud of them boots. His old ones was just about rurnt from walking up and down the ridge. Then, after I left the bake sale, I kept bumping into folks I hadn't seen in a coon's age, and I had to stop and talk." She chuckled. "When you get old, talking to folks is about all you got to look forward to."

"Why didn't you bring Harley up here with you?" Jake asked. "He's welcome to eat with us if he wants."

Miss Agnes dismissed this with a wave. "I told him he ought to come over and get a bite. He said maybe later. He was busy walking around looking at all the doings, watching folks—you know how he does."

Jake brought Miss Agnes a plastic cup of iced tea. "I had an interesting conversation with a trail tramp the other day," he said. "He told me Harley's building a bit of a reputation for himself. Said there are rumors all up and down the mountains, hikers talking about some kind of 'holy man' up on Chestnut Ridge. Turns out he was talking about Harley. What's going on up there?"

Orde half turned to face Jake and Miss Agnes, fanning smoke away from his face with the spatula. Miss Agnes sipped her tea with a wry smile.

"I don't know," she said. "He don't tell me everything. I know he spends a good deal of time up on the mountain, and he runs into folks now and then. He gets up every Sunday morning way before daylight and goes up to Joshua's Knee and stays most of the day. He says there's almost always a bunch of hikers up there on Sundays."

Orde had come to a full stop, listening to Miss Agnes. "I guess that's why he hasn't been back to Sunday school," Orde said, a suggestion of a smirk curling the corner of his lip. "He goes hiking."

She shrugged. "Says he goes up there to listen to God. Far as I know, he just sits on the Knee and reads his Bible. He says he hears better up there."

"He hears better." Orde's face was blank. He carefully lowered the lids on the grills to control the flame on the burgers before turning his attention to Miss Agnes again. He wiped his hands on his apron. "He hears better," he repeated. "So now our local bearded unemployed bum is making himself out to be some sort of guru, and he's putting together his own little cult up on the mountain. How nice."

Miss Agnes's mouth hung agape and she looked at Jake, who had no choice but to jump in.

"I think *cult* might be a little strong, Orde. I mean, he just goes there to read and meditate."

"Meditate. Right," Orde snorted. "Does he chant while he's doing it?"

"It's not like that, Orde. He just likes a little quiet time. And sometimes other people show up and sit with him and they talk, that's all."

" 'Evil men and impostors will go from bad to worse, deceiving and being deceived,' " Orde said, his eyes narrowing.

Jake shook his head. "I've talked to him. I've spent time with the man, and I don't see him trying to deceive anybody. I don't know if it's wise to slander somebody you don't even know."

"I wasn't slandering, I was quoting Scripture," Orde answered flatly.

"Still, I wish you could have talked to the trail tramp I met the other morning. He'd had an amazing experience up there. It was *real,* and Harley had something to do with it. There's no question about that."

"Yeah, well, I guess tramps are going to stick together, aren't they."

"Oh, come on, Orde. This guy was no bum, he was a retired stockbroker. He took to the trail to try and sort his life out after his wife died."

"What happened to his wife?"

"She had lung cancer."

Orde stroked his chin. "Did she smoke?"

"What difference does it make? She's still *dead.* If you want to play God and decide whether or not she deserved to die, the answer is, Yes! From God's point of view, we all do. The question is, What are we going to do about it? What do we offer each other—judgment or compassion?" Jake was a little surprised to hear himself talking this way, especially to Orde, a teacher he had always respected. He figured Harley must be rubbing off.

Orde's face reddened perceptibly and he aimed his spatula at Jake. "You told me yourself, Jake, that bum never set foot in a church. What could he possibly know? What right does he have going around pretending to be some kind of preacher? Has he ever been to seminary? Frankly, I care enough about people's souls to want to put a stop to dangerous heresies and illiterate fools passing themselves off as prophets. I think somebody should do something about this fledgling Jim Jones before the whole thing gets out of hand and we end up with a full-blown cult right here in Sutter's Cross!"

Orde glanced briefly at TJ Nalley as if he expected his cousin to back him up. The corners of TJ's eyes crinkled, a clear warning that his sense of humor had kicked in. He shrugged.

"Just don't drink the Kool-Aid, Orde," said TJ.

The little crowd erupted in laughter. Tony Shepherd, caught off guard by TJ's remark, choked and sprayed iced tea across the lawn. His wife pounded him on the back.

Orde turned back to his grill, yanked up the lid, and started flipping burgers with a staccato ferocity. His face was grim, his lips drawn tight.

Jake decided he'd better try to smooth things over.

"Look, Orde, I didn't mean to insult you or question your authority on biblical matters. It's just that, well, it seems wise to me to wait and see. I figure God has a better handle on things than we do, and if somebody misrepresents Him, for whatever reason, he'll come to a bad end soon enough. But I don't think we should jump to conclusions. We could find ourselves fighting against God."

Orde spun around, red-faced, and pointed with his spatula in the general direction of Harley. "Jake," he hissed, "if you're trying to tell me that *freeloader* is some kind of prophet, or that God sent him here, then I'd have to say I'm starting to wonder where *you're* coming from!" The end of the spatula quivered with his rage. "That's borderline blasphemy, friend!"

Jake stared, openmouthed. He could see no way to approach the man.

Miss Agnes, who had been listening quietly with her gnarled hands folded on her lap, leaned forward and captured Orde with her eyes. She spoke calmly, and her thin voice cut the silence like a knife.

"He wasn't blaspheming," she said. "He was quotin' Scripture."

TJ had risen from his chair and turned his back during Orde's tirade. Jake thought he was about to slip away and evade his cousin's ire, but then TJ stopped and stared across the park toward Harley and a big grin lit his face. "Orde!" he shouted. "That's your guy! *That's* where I've seen him! He was your model, wasn't he?"

Orde adjusted his glasses a notch and stared at the bearded figure across the park, then fastened his frown on TJ. "What are you talking about?"

"That guy! The one with the beard. What's his name—Harvey? He's the face on your billboard down by the river, the Jesus one! You used him for a model, didn't you? I mean, he's the spitting image."

Jake peered across the park and found Harley again. Harley had knelt down to pet a dog, and Jake realized suddenly that the tilt of his head, the way the slanting sunlight broke across his face, the outstretched hand, the smile—all of it perfectly matched the pose of the Jesus on the billboard. The likeness was astonishing. People nudged each other and snickered behind their hands as they picked out Harley and compared notes on TJ's observation.

It was *Harley's* face that beckoned people into Sutter's Cross, and Orde had painted it with his own hand. He had painstakingly removed a lunatic from the picture, only to leave Harley in his place.

Orde said nothing. He stood very still, his jaw muscles flexing and his eyes boring into the scraggly figure in the distance. Smoke wafted around his head from the burning hamburgers on the grill behind him. Finally he turned and bent over his work, grim and silent.

The concert began, and the irrepressible "Till Eulenspiegel's Merry Pranks" leaped cleanly from the strings of the Charleston Symphony Orchestra, bursting out of the amphitheater and spilling across the broad green expanse. Once or twice Orde glared, briefly, across the park, but he said very little for the rest of the evening.

Chapter Thirteen

A few minutes after Miss Agnes's old pickup truck chugged up River Road toward the celebration in town, a red Cherokee pulled in and eased up the rutted driveway between the trees. Guinea hens heralded the arrival and Buster bayed a soulful warning, but Benny T paid no attention. He knew no one would hear. He shut off the engine and, from force of habit, dropped his keys under the seat before climbing out. Keys jingling in a pocket could give a man away, and Benny had long since cultivated the practices of stealth.

He got out and stretched, then sauntered around the front of the Cherokee, keeping an appraising eye on Buster, who advanced a step toward him, growling, his hackles raised. The man with the ponytail held his ground and spoke in low, soothing tones to the dog. He squatted and held his fist out, fingers down, for Buster to sniff. In less than a minute Benny had him literally eating out of his hand—a Beefy Treat fished from a bag in the pocket of his jeans, brought along for just such a contingency.

He walked all the way around the house once, careful to avoid soft ground so his flat-bottomed deck shoes wouldn't leave any clear prints, and then went up onto the porch and rapped gently on the front door. He knew nobody was home, but he had been surprised before and had learned to err on the side of caution. The door was not locked.

Either the old woman doesn't believe in locks or she doesn't have anything worth stealing, he thought. But no matter—he wasn't here to steal. He propped his sunglasses on top of his head and closed the door behind him.

It was a lonely old woman's house, full of silence and memory and smells—the aroma of fresh-baked bread and tired upholstery, overlaid with a faint whiff of wintergreen. The cramped little living room held a collection of overstuffed chairs, lamps, tables, and a country sofa. He paused for a moment, scanning the room, wondering what was missing, then realized it was the television. There wasn't one, nor was there a stereo or even a telephone. The only sound was the patient ticking of an antique wall clock. One wall was a mosaic of pictures, mostly black-and-white snapshots, yellowed with age and slightly out of focus, in cheap frames. There were two old men in dirty T-shirts grinning around a stringer of trout, a boy in the front yard in a baseball uniform with a bat on his shoulder, and endless family shots of spectacled men and women posing in Sunday clothes in front of houses. Above a small corner table bearing a faded tri-folded American flag hung an eight-by-ten color portrait of a smiling young man in a uniform.

"Hello, Robby," he whispered. He lifted a doily from the arm of an ugly green corduroy chair and touched the threadbare arm underneath where the beige backing showed through from thousands of hands having gripped and rubbed it. He carefully replaced the doily and moved on.

He eased into the kitchen, sagging floorboards creaking under his feet.

It struck him that the kitchen was amazingly clean, considering the age of the appliances. The refrigerator and stove were the old, white porcelain-finished, round-edged dinosaurs only found in junkyards these days, yet they were spotless, kept unstained despite decades of use. He stepped around the little oak table and stuck his head out the back door. The screened-in back porch held nothing of interest: a washing machine, a stack of firewood, a chest freezer. No dryer—there was a clothesline in the backyard.

The rest of the house yielded much of the same, everything old but well maintained. There were no surprises. In one of the two small bedrooms he found an old iron double bed, neatly made up and covered with a threadbare homemade quilt. Miss Agnes's bedroom. It was in the closet of the other bedroom that he found what he was looking for—a small, plastic, portable filing cabinet. He carried it back to the kitchen, sat down at the table, and started going through the files one at a time.

He had two objectives. First, he wanted to learn, if he could, the name of the man who had accosted Web in the yard. Benny didn't know what had tripped Web's trigger, but whatever it was, Web wanted this man badly. He wanted to take him down. From what Benny had seen of Harley, or whatever his name really was, he figured there was bound to be a way to nail him. He didn't have the look of a saint.

His second objective was to learn exactly what Miss Agnes was up to *lately.* Her financial history could be, and had been, obtained from various sources and through various means, but that information, complete though it was, only told them she was broke. It told them she was behind in her taxes and scratching by on a fixed income. It did not tell them, however, what she planned to do about it. There was also the possibility that she had some money squirreled away somewhere that didn't show up in her credit report.

He found nothing new in her bank statements, but in the third folder, the one marked Farming Expenses, he found an interesting invoice. Dated only two weeks ago, the invoice was from Parks Seed Co., and it listed a large shipment of seed corn.

He stared out the window. He'd seen no new crop from the road—the trees obscured everything—but it wouldn't be hard to find.

He smiled. "So the old bird has ambition," he muttered.

Finding nothing else of interest in the files, he closed the box and put it back in the closet, exactly where he'd found it.

He eased out the back door and crossed the yard. Buster followed him into the barn, hoping to wrangle another Beefy Treat from his newfound friend. A disk harrow sat parked to the side, its blades looking like a row of woks turned sideways. The edges, resting on the dirt, were shiny from recent use. The tractor sat with its back to him, the head-high rear wheels still cupping lumps of red clay in their treads. He pulled off a chunk and squeezed it in his fist. Still damp. There was some sort of complicated contraption attached to the back of the tractor, built around a metal hopper the size of a laundry hamper. Benny opened the lid and looked inside. There were kernels of dry corn stuck in the corners. Obviously it was a planting machine of some sort.

But he already knew what they were up to. Now he wanted only to find something, anything, that would give him a clue to the mystery man's identity. Web didn't say what had happened between them to kindle such a fierce determination. Still, the fire was there, in his eyes and in his words.

"His head on a platter," Web had said.

It didn't take Sherlock Holmes to figure out Harley slept somewhere in the shed; he didn't sleep in the house, and the other outbuildings were too small. Stepping past the tractor, taking care to step on clumps of straw so as not to leave any footprints in the dry silty dust of the barn floor, Benny stopped at the workbench by the back arch of the drive-through. The bench was clean, the tools put away, but the air still smelled of grease and mineral spirits.

There, in the shadows at the far end of the workbench, was a door. He eased it open and felt for a light switch, but there was none. He realized then that he'd seen no wiring anywhere in the shed. Sighing, he reached into the back pocket of his jeans, pulled out a small flashlight and clicked it on.

The room was tiny, no more than eight feet square, and windowless. A cot, neatly made, lined the back wall and butted up against a rough plywood trunk in the corner. A set of crude shelves rose to the ceiling beside the door. On the shelves he found a Coleman lantern, a small stack of folded clothes, a bag of sunflower seeds. A brief search of the clothes turned up nothing; he left them looking as if they hadn't been touched. He sat on the end of the cot and lifted the lid of the trunk, holding the flashlight in his teeth, wincing at the blast of camphor from the mothballs. Nothing there, either—just some extra blankets and a faded box of rat poison. He put everything back exactly like he found it. As he started back out the door he turned and made one last sweep of the little room with his flashlight. Nothing on the walls, nothing interesting on the shelves, but wait...

On the floor under the cot, he glimpsed the toes of an old pair of boots he hadn't noticed before. He knelt down and pulled them out, turning them over in his hands. Just an old pair of black, rubber-soled work boots, with the heels worn down and a crack clear through the sole on the ball of the right boot. The polish was scuffed nearly off of them, and the nap of the leather showed through on the toes. He looked inside one, pulled the tongue back to see the underside of it, and a Cheshire-cat grin spread out around the flashlight in his mouth.

On the underside of the tongue was a name. It was old and faded and sweat stained, but the letters left by the black felt-tipped marker were still perfectly legible in the soft leather. He patted his pockets for a pen, then realized he'd left it in the Cherokee.

No matter. He would remember the name. He knew instinctively that a man who hid his real name did so for a reason: He had a past that needed hiding. Find the name and you find the past. Find the past and you own the man.

The magic of Strauss coaxed the blue shadow of the western ridge across the green, where a thousand little commotions slowed and stopped as people settled onto blankets to listen. The Charleston Symphony Orchestra serenaded the purple end of a perfect day while the Elder River carried the cool of the evening down from the heights and a gentle mountain breeze rolled it across the park. The golden glow from the amphitheater became the focal point of the evening.

Everyone had settled in except for a group of children, about twenty of them in all, who chased each other and screamed and tagged and teased and laughed, an ardent counterpoint to the clear sweet note of an oboe from across the green. "Death and Transfiguration" had begun; those with programs knew the end was near, but they didn't mind. The encore was what they had come for.

To Marcus it looked like Eddy was making a fool of himself over Ashley—chasing her around, showing off in front of her, hanging on her every word—but with Darryl Snyder for competition it wasn't hard to see why. Snyder, a solid, broad-shouldered tank of a boy, was nearly a head taller than Eddy and Marcus, though he was the same age. Marcus could see the competition developing, but the rules of engagement were beyond him. He couldn't figure out why Eddy didn't just tell Ashley he liked her, unless he just didn't want to say it in front of Brittany.

Eddy finally resorted to the time-tested tactic of putting a firefly down the back of her shirt. She screamed and squirmed, arched her back, crooked an arm and tried to reach it, failed, jerked her shirttail out, shook it and danced in a circle until the firefly fell out and flew off in an arc of phosphorescence, then tripped over her own feet and sat down heavily on the turf, glaring at Eddy.

Eddy moved to help her up, but Darryl Snyder beat him to it. Smiling cavalierly, Snyder offered Ashley a hand and pulled her to her feet. As she dusted off the back of her shorts, Snyder took a step toward Eddy and gave him a shove. Eddy staggered but planted a foot and stood his ground. Snyder closed the gap, stuck his chest out and loomed over Eddy.

"I wasn't trying—" Eddy started to explain when Snyder shoved him again, hard. Eddy managed to keep his feet, but Snyder advanced again.

Marcus stepped between them. "He was just...just..." The word stuck in Marcus's throat, and his face twisted around it.

Snyder's face warped into a caricature of Marcus's grimace, and two of his friends howled with laughter. He brushed Marcus aside to sneer at Eddy. Marcus tripped and fell, but he bounced up and stood beside Eddy, glaring at him. He wouldn't try to talk again; he wouldn't back down, either.

Snyder laughed. "What you gonna do, Holcombe, sic your *monkey* on me?"

Marcus blinked, unconsciously raising a hand to his ear. He hadn't heard the name Monkeyboy since the end of baseball season. He really thought it had died, but apparently it was alive and spreading.

Eddy's chin jutted, his eyes narrowed, and his fingers curled into a fist as his right elbow drew back a notch.

Ashley stepped between them, brushing Eddy back with a shoulder and planting a hand on Darryl Snyder's chest. "Leave him alone, Darryl. He was just playing. He didn't mean anything."

"EEEEUUUUWWWWWW! Get it OFF OF ME!" Brittany screamed. She had bent over and was flailing furiously at her hair, which hung almost to the ground. Ashley went over and calmly plucked a blinking firefly from Brittany's hair.

Brittany stood up, flung her hair back and shuddered, smoothing her tresses. "They're *everywhere*!" she griped, swatting the air, the disgust plain on her face.

They were everywhere. Fireflies had descended around the crowd of kids by the hundreds, painting chartreuse arcs in the air and pulsing yellow on the grass. Children scattered, tearing off in every direction, leaping and grabbing, the skirmish between Eddy and Snyder forgotten as quickly as it had started. They caught fireflies, peeked into their fists to watch the private light show, and then threw them on each other, giggling, and watched them fly away again. Bookish Randy Gurley, with his thick glasses, ran off to get a jar from his mother to put them in.

Marcus tried. He tried very hard to catch a firefly in flight like the other kids, but he couldn't. It was a small thing, and nobody else noticed it amid the chaos, yet when he leaped and grabbed, his hand would always arrive late or close early and the green ember would throb on its lazy way, untouched. It was a very small thing, but frustration is cumulative, and over his lifetime a host of little things had accumulated and merged into a matter of some importance to Marcus. He spotted a firefly resting on the grass and managed to trap it under his hands, but when he opened his fist to look at it, the alert insect buzzed through the opening and made a getaway. He blundered angrily after it, leaping, his face a picture of fierce concentration in the middle of a crowd of laughing, leaping faces.

He didn't see it coming. When Darryl Snyder threw a shoulder into him in midair, it knocked the wind out of him and sent him skidding across the turf on his back. He didn't even know it was Snyder who had blindsided him until, gasping for breath, he looked up and saw the crew cut head bent over him.

The face sneered. "You should watch where you're going, Monkeyboy. You could get hurt." And then he was gone.

Marcus rolled onto his side and pulled his knees up, fighting for a breath. About the time he got his wind back, a pair of strong hands gripped his shoulders and lifted him to his feet.

The hands turned him around, and he found himself looking into the face of a strange man with shoulder-length dark hair and a beard, kneeling in front of him. The gray eyes were kind and soft, and Marcus saw only concern there. But the man was a stranger. Marcus had been warned all his life about strangers. Especially strangers in parks, at dusk. As his breathing leveled out, he straightened up, glanced sideways and spotted his mother sitting in a lawn chair among the little cluster of people from the church. She had seen the whole thing. Even in the twilight, lit only by the distant glow of the amphitheater, he could make out the look of alarm on Myra's face as she started to rise from her chair. Then Lori Mahaffey put a hand on her arm and said something to her, and she sat back down.

"Are you all right?" the man said to Marcus. "You took a pretty good shot."

Marcus nodded, still gasping and holding a fist against his stomach.

Eddy materialized at the dark man's shoulder. "What happened?" he asked.

"Nothing." Marcus shook his head. "I'm okay."

But he wasn't. The shrieking, clamoring tumult continued unabated around him, and Marcus wanted no more of it. He thought he might just go sit with his mother. His gaze fell to the ground. He turned to walk away.

"What about the fireflies?" the deep voice behind him asked, and he stopped.

"I can't catch 'em. They just fly away," he muttered and took another step toward his mother. The voice stopped him again.

"You giving up?"

He nodded without looking back.

"You sure?"

Marcus turned, curious. He suspected that the man's question was larger than his words, but he wasn't sure. Uncertainty was the only constant in Marcus's life.

He nodded again.

"Good." The man was smiling. "That's the only place to start." He crooked his fingers, silently beckoning Marcus closer. He hesitated, but curiosity got the better of him and he trudged back, stopping right in front of the man, his eyes still downcast.

The man leaned closer so that their foreheads almost touched, and whispered, "Do you believe in God?"

Marcus granted him a shallow, perfunctory nod.

"He believes in you, too," the man said softly, then touched a finger to Marcus's chest. "He said so."

Marcus didn't move.

"He wants you to know He loves you. Wherever you stop, that's where He starts. All you got to do is ask."

Marcus looked up and met the man's eyes. He saw no trace of pretense and none of the condescension he'd seen in so many grown-ups. "God talks to you?"

The bearded face nodded. "I think He talks to everybody. Some people can't hear on account of the noise, and some aren't listening, but that don't mean He ain't there."

Marcus stared blankly. He was pretty sure *he* couldn't hear God talking.

"Ask for help," the man said.

Marcus's brows furrowed, and his mouth made a little suspicious O. "You want me to tell God to catch me a *bug*?"

"Don't tell. Ask. Just ask for help. He probably already knows what you need. Maybe it's got nothing to do with bugs. Besides—" he shrugged—"they're His bugs."

Marcus's mouth twisted to one side. His head didn't move, but his eyes rolled upward. The unblinking certainty of this strange man was contagious. "I *could* use a little help," he murmured.

Eddy, who had been listening, held out his fist to Marcus and offered him a firefly. Marcus held out a palm, and Eddy dropped the tiny insect onto it. But before Marcus could close his fingers, the firefly spread its wings and buzzed away. The disappointment in his face melted into a look of puzzlement, and then awe, as the firefly made a slow loop overhead, dove back down almost to the ground, swooped back up in a graceful arc, and flared to a stop in the middle of Marcus's chest. He stared blankly from the firefly winking against his dark T-shirt to the smile growing on the bearded man's face.

"Be still," the man whispered, putting a finger to his lips. "Be very still." He rose to his feet then, towering over the two boys, and took a step backward, watching Marcus. Another firefly swooped down, arcing cleanly onto Marcus's chest. The two insects crawled about and flexed their glossy wings, pulsed their pale lights, and threatened to fly away. But they stayed.

Another firefly zoomed low over Eddy's head and plopped unceremoniously on Marcus's shoulder; another fell straight down from above and arrested itself on his back. Eddy called out to the other kids, "Come here, guys! You gotta SEE this!"

One by one they crowded around, *ooh*ing and *ah*ing as fireflies continued to zero in on Marcus, who stood very still with his arms out and gathered tiny lights in a growing constellation against the night sky of his shirt.

The theme of hope welled up from the orchestra, sweet and strong. Marcus became fully aware for the first time of the music flowing around and through him, and he *owned* it. The summer night sang with a voice far bigger than Marcus, bigger than the park, bigger than the Elder Valley. The night sang for *him,* for the first time in his life, and his chest swelled with the fullness of it. The circle of faces around him gaped in astonishment as fireflies swarmed to him—dozens of them. His heart surged in harmony with a tide of violins. The rolling timpani came from inside him. Fireflies spread out onto his arms and down his legs; one even crawled up onto his face and sat blinking on the bridge of his nose. He stared in cross-eyed wonder while soaring French horns lifted his heart on newfound wings.

The other children hardly dared breathe. Girls whispered to each other behind fingertips, unable to take their eyes from the human Christmas tree before them. Boys stood very still with their hands in their pockets and said nothing, all except for Snyder, who stood behind Ashley with his arms crossed, scowling, and said loudly enough for everybody to hear,

"Clumsy little twerp, probably got peanut butter and jelly smeared all over his shirt."

The music quieted and slowed, layering ghostly echoes upon each other as Strauss drew the curtain down gracefully, peacefully.

Marcus began to twirl, holding his arms wide, a broad grin on his face.

"Awesome," Eddy whispered as Marcus's feet pivoted and danced, spinning him faster and faster. The violins and French horns paled. The dying melody lifted a storm of sparks from the whirling child and sent them spiraling into the night sky as he collapsed, laughing, on his back, to watch.

The music lingered for a few seconds on a single clear note and then winked out. Dead silence reigned until a sea of people rose to their feet in thunderous applause.

And when the cheering reached Marcus's ears, he owned that, too.

The applause died abruptly and an expectant hush fell. The conductor turned his back to the crowd once again. He raised his baton, held it for a moment, and when he brought it down the orchestra exploded into "The Stars and Stripes Forever." This was what most of the people had waited all evening for—knowing the symphony's encore would be Sousa and that it would be timed to coincide with full darkness.

The fireworks began.

Thousands of faces bobbed in time with the brilliant march, tilting skyward like sunflowers to see weeping willows and trumpets splashed against the night in broad strokes of diamond-dusted fire. The piccolo ruled; bright eyes and open mouths were lit from above as one and all became children again.

But one child, looking up, saw farther and deeper and wider than the others. He saw the glittering bursts and showers but he saw fireflies too, and stars, all of them sparks of hope flung upward like prayers into the night. For in one quiet, unexpected moment, he had looked beyond the stars and caught a glimpse of God.

Chapter Fourteen

"The best of men, in the best of times,
is hard pressed to know ill wind from fair."
JAKE MAHAFFEY

It was a season of extremes, that summer, a roller-coaster ride between euphoria and despair, a time when, for better or for worse, there were no small things. In mid-July, Jake and Lori found out they were going to have a baby.

It hadn't been easy. They had been trying for a long time, and the very idea that Lori was pregnant seemed like a dream, as fragile and tenuous as a soap bubble, a thing that mustn't be touched or intruded upon until it grew stronger. They decided to keep it to themselves for a while, at least until after the first trimester. But, after the doctor confirmed the miraculous news, they had to celebrate—the three of them. Jake made dinner reservations at The Gristmill.

As part of Web Holcombe's magical transformation of Sutter's Cross over the last ten years, he had bought the abandoned gristmill on the edge of town and completely renovated it, leaving the old beam structure intact and even restoring the waterwheel to working order, although he removed the milling machinery. He hired a landscape designer to clean up the front lot and sculpt it into a gardener's dream, with weeping willows sipping from the reflecting pond over the shoulders of thick banks of pink and white azaleas and a beautiful stone arch footbridge over the millrace as part of a walking path around the grounds, where children could throw bread crumbs to the ducks. Then he personally went headhunting in New York and came home with a world-renowned chef to head the staff of The Gristmill, the first four-star gourmet restaurant in Sutter's Cross. Jake took Lori there to celebrate their private miracle, and it was there that he first got to know Web Holcombe.

When Jenny glided into the crowded restaurant on Web's arm, heads turned in unison like schooling fish. Web was a commanding presence in his own right, but despite his charisma, he seemed relegated to the status of escort when he was with her. When Jenny entered the room, husbands stole glances at her; wives stole glances at their husbands.

Jake's head turned along with everybody else's—and Lori noticed. It was only an innocent glance, but Lori was feeling very maternal and vulnerable at the moment. She gave him that gunslinger look, raised an eyebrow and made a small tooth-sucking noise.

He reached across the table, took her hand, gazed into her eyes with exaggerated sincerity, and affected a redneck drawl. "Now darlin', you know I don't care nothin' 'bout purty women. I don't want nobody but *you.*"

She tried to stifle the giggle but she couldn't do it. "You silver-tongued devil," she said. "Look, they're coming over here. She must have seen you leering."

Jenny breezed over to their table with Web trailing behind, and Jake rose to meet them. The men shook hands; Jenny kissed the air near Lori's cheek.

"Lori, how are you? It's so good to see you. I looked for you at church the other day, but you must have been in the nursery."

Lori nodded. "I'm always in the nursery these days. I can't help it, I like babies." She cast the briefest sideways glance at Jake. *Be quiet,* the look said.

"Well, we never see you here at the Mill. Is this a special occasion?" Jenny flashed a questioning smile at Jake.

"Birthday," Lori lied. "Sort of." She gave Jake another *shut up* look.

"Listen, Lori, there's something I need to talk to you about whenever you have a few minutes. You're off all summer, right?"

"Yes! I've got seven more weeks ahead of me with no papers to grade. I'm not even taking any classes at the community college this year. But then I am working with a couple other women, trying to get the Sutter's Cross Women's Center going, and it looks like that'll keep me very busy the rest of the—"

"But that's exactly what I wanted to talk to you about! I heard you were working on something like that, and Myra has this friend—well, it's a long story. But call me, please."

"Well, hey, if you're not meeting anybody, you're welcome to join us for dinner and we'll talk about it."

"How sweet! But we don't want to intrude on your birthday party."

"Not at all. We'd love the company, and I'd like nothing better than to talk about the Women's Center."

Jenny laid her fingertips on Lori's arm. "Are you sure you don't mind?"

Even before Web finished sliding Jenny's chair under her, the waiter appeared and whisked down two more place settings.

Jenny leaned on her forearms. "So tell me about the Women's Center. What is it you're trying to do?"

"We've been talking about it for a long time—Megan Clark, Paula Whitehead and I. You probably know Paula—"

"Oh, yes." Jenny leaned forward and lowered her voice. "The one whose daughter committed suicide last year."

"That's her, yes. Megan and I went through a lot with her. She really had a hard time with it, and that's what started us wondering what we could do. There are young women in this town who need help and don't have anywhere to turn. You know—bad marriages, drug and alcohol problems, abusive husbands—too often the law doesn't offer them any protection until it's too late. And then there are the teenage pregnancies. You don't hear much about it because people tend to keep that sort of thing quiet in this town. But they're there, and a lot of them don't see any option other than to abort the baby and get on with their lives. There's nowhere to go, nobody to turn to. Once we started looking and listening, talking to people, asking questions, we were appalled at the number of young women who were hurting and needed help.

"We talked about it a lot, thought about it, prayed over it, and we felt there was a genuine need that we could do something about. Megan has a background in psychology, I've got a lot of experience with young people from teaching school, and it occurred to us that with a little help we could put together a women's center. Of course, we don't pretend to know everything, but we're willing to learn—and we really want to do something."

"It sounds like a great idea."

"I think so. We needed to find a place, though. That's been the real stopper up to now. We just didn't have the funds to build the facility we needed, but last month Mrs. Barfield passed away and left everything to her daughter, Judy Simpson. You know Judy, right?"

"Doesn't she sing in the choir?" Jenny asked.

"Right," Jake chuckled. "She's the one with the tall blue hair, and she nods off sometimes."

"That's her," Lori said. "You know, her husband's a retired judge, so they didn't need the house. Somehow she found out what we were doing and offered to donate it to us. She said they were going to rent it out, then decided they didn't want the hassle."

"That's wonderful! I think I know the place. Mrs. Barfield lived in that big old white house right behind the church, didn't she?"

"That's it. It backs right up to the church property. Which brings us to the next big hurdle—zoning. I'm sure you're aware of all the zoning restrictions in Sutter's Cross and how hard it can be to get anything past the city council."

Web smiled, but he didn't say anything.

"We've applied for all the necessary permits and established ourselves as a nonprofit organization. We've started cleaning the place up and getting it ready, but the house is zoned residential. Before we can open, we have to have it rezoned and bring it up to commercial code standards—fire alarm system, extinguishers, exit signs, and a zillion other little picky things."

"But your husband's a building contractor." Jenny looked at Jake. "You shouldn't have any problem bringing it up to code."

"Not at all. Jake has already volunteered to do the work."

Jake's eyebrows went up. "I have?" Lori had mentioned it, and she knew he would do it, but to the best of his knowledge he hadn't volunteered.

"Oh, didn't I tell you? You volunteered. I'll explain the terms later. But anyway, we have to get it rezoned and we expect some flak from the NIMBYs."

"Nimbies?" Jenny said.

"Not In My Back Yard," Lori explained. "We've posted all the public notices, and we meet with the city council in a few weeks to vote on the rezoning." Jake glanced at Web as she said this. It was common knowledge that Web practically owned the city council, but his face remained noncommittal.

Jenny was visibly impressed. "I had no idea you were putting something like that together, Lori. It's *terrific.* Like I said, I'd heard rumors, but I didn't know you were so deeply involved. That's absolutely fascinating!

Oh! Let me tell you about Myra's friend. She's in exactly the kind of situation you described—"

The waiter appeared and took orders while Jenny and Lori discussed Myra's friend's history with an abusive husband.

Web and Jake talked about building construction and sports. Web steered clear of Jenny's conversation, Jake suspected, because it kept going back to Jenny's and Lori's friends at church. In the South, everybody keeps track of who goes to church and who doesn't, and the fact that no one in Sutter's Cross ever broached the subject with Web was a clear sign of his rank in the community.

Jake had built a few houses for Web's development company but he had never dealt directly with Web, so he didn't really know him; they had only met once or twice. Web seemed pleasant enough, if a little aloof. He struck Jake as the sort of man who guarded his words very carefully lest he let something valuable slip out. He asked Jake a few questions about Fox Chase and the development company behind it, though Jake had the distinct impression Web already knew everything.

Web made him nervous. Business was bordering on dismal, and here Jake was, out of the blue, having dinner with the biggest developer in the valley. He wanted to make an impression, so he offered opinions freely about anything and everything—the new tax laws, the proposed sites for a new water treatment plant, the Braves' chances at the playoffs—but he never really felt as though Web was listening to him. Or rather, he had the impression that Web listened to *everything.* He was sure Web heard what he said, but he also heard what the wives said, every word said by the elderly couple at the next table, and every word uttered by any waiter within twenty feet. He seemed to be constantly collecting data on everything and everybody, when something Lori said obviously got Web's full attention. He lowered his fork to his plate and focused on Lori as she spoke.

"Yeah, Harley's still around. He took up at Miss Agnes's place after the big scene at the church picnic. She even took the wires out of his jaw, can you believe that?" She smiled her admiration. "Miss Agnes is a piece of work."

"I know what you mean," Jenny said. "There's just something about those Depression-era people. They're so strong. She lives out there all by herself and gets by just fine without any help from anybody."

"Agnes?" Web interrupted. "Agnes Dewberry?"

"Yes, do you know her?" Lori asked.

"We met, once. Is she a friend of yours?"

"We sort of look after her, if you can call it that. Her house is on our way into town so we check on her once in a while. But she's so independent I don't think she'd put up with us at all if she wasn't so sweet on Jake." Lori shot Jake a devious grin.

Web smiled, nodded and resumed his dinner, saying nothing else. Then later, after he finished his dessert and started on his coffee, he turned quietly to Jake and said, "Why don't you drop by my office sometime? I think we may be able to help each other out."

"Really?" Jake tried to stay calm. "What have you got in mind?"

"Oh, I don't know. There are a couple of projects coming up where you and I might be of some benefit to each other—if you're interested."

Interested? Jake was desperate, but he tried not to let it show. He shrugged and replied, "Okay. When would be good for you?"

Web dabbed at his mouth with a napkin. "I have to go down to the Atlanta office and work next week. I'll be gone the entire week, and then I'll be busy trying to catch up here for another week after that. Call my office sometime and have Catherine set something up. She knows my schedule a lot better than I do."

Lori and Jake stayed and each had a cup of The Gristmill's famous coffee after Web and Jenny left. When the waiter returned to refill their cups they declined, and Jake asked for the check.

"There is no check, sir. You and your wife are the guests of Mr. Holcombe. Have a pleasant evening."

They had a very pleasant evening.

Chapter Fifteen

July, down in the flatlands, is the doldrums, a time for watching the corn and cotton grow, watching the sky, and finding shelter from the white midday heat; but in the backward economy of a mountain resort town, July is a time of harvest and the busiest month of the year. Tourists clog the trails and rivers until sundown every day, and the streets until midnight every night. The frenzy is contagious, so that it seems even the local people's projects all come to a head in the middle of the summer.

Jake was finishing the last of his houses and didn't have anything new on the horizon, so he spent a good deal of time helping Lori and Jenny remodel the old Barfield place, on Elm Street behind the church, transforming it into the new Women's Center. He pestered Lori continually to take it easy, constantly reminding himself not to say things like "in your condition" lest somebody figure out she was pregnant. Still, he didn't see how anyone could have missed it; the woman positively glowed.

Several of the walls and doors in the Barfield house had to be rearranged to accommodate office space while guaranteeing privacy and protection for women who came there to escape harassment of one kind or another. Jake knocked down old plaster walls, framed new ones, hung sheetrock, and patched holes made by volunteer electricians and plumbers who left a trail of destruction in the process of bringing the old house up to code. Lori supervised the refinishing of the hardwood floors. Megan Clark turned out to be a tireless worker, spending a lot of time down on her hands and knees patching and sanding. Paula couldn't do much because of a perennially slipped disk, but her husband spent many afternoons painting. A few donations covered the cost of the materials, and Jake's friends in various trades supplied labor and expertise. Lori and Jenny worried constantly about money and the rezoning, but Jake knew the codes and he had plenty of friends with tools. The fire chief would be the hardest to satisfy. Jake assured them that after the fire extinguishers and exit lights were in place the rezoning would be just a formality.

Once or twice Jake tried to pry a hint out of Jenny as to what Web was working on that might involve him. It didn't take long for him to figure out she really didn't know. Web and Jenny kept their business affairs separate. She didn't ask about real estate developments, and he didn't ask about the Women's Center, which explains why she didn't offer much help in the way of funding—she was working strictly with her own pocket money. She proved to be a good decorator, though, and Jake figured down the road Web Holcombe's wife would carry serious weight with the local politicians.

There was a lot of traffic in and out of the place while they worked on it. Neighbors, out for a stroll, curious about what sort of "halfway house" this was going to be, would poke their heads in and ask a few terse questions. Generally they'd leave without saying much, wagging their heads and muttering to each other as they resumed their afternoon walks. Neighborhood kids made the rounds regularly until Brady Toler blew through one afternoon with his Rottweilers and tracked up one of Lori's freshly varnished floors. Jake watched in awe as she ran the kid down and threatened him with bodily harm. When she finished with him, Brady took off, looking over his shoulder in terror, thoroughly convinced she would kill him graveyard dead the next time, and Jake couldn't help noticing that she accomplished this without actually saying anything Brady could use against her in court. She'd always had a certain economy with words, and six years of teaching school had sharpened this skill.

On a Wednesday afternoon, right after lunch, Jake heard Miss Agnes's rusty truck pull into the driveway of the old Barfield place. Miss Agnes had known Miss Lillian Barfield all her life, had been in her house several times over the years, and was curious about the changes being made to the place. She and Harley walked around downstairs, checking out the new reception area where the parlor used to be, and then she touched all the new surfaces in the kitchen with a reverent hand. Jake took Harley upstairs to show off the new living spaces he was building in what was once an attic.

Miss Agnes didn't stay long—she had recently changed her blood pressure medicine and wasn't feeling too spry—but Harley volunteered to hang around and help. Jake promised to bring him home later.

"I'm not real good at hanging sheetrock," Harley said, "but I make up for it by being slow."

He turned out to be a pretty fair hand at measuring and cutting. He and Jake passed a pleasant afternoon building walls and talking. Absorbed in his work, Jake let the time slip by until Lori padded up the stairs and told him it was time to go to church. He looked at his watch: four-fifteen. As usual, he'd forgotten that Lori had children's choir practice, and he had a Building and Grounds Committee meeting at four-thirty. Megan and Paula needed to go home and cook supper, so Jake, Lori, and Harley closed the place up, dusted themselves off, and walked across the lot to the church in dusty, paint-spattered work clothes. Harley went with Lori, while Jake headed toward the offices in the main building for the committee meeting.

Orde Wingo arrived at the same time and stopped, with his hand on the back door, watching Harley follow Lori into the children's building. When Jake caught up to him in the vestibule he gave Jake's clothes a once-over.

"I hate to come to church looking like this, but I forgot the time and didn't have a chance to go home and get cleaned up," Jake said.

"I guess it can't be helped. What are you working on?"

"We're remodeling the old Barfield place, turning it into a women's center."

"You mean the big white house behind the church?"

Jake nodded.

"What kind of women's center? What do they plan to do there?" The frown Harley had planted on Orde's face grew roots.

Jake shrugged. "I don't know, something about pregnant teens, runaways, battered women—you know."

Orde stopped in the middle of the sanctuary, hands in pockets, head tilted, frowning. "Like a halfway house?"

"No, not exactly, but Lori and the others could explain it better than I can. It's their project. I'm just the hired help."

Orde pushed his glasses up and stared at him. "I'm not sure that's a good idea, Jake. I mean, I guess places like that are necessary, but does it need to be right next door to the church?"

"Well, they got the old house for free, and they don't have any other options. There's no money for buying a house somewhere else. With a little elbow grease we can fix up the Barfield place for next to nothing. Is there a problem with having it next door?"

"Come on, Jake, you know as well as I do what kind of people end up in a place like that. This is a house of prayer. A lot of us work very hard to provide a place where people can come and be silent before the Lord. You go putting yourself in the middle of women's domestic disputes and the next thing you know their husbands will come looking for them. And I guarantee you, a mad husband won't care anything about the sanctity of worship."

"I don't know, Orde. I can sort of see your point, but what are we here for? I mean, what's this church for if it isn't for people to help each other?"

"There are government social programs for that! That's what we pay taxes for! We provide people with a place to observe the Sabbath, and we have an obligation—to God and to those people—to maintain an atmosphere of reverence in God's sanctuary. We're breaking records in attendance right now because we provide what people want. If you put this thing in our backyard, you're going to offend some *good* folks, folks who work and contribute. People follow trends, Jake. A couple of decent families get fed up and leave and the next thing you know there's a stampede. Then we're right back where we were ten years ago. Is your halfway house worth that?"

"It's not a halfway house, Orde, it's a women's center, with a Christian focus, Christian values. Sure there are bound to be some problems, but I still think we ought to help—"

"You want to help those people, invite them to church! Tell them to clean up their act and get right with God! The good Lord knows they *do* need help, but that doesn't mean we have to *live* with them. 'What fellowship has righteousness with unrighteousness? What communion has light with darkness?' I'm telling you, Jake, you need to be a little more careful about who you hang around with."

His eyes flashed, and suddenly Jake understood. He couldn't connect all the dots, yet he began to see the outline of Harley behind Orde's anger.

The mood carried over to the committee meeting, which Orde ran like a drill sergeant. There were six men on the committee, and they all knew enough to stay out of his way. The meeting clicked right along through the reading of the minutes and the old business. They even decided on a contractor to replace the rusted-out rain gutters on the children's building.

But when they came to new business they found out what was *really* bothering Orde Wingo. He informed the committee that he had painted over the billboard down by the old trading post, completely whited it out, and he was hereby washing his hands of the whole matter. The church could *have* the sign as far as he was concerned; he wanted nothing more to do with it. There had been a lot of snickering over the past month, and the sign had come to be known as "the Harley sign." His jaw tightened at the mere mention of Harley's name.

Jake knew better than to try to talk to Orde about it—it was clearly an open wound—but he finally mustered the courage to ask, "What are we supposed to do with it, Orde? We're not artists. What are we going to put on the sign?"

"I couldn't care less," he answered. "I'm hereby informing you that the matter is now officially in the hands of the Building and Grounds Committee. There's no money budgeted for an artist, and I'm not about to pay for it. I'm just donating the advertising space. Do whatever you want. It's *your* problem now."

The two newest men on the committee were assigned the task of coming up with something to put on the billboard. Orde refused to discuss it any further.

Meanwhile, over in the children's building, Lori was jousting for control over fifteen summer-wild kids in shorts and T-shirts. Harley sat in the front row and tried not to laugh while she shouted orders, waved her arms, pulled her hair, played the piano, sang, clapped her hands to show them the beat, chased little boys back onto the stage after they bolted around the floor, and tried to get little girls to stop talking long enough to learn something. The play centered on Daniel and his friends in Babylon—the fiery furnace and the lion's den. Heavily outnumbered, Lori eventually managed to bring the proceedings to some semblance of order and even somehow got the kids to sing a couple of the songs from the play.

She held her own until help finally arrived in the form of Nancy Taggart, who was in charge of the set and costumes. Nancy dropped in late with an armload of wardrobe material, planning on assigning outfits and figuring out just how many she had to make for what parts. Of course, when the kids saw the costumes they abandoned any thought of singing and poured off the stage in a wave, anticipating a major dress-up session. Lori gave up and pitched in with Nancy in helping the kids try on various costumes.

The Nebuchadnezzar part was assigned to Brandon Teague, the littlest boy in the show, because the king costume included an enormous gold-foiled cardboard crown that kept falling down around his small head when he talked. He was a serious kid, and his natural gravity while constantly pushing the crown back up off his nose was devastatingly funny. He liked the part because he got to wear lots of gold. Lori chose one of the older boys to play Daniel, and he was pleased with his role, despite the drabness of the robes, because he knew the story. Daniel was cool, especially with the lions.

The trouble started when it came time to assign costumes to Daniel's three friends and the lions. Nancy had brought an assortment of towels and old bed sheets to cut and sew and modify until she created just the right "slave look" for Shadrach, Meshach, and Abednego. She'd also made the first lion costume, using her son Cody as a model. The foundation of the outfit was a pair of tawny beige footie pajamas, and she'd sewn a prodigious tail on the back, complete with a mop of brown yarn at its end, and sewed together a hood that covered Cody's head in a shock of brown yarn to match the tail.

All of the smaller kids wanted one, so a fight broke out when Lori tried to assign parts. The kids discovered that three of them were going to wear sacks and be guys with funny names and three of them would get to wear the fabulous lion costumes.

Thus began the Great Costume War. Before they knew what was happening, Lori and Nancy were awash in a sea of angry Lilliputians, all shouting and shoving. Lydia Franklin, a little girl with long, silky blond hair, a little girl who had always been the quietest, most demure, sweet-faced child in the world, had ripped Cody's tail off and was beating him over the head with it. Lori tried to wade across and stop Lydia but was too late. Cody, whose mane had twisted sideways in the melee and covered his face, spun around and flailed blindly at whoever was pelting him over the head. A wild backhand caught Lydia in the ribs and sent her sprawling into the first row of seats, where she whanged her elbow against a metal folding chair. She sent up a howl that instantly quieted the mob.

Lori rushed to her, but before she could pick Lydia up, Harley reached down and pulled the screaming child up onto his lap. He hugged her to his chest, cupped her throbbing elbow in his hand, and spoke soothing words into her ear until she quieted to a snuffle. The bedlam had ceased. All eyes were on Lydia.

"Are you all right?" Lori asked softly.

Lydia nodded, still rubbing her elbow. She wiped her red nose with the back of an arm and shot Lori an indignant look. "But I *still* don't want to be no stupid Shadrach!" she shouted. "I want to be a lion!"

Harley's long face split into a sympathetic smile. "That's a pretty common ambition, kid. But if everybody was a lion, it wouldn't be much of a play, would it? Be nothing but a lot of growling and biting." He illustrated this with a playful pinch of her ribs. "Some people get to be lions, some get to be kings, some get to be prophets, and some just get to be people. Want to know a little secret? Some people grow to be old and bearded and ugly before they figure out that we don't get to decide what we are. Nobody does. It's best to just hit your mark and say your lines. God made every one of us the way we are for a reason, and you won't ever be happy till you get used to it—till you figure out what it is God wants you to do with what He gave you. Just be what you are today and let go of tomorrow. Today's hard enough."

He ran a gentle hand over Lydia's fine hair, and Lori saw a trace of wistfulness in his eyes.

Lydia looked up at Harley's odd face and said with all the sincerity a five-year-old can muster, "What in the Sam Hill are you talking about?"

Chapter Sixteen

Web Holcombe was a busy man, but Jake was finally able to make an appointment with him the last week in July. Jake had never been in Web's office before. He was impressed with the view.

"This looks like a postcard," he said, looking out the glass wall of the corner office. The valley spread out before him at such a perfect angle that he could see all the way to Joshua's Knee. In the middle distance, the Elder River wound through the heart of the valley. He could look straight down the steep slope of Laurel Ridge and see Main Street, the flower-spangled spine of Sutter's Cross, and cars creeping steadily in a line from one end of town to the other, pulsing and coursing to the rhythm of the red lights. It was a humbling experience to realize that the man standing next to him was responsible for so much of what he saw. "You've really made your mark here, Mr. Holcombe."

Web smiled. "Please, call me Web. Oh, I'm just getting started. Look at Chestnut Ridge." He pointed but didn't need to. The unusual contour of the escarpment halfway up the ridge would have made it instantly identifiable, even if Jake hadn't lived there. "What do you see?" Web asked after a moment.

"Nothing." Jake shrugged.

"Exactly. But the right developer could really make something of that ridge, couldn't he?"

"I suppose. It's a pretty piece of land, especially up close. What have you got in mind?"

Web went to a cabinet, brought out a large black portfolio, and laid it on the conference table. Unzipping it all the way around, he flipped it open and spread drawings all down the length of the table, not blueprints—although they were the size of blueprints—but huge, bold, handmade sketches. Jake had never seen such drawings. Some were done in pencil, some in pastels, but all of them had been drawn with the same clarity of vision. Spare but clear. They were detailed drawings of a golf course that weaved itself into the landscape around waterfalls, streams, rock formations, and standing timber in such a way that it looked as if it had always been there. Every drawing had a photograph clipped to the upper left corner, and as Jake studied the photographs he realized what he was seeing was a before-and-after study. The photographs were of the exact same views, taken from the same angle as the drawings. In every case, the drawing, the architect's vision, appeared to be a vast improvement. The views were spectacular.

"Ian Stewart," said Web as Jake perused the drawings. "He's an eccentric old coot, but he's got a reputation as the best designer in the world. Packing all that stuff up there and hand-drawing perspectives on site is pretty archaic. Still, you can't argue with his results. From what I understand, that's how he's always done it and he refuses to change. Says he likes to get dew on his boots. Anybody else would have started with a computer analysis of the topo maps. He says he'll have the construction drawings ready by spring."

Before Jake finished looking over the drawings, Web rolled out another set of plans, this one a complete set of blueprints for the lodge, shops, and convention center at the heart of the country club, all poised dramatically on the edge of the escarpment. While Jake was scanning these, Web brought out *another* set of plans, this one of a palatial estate that was set, according to the plot plan, on the north end of the ridge above the Pyramid.

"Whose is that?" Jake asked. He could see from the plans it was a residence, and one worthy of a king, not the sort of thing anybody would design without a buyer in mind.

"Gerhard Klauss," Web answered.

"Of Gerhard Klauss Wineries? *That* Gerhard Klauss?"

Web nodded. "This is his dream house. We're looking into purchasing the whole back side of the ridge for a vineyard and winery. I didn't understand half of what they said, but his growers got all excited about things like elevation, acidity, and drainage. Gerhard just likes the view."

He rolled out another plan, a topographic map of the entire ridge. A long, narrow section curving back and forth along the top of the escarpment had been outlined with a yellow highlighter.

"That's the preliminary outline of the golf course and country club," Web said. "But look how much land is left between the golf course and the crest of the ridge." His finger traced the crest over its eight-mile length, ending at Joshua's Knee. "Imagine what that land would be worth if it overlooked the finest, most exclusive golf course this side of Augusta. How many mansions do you think we could sell?"

"We?" Jake's pulse had quickened and his breath came up short. The scope of something like this was beyond his comprehension.

"When all this breaks loose next spring, I'll need a project manager. Your experience meshes nicely with the people I already have in place."

"I just build houses," Jake muttered numbly.

"Yes, but you build *good* houses, not the pasteboard palaces a lot of the others are selling. I know. I checked. The clients I'll be dealing with will expect quality, and they won't mind paying for it. But that's down the road a ways. In the beginning I could use you on parts of the lodge and the Klauss estate. I can start you out at five times what you're making now."

Jake was staring at the perspective drawing of the Klauss estate. It could have been a castle on the Rhine, it was that grand. It slowly dawned on him that men like Klauss and Holcombe did not get where they were by giving things away.

"This is *huge.* So what's the catch?" he asked, looking up from the prints. "How do I scratch *your* back, Web?"

Web smiled, looked away, tapped a pencil on the glassy surface of the conference table, then leaned over the topographic map. With his pencil he slowly circled a long, flat stretch below the escarpment in the middle of Chestnut Ridge.

"Let me tell you about my airstrip," he began.

Chapter Seventeen

Like most caged animals, when Marcus and Eddy were first released from a week of house arrest, they approached freedom with small, tentative steps. They were afraid to go too far from the house, and they couldn't ride the four-wheeler anyway; it was off-limits for the rest of the month. For the first couple of days the two boys hung around in the yard playing catch. Perfect angels.

Eventually they ranged farther from the house yet stayed within the boundaries defined by Eddy's father. The Holcombe property extended all the way down to the river, but it was made abundantly clear to the boys that they were not to cross the road, a quarter mile on this side of the river. They were not to set foot on the other side of the road, no matter *how* they got there. Now, with the scope of their adventures limited to a mere eighty-seven acres uphill from the road, the boys turned their attention to Pearl Creek.

Apart from the occasional crawfish hunt, the boys had never paid much attention to the creek, with the river so close by. The creek was too small for swimming and the water too shallow to make even a satisfying *kerplunk* when they tossed a big rock into it. It angled across the ridgeline on a gradual slope with no major drop-offs, and in a few places the banks were low enough and the undergrowth thin enough to allow the four-wheeler in and out of the creek bed, so they had used it mainly as a highway.

Eddy hopped down the bank and picked his way downstream from rock to rock. Marcus tried to watch which rocks Eddy used, but he sometimes got confused. Marcus's feet slipped out from under him three times before they reached the bridge. He never said a word but instead got himself up and tried again. The third time he fell, Eddy saw what happened.

"I'm okay," Marcus said, wiping his hands on his shirt.

"You got to jump to the *dry* rocks, goofball," Eddy chided. "The wet ones are slick."

On reaching the bridge Eddy stood in the middle of the creek with his arms crossed, staring underneath the bridge to the forbidden land beyond.

"I don't see why we can't go down there," he said. "All we ever did wrong was take a little stuff from the Snyder house, and we promised not to do that anymore. There's no harm in going to the river."

"Your mama's scared for us to go down there, Three," Marcus said.

"Mom's not home. She's helping Miss Mahaffey at the Women's Center."

"Yeah, but my mom is. She'll put us on restriction again."

Eddy's lip curled. "Nah. You heard what she said—if she had to spend another week with us in the house she'd hang herself."

"Don't matter." Marcus shrugged. "Your daddy done laid down the law, said he'd whip your butt."

"He never has before."

Marcus's eyebrows went up. "You want to try him, Three?"

Eddy thought for a minute, then shook his head. "No, he'd do it. All he ever does is growl at me. It's what he lives for. He's never home, and when he is he just tells me what I can't do." He turned and started back upstream, jumping from rock to rock. As he took off, he flung a comment over his shoulder that made Marcus flinch.

"Be glad you don't have a daddy, Marcus."

Marcus stared after him, trying to comprehend. He would have given anything to have his father in his life, no matter how many rules he laid down.

They raced up and down the creek for a while, turned over a few rocks and chased some crawfish. They found a stout limb over the creek, stole a length of rope from the garage, and made a T-handle swing. Tired of that, they then found a pine leaning the right way, with only a tuft of limbs at its top, and decided they would cut it down to make a footbridge. Eddy took an ax from the tool shed, but it was Marcus who did most of the chopping. He didn't know how to cut a wedge, so he hacked and gnawed at the tree all afternoon. At first he choked way up on the ax and swung timidly, but before long his experience with the hammer came back to him and he began to swing the ax with authority, letting the weight of the ax head do the work. The soft white pine finally gave up and toppled over, still hinged on the bottom to the splintered stump. Marcus actually shivered with the pride of accomplishment when the tree groaned through a long slow-motion arc and whumped down across the creek—a perfectly positioned footbridge.

Marcus was reluctant to walk across it at first, afraid of falling, but Eddy waltzed across immediately, arms out for balance. He stopped right in the middle on the way back and prodded Marcus.

"What's the matter? Scared?"

Marcus shrugged, a silent admission.

"Come on, it's easy. Just keep your eyes on the log."

Marcus finally tried it and found to his amazement that he could walk across the log bridge without falling, as long as he focused on the log.

"Look, Three! You were right! All you gotta do is keep looking where you want to go!"

They chased each other back and forth across the log a few times before the inevitable happened and Marcus fell off, landing harmlessly in a broad, shallow pool with a sand bottom. Once they realized it was fun to fall off, they used the ax to trim a couple of saplings into staves and fought over the footbridge until Eddy busted a knuckle. Then they raced each other up and down the creek, across the log, back across on the swing and down the creek again.

Without realizing it, they had made a formidable obstacle course out of Pearl Creek, and Marcus couldn't get enough of it.

Chapter Eighteen

Jake waited a week before giving Web an answer about whether or not he wanted to put aside contracting and go to work for him, and another week to get up the nerve to go talk to Miss Agnes about selling her land. When he finally got around to it he found her in the garden, cutting okra with a paring knife and dropping the heads into a basket hung from her elbow.

"I know what you come here for." Her straw hat turned, and she gave Jake a knowing look. "Mr. Web Holcombe come around about a month ago, asking about the land, wanting to know would I sell and how much I'd take. He made me a offer and I told him no. I think he felt a little put out, so I figured sooner or later he'd be sending somebody else around to talk me into it. I didn't figure on it being you, but I reckon the answer's still no."

She didn't look angry or even upset. She was her usual cordial self, but she didn't give an inch. Jake just stood there for a minute, not sure how to proceed. He knew she wouldn't budge, yet it was his job to say his piece and he was going to say it. He wouldn't have agreed to talk to her about it if he hadn't been convinced that Web was right.

"Miss Agnes, Web's willing to pay you a lot of money. You'd never have to worry about anything again."

He looked around at the ramshackle house, the gray, weatherworn boards on the porch, the rickety screen door, bare dirt yard, and the battered old outbuildings leaning ten degrees off of plumb. Everywhere he looked, things needed work.

"You could have a new house anywhere you want and have enough money in the bank to live off the interest. You wouldn't have to raise your own food anymore, wouldn't have to work a truck patch just to meet your tax bill. You could live *well.* You're not getting any younger, you know. You could retire and live easy the rest of your life."

"If I did that, the rest of my life wouldn't be no long time. If I was to sit down and take it easy I'd be dead in six months."

"But, Miss Agnes, you're probably going to lose the land sooner or later anyway. You can't raise enough crops to pay the taxes anymore. Not by yourself."

"I got Harley. He'll help me." Her chin jutted a bit, and Jake saw a mischievous gleam in her eye. "He's already helped."

"But you got a hundred and fifty acres here—way more than you could ever take care of, even *with* Harley's help. What do you want with that much land?"

She drew a long breath, tugged the straw hat from her head and looked him in the eye. "I'll try and explain it to you," she said as she took Jake's arm and headed back up toward the house. "I don't know that I can, but I'll try."

She set the basket of okra and tomatoes on the steps, then plucked a large pod of okra from the basket and rolled it back and forth in her hand.

"Late season okra," she said and pressed her thumbnail into it. "If you don't cut it early, it gets so tough you got to boil it a week before you can drive a nail in it." She dropped it back into the basket, laid her hat and apron down, and ambled off across the yard. "You coming or not?"

She'd tossed the words over her shoulder as she angled toward a path leading down to the woods. Jake caught up with her before she reached the oaks at the edge of the yard, and she took his arm again. Her eyes wandered constantly as they walked through the trees along a trail that was older than she was. Once or twice she reached out and dragged her fingers across the bark of a tree as if to say hello. Strolling along with Miss Agnes at his side, at her unhurried pace, watching her watch the woods, Jake began to feel there were things being said which he wasn't privy to, messages in a silent language between the woman and the land. He felt as though he were slipping into another time. Her voice, when she finally spoke, surprised him. Not that she intruded upon the mood. On the contrary, she deepened it and fell in step with it.

"Jake, have you ever taken note of what people hold dear?"

He shook his head, not sure he understood the question.

"You ever ask folks what they'd save if their house was on fire?"

He chuckled. "I guess everybody'd probably give you a different answer. It depends on the person."

"I expect you'd be surprised. Most folks'll save what they can't replace. They can *buy* a new tee-vee set or a new diamond ring. But most folks—especially old folks like me—will save their picture books. Their pictures can't never be replaced."

Jake waited, saying nothing. About half a mile from the house they walked out of the woods into an open meadow full of the lazy buzzing of insects and the dry, dusty scent of late summer grass. He could see a tangled pile of bent steel, old and rusted to the color and texture of coffee grounds, sticking up out of the tall grass.

"This place is my picture book," she said. "I got a drawer full of old pictures at the house, like everybody else, I reckon. Pictures of family standing up grinning, or sitting on the porch. Pictures I have to look at sometimes just to remember what folks looked like. But my best pictures are in the land. Look here."

She parted the tall grass and stepped in between two long I-beams lying next to a jumble of heavy machine parts so old and decayed Jake could hardly tell what they'd once been—the skeleton of some long-dead steel dinosaur. She turned and looked across the meadow, down toward Bobcat Creek, shading her eyes with her hand. Her face lit up and she actually giggled for a second, as if she were watching something strange and funny unfold in front of her eyes. Jake saw nothing but Johnson grass, accented by yellow spires of goldenrod, and the shade trees down near the creek.

"I had forgot about that dog," she said, then chuckled again. "Wilbur didn't have the money to buy lumber when me and him got ready to build a house, so him and his brother Ben got the bright idea to build their own sawmill, right here. They made it out of junk cars and scrap iron from an old mill that got hit by a tornado over in Kate's Cove. They didn't have money for a gas motor, so Ben designed the thing so they could use Wilbur's Model A pickup to drive it. They'd back that old Model A up onto some rollers right about there—" she pointed at the ground ten feet away—"and put it in gear and just let it run. The rollers spun a pulley that drove a big old saw blade right there." She turned around and pointed to a piece of machinery that no longer existed, but Jake understood. He could see it.

"Ben had a prize coon dog he brung with him sometimes when they sawed lumber, and that dog was bad to get under his feet, so he'd tie him to the door of the truck just to get shed of him. Well, him and Wilbur was down here sawing planks one day, and halfway through a log one of the clamps broke and the log twisted and the blade seized up." She cackled, remembering it. "That truck jumped off them rollers and took off down to the creek like a turpentined cat, with Ben's coon dog tied to the door handle, just a-galloping to keep up."

Laughing, watching the phantom comedy play out in her head, she pointed, describing an arc across the meadow to a stand of tulip poplars on the edge of Bobcat Creek, a hundred yards away.

"There's a swimming hole down there—the only deep pool in the whole creek—and that old truck run right down there between the trees and hit smack dead center of that pool. Wilbur and Ben like to have drowned getting that dog loose. Took two days to winch the truck up out of the creek."

She stared into the darkness under the trees for a long time, as if she expected to see someone emerge from the blue-black shadow of the woods into the rude light, cooled and dripping, with a towel slung over his shoulder. Then, without a word, she turned and started up along the edge of the meadow. Jake followed, caught up to her, and she took his arm again.

"That pool don't seem so big to me now," she said. "But I still see it just the way it was—" she touched her forehead—"up here. Sometimes in the heat of the day we'd go down there to cool off and to be still. On a summer day when the sun hurt your eyes, you'd go into them woods and it'd be a while before you could see, the shade was so deep. There was cottonmouths down there, in the shadows on the other side of the pool, curled up asleep on the rocks. We swam quiet so as not to wake them up. That water was stinging cold and clear as crystal. It looked black till you got up on it, and then you could see slap to the bottom. We used to take a picnic lunch down there of a Saturday afternoon, when the chores was done, and take the heat off the day. There was a passel of us back then. Sometimes there'd be fifteen, counting all the cousins and aunts and uncles and Grandma. Oh, how that place could cool the blood. We'd come out of there toward sundown and stay cool the rest of the day, right on into the night."

From the high side of the meadow they entered the stuffy shade of a grove of huge eastern pines, where the air was thick with the scent of pine sap. A deep carpet of needles muffled their footsteps, and the walking was clear and easy where the shade had long since choked out the undergrowth.

"I remember when Robby was little," she laughed, "him and Danny O'Brien used to go down to the river and grabble for catfish. They'd get in the water and reach up under the banks, in amongst the washed-out roots and rocks, and feel around. He caught a few catfish that way, but once in a while they'd get hold of a muskrat and get a pretty good scare. Then one day Robby reached up under there and grabbed aholt of what he thought was a big old fat catfish, but it hung on to the roots and wouldn't budge. Danny said he commenced to hollering about how big it was and tugging for all he was worth. It still wouldn't come out. Then this little white head popped out of the water in front of him, and he seen it was a cottonmouth." She let out a high, tittering laugh. "That was the *last* time he ever went grabbling. Cured him, it did. Danny swore the only thing kept my boy from getting bit was he popped clean up out of the water and ran across the top of it to the bank."

She squeezed Jake's arm and bent over with laughter. Catching her breath again, she continued, "He bought him a pole and took up trout fishing after that. On up the creek, above Sliding Rock where it thins out and runs shallow over the rocks, there used to be trout. Native, cutthroat trout. It's about fished out now, but that sure was some good eatin' then."

A little ways up ahead the shade opened out to the bright light of a wide open space, and Jake realized they were coming up on the bottom side of a cultivated field. He could see something growing there, though he couldn't make out what it was through the tangle of blackberry bushes lining the edge of the woods.

They picked their way through a break in the prickly blackberry hedge and came out on the edge of the field where they were faced with a vast crop of immature corn, a five-foot high sea of bright green, waving and whispering. The woods rose dark from the other side of the field and climbed up the side of the mountain.

Jake let out a low whistle. "Miss Agnes, did you plant all this?" He couldn't contain his admiration. There was more to this little old woman than met the eye.

"Me and Harley," she said, with more than a hint of pride. "Harley's a good hand with a tractor. He's got a green thumb, and the weather's been good to us. I ain't never seen anything grow so fast."

But a grim thought worried Jake as he stood looking at her corn crop. The stalks, while they looked healthy enough, were far too small for this late in the season. And the ears were tiny. They looked peculiarly stunted.

"I hate to say it, Miss Agnes, but I still don't see how you're going to make it. I'm no farmer, but even I can see that you started too late with this crop. August is nearly gone, and the stalks are only chest high. First frost will probably hit in less than a month, and this crop won't be anywhere near ready in time."

She smiled, nodded. "Things ain't always what you think they are," she said. "This ain't no ordinary corn crop. It's Indian corn. It's not for eating—it makes little bitty ears, all motley brown and orange and yellow, and hard as a rock. Folks use them to make decorations like wreaths and table settings and such in the fall. Grows like weeds, don't take a whole lot of nitrogen, and it's got a lot shorter growing season than sweet corn. I figure it'll be ready to pull by the first week in September, second at the latest."

His admiration was growing by the minute. "You got a market for it?"

"I sent a letter to a old friend of Wilbur's down in Atlanta. He buys stuff like this wholesale and sells it at flea markets. I told him the fix I was in, and he said he'd take all I could grow if I could get it in by the middle of September, and he'll give me top dollar. There's a shortage this year."

He shook his head. "Still, it's only about forty acres. Will it be enough?"

She took Jake's arm and gently started him off along the edge of the field, back up toward the house.

"It's worth a good deal more than regular corn," she said. "It's a small fortune. Seems people are willing to pay more for decoration than for food. Harley says everything's going to be fine, and he always seems to know. You need to let go of all that worry, son. God knows what He's doing."

"Seems to me *you're* the one ought to be worried."

She laughed again. "I done been down too many dirt roads and got too many gray hairs to worry anymore. Tomorrow'll take care of itself. All I can do is plant and hope. After that, it's out of my hands."

Rocks of all sizes littered the ground in front of the blackberry hedge, scattered along the field's edge in both directions as far as Jake could see. He had to watch his feet to keep from tripping. "Where'd all these rocks come from?" he asked.

"The plow. My daddy cleared this field by hand when he was young and plowed it with a mule for fifty years. Every time the plow hit a rock, he'd stop and dig it up, bring it over here and dump it in the edge of the woods. Then Wilbur done the same thing after Daddy died. Every one of these rocks got sweat on it from one or the other of them. People used to sweat; it was part of life. Now they got special clothes for sweating in and they don't want to do it nowhere else. Seems like everything's air-conditioned now, and sweat's a bad word."

"You don't like air-conditioning?"

She screwed her face up. "Stale. Ain't no sunshine in it."

"So this was your daddy's land?"

"Oh, yeah. I thought you knew that. Both my brothers was gone by the time Daddy died, and the land fell to me right after I got married. I was born here, in a house my daddy built. Folks didn't used to be born in no hospital. I was born right up there in them woods."

"I didn't know that."

"Come on. I'll show you."

She led Jake around the end of the cornfield, then turned uphill. Above the field the trail merged with a tiny brook, trickling no more than a foot wide, half buried in its little course by ferns and rocks and decaying tree trunks. The woods smelled of sweet, damp, rotten leaves. Miss Agnes followed the trail alongside the brook diagonally across the foot of the mountain, stopping occasionally to catch her breath. The forest here was different somehow, and Jake began to notice that the trees, while grown, were generally smaller than what he'd seen on the way up. They were mostly young trees, about a foot across at the trunk. Their lower limbs were sparse, small and twisted because there were too many trees too close together. In their fierce competition for the sunshine they had robbed each other of light and water. The shade here was too thin to choke out the undergrowth, and they had to hold to the trail because of the tangle of vines and briars on either side.

They came to a small clearing where the brook turned aside and ended at a little black pool, a freshwater spring seeping from the side of the mountain. Miss Agnes went to the pool and, folding her dress up under her knees, knelt down, brushed back a few leaves on the surface and cupped a handful of clear water from the spring. Gazing down across the valley through the opening in the trees, Jake could see the back of her house a quarter mile down the slope. While not very high up on the hillside, relatively speaking, he thought the wide view of the valley was utterly spectacular.

"Afternoon, Jake." Harley's deep voice came as a shock in the whispering stillness of the woods. Jake spun around to see him sitting cross-legged on a head-high granite outcropping a little ways uphill.

"Harley! I didn't see you on the way up. You're a quiet man," Jake said as he approached Harley's perch. Harley spat a sunflower hull off the rock.

"I hear better that way," he said.

Miss Agnes joined them. "Where you been all mornin', young'un? I was worried when you didn't show up for breakfast."

"I'm sorry, Miss Agnes. I had to get up in the middle of the night and go up to the Knee. Shoulda left a note, I guess."

"Why'd you have to go up there in the middle of the night?" Jake asked.

Harley smiled. "I don't know." He saw the usual confusion in Jake's face and tried to explain. "I just woke up and knew I needed to go. I went up there and sat and listened for a couple hours. Awesome sunrise."

"You had anything to eat?" Miss Agnes asked.

He spat another sunflower hull and shrugged. "Seeds. I'm okay, but thanks for asking. What are you two doing up here?"

"Oh, I just brung Jake up to show him the old home place." She flicked a wry smile at Jake. "And to answer a question."

Harley stared at Jake. "It ain't gonna happen, you know."

"What's not going to happen?" Jake always felt like he was a page behind when he tried to talk to Harley.

"Whatever Mr. Holcombe's got planned for this place." Harley raised his eyes and looked out over Jake's head to the valley beyond. "It ain't gonna happen."

Miss Agnes said nothing.

Jake tried again to cut through Harley's words and bring the conversation back to a place where he could get a grip on it. "Harley, how do *you* know what Web's got planned for this place?"

"I talked to him, the day he came around trying to buy the place. I told him the same thing—it ain't gonna happen."

"Because she's not selling."

"No, that's not what I'm talking about. I don't guess her plans are any more important than anybody else's." His gaze remained fixed on Jake. He didn't seek Miss Agnes's approval or apologize for his assertion.

Jake blew out a frustrated breath. "Then what *are* you talking about?"

He looked out on the valley again, spat another sunflower hull. "The face of this place. I don't think it'll change, at least not the way anybody plans."

"What is it you see, Harley, and how do you see it?"

"It's not *seeing*, exactly. I just know."

The thing Jake found frustrating about Harley's obtuseness was that he believed him. In all his experience with the man, Jake could find no trace of an ulterior motive, and furthermore, he had to admit he'd never known Harley to be wrong.

Harley unfolded his long legs, scooted forward and slid down off the rock ledge.

Miss Agnes spoke up. "Y'all want to see where the old house was?"

"You mean your old home place?" Harley asked.

"Yep." She was already turning away and heading up the hill. "I was born in the old house right up here."

Harley and Jake followed her up a slight rise above the rock ledge to a flat spot in the mountainside. The little plateau was maybe a hundred and fifty feet wide and half that deep. In the middle, scattered among a flurry of sassafras and dogwood saplings, lay a few crumbled cinder blocks and the toppled, broken remains of an old stone chimney. Covered with moss and wound about with a thousand vines, the chimney would not have been distinguishable from a large dead log had it not been for its square shape.

"My daddy built this house with his own two hands when he first came to this valley. I was born and raised right here. Long as he lived, Daddy wouldn't have no window screens on this house. Said they cut off the breeze." She turned back toward the valley, and a sadness crept over her face. "Used to be chestnut trees all around here—*big* old trees—bigger by half than anything else around. When I was little, me and my cousins made good money selling chestnuts in the fall. There wasn't nothing like them." She sighed. "That's how come it's so growed up around here now, 'cause the chestnuts are gone and all the young trees have sprouted up, fighting over the space. Used to be clear shade here, under the chestnuts. Daddy loved them old trees. That's why he built the house so far back off the road, on account of that little spring over yonder and the chestnut trees. This ridge was covered with them."

"What happened to them?" Harley asked with a frown.

"They died. They all died, every last one of them, in the space of about ten years when I was a child. Somebody brung a disease, a fungus, into the country in some logs from somewhere else, and it spread. It come down through the mountains like a plague and killed them all. It was one of the most heartbreaking things I ever seen. For years after that, anywhere you went in these hills, you could look out and see them giant skeletons standing gray and dead, stickin' up over the other trees. It was like a reminder of what we lost, and you just couldn't go nowhere but what it was right there in your sight."

"There's none left anywhere?"

"Well, in a manner of speaking there is. Come on, I'll show you."

She walked carefully back down the hill and led Harley and Jake to an area no more than fifty feet from the ledge where Harley had sat. She pointed to a ring of raised earth about twelve feet across, sunken in the middle and full of dead leaves and humus. The ring around the outside was humped up more than a foot above the forest floor, like the work of a giant mole. The deep carpet of moss and leaves threatened to obscure the whole thing, but the outline of the massive trunk was surrounded by little mounded sprigs with dark, glossy, spear-shaped leaves.

"That ring there is the footprint of a stump where a chestnut used to stand. This one was mine—my own private tree when I was just a little girl. I had a swing hanging from it, and this was where I'd come to play. That rock where you were sitting was my rock, in the shade of my tree. This was a magic place. I could come here and feel safe, like there was something powerful lookin' over me. There was great comfort somehow, sitting in the shade of something that old and big and strong."

She pulled a handkerchief from her apron, dabbed at her forehead and continued. "Back in them days it seemed like life was hard on the body and easy on the mind. Now life's easy on the body and hard on the mind. Details beget more details. People are going crazy with it, fighting for their share, and they're working so hard and running so fast they don't see they're using up their lives. The thing is, there ain't no magic no more, no big things. Just little tight spaces, little shiny things, little mean people in neat, clean packages, all the same. The giants are all but gone. People ain't got faith no more, they don't need it—they got in-surance."

She pointed to the little mounded shoots sprouting from the ring of raised earth.

"See them sprigs? That's what's left. I reckon there's still life in them old roots. That tree's been dead near sixty years now, and the roots are still putting out shoots."

"What happens to the shoots?" Jake asked. "Why don't they live?"

She shrugged. "When they get up fifteen or twenty foot, the fungus gets to them. See this one here?" At the lower edge of the ring, she put her hand on a spindly sapling, twelve feet tall and about an inch and a half in diameter, leaning, too weak to stand up straight, and sprouting only a few sickly limbs. But it was alive, its saw-toothed, spearhead leaves trembling in a light breeze.

"It's about topped out. In another year or two this smooth bark will start to crack, trying to turn into a grown-up tree. Soon as the bark starts to crack the fungus gets in and kills it."

"Isn't there anything they can do?" said Jake. "Seems like a fungus wouldn't be that hard to beat with all the technology we've got nowadays. If they could find a way to kill the fungus, the chestnuts could come back, couldn't they?"

"Lots of folks have tried. I reckon somebody or other has been trying for years to find a way to kill it. But so far nothing works."

Harley squatted down and fondled the leaves on one of the low mounds. "The key is in the roots," he said. "You can't go around treating every tree after it's sick, after the fungus has already spread everywhere. You can't treat the disease. You got to make the tree stronger, strong enough to beat it. All it would take is for one tree to overcome it, and then when it fruited you'd have the seeds of a whole new crop. But you can't cure it by treating the leaves. The answer is in the roots."

Miss Agnes nodded. "I reckon so. The power of a thing is in its roots." She wasn't looking. She was standing with her back to him, gazing out across her valley.

Harley rose and stood beside her. "It's a fine place you got here, Miss Agnes. I like it here."

"It's more than that," she said. "It's all I know. I come from this dirt. I'm made out of the beans and taters and corn and hogs and chickens that grew up out of it. I *am* this place. And Robby was, too, even more than me. Ever since he left, I been waiting for him to come back home. They never found him. I never got nothing back. Part of me is lost and gone and I can't find it. I could accept that he was dead—I felt that in my bones, right from the start—but I still want him here, even if he ain't nothing but some dust in a box.

"He was my boy—my only boy, and oh, how he *shined.* Me and Wilbur waited a long time for him to come home so we could bring him up here and put him back in the dirt he come from. When Wilbur died I wanted to bury *him* here, but the county wouldn't let me." Her voice quavered, and she reached out to steady herself against the twisted stalk of the chestnut sapling. "I'm still waiting," she whispered. "If Robby ever comes home, I'm gonna lay him right here. I don't care what the county says."

Chapter Nineteen

"Miss Agnes came from another era, a time when there was honor, even among thieves. Her time is past."

Jake Mahaffey

"Web, there's got to be another place you can put an airstrip. That's all there is to it." Jake was sitting in a studded leather armchair in Web's office, sitting on the edge to keep from touching anything, feeling very much out of place in his concrete-spattered work clothes among the brass and marble and teak and mahogany and Persian rugs and original paintings imported from some studio in New York.

Web was leaning against the glass wall of his office, his bronze hands braced against the mullions, his lean frame angling tensely as if he were trying to push the wall down. Even from behind him, Jake could see the tension in his shoulders and the flexing of his jaw as he surveyed his valley.

"No," Web answered without turning. "It's the best site within a hundred miles, the only natural site with workable ridge lift on both sides of the valley and plenty of open fields nearby for emergency out-landings. It's perfect. The strip goes where I say it goes."

"But it's not even part of the country club plans. There's no hurry. Miss Agnes is old. She won't live forever, and she's got no living relatives. You could go ahead with the country club and wait her out. If you can't wait, then, with your resources I'm sure you can find something else, even if it takes a little grading—"

"You just don't get it, do you?"

Web pushed away from the window and turned on Jake. His eyes narrowed, his lips tightened, and an incongruous rage boiled to the surface for an instant.

"The strong *take*," Web said. "It's nature's way. The strongest lion takes the slowest antelope, and the lion and the antelope are *both* made stronger in the process. It's how things work, Jake. Life's hard, and it runs on competition. The strong take!" he thundered, slamming a palm on his desktop. "It's my place. And in the process I make the world better and stronger, and everybody wins in the long run!"

"That might be true if we were lions and antelopes," Jake said weakly. "But we're more than that."

Web sat down at his desk, leaned back in his chair, laced his hands behind his head and crossed his feet on the desk. "So tell me, Jake, what are we? If we're not lions and antelopes, what are we?"

"We're people, set apart by reason and compassion. Human beings, made in God's image."

"I see. So it's a religious thing, is it?" Web's lip curled, and he fairly hissed the word *religious*. He spoke quietly, but the note of sarcasm was unmistakable. "Okay, teach me. What image is that? What does your God look like? How tall is He? What color hair does He have? What does He sound like when He talks to you?"

Jake hesitated, trying to keep from squirming. "It requires faith," he mumbled. It was all he could think of under Web's intense glare.

"Faith. I see... I'll tell you what, Jake, you take the antelope and give him faith. I'll take the lion and give him speed and claws and strength and cunning, and we'll see who eats whom. When faith comes up against knowledge and strength, faith is dinner. Now, let me teach *you* something, teacher. The reason you can't make it in business isn't because you don't know what you're doing—you build good houses, I'll give you that. So, why are you going broke? Why is it, with all the houses being built in this valley, nobody's hiring you to build them? I'll tell you why. It's because you don't have the killer instinct. You like to think you're being fair, giving value for value, but where has it gotten you? You're about to be out of business because people don't want fair; they want a *bargain*. Everybody wants a Cadillac at a Volkswagen price, so if you're smart you learn to build a Volkswagen that looks like a Cadillac. And if you can't do that, you can't last, Jake, because even your customers won't buy into your principles. Then," Web added, pointing out the window, "when you need to be building your business, instead you spend your time down there working on a shelter for a bunch of trailer-park refugees, when we'd all be better off if they'd just take their little problems someplace else!" He laughed derisively. "Jake, you're going to have to rise above your principles if you expect to make it in the *real* world."

Jake rose and leaned on his fists on the front of the desk, seething.

"I really don't care at this point what you think of me, Web. You still can't take Miss Agnes's land from her. Not if she doesn't want to sell."

"Oh, but I can. All I have to do is take away her choices. I'm in control and I own this valley. Do you really think her little forty-acre patch of Blue Maize is going to save her? Up to now I've tried to play nice, because this is a small town and I don't like to make enemies unless I have to. I've gone to her myself and offered her more than the place is worth. I've sent you, her friend, to try and persuade her—for her own good. It's in her own best interests. I've done every—"

"You don't get to decide what's best for everybody, Web. You're not God."

Web chuckled, sat forward and clasped his hands on the desk. "Prove it," he said, then waved a hand, dismissing the issue. "But you're right. I have no idea what's best for her, and frankly I don't care. I do know what's best for *me,* and I know what's best for this town, and I won't be stopped, or even delayed, by one stubborn old lady."

"Well, I won't be any part of it," said Jake. "You can't take her land against her will. I will personally do whatever I can to stop you."

Web shrugged. "Fine with me. You're fired. I can replace you. Can you replace me?"

It was an odd feeling. Jake's bright future had dissolved before his eyes, but all he felt was relief. He straightened up and stuck his hands in his pockets. "I feel sorry for you, Web. I didn't know your father, but from what I hear, you're not cut from the same cloth. I don't know where you learned your back-alley tactics, but they'll come back to haunt you one day. There's a price. There's such a thing as justice."

The intensity of the rage blazing from Web's eyes as he rose and leaned across his desk seemed all out of proportion. Jake had obviously scratched an old wound. Web's head shook as he spoke through gritted teeth.

"I'll *tell* you where I learned most of what I know," he hissed. "I learned it in the management school of Southeast Asia, in a place where a man only had two choices—he could be a dead antelope or a living, breathing lion. Justice? I'll tell you what justice is. Whether you're in a bamboo cage on a mud flat in the Mekong Delta or right here in Sutter's Cross, justice is whatever *The Man* says it is, and in this town I'm The Man! I'm still alive because I understand that security lies in controlling your surroundings, including the people. Especially the people! And people are all the same. You can own most of them for a smile and a candy bar. If that doesn't work, you raise your voice and rattle your weapons. But every once in a while you run across somebody who won't be persuaded no matter what you do.

"Then," he said, lowering his voice, "you burn their village."

Over the next few weeks Jake talked to everybody he could think of in the housing market. All he got for his time were blank stares and condescending smiles. Everybody made promises, offered platitudes about how they would be sure to call him "as soon as something comes up," although they wouldn't look him in the eye. Word had gotten around that Jake was on Web Holcombe's list, and nobody wanted to cross Web Holcombe.

The last thing Jake wanted to do was go out of town looking for work, but the situation was becoming desperate. The first week in August he received a call from an old friend over in Kate's Cove who wanted a new house built. It was an hour's drive over the mountains, and he didn't want to be that far away from home with Lori pregnant. But she still had a long way to go, and Jake figured he could finish the house well before Lori's due date.

He was surveying the site in Kate's Cove when the rezoning of the Sutter's Cross Women's Center came before the city council. When he arrived home that evening Lori was still at the meeting. He had heated some leftover spaghetti and plopped down in the recliner to watch the Braves game when he heard Lori's car pull into the garage.

The whole house rattled when she slammed the back door, and her pocketbook hit the kitchen counter with the force of a small meteorite.

"That TURKEY!" she railed. "Of all the unmitigated… RRRRRRGH!" She stomped into the living room and flung herself down on the sofa, red hair flouncing unheeded across her eyes as she crossed her arms and glared at the TV.

Jake waited a full minute before he said anything, reluctant to toy with a ticking bomb. Lori was in Global Warming mode.

"Is there a problem?" he asked, bracing himself.

She took a deep breath. "The NIMBYs showed up!" she said. "All the people we were expecting from the neighborhood and then some. They took turns cackling like geese about how the Women's Center would degrade the atmosphere of their fine old tranquil street. Remember the little guy who was so nice when he dropped in to see what we were doing and wished us all the luck in the world? Well, he whined for thirty minutes! Said he'd be afraid to let his grandchildren out of the house when they came to visit. Said the street wouldn't be safe anymore with all the 'rabble' drifting in and out at all hours!"

"He was the turkey?"

"NO! That wasn't the worst of it. That no-good, low-down, backstabbing Orde Wingo showed up at the last minute! He told the council he was there in his 'official capacity as the chairman of the Building and Grounds Committee, representing Sutter's Cross Community Church, if you will.' " She'd retracted her chin and was doing a passable impression of Orde's public voice. "And he told them the church opposed the opening of the Women's Center 'on the grounds that it would create unwelcome disturbances, violate the sanctity of our worship services, and flood the church with undesirables.' He made it sound like he'd have to come to church a half hour early just to kick all the drunks out of the stairwells. He said we should consider putting it out on County Line Road, by the dump and the prison and the pawnshop and the bail bondsmen, where it belongs. We were holding our own against the NIMBYs, but Orde killed us."

"What did Jenny have to say? I'd have thought Web Holcombe's wife could put a new stadium past the city council if she wanted to."

She looked at Jake with hurt and confusion in her eyes. "Jenny wasn't there, Jake. She called at the last minute and begged off. She was crying, and she said something about Web. If I understood her right, she won't be working with the Women's Center anymore." Lori rolled her eyes. "As if there *were* a Women's Center. It's dead, Jake. Just like that, we're dead in the water. I don't know what we'll do with the Barfield house, but we can't use it for the Women's Center. The vote was unanimous. Craig Stafford is Paula's brother-in-law, and even *he* voted against us. I just don't get it."

Jake was nearly as shocked as Lori. He didn't know what to say, so he got up, walked over to her, pulled her to her feet and wrapped his arms around her.

"It's all right," he said. "A hundred years from now nobody'll remember the city council meeting, or the Barfield house, or Orde Wingo." He took her face in his hands and turned it up to meet his. "Anyway, I don't think you should be getting so worked up. It can't be good for Elmo."

She scowled. "So you've decided it's going to be a boy, huh?"

"I didn't say that. What's wrong with naming a girl Elmo?"

"I'd prefer something with a little class," she said. "Like Dagmar, or Zenobia."

Jake made a face. "Nah—too common. These days you can't swing a dead cat without hitting a Zenobia. Besides, you've lived in this town long enough to know how people name a kid if they expect him to grow up to be a Supreme Court justice."

"How?"

"Easy. You give him a first initial and two last names."

She brightened instantly. "You know, you're right. I never thought about it, but I've seen tons of kids in the nursery with names like that. There's little T. Walton Hutcheson who likes to play doctor, and G. Harbin Thurber who used to leave teeth marks on a new victim every week—definite corporate lawyer material. And R. Burns Newsome, the cabinet climber; he'll probably be an astronaut. By george, I think you're on to something. But, well—and please don't be offended by this, it's just that I know the possibility hasn't occurred to you—but what if it's a girl?"

Jake shrugged. "Same thing. I mean, it's not going to be a girl, but just for the sake of argument I can recall a Taylor Bainbridge, Morgan Stratton, Connelly Upton—"

She giggled. "Nnnnnah, those just don't do it for me. I really had my heart set on Dagmar Zenobia. Maybe a compromise. Dagmar Elmo Mahaffey has a nice ring to it."

"She'll never make the Supreme Court without at least two last names."

"That's okay, so long as she's like her dad," Lori said, and kissed his cheek. "Maybe she can get a job as a welder."

Jake got up at four the next morning, as usual, starting his day with quiet time. He stared at his journal for an hour and a half, drank coffee and doodled on a pad. He did everything but write. He couldn't make himself write down what he really thought about Orde Wingo. He couldn't get over the fact that Orde would go so far as to set out to squash the Women's Center at the rezoning hearing. This was still on his mind as he drove through town on his way to Kate's Cove at daybreak. As he approached the river he noticed that the guys on the Building and Grounds Committee had finally done something with the billboard beside the bridge. They'd painted a simple text message on it that meshed nicely with the "Bring a Friend to Church" theme of the upcoming Fall High Attendance Day. Leaving the background entirely white, they had stenciled across the middle of the sign in bold, black, sans serif letters the rhetorical question, *Where would we be without friends?*

Centered on the solid white field, the message was large enough to read but small enough to draw the eye. At first glance it seemed an effective use of the space, in a minimalist sort of way. But then, as Jake's truck tilted down the grade toward the river, his headlights raised the bottom half of the sign, which had been left unchanged. Counterbalanced as it was on the same white background, in bold black letters of the same size and weight, it struck his eye, not as the signature they had intended, but as a coldly ironic answer to their own question: Sutter's Cross Community Church.

Chapter Twenty

Jake told Miss Agnes everything that had transpired in Web's office. She shrugged it off, told him she knew everybody in the valley, knew their kids and grandkids, and there was no way in the world her place could be taken from her; she couldn't conceive of it. Jake suspected that, never having possessed, or needed, a lot of money, she underestimated the power and influence it could wield in the right hands. Or the wrong ones.

Coming home from Kate's Cove one afternoon at the dog end of August, Jake was driving down River Road in front of her place and he happened to look up toward the ridge. Through a break in the trees he saw Harley's unmistakable storklike figure running pell-mell across Miss Agnes's upper field toward the house, gangly legs pumping, eating up ground at a prodigious rate. For no apparent reason Harley dropped and rolled for a second, jumped up, spun around, slapped himself a couple of times, and broke for the house again. Jake slowed down and turned into Miss Agnes's driveway to see what was going on.

He found Harley sitting at the edge of the yard, still flushed and puffing from a hard run, rubbing his neck. He had little welts all over his face and arms.

"Yellow jackets," Harley said. "I was Bush-Hogging the field and I ran over the biggest nest in the western hemisphere—Bee Central. Man, there must have been a million of them. For something so little, they sure pack a wallop."

"You're not allergic to beestings, are you?"

"No, they just *hurt.*"

"Let's go in the house and see if Miss Agnes has anything to put on them."

Harley got up and started for the house, but then he looked over his shoulder and stopped. "We probably should go see if we can find the tractor," he said. "No telling where it is by now."

"You left it running?"

"Well, it didn't seem real important at the time." One of his eyelids had swollen to half-mast, and he rubbed it with a forefinger.

They took Jake's truck up across the field—with the windows rolled up tight. It wasn't hard to track a running Bush Hog through waist-deep grass. Halfway across the field an impressive cloud of yellow jackets marked the point where the freshly mowed eight-foot swath bent toward the road in a long curve, disappearing into the woods on the north end of Miss Agnes's property. They found the tractor wedged up against a hickory trunk on the far edge of the field, still running. The back wheels had dug themselves almost to the axle, and the blades of the Bush Hog churned and clattered in the dirt, clanging against roots.

After disengaging the mower deck and raising it out of the way, the tractor backed out of the hole more easily than they expected. Harley drove it back to the shed.

"It don't run straight," said Harley, wiping his hands on his jeans as they walked to the house. "The wrinkled grill ain't much of a problem, but the tie rod's bent and it's cracked on one end. Gonna need a new one."

He sat down at the kitchen table and told Miss Agnes what happened. She cackled, bustling off to the back of the house for something to put on his welts. Harley pulled off his boots and scratched his feet.

"I've about got these new boots broke in. They're still hot, though. Never should have got insulated boots. They make my feet itch bigtime."

Miss Agnes came back with what looked like a baby-food jar containing a thick, white, foul-smelling paste, which she proceeded to gob onto all the welts she could find on Harley's face, neck, and arms. By the time she was done he looked like a Sioux warrior with a beard.

While she was plastering Harley, Jake tried talking to her about the seriousness of her situation and the plain fact that Web wasn't going to take no for an answer. Web was a powerful man, and he had his sights on her property. Jake had no idea what Web might do, but it was a safe bet that whatever it was would be formidable.

She shrugged. "I reckon we'll deal with that when we come to it." She grabbed Harley's chin and tilted his face upward, checking to see if she had missed any spots. Jake didn't see how she could have; Harley was pretty thoroughly speckled. She screwed the top back on the evil poultice and set it on the counter. "Now. Tell me about the tractor."

Harley explained to her about the cracked tie rod.

She picked up the jar of poultice and disappeared to the back of the house for a minute. She returned holding a plastic file box, put it on the kitchen table, and pulled out a dog-eared file marked Farming Expenses.

"I'll need the name of that parts place we got the fuel lines from when we were planting the corn," she explained, opening the folder. She propped her half glasses on her nose and stared at the first invoice in the file. "This ain't right," she said. "The last thing I put in here was the receipt for the tractor parts from that place in Dalton." She lifted the first invoice. "It's here, but it's out of order. The one on top now is the one from Parks, for the corn. Somebody's been messin' with my files."

Harley leaned over the table to look. "You probably just stuck it in the wrong place," he said.

"No, I remember putting the receipt for the parts right on top; it was the last one I got. I'm particular about my files because I have such a hard time finding things. Look at the dates."

Jake looked over her shoulder to see what she was talking about, when something on the invoice caught his eye. The right-hand columns bore the quantity and price, while under the Description heading it said Blue Maize. The words gave Jake a chill when he remembered where he'd heard them before.

"Miss Agnes, what is Blue Maize?"

Her eyebrows rose. "I guess that's the breed name of the corn I bought. There's several different kinds. I just told them to give me the one with the shortest growing season."

"Is it a pretty common name, something anybody might know?"

"No, I don't think so. Fact is, I didn't recall it myself until now. Why?"

"Because when I had the argument with Web, he mentioned it by name—Blue Maize. Is it possible he might know enough about corn to know that's what you planted?"

"Pshh. Web Holcombe ain't no farmer. He wouldn't know Blue Maize from a rutabaga."

Harley stirred. "Are you saying Web's been snooping around in her house?" His eyes smoldered.

Having never seen Harley angry before, this reaction seemed completely out of character.

"No," Jake answered. "I doubt Web would do something like that himself. But he's not above hiring somebody else to do it. How else could he have known what was in her files when even she didn't know it?"

Harley's fist rapped absently on the tabletop. His knuckles were white. "Whoever it is," he grumbled, his nostrils flaring as he spoke, "he better not let *me* catch him around here."

Jake might have been able to take him more seriously if he hadn't had one eye swollen shut and his reddening skin polka-dotted with stink cream. As it was, Jake and Miss Agnes took one look at him, glanced at each other, and cracked up.

Chapter Twenty-One

"A child, at least in the beginning,
is made almost entirely of parents' dreams."
Jake Mahaffey

Lori bought all the latest baby books and pored over them every evening, memorizing pictures of fetal development and smiling that smile. She knew what the baby looked like inside her, knew that it already had eyes and a mouth and a nose, ten little fingers and toes, that it stretched and curled and made itself comfortable floating in its dark private sea. Its butterpea heart pumped and fluttered, alive—her very own child. Its personality was already assigned, the color of its hair and the size of its ears already set in its DNA. She dreamed of holding little Elmo warm against her breast, and she saw bright eyes and blond curls and frilly dresses and piano lessons and soccer games and skinned knees and boyfriends and proms and a good college and one day a handsome son-in-law—and grandchildren. She hid these things behind a Mona Lisa smile as she sat on the couch and ran her fingers over her belly and touched the pictures in the books.

At the end of August she went for a checkup. She had arranged the appointment for the afternoon because it was the last week before Labor Day and she and the other teachers had already reported for work. School would open the following Tuesday, and all the rooms and teaching plans had to be made ready.

Lori's midwife, a big, blond, friendly girl named Brenda, met with her in the exam room. Exam rooms had changed since the last time Lori had seen one. The salmon pink wallpaper with the teal border around the top, the hand-painted folding screen in the corner, the rocking chair, and the framed print of a rosy-cheeked seventeenth-century schoolgirl all combined to create a cozy, homey atmosphere. The exam table itself hadn't changed, however. It was still a stiff, straight, stainless steel rectangle supporting a thin mat covered with roll-out paper. A brass floor lamp with a flexible gooseneck stood next to it.

Lori sat patiently on the foot of the exam table and answered all the questions. She didn't smoke or drink, didn't work in any hazardous environment; she ate right and exercised. Brenda was proud. This one would be easy and fun. The questions took too long, and Lori had begun to fidget and squirm before Brenda finally laid aside her clipboard, clapped her hands together and asked, "Would you like to hear the heartbeat?"

Lori only nodded, her feelings at the prospect of hearing the sound of her baby too deep for words.

Brenda had Lori lie back, pull up her shirt and undo the top of her pants. She hummed a happy little tune as she took some sort of electronic device from a charger on the counter by the sink and switched it on, a white plastic thing not much bigger than a bar of soap.

"This is a Doppler," Brenda said. "It lets us eavesdrop on him. And the number in this little window right here tells us whether he's asleep or riding his bicycle."

She squirted a line of clear gel on the rounded end of the Doppler, then stuck the wet end unceremoniously to Lori's belly.

The tiny speaker emitted a grainy static, like the ocean in a seashell. She moved it up toward Lori's ribs and pressed down harder.

Nothing. Brenda stopped humming and her smile began to fade. "The little dickens is hiding from us," she said, but her sprightliness sounded forced.

She moved the Doppler again, leaned it this way and that. More static. Faintly, above the hollow hiss, the rhythmic thrumming of Lori's heart could be heard, beginning now to quicken its pace, but there was no other sound. Neither of them said anything.

Lori bit her bottom lip. It crossed her mind that a seashell had never sounded like the ocean to her; it had always sounded like a toilet flushing. She knew, even then, that something was terribly wrong. She wanted Jake.

Brenda retreated to the sink, giving up on the Doppler. "I never could work this thing right," she said as she cleaned it and popped it back into its charger. "Listen, everything's probably fine, but let's get an ultrasound just to make sure, okay?" She patted Lori's knee lightly and flashed a strained smile that said everything was definitely not fine.

Brenda disappeared for a couple of minutes, leaving Lori completely alone with the rosy-cheeked schoolgirl in the painting. Lori stared at the eyes, focusing on them, trying desperately not to think. The girl stared back, but her expression, which had seemed an innocent, almost congratulatory smile when Lori first entered the room, had somehow changed. It was the same face, the same smile, yet now the little girl's eyes held a trace of a smirk.

The door bumped open, and Brenda trundled a beige plastic cart loaded with electronic paraphernalia into the room. "So how are we doing?" Brenda chirped, a little too brightly.

"I don't really know yet, do I?" Lori was at the edge of a cliff.

"Well, let's just take a look and see what's going on. Junior's probably just playing hide-and-seek."

She rolled the ultrasound equipment close to the exam table, plugged it in, and punched a few buttons on what looked to Lori like a fax machine. Numbers appeared in the corners of the black-and-white monitor mounted atop the cart.

Brenda greased Lori's belly with the gel.

"This is a transducer," she explained, wielding a device the size and shape of an electric shaver, holding its thick cord out of the way with her left hand. "It's harmless. It just makes pictures out of sound waves so we can see what's going on in there."

She moved the transducer around on Lori's greased belly as she had done the Doppler, trying different spots, leaning it different ways, searching for Elmo. They stared at the monitor. At first there was only blackness on the screen, with quivering white striations across it. Then, as if it had bubbled to the surface of a tar pit, a peanut-shaped outline appeared. It was small, its full length taking only about a quarter of the width of the screen. The white outline was clear and it was the right shape for a fetus, but inside the white outline was only blackness, a void darker than the background and without the snowy striations.

Brenda moved the transducer slowly, looking at it from various angles, but all the angles said the same thing. Lori heard her mumble something about a "fetal pole," but she was talking to herself, intense and concerned, and Lori couldn't follow it.

There was something there, only it was not a baby.

Lori still made no sound, and she held her face tightly in check, though tears pooled and ran. Even through the tears she could see there were no fingers and toes, no face, no little heart beating quick like a bird—no prom, no grandchildren.

She wished Jake were here.

"What you've had is a missed abortion," Dr. Nordlinger said in as clinical a tone as he could muster.

Lori sat facing him in his office, a book-lined, carpeted study in muted browns and grays. Most patients never saw his office, but he was a kind and sensitive man and so knew when a special touch was needed. Dr. Nordlinger, who was in his sixties and had seen everything at least once, sat behind his desk with his hands clasped on top of it. What Lori saw in his eyes now was a faded kindness, worn smooth by having faced situations like this a thousand times.

"Sometimes something happens to the fetus," the doctor said, "and Mother's body just doesn't get the message. All the hormonal changes keep occurring on schedule, just like a normal pregnancy."

"Why did it . . . die?"

"We don't know that it ever lived, not really, not in a form more advanced than a fertilized egg. Again, there's no way of knowing these things unless we see it happen."

"But *when* did it happen?" Lori asked, her voice thin and high. She was thinking in circles, asking questions he'd already answered.

"I don't know. It could have been at the very beginning, or it could have been last week. We have nothing to measure such a thing."

"But was there ever a baby? I feel like this was all just a cruel joke."

"Well, it is likely there was a viable pregnancy, at least at first."

"How could this happen without my knowing it? Why was there no change? I mean, I had morning sickness up until a week ago."

"As I said, your body just didn't get the signal. It's a simple case of missed communication. Sometimes it happens. Eventually it would have aborted, but there's no telling when."

"What do we do now?" she asked. She ransacked her mind, trying to find what she had done wrong that had resulted in little Elmo's death.

"I recommend a D&C as soon as possible—that's dilatation and curettage, fancy words for removing the fetal remains and placenta."

She shuddered. "And I didn't think it could get worse."

"It's necessary," he went on. "There are some minor risks involved in leaving it there, and this way you avoid the trauma and discomfort of an inevitable miscarriage. Trust me, this is the best way."

Lori's gaze returned to her lap. "When?" she muttered.

"As soon as possible. If you'll see the receptionist, she'll arrange everything. I'm sure we can take care of you sometime this week."

Jake and Lori grieved as if they had lost a child. Which they had, in most ways. They hadn't held an actual warm little body in their hands, nor heard the rusty cry, but in every other way they had indeed lost a child.

Jake didn't know where she got the strength, but the next morning Lori called the school and told them what had happened, and she managed to keep her poise while doing it. The school was completely supportive. The principal told her to take off as much time as she needed, but Lori insisted she would be there next Tuesday for the first day of school. She said she would need something to occupy her mind and her hands. Twenty-seven third graders should do nicely.

On Thursday morning Jake sat in a vinyl-and-chrome chair in the waiting room and stared at the television monitor hanging in the corner. A precisely groomed, perpetually smiling weatherman pointed and jabbered in front of a satellite photo of the Atlantic while a team of sterilized professionals vacuumed away the messy remains of shattered dreams. The weatherman on TV prattled on cheerfully, pointing at three distinct white swirls, one in the Gulf, one near Venezuela, and one in the middle of the ocean. Names appeared next to the swirls as he pointed to them. The smallest one, the one in the bottom right corner of the screen, said *TS Elise.*

Jake couldn't have cared less.

A receptionist in a pale green smock stuck her head into the waiting room and called his name.

"The doctor wants to see you for a minute. He's done, and everything's okay. If you'll just follow me?"

She led Jake back to a little room just off the operating room where he found Dr. Nordlinger still in his green scrubs, with his mask dangling from his neck, rinsing his forearms.

"Everything went well," said the doctor, grabbing a towel and drying his hands. "Mrs. Mahaffey is fine and she's in recovery now. You should be able to go back and see her in about thirty or forty minutes. We'll send samples to the lab this afternoon—"

"Samples? What for?" The word triggered alarm bells.

Dr. Nordlinger smiled and waved the matter into insignificance. "It's routine—we always send samples to the lab after a D&C. They run a few tests and make sure everything's all right. It's just a formality. Have your wife call and set up an appointment in about a week, for follow-up."

Chapter Twenty-two

The Friday before Labor Day turned out to be a scorcher, a heavy, hazy day with temperatures in the high 90s and not a breath of wind. Such days were rare in Sutter's Cross but not unheard of. Miss Agnes sat on the porch in the shade, sipping iced tea, fanning herself with an old funeral home fan from the church and complaining about the dog days. The church hadn't had August revival meetings in twenty years, although they still handed out pasteboard fans on a couple of Sundays in August, relaxed the dress code a bit, and called it "Camp Meeting Days" for nostalgic effect. The younger people really didn't care; however, the funeral home fans were a hit with the older crowd.

Harley walked up in the front yard, wiping his face with a dirty rag. He'd been in the shed pounding out the wrinkle in the tractor grill.

Miss Agnes squinted off into the woods below the house. "Sourwood's finished," she said. "We need to move the hives."

She kept four beehives on the edge of the woods down by the vegetable garden. In the summertime, serious beekeepers had been known to bring whole truckloads of beehives to the valley to make honey from the blooming sourwood trees. Some people claimed Elder Valley's sourwood honey to be the best in the world.

"I don't know if I'm ready to take on any more bees just yet," Harley said as he scratched at his neck. For the most part, the stings had cleared up, yet some of them had left little hard brown spots that itched constantly. "Corn'll be ready in a couple weeks. I need to get the tractor fixed."

"We can make do with the truck if we have to," Miss Agnes replied.

He nodded. "I'm going to check the mail," he said, then headed off down the driveway.

"They won't be putting no tie rod in the mailbox—they'll bring it up to the house," Miss Agnes called after him.

"Still gotta fetch the mail," he said without breaking stride.

Five minutes later he returned, and his pace had quickened. When he hopped up on the porch and handed her a sheaf of junk mail she saw anger in his eyes.

"There's a sign down by the road, little white sign about so high—" he illustrated with a palm, thigh high—"that says there's gonna be a rezoning hearing next month about this piece of land. *This* piece of land," he repeated and pointed at his feet. "The sign says it's going to be rezoned C-1, whatever that is. Do you know?"

"Yeah, I believe it means Commercial. They made Mr. Walt Drummond rezone part of his farm when he built a roller rink on it, and it 'bout broke him. His taxes went from three dollars a acre to nearly three hundred, best I can recall. I sure don't need that."

"Did you ask for it to be rezoned?" Harley started to pace up and down the porch.

"No."

"Well, did you know about it?"

"No."

"Then why would they rezone it? It don't make any sense."

Miss Agnes rocked steadily, head back, fanning under her chin, her expression unchanged. "It does if you think about it long enough. The law'll come take me off this place if I don't pay my taxes, and I can't pay no three hundred a acre in taxes. That's a heap of corn."

"But the city doesn't do stuff like that on their own, do they? Somebody would have to ask them to rezone it. And if you didn't, who did?" His frown deepened.

"Who wants me off this land?"

He stopped pacing and stared hard at her. "He can't do that, can he? Can you rezone somebody else's land?"

"I reckon you can do whatever you can afford. City councilmen ain't all that expensive, from what I hear."

Harley's eyes narrowed, and his chin got that belligerent set to it. "Give me your keys," he said, holding out his hand.

"Where you going?"

"To see Web Holcombe. This has got to stop. Give me your keys."

"No. You don't even have a driver's license. You'll get locked up."

"I'll take that chance. I been busted before."

"No. You need to calm down, Harley, you're too riled up. You know good and well, running off up there and hollering at Web Holcombe ain't going to solve anything. You won't change his mind, and you'll most likely end up in jail. Why don't you just take a walk?"

His eyes flared and he withdrew the hand. "I think I will," he said. He bounded off the porch and struck a course for town, straight across the upper field at a fast march.

Web was at the conference table with Gerhard Klauss and his entourage when Catherine came in and handed him the note. No words were exchanged, but he had told Catherine to hold his calls. If she thought it necessary to interrupt him, her message was extremely important.

Gerhard Klauss was expounding on some obscure bit of wine lore while his impressive following of lawyers and architects, and Web too, pretended to be fascinated. Privately, Web disliked the man's Teutonic arrogance so much that he mentally assigned him the nickname *Blowhard Klauss.* Publicly, he smiled and nodded. Klauss was, after all, worth just over a billion dollars. Fortunately the man was too busy to make such personal appearances regularly, but this new estate was to be a gift to his most recent wife, a twenty-year-old French cover girl, and he wanted his thumbprint on it.

Web opened the folded note and glanced at it as Klauss rambled on. It contained only one word, in Catherine's precise hand: *Trouble.*

"Excuse me, please," Web said, glancing at the note for effect as he rose to his feet, "but it seems the morons I have in the field are incapable of the smallest decision." Web knew the quickest way to a man's heart was to share his attitudes. Klauss graciously excused him.

"What is it?" Web asked, once out of the conference room.

"I'm not exactly sure." Catherine frowned. "My son, Eric, called just a minute ago—you know, he works at that leather goods store on Main Street by the ice-cream shop—and he said some guy just stormed into his store asking where he could find Web Holcombe. Eric said he was a rough-looking character and he was, um, extremely agitated about something. So, to get him out of the store, Eric took him out on the street and pointed out our building to him. He's pretty sure the guy was on foot; he made a beeline straight into the woods and up the ridge."

"Did Eric say what this man looked like?"

"Tall, dark, thin, has a beard—'cheesy looking,' whatever that means."

Web went to his office and closed the door. He dialed a cell phone number he had come to know by heart.

"Hey, it's me," said Web. "Are you still in town?... Good, I'm glad I caught you. How would you like to pick up a little bonus? There's a minor problem coming my way, and you're just the man to head it off."

Benny T put away the cell phone and turned onto the winding switchback road that cut back and forth across the steep face of Laurel Ridge. Slowing the Cherokee every time he crossed what he guessed to be an imaginary line directly between Main Street and Web's office, his sunglasses turned constantly from side to side like radar, scouring the woods for Harley. He never spotted him, but when he arrived at an overlook high up on the ridge, he felt safe in assuming that Harley could not possibly have climbed this far yet. Looking uphill through the trees, he could see the sunlight glinting off the glass of Web's office building no more than two hundred yards away. He nosed the Cherokee up to the low stone perimeter wall of the overlook, then got out and lit a cigarette as he walked back to sit on the end of the wall and wait. This was going to be easy. Having climbed this far in a heated rush, Harley would be winded when he got here. About the time he flipped the cigarette butt away, Benny's eye caught a slight commotion a hundred yards downhill.

He was impressed that the raggedy man had gotten this far this fast. He watched calmly as Harley scrambled over rocks and blowdowns and finally emerged, dripping with sweat, through a rhododendron hedge onto the curve of road beside where Benny sat. Harley stopped on the shoulder of the road, leaned over and propped his hands on his knees, catching a breath before plunging ahead. He glanced at Benny and the red Cherokee once, but his eyes showed no sign of recognition. Straightening up, planting his hands on his waist and arching his back, he began to move, almost staggering across the road, still panting heavily.

"Yo, Johnny!" Benny called out.

Harley paused on the centerline. When he started to move on without looking back, Benny shouted a little louder.

"John Aaron Alexander!"

Harley stopped again, still in the road, and turned around.

"Do we know each other?" Harley asked, breathing heavily. He started ambling toward Benny, looking him over with what appeared to be no more than ordinary curiosity.

There was no suspicion in his eyes. *Good.* Benny maintained a casual air as he rose from the end of the stone wall, smiling amiably as if they were old friends. Harley kept his body loose, wiping his right hand on his jeans as he drew close to Benny, swiping away sweat, preparing to shake hands. At least that was what Benny thought until Harley's fist lashed out. The uppercut caught Benny by complete surprise and nailed him flush under the jaw. His head rocked back, his sunglasses flew off, he stumbled backward and crashed to the gravel. He raised up on an elbow, wiped his mouth with his fingers and looked for blood, then glanced sideways at Harley, and his blue eyes twinkled.

"Nicely done," he said. "Didn't telegraph a thing. But then, this ain't your first rodeo, is it, Johnny?"

Harley circled him slowly, fists clenched at his sides. "You're him, ain't you? You broke into Miss Agnes's house. Web Holcombe's errand boy."

Harley stopped circling when he came to the sunglasses. Benny held his breath; he was coiled and ready now. Harley's boot smashed down on the sunglasses and ground them into the gravel. It was all the diversion Benny needed. In the split second that Harley's eyes were on his own boot, Benny's heel shot out and drove hard into the side of his knee. Harley went belly down in the gravel, and then Benny was on top of him, pinning him down and delivering a paralyzing blow to his kidney.

Benny walked around him, adrenaline lighting his eyes. He quickly pinned back the hair that had escaped from his ponytail. "That was for the sucker punch," he said, then he fired a wicked kick into Harley's ribs. "And *that* was for my glasses. Those were hundred-dollar sunglasses, man."

Harley writhed, still trying to get a breath.

"You want to know who I am, Johnny?" He leaned over near Harley's ear and the sly smile crept back onto his pocked face. "I'm your worst nightmare. I'm your past come a-calling. I'm four DUIs and twenty-seven grand in unpaid credit card bills. I'm your burned-down house and your two outstanding mortgages." His voice dropped to a whisper. "I'm your poor dead daughter, Amanda."

Harley sucked a sharp breath and curled into a tight ball.

"How's your heart, Johnny? Didn't think you'd live this long, did you? But here you are, still walking and climbing and planting corn and butting in where you're not wanted. Must be the mountain air, huh?"

The fight was gone out of him, and Benny owned him now. At that moment the man writhing in agony at Benny's feet was not Harley; he was John Alexander. He had stormed through town in righteous rage to take on an enemy, but Benny had brought him face-to-face with himself.

"Feeling a little sick, *Harley*? A little small and helpless, maybe? Wishing you were somewhere else, *Harley*?" He accented the name with a sneer. "Think about it, *Harley*. Wishing you were somewhere else is the story of Johnny Alexander's life, isn't it?"

Benny leaned over, gripped Harley's shoulders, and helped him to stand upright. Supporting him, he guided Harley back to the roadside near the overlook. Slowly, Benny turned him about so they faced each other and, still smiling, drove a sledgehammer fist into his stomach. Harley bent double and dropped to his knees, retching.

He bent down and gripped the sides of Harley's head, whispering into his ear, "Your days are numbered, Johnny, no matter what you do. But stay away from Mr. Holcombe just the same. Okay? Good. I knew you'd understand."

Benny took a step back and launched a vicious kick into Harley's lowered face. Harley vaulted backward, landing on his shoulders and tumbling down the mountainside, bouncing off rocks and trees for what seemed an eternity before he fetched up against a hemlock trunk and went limp.

"Oooh, that's gotta hurt," said Benny, and then he happened to look down and notice a spot of blood on his white athletic shoe. "Aw, man," he whined, "these were brand-new shoes. Jerk."

Chapter Twenty-three

Marcus was hoping the crowd would be sparse for the Little League season opener the Friday night before Labor Day, but he was disappointed. The bleachers were nearly full. He hadn't wanted to sign up for fall ball—a whole summer hadn't been enough to erase the humiliation of the last game of the spring season—but Eddy said he wouldn't play unless Marcus did, and that settled it.

The reason for the crowd soon became apparent: the Giants, the team in the other dugout for the Dodgers' opening game, had picked up a new kid, a real phenomenon, a pitcher with an unhittable fastball.

His name was Darryl Snyder.

Snyder could *hit,* too. Batting fourth in the Giants' lineup, he came up in the first inning with only one out and runners on first and second. He scorched a line drive toward right-center field, but Eddy Holcombe was playing second base, and on this night he was focused. He timed his leap perfectly and snagged the ball in the web of his glove, then stepped on second for an unassisted double play, ending the inning.

When Snyder took the mound he looked over at the Dodgers' dugout and sneered. Marcus's stomach caved a little, the way it did sometimes when he sat down in a too-hot bath. Snyder's warm-up pitches smacked the catcher's mitt with a sound like a firecracker, and a couple of times the catcher even took the mitt off and flexed his hand to chase the bees out of it. Snyder's last warm-up pitch went wild, smashing against the chain link halfway up the backstop, and Marcus gulped. The only thing scarier than a killer fastball was a wild killer fastball.

Snyder struck out the side in the bottom of the first. When the last hitter fanned at the third strike, Snyder six-gunned him from the hip, then blew imaginary smoke off his forefinger. His dugout went wild.

The second time Snyder came up to bat, in the third inning, Eddy frustrated him again. With one out and a runner on first, Snyder hit a blistering ground ball up the middle, but Eddy dove to his right and speared the ball, got up, ran to the bag and fired a strike to first, nipping Snyder by a step for his second double play of the game. As they passed each other on the way to their dugouts Snyder pointed at Eddy and snarled something, but Marcus couldn't hear what he said.

Marcus, who still hadn't gotten into the game, was the first one in the dugout to give Eddy a high five. But when Eddy brushed on past him and sat down without smiling, it dawned on Marcus that he'd been too quiet the whole time. Eddy's mind tended to flit about in search of entertainment most of the time, yet he was capable of laser focus—especially when he was angry. He played his best when he was mad about something, and on this night Eddy was having the game of his life. Marcus twisted around on the bench and scanned the faces in the stands. Myra and Jenny were there, but Web Holcombe was not. Marcus sighed and settled back into his accustomed spot on the bench. There was nothing he could say.

Snyder's fielders didn't have a lot to do; his fastball was truly unhittable. Eddy's team struck out, popped out, and dribbled weak grounders to the right side. Nobody made solid contact all evening. Snyder grew increasingly cocky, so that around the fourth inning his showboating intensified. Every time he got a strikeout he sneered, jammed his glove under his arm, and hip-fired two imaginary six-guns at the retiring batter.

The Dodgers' coach scratched his head and paced in frustration. He made substitution after substitution trying to find somebody who could handle Snyder, but nobody could do it. Amazingly, there was still no score going into the last inning.

Ricky Skidmore had been on the mound for the Dodgers the whole game. Skidmore was no match for Snyder. Only a sparkling defense and pure blind luck had kept Snyder's team from scoring. The only substitution in the final inning was in right field, where the coach always put Marcus for his obligatory playing time, where he was likely to do the least harm. Marcus understood this and so stood very quietly in right field with his fingers crossed, hoping no ball would come his way and that Ricky Skidmore's incredible luck would hold just a little longer.

Snyder came to bat with two out and a runner on second, still no score. Skidmore threw him a fastball, shoulder high, and Snyder pounced on it, banging a line drive off the fence in left. The runner on second raced around for the score, but the ball had been hit so hard it caromed back to the left fielder quicker than Snyder anticipated. The fielder, who had the best arm on the team, wheeled and fired the ball back toward second base. Eddy, standing on the bag, took the throw and turned low to sweep a tag, expecting the runner to be sliding. But Snyder chose not to slide, and when Eddy spun around to make the tag, Snyder plowed him under and knocked the ball out of his glove. Eddy rolled on the ground, grabbing his left knee and wincing, while Snyder flashed his characteristic sneer and six-gunned him from the hip. His family cheered.

The next hitter popped up to end the inning, but the damage was done. The way Snyder was pitching, one run would be enough.

Marcus watched from the dugout as the Dodgers' first hitter struck out in the seventh and Snyder's cheering section went crazy. They were two outs away from a one-to-nothing shutout. Snyder was grinning and doing that head-bobbing thing.

Eddy was up next, and as he walked to the batter's box adjusting his helmet, the coach called out, "Who's on deck?"

Danny Putnam, the regular right fielder, piped up, "You put Marcus in for me, Coach, so he's up next."

Marcus jumped up and started to grab a batting helmet when the coach rolled his eyes, scanned his lineup card, and said, "Tyler, get in there for Marcus."

Tyler leaned forward on the bench, pushed his thick glasses up, and stared at the coach in obvious surprise. "I can't, Coach. Remember, I already played."

The coach ran his finger down the list, checking off the names of the boys who had already played, his face sagging as he reached the bottom of the page. He raked his cap off and ran his fingers wearily through his hair, then drew back and kicked the dugout fence. "Marcus," he growled, "grab a bat. You're on deck."

Snyder had started to tire. He had trouble finding the strike zone. And

Eddy had a good eye; he drew a walk and trotted down to first with a noticeable limp, his knee still smarting from the collision at second.

Snyder, seeing Marcus approach the batter's box, stuck his glove under his arm and walked off the mound toward second base, rubbing the ball. He waved his fielders in closer and shouted, "Move up, guys! It's the monkeyboy!"

Eddy stood on first, squeezing his knee, glowering at Snyder as the fielders strolled casually to within a few yards of the infield and started to chant at Marcus. A darkness crept over Marcus's face—knit eyebrows, a down-turned mouth.

Then Snyder fired a fastball right down the middle, and Marcus waved at it weakly, and late. He didn't even see the pitch, for his eyes were closed. Eddy winced and put his hands on top of his head.

"Make him pitch to you!" the coach shouted, baseball code for "Don't swing!" If Marcus kept his bat on his shoulder, the worst he could do was strike out. But he would only be the second out, and the boy behind him could *hit.* There was also the outside chance that Snyder might walk him.

Snyder rubbed the ball and turned toward the outfield, motioning them in even closer. The outfielders, joining in the insult, met each other at second base for a chat and passed around a pack of chewing gum. They were laughing, all of them, and ostentatiously ignoring Marcus. Even Marcus's own coach was snickering at Snyder's antics.

"You can take a break," Snyder told his third baseman. "There's no way Monk's gonna pull my fastball." The third baseman, a redheaded kid called Poke, sat down in the dirt, grinning, and hugged his knees.

The second pitch was a foot outside, but Marcus was so flustered he forgot himself and started to swing, losing his balance and stumbling across the plate as he checked his swing. The coach screamed at him this time, for even thinking about swinging. The Giants' bench hooted. Marcus's shoulders slumped.

Snyder smoked yet another fastball down the middle. Marcus didn't even look at it. Strike two.

Eddy turned to the infield umpire, called time and hobbled toward home plate. Marcus saw him yet didn't move to meet him right away. It was unusual for a runner to want a conference with the batter. Marcus trotted out with the bat on his shoulder and met Eddy halfway up the first base line.

"I'm going on the pitch," Eddy said.

"You what?" Marcus's eyes widened.

"I'm going."

"But the coach told me not to swing!"

"Forget the coach. I'm going."

"But there's only one out. You can't run, Three. I saw you limping. I can't hit his fastball, and that catcher's got a cannon…" Marcus's voice trailed off and he stared at the ground.

"I'm going!" Eddy repeated. "You're gonna hit the ball and I'm gonna score. Don't listen to those idiots. Don't think. Hit."

Marcus nodded perfunctorily.

"Choke up and stick the bat in front of the ball. And if I see you close your eyes again I'll come thump your head myself. If he beans you, at least you'll get on base."

"If he beans me, I'm dead. I still can't hit his fastball."

"AIN'T NO CAN'T, MARCUS!"

Marcus's head recoiled an inch. Eddy was capable of rage, but Marcus knew his friend well. He knew this explosion wasn't really aimed at him. Marcus's eyes wandered to the stands.

The plate umpire strolled out to them with his mask under his arm. "Get his phone number, Eddy. We got a game to play."

Eddy nodded at the ump and started to turn. Marcus grabbed his sleeve.

"I'm sorry your daddy didn't show up, Three. He's a busy man."

Eddy glared and said, "I'm going."

There was no hope. Marcus was doomed. He wanted to run away and hide. He trudged back to the batter's box knowing he would strike out and Eddy, with his gimpy knee, would be thrown out at second to end the game.

But as he turned to walk back to home plate, Marcus happened to look out beyond the empty outfield. There, leaning against the fence, was the tall bearded man Marcus had met in the park at the Fourth of July celebration, the night of the fireflies. The man stood with one foot on top of the other, his forehead pressed up against the chain link and his arms outstretched, holding on to the top rail of the six-foot fence. He was a long way off and he looked different. His clothes looked torn and dirty, his face was splotchy, and his hair was all over the place. Still, Marcus was sure it was the same man, and the mere sight of him fanned an ember in his chest, as if a firefly had suddenly landed on his shirt. He'd almost forgotten what the man said that night.

"Where you end, that's where God starts."

Marcus dug into the batter's box in a wider stance than he normally used, and a little closer to the plate. He started to choke up on the bat, and then, remembering the feel of an ax, he moved his fists right down against the knob. "Let the bat do the work," he said to himself. Then, before Snyder went into his windup, Marcus glanced once more at the strange man beyond the outfield fence and stepped out of the box.

The umpire rolled his eyes and said, "What *now*?" He held his hands up, signaling time-out. Marcus thumped his cleats with the bat and looked down to hide his face behind the bill of his batting helmet for a moment.

"I could use a little help," he muttered. He would do all he could, but Marcus knew for a fact that there were things well beyond his understanding. He stepped back into the box.

Snyder held the ball up for Marcus to see. "Fastball, Monkeyboy! Belt high," he snorted, then went into his windup.

Blowhard Klauss and his entourage finally left after an unbearably long session. Web leaned on his fists on the conference table looking over the stack of papers Klauss's people had left—drawings, specifications, endless red tape Web's lawyers and architects would have to sift through before a final contract could be drawn up. He straightened, arched his back, stretched and went into his office to get a highlighter. He wanted to make some minor revisions and suggestions and underline his own personal stress points in the tangle of documents so his lawyers would know what was on the table.

While he was there he poured himself a glass of twelve-year-old scotch from a crystal decanter and stopped in front of the full-length glass wall, sipping his scotch and staring across his town at Chestnut Ridge—*his* ridge now—its crest still lit by the setting sun as blue shadows crept up the hillsides. His eye was eventually drawn down to a bank of bright lights peeking through the trees from the darkening valley in the middle distance, and he suddenly remembered.

He groaned, ran a hand over his sagging face, and glanced at his watch. 7:28.

He turned to his desk and punched a button.

"Catherine, what time is Eddy's game?"

Catherine's voice crackled over the intercom, tinged with regret. "It was at 6:15. I'm sorry, Web—you were in conference and I didn't think you wanted to be disturbed."

"It's all right, Catherine. Not your fault."

"If there's nothing else, I'm going home. See you in the morning."

He clicked off the intercom and drained his glass. "No," he whispered. "There's nothing else."

Marcus coiled himself and looked into Snyder's eyes, then consciously shifted his focus to the glove where the ball was hidden. Time seemed to slow down. Marcus saw the ball, only the ball, as it came out of the glove, dipped, made its rapidly accelerating arc up over Snyder's shoulder and came whistling toward him. He felt his own weight shift forward in response and his arms start to move. He saw the red seams on the ball as it hurtled toward him, felt his wrists whip the bat, like swinging an ax. His eye followed the ball all the way to a place right in front of him, belt high, where it met with his bat and rebounded from a metallic *PLINK*!

He watched in shock as the ball looped high over third and kicked up chalk when it dropped on the foul line, bounding toward the left field corner. An umpire boomed, "FAIR BALL!" He watched until the screams of his teammates got through to him and he caught sight of Eddy rounding second base at half speed, limping. He remembered to run then.

And it was then, racing toward first base to claim his base hit, that Marcus became aware of the changes in his own body. For the last month he'd spent most of his waking hours charging up and down the slippery rocks of the creek, swinging on a rope swing, and running back and forth over a log bridge. His legs pumped as true and hard and regular as pistons, and his arms knifed up and down tightly by his sides. He felt the wind billow the back of his shirt as he glided around first and turned on the jets.

The left fielder had been standing near second base, horsing around with the infielders, pointedly ignoring Marcus until he heard the *plink* of the bat. As Marcus rounded first he saw the left fielder streaking toward the corner leaving a trail of curses in his wake. He was closing in on the ball when Marcus banked around second.

Marcus ran out from under his batting helmet on the way to third. Leaning into the turn, he watched Eddy thump across home plate with the tying run. Marcus missed seeing the frantic stop sign of the third base coach and so banked off the bag at full speed. There, at home plate, was the catcher with his mask off and glove at the ready, waiting for a throw that, judging from his eyes, Marcus knew was already in the air.

And there was Eddy, off to the side, grimacing, waving his arms and screaming, "NO! GO BACK!"

But there was no going back. The wind had taken over Marcus's legs, and he barely felt the ground passing under him. He was flying!

The throw wasn't perfect; the catcher had to sidestep up the first base line to corral it, while Snyder hustled in to cover the plate. Fifteen feet up the line, the catcher caught the ball and flipped it to Snyder as Marcus left his feet in a headfirst dive. He dove wide and reached out for home with his left hand, sliding past on his stomach. Snyder swept the tag and caught Marcus on the thigh as his fingers dusted three white streaks across the rubber.

The umpire, waist deep in a red cloud, flung his arms wide, palms down, and roared the magic word.

Then Marcus did one more thing that was entirely new to him. He sprang to his feet, spun around to face a stunned Darryl Snyder, and emptied two imaginary six-guns into him. From the hip.

Chapter Twenty-four

Tropical Storm Elise was a precocious child. Within three days of her birth in the middle of the Atlantic she capsized an old freighter limping south of the shipping lanes on two bad engines. When an oil tanker heard the SOS and came to the rescue, Elise almost sank that ship, too. But not quite; she was young yet.

She swung southwest, slowing to feed on the ocean's warmth, and took careful aim at Puerto Rico, although at the last hour she altered course, repulsed by some force of weather, water, or prayer. She grew to a Category 3 as she sucked energy from the Gulf Stream, churning to the northwest. The next day she changed her mind again and bent her path slightly westward, toward Florida. By the time she raked the north shore of the Bahamas she had grown to a Category 4.

Daytona battened down the hatches. Fair-weather cumulus thickened, merged, crowded out the sun and darkened to battleship gray. Flags stiffened and snapped in the freshening wind. The ocean rose, beat against the piers, and radical surfers gathered to worship when something repulsed Elise again, turned her up the coast and out to sea before her great fist could hammer the beachfront.

She rolled northward as meteorologists up and down the East Coast waited, watching as she veered ever so slightly away from the coast, growing, feeding. They smiled nervously into the cameras and said, "We can all breathe a sigh of relief," and they thought to themselves, *She'll be back. She's a treacherous, spiteful child, this one. She'll be back.*

Chapter Twenty-five

On Sunday night the first of the fall cold fronts rolled through Sutter's Cross and wiped away the summer haze. Labor Day dawned gloriously clear and found a steady stream of heavily laden minivans and SUVs carrying summer people reluctantly away, back to the suburbs for nine months of school and work. Eddy and Marcus didn't have to leave town, but it was the end of their summer nonetheless. Having served their sentence, they were given back the key to the four-wheeler, and they made the most of their last day of freedom ripping up and down Laurel Ridge, blazing new trails and reacquainting themselves with old ones.

After lunch they rode down to their obstacle course on Pearl Creek, parked the four-wheeler, and played on the ropes and logs for an hour. But they grew tired of it and began to feel confined by the restrictions Web had placed upon them. It was Marcus who first mentioned the tree house.

"I miss it," he said, gazing longingly toward the bridge that marked the lower boundary of their range. "I wish we could go back there just once before school starts."

Eddy climbed up the bank without a word, hopped on the four-wheeler, cranked up and drove down into the creek bed. Stopping in front of Marcus, he revved the engine and grinned. "You coming?"

Marcus hesitated. He hadn't meant to suggest it. He was only wishing. "Your daddy said we can't go down there, Three."

"Ain't no can't. Besides, he's gone to the gliderport today. He's not here. He's *never* here. What's he gonna do, send me a memo?" He popped the gearshift with his toe and the four-wheeler lurched impatiently.

Marcus shook his head and frowned, but he climbed on behind Eddy and the four-wheeler forged ahead, waddling down the rocks of Pearl Creek, underneath the bridge, down toward the river.

From a distance the tree house looked the same, as if it had sat untouched for a month, awaiting their return. Only when they pulled up near the great dark tree and killed the engine did Marcus notice that the rope ladder was gone, or rather it was pulled up, because he could still see the knots where it was tied to the two-by-four at the lip of the trapdoor. He then heard subdued giggling. Darryl Snyder's grinning face appeared in the window of the tree house.

"Hey, look, guys!" Snyder said to someone behind him. "It's Little Lord Fauntleroy and his pet monkey!"

The freckled face and red hair of Snyder's friend Poke appeared in the window, then Ashley, and then Brittany, pulling her hair back and scowling.

"Thanks for the tree house, guys. It's great!" Snyder gloated.

Eddy's eyes narrowed and his nostrils flared, but Marcus could see he wasn't looking at Snyder. He was staring at Ashley. Her eyes roamed; she looked everywhere except at Eddy.

"It's ours!" Eddy said. "We built it."

Marcus said nothing.

"Yeah. On our property, with stuff you stole from our house. You did a nice job, though. We really like it. Say, Richie Rich, does your *daddy* know you're down here? I heard you weren't allowed here anymore. I heard you were supposed to stay where your mommy could see you." Snyder chortled and elbowed his buddy.

Poke handed Snyder something beneath the window—Marcus couldn't see what it was. Ashley glanced at Eddy, flashing him a strange look that Marcus thought might have held a trace of alarm, then she turned away and left the window. Snyder raised his hands above the sill. Something metallic was sticking up from his fist, though Marcus still couldn't tell what it was. Snyder's grin turned evil as he bent his head to aim and drew back his other hand. Then he let go.

Marcus realized too late what Snyder held in his hand. He heard the distinctive ripping sound as something tore through the air and stung him on the shoulder like a hornet. He turned away, yelping, then saw an acorn trickle away down the bank and plop into the edge of the water.

Snyder howled, "Look at the monkey *dance*!"

Poke raised his own slingshot and nailed Eddy in the ribs. Eddy jumped on the four-wheeler, and Marcus scrambled on behind him while he fumbled with the gearshift, frantically trying to find neutral so he could start it up. They finally sped away, fishtailing through the deep leaves, but not before Eddy took another hit in the leg. Marcus was stung once more in the back when they were almost out of range. They could hear Snyder and his friend whooping and laughing long after they were out of sight.

Web cruised back and forth on the cushion of lift on the windward side of the ridge above Blue Ridge Gliderport for nearly an hour before he saw the first lacy tissue of cumulus forming, first above the ridgeline, then scattered across the flatlands. He made one last circuit to give the thermals time to build and then picked out a nice, tight little cumulus cloud in the direction of Edenville and headed straight for it. A few minutes later he felt the sailplane mush upward as he entered the thermal two thousand feet below the cloud. He instinctively pulled the nose up to cut his speed and began to circle, glancing occasionally at his variometer, a sensitive instrument that told him his rate of climb. The variometer needle stayed buried on the plus side, indicating a climb rate of nearly a thousand feet per minute. This promised to be a *very* good day.

Constantly adjusting his pattern to compensate for wind drift, Web deftly kept himself centered in the powerful updraft for several circuits until he neared the bottom of the cloud and felt the chill of the air at five thousand feet. He then dropped the nose of the plane, increasing his speed to a hundred knots, and rolled out precisely on a course for Edenville, a sprawling cluster of buildings thirty miles to the north, bisected by the highway.

Over Edenville Web struggled a bit. The thermals weren't as strong as he had expected, and they were narrow, difficult to center. Apart from that, he just couldn't concentrate on soaring. His mind kept drifting, as it had done during the drive over to the gliderport and during the leisurely hour cruising the ridge. He couldn't stop thinking about the raggedy man Benny had intercepted on the road below the office.

"I cleaned his clock," Benny had said when Web met him afterward at a secluded spot. Benny was still a little pumped when Web saw him, the

adrenaline residue of battle causing him to light one cigarette from another.

Benny had only followed orders, but now it ate at Web's mind, ruined his concentration. In the seclusion of his sailplane, Harley tugged at his conscience. In the attempt to calculate his glide path to the next turn point, his father's voice intruded.

"I didn't say it was illegal, I said it was wrong."

And his own voice answered, *"What's the difference?"*

From Edenville he struck a course for the twin towers of the power plant to the southwest. Belching banners of steam into the polished sky, the thousand-foot stacks provided an unmistakable landmark, even from almost forty miles away.

He soared high over quilted farmland in the low, rolling country around the river. He ghosted past the expressway, a counterpoint to the random wandering of the surface roads with its long straightaways and occasional shallow angles dotted with cars like ants in procession. Keeping his radio off as was his custom, Web heard only the wind whispering past his canopy, but still he struggled to keep his mind centered as he made constant small adjustments to his flight path and glide angle, speeding up in sink and slowing in lift.

The winds at altitude were stronger than on the ground, and it took considerably longer to complete the second leg of the triangle against a headwind. As Web neared the power plant he was struck by an alarming sensation that he was flying closer to the ground than he should be; the thousand-foot stacks reached up entirely too close to the level of his plane. Web reviewed his mental calculations and finally realized his error. Though his altimeter told him he should still have twenty-five hundred feet of altitude, he now remembered that he'd zeroed his altimeter to the elevation of the gliderport. A quick check of his charts confirmed that the ground here was nearly a thousand feet higher than the gliderport. His altimeter, then, was off by a thousand feet.

He looked around for a new source of lift and quickly became aware that there was none. In fact, Web didn't see any clouds within thirty miles, so he had no visible means of locating a thermal. He had seen such a thing before but it was rare. Soaring pilots called it "cycling out," when a momentary inexplicable bobble in the barometric pressure killed the convective process and the clouds faded away until there was nothing left but clear blue sky. Usually the condition was temporary, lasting only thirty minutes to an hour. Web knew if he could hang on for half an hour or so, the thermals would return.

But for now the sky smiled down on him sardonically with endless, unmarked, unforgiving blue.

Directly over the power plant his variometer betrayed the intermittent presence of faintly rising air—unstable bubbles of heat rising from the mass of sun-baked steel and concrete in the plant. He banked into a series of tight circles, gaining, losing, in the end breaking even and barely maintaining altitude. His own rare mental error had put him at the brink of deep trouble. Struggling in weak lift over the power plant, he didn't take time to chide himself. He reviewed his options.

First, he carefully examined the terrain around him. Below lay a small lake a mile to the south, a cooling pond for the plant. It might be long enough for an emergency water landing as a last resort, but the plane would be lost. The power plant dominated an area of roughly two square miles carved out of the surrounding forest, except most of it appeared cluttered with buildings and equipment. High lines radiated like the spokes of a wheel in five different directions, making any sort of landing extremely tricky and dangerous. The only flat stretch in the plant was the coal reservoir at the north end, where the loaders had smoothed a long ramplike scrape by hauling off coal to be burned. But it was bracketed on the ends by diverging high lines, and he estimated the space between the 100,000-volt power lines at only a few hundred yards. He would have to skim the power lines and plow his flawless white bird into a coal pile.

Web didn't like it, but there were no other options. He was now too low to glide beyond the forest.

It became increasingly clear that he wouldn't be able to remain aloft long enough for the clouds to reappear. He was down to twelve hundred feet, adjusted for the altimeter setting. The stacks loomed larger and larger. With every circle of the sailplane he studied the approach to the coal pile for as long as he could, carefully visualizing all the moves he'd have to make to put the Discus safely down between the obstructions. At the same time, he desperately scanned the skies for any sign of a cloud beginning to take shape.

On his last turn, as he was about to pull out of the weak lift and set up a long, deliberate approach to the coal pile, he looked across the valley toward the gliderport. Nearly a mile away, he saw a black check mark on the sky. As the mark banked slowly into a circle and presented its underside to him, he saw it was a turkey buzzard with its broad wings spread wide to catch a thermal.

A mile. With only a thousand feet between him and the trees, Web knew it would be close. If he flew to the buzzard's thermal and it turned out to be nothing—sometimes a bird would circle in lift too narrow to do a sailplane any good—he'd be trimming treetops on his way back to the coal pile where he would then have to make a desperate, no-margin-for-error, last-chance landing.

But Web knew himself. Desperate, no-margin-for-error situations were his forte. Those were the times when he shined. He made a beeline for the buzzard and trimmed the Discus for best glide speed.

In just over a minute he cruised directly underneath the buzzard, expecting, hoping any second to feel the lift in the pit of his stomach. Looking up, Web could see the bird, now five hundred feet above him, still climbing, shifting his weight this way or that and flexing the feathers that stretched like fingers beyond his wing tips, but never once flapping a wing. Web's pulse raced, his senses sharpened to a diamond edge. He tracked the bird, the altimeter, the variometer and a dozen other things, all the while keeping the Discus perfectly coordinated.

Gripping the stick a little too hard, he passed beyond where the thermal should have been.

Nothing. Not a quiver from the variometer, which hovered stolidly just below zero.

He banked smoothly, lining himself up on final glide to the coal pile. As his wings flattened out, aimed once again toward the power plant, his left wing jerked upward slightly. A quick glance at the variometer told him nothing, but his instincts begged to differ. He shoved the stick hard left, and his wings tilted effortlessly into a turn.

While banking he felt a powerful elevator surge in his seat and up through the pit of his stomach, as if a giant hand had reached up under the Discus and shoved it suddenly skyward. The vario pegged immediately, and Web rolled the plane harder to the left, adjusting his circle until he centered the muscular thermal. Before he knew it he was climbing past two thousand feet; in two minutes he had caught up to the buzzard at three thousand.

The buzzard, not to be outdone, widened his circle and kept pace with the Discus for a while, dancing with it. He surfed for a moment in the vortex off the wing tip, coasted in to sample the miniwave directly above the canopy, and finally took up a position just above the wing. Web watched the bird work the thermal, extending and flexing his wing-tip feathers, exercising a subtle and beautiful control. Nearly a mile from the ground, as the strength of the thermal began to wane and Web could see the mist of a cumulus cloud congealing overhead, the buzzard flapped his wings once, as if to wave good-bye, and cruised off to the north.

Web headed back to the gliderport in a dark mood, despite the surreal dance with a buzzard. He was angry with himself, embarrassed over having set the altimeter wrong in the first place—an inexcusable oversight. But there was something deeper troubling him. It wasn't anything anybody else would have to know about, just a private thing between Web and himself.

He had lost control.

He could live with a mistake. He had been distracted, and people make mistakes. The thing now gnawing at him was the fact that, in spite of his conscientious training, his finely tuned flying skills, and his state-of-the-art sailplane, in the end it was a buzzard that had lifted him up and shown him the way home.

Lori and Jake spent Labor Day alone together. Jake cooked a big breakfast, very little of which Lori ate. They lounged around the house for a while, then went for a long walk in the woods. The trees were restless, murmuring to each other, and there was a strange quality of light. The sky was blue but there wasn't enough light in it, as if they were in the shadow of something very, very large. Lori seemed drawn to the creek where the soft gurgling of water over stones might offer her some therapeutic balm. She spoke little, and Jake didn't press her.

The dogwood leaves had taken on a delicate peach tone, marking the end of summer. September was in the wind. Little clusters of purple aster and deep blue spearheads of lobelia poked through the undergrowth of ferns, and the leaves of an occasional sourwood tree caught the sunlight and turned it to wine. It was a gorgeous day, and Lori had no difficulty with the leisurely pace. It appeared as though she'd already recovered physically.

It wasn't the physical wounds that worried Jake.

Tuesday morning he hung around much later than usual before he left. He made excuses about not having anything scheduled for the morning so he could hover over Lori. Though he was privately worried about her going back to work so soon after such a loss, he didn't say so. Yet he couldn't leave her alone.

Finally she looked at him in the mirror as she was rolling her hair and said flatly, "I'm fine. Go to work."

So he left. The weatherman had hinted at the remote possibility that the hurricane off the coast might turn around and brush near the lower piedmont. The worst they could expect, he said, was a day or two of heavy rain in the middle of the week, but Jake wanted to get footings dug and concrete forms set up for the foundation and the basement walls of the house in Kate's Cove, just in case. A couple of days of heavy rain before he got the concrete poured would cost him a week's work and throw him off schedule. He had a lot to do.

Chapter Twenty-six

The residents of Bermuda have sometimes described themselves as "ten thousand alcoholics clinging to a rock." They clung a little tighter to their rock as Elise drew near, slowed, and stopped short. She hovered close enough to hide the island under her broad skirts, tickling the cliffs with gale-force winds and slapping the rocks with heavy seas, but she spared them the brunt of the fury that lay at her heart. For a full day she paused, brooding, deliberating.

It was not Bermuda that she wanted. Hungry and vengeful, she wanted the mainland. A beast of uncommon strength and determination, she churned at a steady 140 miles an hour near the eye, and twice now, the woman had been scorned.

She moved. Almost imperceptibly at first, she crept westward. Meteorologists' faces hung in the blue glare of monitors, comparing satellite photographs, nodding gravely, wincing. She gained momentum slowly, ponderously, like a long train. Elise would not alter course again and everyone sensed it.

She bore down on Cape Hatteras.

Chapter Twenty-seven

Pssst, Marcus. Wake up."

Marcus sat up, rubbed his eyes, blinked. Eddy's face hung over him, ghostly in the faint glow of the night-light. "Whassup? What time is it?"

"I don't know. Two, I think. Come on, get dressed. I need your help."

Marcus threw the covers back and swung his feet out. He gave his face a vigorous rub and then reached down for the jeans he'd dropped beside his bed the night before. When he picked up the jeans, a tennis shoe rolled off and thumped to the floor.

"Shhh! Be quiet, man," Eddy whispered. "If your mother wakes up, we're dead."

Marcus finished dressing in silence and followed Eddy. Stopping only to disarm the alarm system, Eddy led him outside and down across the front yard with a flashlight. Dressed in a T-shirt, jeans, and tennis shoes, Marcus was surprised at the warmth of the night. The trees rustled anxiously, and the air smelled like rain. Only when they had reached the woods did Marcus break the silence.

"What are we doing, Three?"

"We're going to chop the tree down."

Marcus stopped. Eddy took several more steps before he realized

Marcus wasn't with him anymore and turned around. He shined the light in Marcus's face.

"You crazy? Why you want to cut the tree?"

Eddy came back a few steps, keeping the light in Marcus's eyes. His anger boiled out of the empty blackness beyond the bright light.

"Because it's *mine*! I made it, and now I can't even go there anymore. That hairball Snyder thinks it's his now, but he's about to find out different. If that caveman thinks he can come here and steal my tree house and my girlfriend, bust me with an acorn and *laugh* about it—it's time he got an Eddy-gram!"

"This is bogus, Three, and I ain't doing it. I'm not chopping our tree house down."

"Fine! I'll do it myself. You can hold the flashlight."

Eddy turned and stalked off. Marcus had to hustle to catch up; he wasn't about to go back in the dark by himself.

They followed the flashlight beam down the trail to the edge of Pearl Creek where they found the ax still wedged in a pine stump. Eddy pried it loose, propped it on his shoulder, and followed the creek bank down across the road.

They came at last to the old oak tree by the Elder River. Ominous clouds blocked out the moon. Marcus took the flashlight and then took several steps back before pointing it at the tree. He wasn't about to get within range of Eddy's rage. The flashlight didn't exactly light the place up, but it was close enough.

Eddy spit on his hands, hefted the ax and set to work, attacking the massive trunk with the fury of an angry man on a mission.

But his aim was bad, his technique flawed, and the tree very large. After a half hour of flailing mercilessly at the tree trunk, grunting and huffing and sweating, he sat down and surveyed his work. The bark was chewed up over a sizable area but he'd cut no more than six inches into the trunk.

"Ain't no way," Marcus said. "You ain't getting through that tree in *two* nights."

Eddy glared sideways at him. Sweat poured down his red face. Anger lit the whites of his eyes. "I could if I had some *help*."

Marcus shook his head, then realized Eddy couldn't see him around the light. "I won't do it, Three. I'll stay with you and I'll hold the light, but I won't chop. And you won't never get through it by yourself. Not in one night."

"Ain't no can't. I'll find a way, with or without you, Marcus."

He rose to his feet as he said this, and tore into the tree with a fresh wave of anger, grunting with every stroke, hurling himself whole into his own righteous wrath.

Within ten minutes he was gasping and heaving. He flailed weakly, harmlessly, at the giant trunk until he collapsed at the foot of the tree.

"You all right?" Marcus asked.

Eddy waved a hand without raising his head. Marcus could see he was still too winded to talk, so he let it go.

Sitting on the knee of the huge root trailing inland from the trunk, Eddy rested, holding his head in his hands. Cold sweat dripped onto his knees from the matted ends of his hair. Raking his lucky cap off his head, he used it to wipe sweat from his face and neck, then stuffed it bill-first into the back pocket of his jeans. An owl hooted nearby.

"Mama'll be up soon," said Marcus, looking back in the direction of the house. "She gets up before daylight to fix breakfast."

Eddy nodded and set his hands on the ax handle to pull himself to his feet, but before he could rise, a powerful gust shoved against the tree. The great tree, with its awkward burden of tree house on one side, groaned and swayed and leaned a little toward the river, and the root Eddy was sitting on bulged up out of the ground. He stared at the root for a second and then turned to Marcus with a new excitement in his eyes.

"Let me see the flashlight," Eddy said, beckoning with his fingers. He studied the crumbled earth pushed up against the root.

"She was right!" A broad smile lit Eddy's dirt-streaked face.

"Who?"

"Brittany! Ashley's snotty cousin. She was right! Look at this root. Remember what she said, the day I accidentally dunked Ashley? She said if this root went, the whole tree would fall in the river!"

Marcus watched for a minute as the wind rocked the tree and the great anchoring root strained upward, lifting the broken soil around it a good half inch. Though the root was bigger around than his waist, it was a lot smaller than the trunk.

Grinning like a madman, Eddy lifted the ax and tore into the root with renewed vigor.

Fifteen minutes later he swung hard into the center of a white, wedge-shaped cleft in the root, and the ax bit through to the earth underneath. He left it stuck there, and he and Marcus got down on their knees, side by side, to inspect his handiwork. The wind gusted, causing the ax head to pivot a little between the grinding halves of the root. The landward side of the root no longer moved, but the side still attached to the tree heaved up a hand's width when the tree leaned out over the river.

Then it settled back.

They watched for a while with the flashlight dimming to a useless golden ember. The wind would rock the tree and the root would rise, then settle back again. The old tree refused to fall.

In a last burst of fury and with a defiant roar that actually made Marcus recoil in fear, Eddy swung the ax from his heels and buried it up longways in the trunk of the tree. He wheeled about then and grabbed the dying flashlight out of Marcus's hands and hurled it into the river.

Without another word, Eddy turned and trudged back up the hill toward home in near total darkness, cursing Darryl Snyder with every breath. Marcus followed close on his heels.

Somewhere along the way Eddy's lucky cap slipped from his back pocket and was lost. He didn't miss it until the next morning.

Chapter Twenty-eight

At dawn Wednesday morning Elise ripped through the outer banks and hurled herself at the mainland. She bludgeoned Shoal Beach with thirty-foot seas and a horizontal deluge, flung sandbags like shotgun slugs, and flipped sheets of plywood like playing cards for twenty miles up and down the coast. She made new reefs out of cars and Ferris wheels, piled rows of broken-backed yachts between shattered vacation homes, and gutted grocery stores. Blue-white flashes marked exploding transformers as the town blacked out. Telephone poles somersaulted through the streets trailing whips of broken wire, followed by shattered oak limbs rolling like tumbleeeds. She uprooted piers and used them to batter beachfront hotels to splinters, and then she strewed the splinters fifty miles inland. So great was her fury that she blasted through the seaside town in less than an hour and raced for the foothills.

But the carnage dulled her rage as the swamps and rolling hills sapped her strength. By late afternoon she had stalled out over the Appalachians, too tired to climb any more ridges, too stubborn to turn around and slink back out to sea. She sat down heavily on the mountains to cry herself out, drifting slowly southward.

Chapter Twenty-nine

After the nasty confrontation with the ponytail man in his driveway earlier that summer, Dan O'Brien had agreed to Holcombe Properties' terms. What else could he do? The money was good—more than he would have thought the little fifty-acre homestead on the north end of the ridge was worth, and enough to convince Libby that the money was the sole reason for his change of heart. He'd told her that he could find another place farther up the valley, or maybe over in Kate's Cove, and save a bundle. If he did a lot of the work himself, building a new house and shop, they might be able to put away a nice nest egg for the kids' college. Libby had understood, or at least she said she did.

Dan talked to Holcombe Properties, and they graciously agreed to give him six months to find another place and build a house and move, although they insisted upon going ahead and closing the deal. They wouldn't begin construction until spring, anyway. Dan and Libby and the kids now lived on land that belonged to Holcombe Properties.

By summer's end, Dan O'Brien still hadn't found the piece of land he was looking for. Nothing quite suited him; nothing quite replaced the beautiful spot where he'd built his first house with his own two hands, the house he and Libby had moved into after they were married, the only house his children had ever known.

In the end he figured a house is just a house; adjusting to a new place would only be a matter of time. But it seemed to Dan that he'd lost more than a house. He had lost a home. He and Libby had grown apart since the incident. She knew nothing of it, but still her attitude toward Dan had changed. Nothing was right anymore. Dan couldn't quite put his finger on it, but things were not the same. With the passing of a few weeks and the growing certainty that Libby would not learn of his little adventure, the edges of his guilt smoothed away and Dan learned to live with a secret. And yet things had changed in ways his simple carpenter's mind couldn't grasp. He and Libby had painstakingly constructed not just a house but also a *life* together. He and Libby and the kids had been a unit, an inseparable collective, different branches grown from a single seed, and there had always been a natural bond between the four of them. Until now.

Although Libby had accepted his decision to sell the place, it seemed she had drawn a curtain between them. She and the kids never came out to the shop anymore when he was working. Before, they had come out for a visit almost every day. Libby would bring him a cup of coffee and sit and watch his big rough hands turn a piece of wood while the kids grimed themselves with sawdust and made guns and cars from wood scraps on the floor, or built castles. The kids built the most unusual castles from odd wood scraps, and sometimes Dan put aside his work to help. Now Libby never came out, and when he went to the house, the kids rarely looked up from their video games. He couldn't say how it had happened, or exactly when, but they had become four separate people. He missed building castles together. He missed it a lot.

Dan developed the habit of going off by himself once or twice a week, but not to Duffy's. He never went to Duffy's again. He always said he was going to look at a piece of land, but sometimes he'd drive back into the hills, up some old washed-out logging trail to a trout stream he'd frequented as a kid, and wade the creek tossing salmon eggs with the ultralight rod he kept behind the seat of his truck. If he caught fish he let them go. He didn't go there to fish but to think and to be alone in the wild, to feel the sun on his back and the frigid water on his ankles.

On the Wednesday morning after Labor Day, Dan got in his truck, drove down River Road, and turned onto a barely visible trail that quickly disappeared into the deep shade alongside Bobcat Creek. He drove past the old swimming hole and followed the faint logging trail, bouncing over ruts and fallen limbs, scraping over thin saplings that had grown up since the last time anybody had driven up that way, and parked his truck well up the ridge past Sliding Rock, where Robby Dewberry had taken him fishing for native cutthroat trout as a boy. He took out his ultralight rod, tied on a small brass hook, fixed a salmon egg to it, and waded up the creek, bending low to work his way under overhanging branches, flipping his bait near the banks and letting it drift over dark pools where trout once lived.

When he reached an open place, he straightened up, arched his back and looked at the lowering aluminum sky. The weatherman had predicted rain for the afternoon, coming from the tail end of the hurricane, and it looked like he was right for once. It was a good day for fishing, but Dan didn't care. His slow-working, methodical, hammer-and-nails mind turned to his wife and family. He took his memories out and held them up to the light as he had done so often, turning them this way and that like a piece of cherrywood, looking for truth in the grain, and he finally began to see.

He and Libby never talked anymore, which on the surface didn't seem like much of a change; he'd always been a taciturn man. But wading up Bobcat Creek he began to see that there was another language, a secret language of knowing looks and surreptitious touches, and this was the thing that was missing between them. It was the quiet language of trust, the bond of mutual understanding, and it had been the glue that held his world together. He began to see that it was he who had withdrawn, not his wife. Cautious of his dark secret, he had slowly drawn away into himself. This was what separated them now. It wasn't a matter of land and houses, or even of words, but of trust and oneness. It was his doing and no one else's. He had brought this state upon himself and only he could correct it.

He weighed the possibilities in his mind and considered what might result from each course of action. In the end, he decided it was better to face the hard truth together than to be driven apart by a lie. He took a deep breath, trudged back to his truck, put away his rod and reel and started for home.

Driving back down the rutted logging road, as he neared the old swimming hole, he got the surprise of his life. It hadn't been there on his way up, but there in front of him sat a red Cherokee. *The* red Cherokee, with the blue-and-white *Nuke the Whales* bumper sticker and a dream catcher hanging from the rearview mirror. He stopped his truck thirty feet away, his big heart pounding, half expecting the ponytail man to emerge grinning, bringing another evil twist of fate.

But the ponytail man didn't appear. Dan inched his truck closer. It was dark inside the Cherokee, yet Dan could see through the windshield, even in the gloom by the creek, well enough to see that it was empty.

He shut off his engine and eased out of the truck, his eyes searching furtively, certain that the ponytail man was not far away. Haltingly, he walked over to the Cherokee and pressed his face to the glass, shielding his eyes with his hands. He glanced over his shoulder once more, then opened the door and looked inside. Clean except for a pair of tennis shoes, the interior smelled of cigarettes and new leather seats.

An interesting thought crept into his mind. He was on his way home to tell his wife the truth—the whole truth—and he suddenly realized he didn't have to be afraid of blackmail anymore. A devilish grin spread across his red face as he climbed into the Cherokee, into the driver's seat. He released the emergency brake, then tugged on the gearshift handle, but it wouldn't move. When he tried to turn the steering wheel it moved only an inch before it locked.

With a sigh he started to climb back out when his heel brushed against something on the floorboard, something jingly.

He found the right key, fitted it into the ignition, and turned it to the first notch. The dash lights came on and the seatbelt warning bonged. Dan pulled the gearshift lever down to N, turned the steering wheel hard right, got out and closed the door.

Hurrying now, flushed with the paranoid urgency of an amateur criminal, Dan went around in front of the Cherokee, spread his big hands against the hood, bent his back and pushed.

When the Cherokee hit the water the impact sent a miniature tidal wave rolling across the little pool, dislodging two moccasins coiled on the rocks on the other side. Dan watched gleefully as the front end tilted under, the back bobbed a couple of times, and the Cherokee sank in a boil of bubbles. Then he remembered himself and literally jumped, nervously scouring the woods, expecting to see the ponytail man bearing down on him, but there was no one there. His heart raced as he hustled back to his truck. He drove down the overgrown track toward River Road, turning on the radio and singing along with an old familiar rock song, quietly at first, until the joy of liberation burst onto his bearded, cherubic face and he belted out the last line.

" 'But if you try sometimes you just might find... you'll get what you nee-eed!' "

Chapter Thirty

Wet, filthy, and exhausted, Jake drove home from Kate's Cove Wednesday afternoon. He felt satisfied, however. He had started early and worked hard to get all the concrete poured before the rain arrived, then stayed to lay plastic over the basement slab and cut it into the drain, hoping to dull the abrasive effect the rain would have on the still-damp surface. The rain hadn't come yet, thank God, but a flannel sky crawled low overhead as Jake topped the ridge above Sutter's Cross.

Then he saw it, and his heart stopped.

A bulbous column of smoke billowed up from the valley on the other side of the river, about halfway down the length of Chestnut Ridge, pumping out of the tree-covered landscape in great round bursts, bending northward on the breeze and fanning out beneath an overcast of darker gray. Jake's first thought was that his own house was burning, but the fire lay to the north of his property and the wind was against it. The smoke looked like it was coming from Miss Agnes's place.

Racing through town, grateful for the thinning of traffic since the summer people left, Jake watched the column of smoke grow. The closer he got the more certain he was, and when Miss Agnes's driveway came in sight around a curve, he saw a sea of lights flashing at the end of it. Two pump trucks and a ladder truck sat by the end of her drive, strung with hoses, lights flashing, engines running, and making no attempt to go up the driveway. They were nowhere near the fire; the smoke rose from a point half a mile up in the woods. Jake whipped his truck into the driveway behind three firemen in full dress trotting toward the house. Two of them carried chain saws. He blew the horn and yelled for them to jump in the back. The man in the lead ran around and climbed in the passenger seat. Jake recognized him after he got in, an old friend of Lori's from high school.

"What's wrong with the trucks?" Jake shouted as he shoved it in gear and tore up the driveway.

"Can't get between the trees," the fireman answered. "Too narrow. We'll try to cut a break before it goes up the ridge, but if the wind shifts we're gonna be in a world of hurt." He shook his head. "Man, you try to tell people, but they just don't listen. Out here there's no water, unless there happens to be a creek in the right place. The pumpers are all we've got to work with, and if you don't cut your driveway wide enough, well, you're on your own."

Jake could hear the caterwauling of the guinea hens even before he reached the yard. The scene was pure bedlam: two police cars and the fire chief's car, lights flashing, Buster barking at nothing and everything, firemen with axes running toward woods alive with the ring-ding symphony of several chain saws already at work. At the south end of the yard Harley was on the tractor, plowing a firebreak across the front of the garden and up through the blackberry hedge. Miss Agnes had drug her garden hose around to the end of the house and was calmly hosing down the weathered clapboard siding.

Jake couldn't see the flames but he heard the roaring, like the sound of a train slowly approaching, accompanied by the sound of twigs snapping and popping. A light breeze stuttered and gusted and swirled, and for an instant he saw flames lashing fifty feet high over the north end of the cornfield. The air was heavy with woodsmoke. Sporadic heat waves buffeted his face. The fire had apparently started at the other end of the cornfield and would soon threaten the house. Miss Agnes's crop of Indian corn was already lost.

A dozen firemen hacked and slashed, cutting a firebreak along the bottom of the slope where the ridge leveled out onto Miss Agnes's garden, but their efforts were clearly intended to keep the fire from spreading up the ridge. As far as Jake could tell, the only people trying to save the house were Harley and Miss Agnes. When he spotted the fire chief down near where Harley was plowing, pacing back and forth with a two-way radio pressed against his head, shouting orders, Jake ran toward him.

"What's going on here?" Jake shouted to be heard over chain saws, fire, and tractor. "The fire's moving this way. Why isn't anybody cutting a break up here between the fire and the house?"

The fire chief lowered his radio. "If this wind stays down, that guy on the tractor is doing about all that can be done. I've got a bulldozer on the way, but it won't be here for another fifteen minutes. If the wind picks up"—he nodded toward a grove of pine trees encroaching on the yard—"those pines will go. And if the pines go up, there'll be no saving the house. So if the dozer gets here in time, I'll have him take them out. My biggest worry right now, though, is what'll happen if the wind shifts. We've *got* to contain it between the ridge and the river. If this thing gets loose on the mountain, it'll take days to bring under control, maybe weeks."

Jake looked at the sky, a solid mass of gray drifting southward, counter to the breeze on the ground.

"Best thing you can do right now is get *her* out of here," the fire chief said, gesturing toward Miss Agnes. "This could get ugly real fast." As if to emphasize his point, a gust slapped a rolling curl of acrid smoke down on top of them, almost obscuring the chief from view, though he stood only a few feet away.

Jake ran, coughing, back to where Miss Agnes was still hosing down the end of the house, as unperturbed as if she were watering the flowers. He took her by the shoulders and spoke straight at her.

"Miss Agnes, we've got to get out of here. The chief says a fire like this can move real fast, and we could get trapped."

She blinked. Her eyes widened as if awakening from a dream. "All right. Just let me get a couple things out of the house."

"Give me your keys and I'll get your truck."

She winced. "It's in the barn, but it won't start."

"What's wrong with it?"

"I don't know. It just up and quit on me. It won't crank."

"Well there's no time to mess with it now. We can load your stuff in my truck."

She laid down the hose, wiped her hands on her apron, and made her way around the front of the house, stopping at the spigot to turn the water off.

Jake was about to dash for the truck when he heard the steady growl of the tractor's diesel grind to a halt. Harley had been in the process of turning around to plow another swath when he suddenly stopped. The tractor sat facing Jake at the edge of the garden. Harley climbed down, walked around front and bent over to examine the front wheels, which were pointing in two different directions. The cracked tie rod had let go; the tractor was finished. There was nothing Jake could do about it, so he turned and ran for the truck.

As he pulled up near the front steps, Jake saw the sheriff's car—two-tone bronze with a big gold star on the door—pull into the yard and add his flashing lights to the confusion. Billy Thompson got out and put his flat-brimmed hat on, then strolled up to the house with a manila folder in his hand. Miss Agnes met Jake at the steps with an armload of photo albums. She reached over the side of his truck and laid them in the back and had turned to go back inside when the sheriff stopped her.

"Agnes Erline Dewberry?" he asked, glancing into the folder.

She snorted and came back down the steps to face him. "Billy Thompson, we been knowin' each other for thirty years. If you don't know my name by now—"

"It's official business, Miss Agnes. I'm sorry." He palmed the folder and hitched up a wide patent-leather belt supporting a prodigious array of equipment, all black, all shiny. "I have a warrant for the arrest of one John Aaron Alexander, and I'm told he lives here. Do you know where he is right now?"

"I don't know any John Alexander. Somebody told you wrong."

"I've been told he sometimes goes by the name Harley. I've got a picture." He tugged a sheet of paper from his folder and handed it to her. It was a grainy black-and-white computer printout of an old photo, a casual shot, head and shoulders in profile, smiling, with a cigarette clenched in his teeth. The face was younger and straighter, the hair shorter, and he was clean-shaven, but looking over Miss Agnes's shoulder, Jake could see that it was Harley.

She gave the picture back to the sheriff. "What did this fella do?"

Billy Thompson consulted his folder, blew out a breath. "Well, he's got outstanding warrants in six states for little stuff, moving violations mostly—speeding, DUIs. But it says he's wanted here in Georgia on nine counts of credit card fraud and one count arson." He looked up from the warrant, pushed his hat back on his head, and nodded in the direction of the blaze that had now reached the garden. "Maybe two."

She thought about it for a few seconds, drug a strand of gray hair out of her face, and glanced at the house. The front door stood wide open. She and Jake both saw him at the same time—Harley, standing by the back door, staring through the house at them.

She turned quickly back to the sheriff. "Last time I seen him he was down yonder fighting that fire," she said, jerking a thumb over her shoulder. It was a half-truth, but loyalty supersedes law in some places. She wouldn't give Harley up until she had heard his side of it.

"You mind if I have a look around?"

"Help yourself. I was just fixin' to hightail it, myself."

The sheriff hesitated, eyeing her suspiciously, then tipped his hat and brushed past her, striding briskly in the direction of the fire chief, who still held his post at the top of the garden.

Jake went through the house with Miss Agnes at his heels. Harley was gone. Jake stuck his head out the back door in time to see Harley slip into the barn.

Miss Agnes gave him a gentle push from behind. "You go talk to him," she said. "I got a couple more things to get out."

By the time Jake reached the barn Harley was already heading out the back way, toward the trail. "Harley!" he shouted, running after him. "Where are you going?"

Harley stopped, turned, and pointed with his eyes toward the ridge. "Time to book," he said. His voice was flat, his eyes tired. "Get Miss Agnes out of here."

A ragged spur of smoke drifted between them, and when it passed on, Harley was gone. Jake started to run back, then heard his name called. Harley had stopped a little ways up the trail, half turned, with one foot still forward. His face had changed. The child was gone out of it. "It wasn't me," Harley said, his eyes indicating the encroaching fire.

"What—?"

The smoke cut between them again, and when it cleared, Harley had disappeared.

There was no time to chase him. Jake heard frantic shouts from the direction of the fire fighters. The hardwood trees in front of him swayed violently with the stiffening wind. He turned and ran. The flames leaped and swirled about the near edge of the garden now, licking at the grove of pines that bordered the yard. He charged into the house shouting for Miss Agnes. Halfway through the house he looked out the open front door and saw her already sitting in his truck. A squadron of official cars turned and jockeyed in the front yard, their lights flashing, and raced single file down the driveway to get out of harm's way. Billy Thompson was standing beside

Jake's truck, pointing to his squad car and arguing with Miss Agnes. As soon as he saw Jake, he waved frantically and raced away, holding on to his hat. Jake jumped into his truck, cut a donut in the front yard, and tore down the driveway right behind the sheriff's car.

Looking over his shoulder, the last thing Jake saw was an impossible wall of flame boiling out of the pine grove, fueled by tons of dry pine straw, rolling across the yard, engulfing the house.

Miss Agnes didn't look back. She sat stone-faced, stared straight ahead with a tri-folded flag and Robby's picture on her lap, saying nothing. She hadn't shed a tear.

"Are you okay?" Jake asked.

There was a hint of sadness in her smile—there was no corner of Miss Agnes that didn't hold a shadow of sadness—but she smiled.

"I'm fine," she said. "It's just a house. I never seen the point of worrying about something I can't help, and I sure can't do nothing about that fire."

"I'm sorry, Miss Agnes. I'm really sorry." He could think of nothing else to say. "What are you going to do?"

She let out a small snort of a laugh. "Got any marshmallows?"

She never looked back.

Jake pulled out onto River Road and parked a hundred yards down, past the police and fire vehicles. Spectators' cars lined the far side of the road. They had pulled off to stand next to their cars and gawk at the huge plume of smoke. From the road they could see nothing of the actual fire. Near the driveway a bulldozer grunted and puffed out black smoke as it clattered down the ramp of a lowboy, shifted into high gear, and chewed up gravel, heading for the fire. The operator wore fireman's gear and a headset, no doubt talking to the chief.

Not knowing what else to do, Jake and Miss Agnes got out of the truck and stood by the tailgate, staring at the black smoke rising from the house. A young policeman walked up behind Jake and put his hand on Jake's shoulder. It was Andy Fisher, a friend from church.

"How's it going, Jake?"

"I've had better days," he said, still watching the smoke.

"Listen, I heard about you and Lori, you know... losing the baby. I'm awful sorry, Jake. That's gotta be tough."

Jake nodded. It was a small town and word traveled fast.

"Is she okay?" Andy asked.

"Aw, she's doing great, considering. She went back to work yesterday, teaching third grade. I thought it was a little early, but she said she needed—"

"No, I meant today..." The young policeman paused and a puzzled look came over his face. "But then, I figured if you're here it must not have been anything major, huh?"

He was giving Jake a very uneasy feeling. "What are you talking about?"

"Lori...the doctor." Andy blanched suddenly. "You haven't talked to Lori?"

"No, what's wrong?"

"Gail—my wife—works in the office at school. I talked to her right before I took this call. She said Lori got a call from the doctor's office late this afternoon. Gail paged her to the office and she called them back. The doctor said for her to come down there right away and to bring her husband with her. Gail said she was really upset when she left. I just assumed... You mean she didn't get hold of you?"

Jake was already cranking his truck. He yelled out the window for Andy to take care of Miss Agnes as he slammed it in gear and peeled out.

He white-knuckled the steering wheel and screamed at himself, racing up River Road toward town. Fumbling through the pockets of the work vest lying on the seat beside him, he fished out his beeper. There was one page on it, the number of the school office. The last beeper he owned ended up immortalized in a concrete wall when it got knocked off his belt, and ever since then, Jake had made it a habit to leave his beeper in the truck when he was pouring concrete. He never got Lori's page, never returned her call.

Before he got to the doctor's office the rain started falling, so when he pulled into the parking lot he took a minute to move Miss Agnes's stuff into the cab to keep it dry. There wasn't much to it—a bunch of photo albums, an antique mantel clock he figured was probably an heirloom, and a couple of cigar boxes full of strange odds and ends that Jake knew must be all that was left of Wilbur.

Lori had already left, but the doctor took a minute to fill Jake in.

He called home—no answer. He ran back out to his truck, too full of angst to notice the steadily increasing rain. When he got behind the wheel he just sat there, wracking his brain, trying to think where Lori might have gone. He didn't know which way to turn. He looked at his watch.

5:15.

What day is it? Think, Jake!

Wednesday! Wednesday, September 9. Why does that ring a bell? What happens on the ninth?

The play! The children's play she's been practicing for! It's tonight! That's where she'll be!

He yanked it into gear and spun out, heading for the church.

Chapter Thirty-one

"I once knew a hard-rock miner who kept a collection of crystals he had found in various tunnels he'd dug over the years, little gleaming cities of quartz dusted with bright pinpoints of iron pyrite, like stars. It was a fine collection of beautiful and unusual formations. When I asked him where he found such things, he said, 'Bad ground. Crevices. Fractured, loose, dangerous places. Always bad ground.'"

Jake Mahaffey

Dense clouds squatted heavy on the valley, compressing the air. Lori took a shuddering breath as she closed the car door. She couldn't breathe. She wondered if the air had thickened or if the anguish in her chest had somehow gelled into a solid mass, displacing her lungs. She dropped her keys into her purse and shoved herself toward the old red brick building.

Approaching the church building from this angle always triggered the same memory, now worn so smooth it played across her mind in a blink, no more than a footnote. Once, as a teenager, she had crossed into the church building from this same parking lot with the back of her skirt tucked into her pantyhose, and ever since she had not been able to approach the building from this angle without the mere sight twisting a deep and secret knot. This time she almost welcomed the twinge as a lesser evil, tried to hold on to it like a yellowed photograph of a world so innocent and golden as to be shaken by trivial things. But the doctor's words swamped the memory, overwhelmed it the way the endless dense clouds overwhelmed the sun.

He'd said something about adhesions—which hit her unexpectedly—about how her insides were "all glued together" as a result of a ruptured appendix as a teenager, and the ensuing blood poisoning. He said this was why it had taken so long for her to conceive. Under the circumstances, he told her, she would probably never be able to conceive again. The rest of what he said became a jumbled chorus of disconnected phrases in her memory, a song of despair.

"*... lab results from the D&C confirmed a molar pregnancy ... microscopic abnormalities ... erratic cell growth ... on the pill for a year ... monitor your blood ... cells can become invasive ...*

"*... never be able to conceive ...*"

The words dipped and swirled around one another like bats and drove out other thoughts. She walked mechanically, on numb feet.

"*... a year ... erratic cell growth ... never be able to conceive ...*"

Jake.

She thought about her husband and speared herself with guilt and regret. How would she tell him there would never be a little Jake bounding down the halls, ruling the house? Often she had heard the question asked in different ways by different people in odd scraps of casual conversation: "Why do you want kids?" or "What good reason is there for bringing a child into this rotten world?" Some people philosophized, spoke of carrying on names and legacies. Some were arrogant enough to talk frankly about keeping "quality in the gene pool." But Jake's answer was always the same: *"A man needs somebody to leave his pocketknife to."* It was one of the reasons she loved him.

Beneath the lonely weight of fear she thought of Jake and wondered what she would say.

You can keep your pocketknife, dear. You picked the wrong woman.

She felt small and dirty and very, very alone. She pushed her leaden feet faster on the walk as if to outrun this evil, this weight. It helped to move, to walk, to put one foot in front of the other. But the weight followed on a short tether, and she knew it would ram her from behind when she stopped. She moved because it hurt less than standing still. *Put one foot in front of the other.*

The door to the children's building bumped open, and Cody Taggart, a cotton-topped five-year-old ball of boundless energy, spilled out and raced across the lawn. He wore the nylon shorts, green-and-white checked shirt, cleats and shin guards of his soccer team. Nancy Taggart, holding two-year-old blond-ringleted Whitley on her hip, backed through the door shouting at Cody, nearly dropping Whitley.

Lori dug into her purse for her sunglasses. Nancy almost walked into her when she turned around.

"Whoa! Lori, you scared me! I'm glad I ran into you, though. Listen—" she shifted Whitley, pushed back a handful of auburn hair, and words tumbled out of her in a breathless rush—"all the snacks for after the recital are in the fridge in the kitchen we'll be here but we'll have to come straight from soccer practice we'll have to grab a burger on the way and I brought Cody's lion costume so he can change in the car." She gulped a haggard breath, jerking her head sideways in a futile attempt to sling her hair out of her face. "Don't you wish you had kids?"

Lori almost staggered from the blow, unintentional though it was. Apparently Nancy hadn't heard. Lori glanced at Nancy's belly, which was now showing signs of child number three. With supreme effort Lori forced a smile and said nothing. It wasn't Nancy's fault; she didn't know. Lori was glad now that she hadn't bragged to the world, but she wondered, too, if she and Jake might've jinxed themselves, and she added another brick to a growing wall of guilt. She hoped Nancy couldn't see through the sunglasses.

"Cody, GET OFF THAT DOWNSPOUT!" Nancy rolled her eyes. "They're such fun. I DON'T CARE, COME HERE THIS INSTANT, YOU'RE GOING TO RUIN YOUR SHORTS! We've gotta run—we're late. But everything's ready, okay? See you at the program!"

"Okay. Thanks," Lori managed to say.

As soon as Nancy turned away, Lori stepped inside the building. Nancy would wrangle her two and a half children into her minivan and dance away to the tune of her humming, whirling, vibrant life, and Lori didn't want to watch.

Everything was ready in the little auditorium, much to her surprise. Nancy's snacks were in the fridge, along with two jugs of juice and four liters of caffeine-free Coke. The backdrop was finished. A brightly colored banner had been strung across the front of the stage bearing the name of the musical, *What Lions?* She found all the sheet music in order, stacked on the desk in the office next to the stage. She picked up her purse and took one last look around, sorely disappointed at not finding something to do, something to occupy her hands and her mind. Only when she turned to go and walked across the spot where the piano normally sat did it dawn on her that the piano was missing. The little upright that belonged next to the stage, the one she played once a month for children's church and needed for the program tonight, was nowhere in sight.

She looked in all the Sunday school rooms off the side of the auditorium, the offices on both sides, the hall leading to the back lot. She even looked in the storage room next to the kitchen. Finally she recalled someone saying that the piano in the choir's practice room had been sent off to be refinished. They must have taken the children's piano for a temporary replacement. She went outside and crossed over to the main sanctuary. A light rain had begun to fall, but she barely noticed.

The sanctuary was all soft shadows and stillness, the only light filtered to a honey gold through intricate stained glass. The still, warm air smelled of furniture polish. The plush carpet vacuumed all sound from the air. She paused at the back for a moment and absorbed the sight: burnished mahogany and rose, the wide, fan-shaped dais with its ornate pulpit, handmade from rare curly chestnut, the silent choir loft and orchestra pit. She stood for a full minute listening, groping from the bottom of a well of desperation for a sound, a sight, a memory to touch her and hold out a gentle answer, to make some sense of her pain.

Nothing came. It was a beautiful, silent, empty place, as if God had crossed His arms in refusal—or worse, indifference. A great wave of despair caught up with her. Shivering, she pushed on instinctively in hopes of stepping out from under the wave.

She found her piano, as suspected, in the choir room. She stepped across the hall to the church office, looking for somebody to help, but the office was empty, lit only by the screen saver on the secretary's computer. From the window she could see that the custodian's truck wasn't in its customary parking place. Hers was the only car in the lot.

Back in the choir room she stood looking down on the squat console piano. In the silence, the doctor's voice intruded again.

"... won't ever be able to conceive ... ever ...

"EVER ..."

Her jaw muscles flexed. She bowed low into the piano and gave it a shove. It was lighter than she expected and had moved much easier than she thought it would on its small bronze casters. Encouraged, she swung the end around and pointed it toward the door. Slowly, with great and satisfying effort, alone, in two-inch heels and a dress, Lori worked and worried and shoved and tugged the piano out the door and down the long, carpeted aisle of the sanctuary to the back door of the church. She stopped to rest in the rear vestibule, her face flushed with effort. Breathing heavily, she turned once again and stared into the silent sanctuary with her hands on her hips.

"Sanctuary," she snorted.

Fueled by a growing resentment, she managed to heft the end of the piano over the threshold onto the sidewalk. The sidewalk sloped gently downward toward the children's building, so she figured even though it was beginning to rain steadily she could cross the fifty feet of open ground quickly enough to avoid wetting the piano too badly. Besides, she had found something to do, a challenge to meet. She had found something to take her focus away from her grim future, however briefly, and her mood would brook no resistance. She put her shoulder into the piano, shoved hard, lifted, and the last two casters dropped off the threshold. Slowly the piano rolled down the sloping sidewalk on its own, its casters grinding and rumbling on the concrete. She grabbed the trailing end and steered it, bracing herself by spreading her feet wide, keeping the piano in the middle of the walk. But it gained momentum as it rolled, and halfway across the open ground, the front casters clicked heavily over a joint in the concrete and veered to the left. She hauled back, which only made it turn harder. The piano spun sideways so that the front casters dropped off the edge into soft ground. The frame settled hard onto the edge of the concrete and ground to a stop.

Rain pattered on the lid.

Near panic, she scurried onto the grass and heaved against the stuck end, but she managed only to snag her dress on a corner and rip a hand-sized hole in it. She threw herself into a second effort, mightier than the first, and the only result this time was her breaking the heel off her shoe when she levered it against the sidewalk. She pulled her shoes off and flung them away.

It began to pour. The deluge had arrived.

She bolted into the building, ransacked the janitor's closet, and rushed back outside with a broom. On her knees in her ruined dress, panting, with cold rain dripping from her hair and the end of her nose, she worked the broom handle under the mired corner of the piano until she felt it grip the edge of the concrete. Gritting her teeth, she squatted, wrapped both hands around the broom handle and pried with all her strength. With a slight grinding noise the piano moved. It shifted sideways, and the casters rose clear of the mud. She saw that she needed just a half inch more to bring the caster onto the concrete. With a grimace, she threw her head back and poured her anger into the broom handle.

It snapped. The piano grunted back into its hole as she hurtled backward, landing flat on her back in a puddle. Sitting up, she tossed aside the broken stick. She smeared mascara with the back of a wrist and noticed blood running down her finger from a fingernail ripped half off. Thunder rumbled in the distance, and she tilted her head back, blinking up into the rain.

"I can't see you from here, either," she whispered, then she collapsed in defeat and wept.

She sat on the lawn in the rain and wept for broken shoes and a torn finger, for a ruined dress and a rain-soaked piano. She wept for her future, for her treacherous body, for shattered dreams and her unfortunate husband and his pocketknife. She wept for her unborn children.

In time, she felt herself shivering and became aware of a profound coldness. She knew she must at least go home. She dragged herself up onto her bare feet and started toward the car but then remembered that her keys, and the pocketbook that held them, were in the auditorium. She turned and went back inside.

She found her pocketbook where she'd left it, on the end of the stage. Wiping her eyes with a tissue, she glanced up at the banner with its slogan beaming brightly in childish letters three feet high.

What Lions?

The pure, sweet voices of children washed over her, an unbidden memory of yesterday's dress rehearsal. She heard them as clearly as if they were standing there on the stage waving their arms, belting out the happy finale of their musical program with the untarnished enthusiasm of the innocent. There was little Jordan dressed in the robes of Daniel with his arm around Cody Taggart, a lion in beige flannel with a shock of brown yarn for a mane, waving a paw in the air. Cody's exuberant and slightly off-key voice stood out over the others, and his southern drawl came through his words as he sang the last joyful lines:

"When you come to the end of your rope
and you just lost your last ounce of hope
when you come to the end of your rope, look up,
shout, 'HELP, LORD!'
and then LET GO!"

The kids loved to shout the last two words at the top of their voices. The memory of the absurd, jangly, bluegrass rhythm of the music, the unbridled joy of the children, and Cody's off-key drawl conspired to bring a chuckle to Lori's throat, and she put her fingers to her lips in surprise. As the ring of voices subsided she silently mouthed the words behind her fingers.

Help, Lord.

She looked down the row of seats, and her mind dredged up a picture of Harley sitting there, quieting a crying child.

What was it Harley had said?

"Just be what you are today and let go of tomorrow."

Let go.

A folding chair leaning against the end of the stage filled her vision, and then a strange notion crept into her mind. She put her pocketbook down, picked up the chair, and went back out into the rain.

Ignoring the deluge, she opened the chair, clanged it down on the concrete in front of the listless piano, and sat. She raised the lid and began to play, softly at first, the finale from the children's program.

She played from memory, note for note, following the music as she had always done, but her mind fastened on one thought.

Let go.

When she launched into the second verse her playing strengthened. She closed her eyes as her hands began to improvise, and the piano took on an amazingly bright tone despite the pounding rain.

The third time through, she abandoned herself completely. She stared in wide-eyed wonder, like a proud parent, as her hands changed keys on their own and took command of the keyboard, improvising, dancing around the melody in spontaneous celebration. A trace of blood from her torn finger mixed with the rain pouring over the keys, washing between them and splashing into the air from the force of her hands. She threw back her head and laughed like a giddy schoolgirl, the laugh of a new-polished soul, a laugh that forced tears of joy to mingle with the rain.

Jake spotted Lori's Blazer in the church lot and pulled in next to it. Even before he got out of the truck, even with the rain drumming on his roof, he could hear the piano, and he thought it odd that the sound should carry so well from the children's building. As soon as he opened the door and stepped out he realized two things. The sound was coming from somewhere *outside* the building, out in the rain, and whoever was playing, the person couldn't be Lori. He knew the sound of her playing as well as he knew her voice, and she could never improvise like that.

He ran splashing through the downpour, heading for the children's building, but he skidded to a stop when he rounded the corner of the sanctuary. The sight and the sound stopped him cold. He watched for a minute or two, just taking it in. It was a piercing sight, one that would remain with him for the rest of his life.

Lori, the piano, and the rain.

He had never heard anything like it; he knew he was seeing something profound.

Waiting until she stopped, with the last perfect chord still hanging in the air, he came up behind her, leaned over next to her ear and whispered, "Need some help?"

The chair went sprawling as she leaped into his arms and buried her face in his shoulder.

"I'm sorry I wasn't there for you," he said. "I didn't know. I left my beeper in the truck—I couldn't hear it." He hesitated, clutching her head against his chest, not sure how to proceed. "The doctor told me about the lab results. It's okay, Lori. Everything's going to be okay."

She pulled back and smiled into his eyes. "I know."

Rainwater parted her hair, ran down her face.

"I went to the doctor's office as soon as I heard," Jake said, "but you were already gone. Then I remembered about the program tonight and I figured I'd find you here."

"You're getting wet," she murmured, clearing hair from his forehead with a fingertip.

He looked over her shoulder at the overturned chair and the mired piano, the broken shoe, the splintered broom flung across the lawn. He gazed at her melted face and ruined clothes, looked deeply into her red-rimmed eyes.

"You are magnificent," he said.

Chapter Thirty-two

The rain knocked Jake out of work on Thursday. "You can't build a house in a hurricane," he wrote. Lori got up early and dressed, eager to get back to school despite Jake's protests. But inwardly he was awed by her resilience. Lori shined. She had played the piano and directed the children's program the night before without a flaw, even with the bandage on her injured finger and the completely different feel of a piano borrowed from the Methodist church down the street. And the program had been a huge success for the kids, though the crowd was small due to the rain.

Jake cooked a big breakfast while she dressed. They had time for an extra cup of coffee before she left, so they sat and talked calmly about all the things the doctor had said. Lori reassured him that all would be well.

She reassured him. She said they would have to wait a year before they could try again to have a baby, but she was only twenty-eight; there was plenty of time. The doctor wanted to monitor her blood so he would know if the errant cells returned and multiplied. He'd never used the word *cancer*; he only talked about erratic cell growth. Neither had he said *metastasize* but instead talked about how such cells could be "invasive." He finished by telling her that if the bimonthly blood tests revealed any abnormalities, she would then need to start taking some very strong medicine.

The words the doctor used—or didn't use—couldn't hide what he was talking about or change the nature of it.

Conception was beyond her control, Lori said, so she let it go. She had left it in the hands of God. With a wistful smile she told Jake again, as she had told him many times before, that she'd always dreamed of four little redheads gamboling about the house someday.

Jake told her all about the fire. Andy Fisher had left a message on the answering machine saying he had dropped Miss Agnes off at Nell Prudhomme's before he went home.

Eventually they came back around to talking about Harley, about the warrant for John Aaron Alexander on credit card fraud and arson charges.

"He didn't start that fire," Lori said flatly. "I don't know who he was before or what he might have done, but the Harley I know wouldn't torch Miss Agnes's place. He loves that old woman."

"I know," said Jake, twisting his coffee cup on the table. "But why did he run?"

After Lori left for school Jake spent two hours writing in his journal, recording all the events of the day before. Warm and comfortable in his study, with a vicious rain slashing at the windows, his thoughts turned to Harley—where he was and what he was doing. Miss Agnes had said that Harley knew of a place on the ridge where he could go to get out of the rain, but Jake couldn't picture it. There were no houses on Chestnut Ridge apart from the ones on River Road in the valley, and there weren't any empty hunting lodges or cabins on the higher reaches of the ridge, as far as Jake knew.

He called Nell Prudhomme's house and talked to Miss Agnes for a while.

She and Nell wore the same size clothes, although Nell's wardrobe was a little too fancy for Miss Agnes's taste. Jake promised to come by later in the day and drop off the stuff she'd left in his truck, and he asked if there was anything she needed. She said she would like to have her own toothpaste—Nell's was tartar control, "like brushing your teeth with sandpaper"—and she said she could use some "drawers" but figured she and Nell would take care of that. This was followed up with, "If you don't mind, you might want to go see if you can find Buster. I never saw him after the fire."

Then, when Nell left the room, Miss Agnes lowered her voice and confided that Nell was driving her crazy.

"That woman can talk the paint off the walls," Miss Agnes said, "and her phone never stops ringin'." It had been less than a day and already Miss Agnes sorely missed the sweet silence of home. She sounded like her old cantankerous self, but her tone darkened when she spoke of Harley.

"He's in trouble, Jake. He ain't right—ain't been right since the other day when he bowed up and went after Web Holcombe and got the snot beat out of him by some fella with a ponytail."

Jake hadn't heard the story, so she told him. She told him how Harley had gone off in a rage to hunt down Web Holcombe and had come home several hours later, beaten and bruised, and holed up in his little room in the shed where he had stayed until the fire started. Now the town was buzzing with rumors. Every time the phone rang, Nell would talk excitedly for a while and then would hurry to tell Miss Agnes the latest version of the story. It began with the warrant and grew from there.

The fire department investigator found the point where the fire started down at the south end of the cornfield and immediately decided that it had been set deliberately. By then the rain had obliterated most of the tracks, but not before he found two partials leading away from the scene. After taking careful measurements and snapping a couple of pictures for checking against the files to determine the size and make of the boots, the investigator called Miss Agnes at Nell's place and asked her about Harley's boots. She told him the truth, that Harley did in fact own a pair of boots like what the investigator described. Nell got on the phone then and within the hour the news was all over town.

Rumor had it that John Aaron Alexander's baby daughter had died under mysterious circumstances, and he'd run from the law and gone on an extended crime spree that ended at Miss Agnes's place. He was a known arsonist who started fires for fun, a drug-crazed madman who had stolen and pillaged indiscriminately across the country. In one day's time the gossip machinery had turned Harley into a dangerous fugitive, a baby killer, a dark and disturbed man with a long criminal record. And he was hiding in the woods nearby. The town was up in arms. A reward of ten thousand dollars had been offered for the capture of the man who had torched Miss Agnes's farm.

"You won't never believe who put up the reward money," Miss Agnes said. "It was Web Holcombe."

Rain hammered the piedmont mercilessly. It rained so hard even the locals crept along the curvy mountain roads with their emergency flashers on. Cars threw up bow waves in the flat places and gave each other a wide berth on the grades. The Waldrens' teenage boy hydroplaned off Tucker Drive and wrapped his new Camaro around a tree. He wasn't badly hurt; apart from his bent car, his relationship with his girlfriend suffered the most. A rabid ecologist, she was inordinately worried about the tree.

Rainwater flowed from the high, steep places and carved out new paths through pine straw and leaves. Joining with other veins to form fresh streams, eager little brooks grew muscles when they merged at the nearest draw. Dry gullies filled and thundered down on normally placid creek beds. Creeks where wheat-haired children once laughed and splashed after crawfish, where clear water once slithered quietly over worn rocks, now swelled and morphed into rollicking, brown, heedless monsters.

On the way to Miss Agnes's place Jake passed over Bobcat Creek and saw just how angry it was. The creek roared under the bridge, throwing up a foaming wake against the quivering limbs and debris it had piled against the bridge supports. Jake could barely see the Elder River through the trees off to the left, yet he could tell it was already running high. The rain hadn't slackened in the least.

Miss Agnes's farm looked like a war zone. The deluge had snuffed out the fire before it had a chance to spread up the ridge. The barn, miraculously, was still standing, with Miss Agnes's truck still parked in the middle. All that was left of the house was a few cinder blocks and a blackened chimney. Buster trotted up, tail wagging, as Jake stood surveying the scene. The view to the south, with all the underbrush burned away, showed fifty acres of black stubble on barren ground. A driving rain pocked and stirred the whole mess, leaving a thousand rivulets of red clay coursing between tiny islands of glistening black. The pine grove now stood as a collection of charred trunks, burned to a point twenty feet up. The lingering residue of woodsmoke and the miasma of wet ash was so dense it made Jake's eyes water.

Buster howled a warning as two cars and a pickup truck pulled into the yard. Five men got out, but Jake couldn't tell who they were because they all wore camouflaged, hooded rain ponchos. Four of them went around to the back of the truck, which was covered with a camper shell.

The fifth one strolled over toward Jake, keeping his head down, shielding his face from the rain. When he finally looked up, Jake saw that the face under the poncho belonged to Orde Wingo.

"What are you doing here, Jake?" Orde tilted his head back, trying to see clearly through fogged-up glasses.

"I was about to ask you the same thing."

"We got us up a little posse," Orde said. He motioned toward the others, who were pulling two large bloodhounds from the back of the camper shell and putting leashes on them. The dogs stood very still with their heads low, their long ears almost dragging the ground, clearly not happy about being out in the rain. "You heard about the reward, didn't you?" Orde asked.

"Yeah, I heard. So you're going after him in this weather?"

He shrugged. "A little rain won't hurt us. TJ's got more work than he can handle right now with the flooding in the low places and wrecks everywhere, so he let me borrow his bloodhounds. Harvey's already got a day's head start. With the rain washing out the scent, we can't afford to give him another day, don't you know."

Jake smirked. "*Harley,* Orde. His name's Harley."

"Yeah, this week. I heard he changes it now and then."

"Why are you doing this? What did he ever do to you?"

Another shrug. "Ten thousand dollars is a lot of money."

"This isn't about money and you know it."

He studied Jake for a long moment, and his eyes narrowed. "I can't believe you're still defending that bum after what's happened. I told you from day one that guy was nothing but trouble. Now he's burned Miss Agnes out, and you're still taking up for him. What's it going to take to convince you, Jake? Does he have to kill somebody's kid?"

"I've heard the rumors. I don't believe everything I hear, and neither does Miss Agnes. Harley didn't start the fire."

"You can believe what you want. According to the police, he's done it before. He's done lots of things."

"Maybe. Maybe not. Even if he has, it doesn't justify a lynch mob."

"Aw, Jake, we're just looking for him—to bring him in. I've hunted just about everything else, but I never got to hunt a man before. It's kind of exciting, don't you know. This is no lynch mob."

The other four men had closed up the truck and were leading the dogs across the ruined yard, heading for the shed. As they passed, Jake noticed two of the men's ponchos tented ominously at their sides, pushed out by something long and straight cradled in their arms.

"Then why are they carrying guns?"

There was something offensive in Orde's sheepish grin. "You never know what might happen if we run up against this guy. We don't know how desperate he is. We don't even know if he's armed. Better safe than sorry, as the fella says."

Before Jake left, he watched them drag Harley's blanket out of the shed to give the dogs the scent, then Orde and his posse hustled off up the trail behind the baying hounds and disappeared into the woods.

Miss Agnes's eyes went wide at the news that Harley was being hunted by men with dogs and guns. Nell Prudhomme put an arm around her and told her everything would be all right, but Jake could see a gleam in Nell's eye that said this was exciting news—grist for the rumor mill. Miss Agnes wrung her hands, sitting on the wicker divan in Nell's Florida room. Her eyes darted occasionally to the window, though she couldn't have seen the ridge from there, even without the dense rain.

"There's got to be something we can do, Jake. Or at least something *you* can do. I know it's out of my hands, but maybe you could go find him. He's up on that ridge somewhere, I know it. He ain't left town. He's still there somewhere. If you could find him before they do, maybe you could talk him into coming down and straightening this whole mess out. He ain't done nothing, Jake, but there's no telling what'll happen if they catch him."

"Miss Agnes, I'll do anything I can to help, you know that. But if five men and two bloodhounds can't find Harley, I don't see what chance I'd have of tracking him down all by myself."

"But you know him," she said. "You know how he thinks and where he likes to go."

She was careful not to mention Joshua's Knee in front of Nell, but Jake knew what she meant. Harley wouldn't be too far from the Knee.

"He's hiding somewhere up there, and if he was to see you he might just come to you. You got to try, Jake. You can't leave him all alone out there in the jungle."

Her eyes pleaded. "Jungle" she had called it. Not woods. Jungle. She didn't even realize what she'd said, but that single word told Jake what was in her heart.

He nodded. "They say the rain might let up tomorrow. I'll see what I can do."

Chapter Thirty-three

Hurricane Elise was tired. Her winds were spent, and now she was losing her shape and drifting listlessly to the northeast. The forecasters seemed to think the clouds were nearly exhausted and that the south end of the mountains might start to see short breaks in the rain by morning. Jake informed Lori of his plan to go looking for Harley, but he still had no idea where to begin.

He called Miss Agnes again after supper and got the shock of his life.

"Danny O'Brien came by to see me this evening," she said. "He was down by the creek right before the fire started. Said he saw a red car down there that belonged to a man with a ponytail."

"Wait a minute," Jake said, alarmed. "Didn't you tell me it was a man with a ponytail that beat up Harley when he was on his way up to Web's office?"

"I did. That's what Harley told me. He didn't tell me a whole lot, but I remember the ponytail man. Harley was scared to death of him."

"You think this guy works for Web?"

"Danny was sure of it, said he knowed it for a fact."

Jake took a minute to think.

"You're saying it was Web's hired man who started the fire?"

"Yep. Don't know as I can prove it, but it's a fact."

"Well then, what are we going to do about it?"

"Find Harley, Jake. Find him before some fool kills him for something he didn't do."

Nell's grapevine had also picked up the news that Orde's posse had come back empty-handed after their first day on the ridge. Lori suggested Jake call Pug Mabry, who probably knew the ridge better than anybody else.

Pug got a huge laugh out of it when Jake told him about Orde scouring the mountain all day in the pouring rain with TJ's dogs. "You wait'll I see Orde. He ain't gonna live this one down. Tracker, my aunt's fanny!"

Jake didn't find the news as encouraging as Pug did. "But, Pug, if five men and two bloodhounds can't track him down, how am I supposed to find him?"

"I'll tell you, Jake. If TJ's hounds couldn't sniff him out, and if he's still up there, there ain't but one place he could be. He's in the Greek's cave."

"I thought that was a myth, an old wives' tale."

The Greek was reputed to have been a Civil War deserter who lived in a cave on Chestnut Ridge for two years, waiting for the war to end. There were a lot of stories about him, but nobody knew the actual location of his legendary hideout. During the war he became a bit of a celebrity, not to mention a sought-after trophy, as several vaunted trackers and their dogs tried unsuccessfully to track him down. After the war he disappeared.

"Nope," Pug said. "It's real, all right. It's just that nobody knows where it's at—not exactly. I don't even know, although I got a pretty good idea. My daddy found it when I was a boy, and he told me all about it. He even said he saw the Greek's name and a date scratched into the wall, but he wouldn't tell me how to find it. Said it was the best hideout he ever saw. He stumbled on it by accident one night, coon hunting, and he said there wasn't no way anybody could find it except by pure blind luck, even with dogs. He wouldn't tell me where it was at because he said he didn't want a bunch of teenagers up there paintin' their names all over it."

"That's not much help, Pug. Even if you're right, how am I supposed to find it?"

"Well, Daddy slipped up once and gave me a pretty good clue. I heard him telling Dred Purdue about a big coon drowning one of his dogs in a creek within a half mile of the Knee, and he said it happened the same night he found the cave. I could be wrong, but the way he told it made me think the cave was somewhere around Joshua's Knee. He said over the years probably a thousand people had walked right by within fifty feet of it and never knew it was there, so I figure it ain't far off the trail. Maybe you could just go up there and holler."

By Thursday night the creeks had overwhelmed several of the small timber bridges on outlying mountain roads. Spoon Creek Bridge had already washed away; three others were in imminent danger. The Elder had gotten out of its banks in the upper part of the valley and flooded a couple of farmhouses, but so far nobody had been hurt. School was canceled for Friday.

Sometime during the night the rain slackened. After breakfast Jake shrugged into a pack and headed up the mountain. Under normal circumstances he would have taken a long, slanting switchback approach to cut down the grade. Jake had done his share of hiking, but he was no rock climber; straight up was not his style. But he knew the lower slopes of the mountain would be sliced up by half a dozen swollen, angry, impassable creeks, and he could be turned back at any one of them. The best way to avoid crossing them was to go straight up the south end, between the tributaries, and hope to find a path up through the escarpment.

He paced himself, stopping often to drink. Even in the gloom, the woods were spectacular. The trees hadn't turned yet; the ground was still rich with thick stands of fern, dappled with daisylike lavender asters. Squirrels skittered constantly on the edge of sight, taking advantage of the break in the rain.

As Jake climbed higher, the trees thinned a little and rocks took up more of the landscape. The escarpment was made up of a layer of granite about three-quarters of the way up the mountain, exposed and washed clean of the softer earth around it by eons of rain and wind. On the south end of the mountain the granite face was much more broken and sporadic than along the western rim above Miss Agnes's house.

When Jake reached the granite layer he found a wide, boulder-strewn cut where the creek tumbled down through the exposed rock. By holding to the right side and scrambling from one rock to another he was able to clamber up beyond the escarpment without breaking any bones or falling into the roaring creek and getting washed all the way back down the mountain. Once on top, he stopped, shrugged out of his pack, and dug out the lunch Lori had packed. In the sandwich bag he found a note that said simply, *I remember.*

The words had come to be a sort of code for Lori and Jake over the years. Lori knew he would be needing a little energy boost around lunchtime. Even though he was on the downhill side of thirty, when Lori looked at him she saw the invincible young man he once was, all full of grand design. He took comfort in the knowledge that no matter what happened to him, no matter what price time and circumstance exacted from his body and spirit, somebody still remembered when he shined.

He folded the note and stuck it in his pocket. The morning fog had lifted and a light breeze drew it to the north in rags so that he could see the valley occasionally through a thin, broken haze. The sky was still heavy and overcast. The whole world smelled like rain and wet earth. The trees dripped constantly, the soft plopping the only sound Jake could hear apart from the rush of the nearby creek. Sitting cross-legged on top of the escarpment in damp silence, he ate his sandwich. The world may not have been his, and he might not have been able to see much of it, but it was beautiful all the same. And he was on top of it.

The distant baying of hounds came to him from the direction of Miss Agnes's place, muffled by the mist. Prodded into action, Jake shouldered his pack and moved on, hiking directly to Joshua's Knee. Standing in the open near the precipice, he turned and called Harley's name several times, hoping Harley would hear and recognize his voice, maybe come creeping tentatively from the shadows.

But he didn't. After a while Jake gave up and struck out northward along the trail in hopes of finding some sign that Harley had been there. All he found were day-old tracks of men and dogs, washed out and blurred by the constant rain. There were no new ones; Harley hadn't passed this way since the dogs were here. Still moving north, Jake followed the trail along the edge of a rhododendron jungle for nearly a mile with no luck. The creeks were smaller at that altitude, and he was able to jump over them. He searched the soft ground around the creeks for large boot tracks, but he found nothing he thought might've belonged to Harley. When he guessed he had hiked a mile from Joshua's Knee he turned back. If Pug was right, he'd gone too far.

He began to get discouraged. There was nothing he could do but walk up and down the trail calling out occasionally, hoping Harley would hear or see him. Twice he saw deer flash through the trees, white tails up in alarm. A wild turkey hen waddled across the path in front of him and disappeared into the brush. Every so often he heard the dogs in the distance. But Harley didn't appear. A quarter-mile from the Knee he stopped at a small brook, no more than three feet across, and squatted down to cup a handful of water. The water on this unspoiled peak remained untainted, safe to drink, and tasted sweet here near the source.

Jake started to cup a second handful of water when something small and bright floated down the brook and caught his eye. He reached down and plucked a tiny object from the water, the size of his little fingernail. His heart raced as he turned it over in his palm.

A sunflower seed hull.

He rose, stepped into the middle of the brook and bent low, following the meandering course up a slight grade through a tunnel made by the dense canopy of rhododendrons. Up ahead he could hear the light spattering of a small waterfall. Twenty yards later the brush ended at a knobby, vine-covered granite cliff where the little brook rained down the face of the moss-covered rock. Looking up, Jake saw what appeared to be a ledge about ten feet above his head. It was almost invisible among the overhanging vines and mountain laurels, and if he hadn't seen the little waterfall breaking over the lip, he never would have known the ledge was there.

He studied the rock for a minute, picked out a few handholds, and started up. It was easier than it looked, and in a moment he poked his head over the top. He saw the dark hole from which the little spring issued, a narrow, pointed crevice no more than four feet high, almost hidden behind a thick hedge of mountain laurel. He pulled himself up onto the ledge and crawled over to the crevice, stopping to fish a small flashlight from his shirt pocket. He could see that the hole widened out a little ways into the cave, so he held the flashlight in his teeth and crawled into the hole on hands and knees. The water numbed his hands and filled his boots, but with a pack on his back there was no other way. Fortunately it was a short crawl. In less than thirty seconds Jake was able to stand up and look around.

He was inside the Greek's cave. He didn't need the flashlight, for a blue shaft of daylight filtered down from a crevice somewhere high above. The cave was roughly forty feet square, with the little brook issuing from a crack in the back wall and running along the left side straight out the entrance.

On a small ledge to Jake's right, wrapped in an orange blanket and watching with his old childlike curiosity, sat Harley.

" 'Bout time you showed up," he said. "I'm starving."

Chapter Thirty-four

Two days of constant rain and darkness had forced everybody indoors. Dampness seeped into people's clothes and houses and spirits and made them edgy and irritable. On Wednesday evening, already bored with being trapped indoors, Marcus and Eddy had gone to the basement to experiment with the chemistry set Eddy got for Christmas. They tried all the stuff the book recommended, but the results proved too tame, so Eddy and Marcus started mixing concoctions of their own.

They drained the acid from an old battery in the garage and experimented with pouring it into bowls of various types of crystals and filings, until finally one of them started to smoke. The mixture liquefied and began to bubble, then glowed faintly red in the middle. When the volcanic mix began to crystallize around the edges, Eddy hypothesized that if it hardened all the way across the top the heat in the center might cause it to explode. So he picked up the little porcelain bowl with a pair of tongs, put it in the utility sink next to the washing machine, and ran a tiny trickle of cold water into it. A column of brown smoke boiled up out of the sink. Frozen by indecision, the boys backed away and watched, fascinated, as thick smoke fanned out across the ceiling, obscuring the lights. It grew dark and pungent. The smoke alarm triggered and a piercing wail shot through the house.

By the time Jenny and Myra ran down the stairs, gagging and screaming, the brown overcast had spread over the entire ceiling and begun snowing little brown streamers like the ones Marcus had seen once when he burned a comb, only much larger. By the time Jenny got the alarm turned off, the smoke had started to clear, and Eddy pointed out that the source of the clouds was a harmless little bowl of "stuff" in the sink. Myra dragged Marcus to his room by an ear, fuming about the two loads of ironing she would now have to wash all over again. Jenny cornered Eddy in the dining room and preached him a sermon.

But Thursday night had been the real disaster—the night of the flying squirrel. After school the boys put on raincoats and went out to the edge of the woods to check the wire trap they kept armed and baited behind the garage. They were hoping to catch a rabbit. Instead, they found a small squirrel-like animal not much bigger than a chipmunk, cowering wet and shivering in a corner of the wire box. But it wasn't a chipmunk. It was gray, a cute little thing, and it had big, oval-shaped black eyes like an alien. They debated for a moment or two about what to do with it. They couldn't let it go; they had never seen anything like it. And they couldn't leave it outside in the rain.

It was inevitable, as unavoidable as the sunrise. Two boys with a strange new animal could do nothing other than take it into the house to show it to somebody; a flying squirrel, cold and terrified and blinded by the lights, could do nothing other than bolt from their hands and race around the room, up and down the furniture and across the drapes.

Myra joined the fray with a laundry basket. Jenny chose a tennis racket. Eddy finally managed to trap the squirrel under a blanket but not before the battle had caused the breakage of two expensive vases and the forefinger of Myra's right hand.

Eddy gathered up the blanket, wiggling squirrel and all, and took it outside to shake it out. The flying squirrel sat there on the fine-trimmed lawn in the rain and stared at him for a minute, thoroughly bewildered, before it finally wandered away in the general direction of the woods.

The Battle of the Flying Squirrel would live long in the memory of the Holcombe household.

The boys lay low on Friday morning, eating breakfast in silence—all of it for once—and walking a thin angelic line. Myra's teeth were still clenched. She was still occasionally pointing her great splinted finger at them, hissing and muttering threats of bodily harm. Eddy didn't appear worried. Marcus, however, wasn't entirely convinced that his mother wouldn't shoot them both. Jenny was seething mad over the loss of her two finest vases. She said shooting was too quick and painless.

The two watched TV for a while, but it was a weekday and the only things they could find to watch were baby shows, so they broke out the video games. Myra passed through twice and made them turn down the volume; the constant *ping-zap-clonk!* was driving her nuts.

Eddy grumbled once or twice, complaining that his father had promised to take him and Marcus to Six Flags the next time they had a day off from school, but Web had risen before daylight and gone off to the Atlanta office and wouldn't be back before Sunday. Marcus defended Eddy's father on the grounds that it had been extremely short notice; they hadn't known they were going to be out of school until the night before. Eddy wouldn't listen to this. He put aside the video game occasionally to get up and look out the window, checking the weather, gauging the misty rain. The drizzle stopped, and by midday the fog started to lift a bit.

Eddy worked the Six Flags angle during lunch. Jenny acted unsympathetic. Still, to Marcus's amazement, after lunch she agreed to let them go four-wheeling so long as they promised not to go anywhere near the river and come home immediately if it started raining again. Myra was reluctant, but by then she was willing to risk almost anything to get them out of the house for a time.

They dressed in old clothes that were about ready for the ragbag, reassured Myra they wouldn't go near the river, then cranked up and took off for Pearl Creek. They had not, after all, promised not to go near the creek. What they saw when they got there was astonishing, even for a couple of twelve-year-old men of the world. The placid little creek where they used to jump from stone to stone had grown into a roaring torrent, tearing at the roots and rocks along the banks. Eddy wanted to walk the log, but Marcus talked him out of it. The creek didn't look like it was in a mood to play.

Eddy was quiet. Marcus had noticed that he'd been quieter than usual ever since the night he tried to chop the tree house down. He threw a few rocks into the torrent but did so without enthusiasm. He sighed and rubbed a hand over his bare head.

"I want my hat," Eddy said, staring down toward the road.

Marcus knew he wasn't really thinking about his cap. He just wanted to go to the tree house, wanted to see it gone, wanted to see the look on

Snyder's face when he told him what had happened to it. They had talked about these things, and Marcus was sure it would lead to trouble. He wished Eddy would just let it die.

"We can't go down there, Three. We promised."

"I never promised I wouldn't look for my hat." He mounted the four-wheeler and gave Marcus a hard look. "You coming or do I have to go by myself?"

Marcus climbed aboard, shaking his head.

They drove across the road and angled off into a thicket, following a trail that would lead eventually to the tree house. Yet it was only one trail out of a dozen that they might have taken in the dark the night Eddy lost his cap. He never stopped to look around and only rarely turned his head from side to side as they headed down to the river.

The tree was gone. Their great big magnificent tree was gone, washed away, and the tree house with it. The river raged and boiled over the spot where the tree had once stood; it was laughing, not the pleasant chuckle of a brook but the rough, roaring horselaugh of an unrepentant bully. The new banks of the rising river, for the little distance they could see, were a solid tangle of broken limbs and logs fetched up against the trunks of standing trees, tossing up churning waves where the current railed against them. Now and then a log would break free of the jam and spin off downstream.

They walked a little ways up the bank, keeping an eye out for Snyder, half expecting acorns to zing at them from an ambush. Eddy was silent, and he kept stopping to stare at the place where the old tree had stood. They tossed a few sticks into the current to see how fast they would go, but in the end the game was too tame. Half a mile downstream, where the river ran through a gorge, hung the swinging footbridge that crossed over to the golf course. They started up the four-wheeler and rode down to check it out.

CHAPTER THIRTY-FIVE

"Geologists say the Grand Canyon wasn't carved out slowly, by the steady erosion of gently flowing water, but by cataclysmic hundred-year storms. People are like that, too. It's the storms that make us who we are."

JAKE MAHAFFEY

Has it stopped raining?" Harley peered out of a cocoon of blanket.

Even in the dim light of the cave Jake could see the dark circles under his eyes. "Yeah, for now. Sky's still heavy, though."

"Let's go up to the Knee. I haven't been out much; I could use some fresh air," Harley said, peeling aside the blanket, unfolding his legs and shoving his feet into his boots. "Man, I'm really starting to hate these boots. They're even hotter when they're wet, and they've been wet for two days now."

"Harley, there are people out there hunting you, did you know that?"

"Yeah, I knew it was coming. Matter of time. They also got dogs. I sat out on the ledge yesterday and watched them for a while. It was kind of funny. They went up the trail to the Knee and back with the dogs yelling and baying the whole way. The dogs could smell me but couldn't follow me up that brook."

"I talked to Miss Agnes," said Jake. "Dan O'Brien told her it was the ponytail man who started the fire. He was there. Dan saw his car. Harley, we know you didn't do it."

Harley chuckled. "I tried to tell you."

When he had finished lacing his boots he stood up and draped the blanket over his shoulders. He looked weary, but the childlike half smile was back on his face, the twinkle back in his eyes.

Jake followed him out of the cave and down the rock face, through the creek, and up the trail to Joshua's Knee. A lumpy sky crawled along just above their heads, threatening, but no rain was falling at the moment.

Harley stopped ten feet from the edge and sat down. Jake sat down beside him, wormed out of the pack, and plunked it down between them. He dug into the pack, marveling at Harley's restraint considering the fact that he'd been living on sunflower seeds for the last two days. Harley watched patiently as Jake opened a pack of crackers and a can of Vienna sausages, then waited for him to fish a plastic fork out of the pack. Harley worried a sausage out of the can and was about to pop it into his mouth when he stopped and looked straight up.

" 'Preciate it," he said and then started eating.

It was the simplest, most unadorned prayer Jake had ever heard. It struck him then that it was also one of the most sincere.

While Harley ate, Jake asked questions.

"So, what have you been doing up here the last two days?"

"Nuff'm." Harley swallowed. "Talking. Listening. Getting right." He crammed another cracker into his mouth. Jake decided to come right to the point.

"Why did you run, Harley? If you didn't start the fire, why did you run?"

He sighed and stared off into the valley, thinking.

"I got scared. Somehow I had it in my head that I was here to protect Miss Agnes, but if that was what God put me here for, then how come I made such a mess of it? The truth is, I went my own way. I quit listening to God and got hurt because of it."

"You mean the day you went after Web Holcombe? Miss Agnes told me you came home all beat up. What happened?"

He told Jake the whole story. He spoke frankly of the rage born in him when he learned that somebody had invaded Miss Agnes's house, how it had festered and swelled and how he focused it on Web Holcombe when he saw the rezoning sign. He told Jake about how Miss Agnes wouldn't let him have the truck and so he stomped off on foot. He said the part of God that was inside him objected, but he spurned the high road and followed his anger. Picturing his thumbs on Web Holcombe's throat, he stalked through town and climbed straight up Laurel Ridge, where he ran into the man with the ponytail, the man who knew his real name.

With downcast eyes, Harley told Jake everything the ponytail man said to him that day, about the DUIs, the burned-down house, the bad debts, and his poor dead daughter, Amanda. Jake could see he still didn't want to talk about it, that he was forcing himself to tell the truth, maybe because he was tired of hiding.

"Why don't you start at the beginning," Jake said softly. "Who is John Aaron Alexander?"

"I was a tin-knocker," Harley said. "I put in ductwork in commercial buildings, mostly in Atlanta. Made a decent living, too. For a while there I had it all. Me and my wife—I called her my wife, but me and Vicky never got married—she lived with me for seven years, and we had a nice little place out in the woods, where we didn't have any neighbors looking in our windows and we could do whatever we wanted. We had a baby girl." He raised his head and gazed southward over the flatlands, into the past.

"She was our light. All blond curls and big eyes and a laugh to melt your heart. And she did love her daddy." He stopped and swallowed hard.

Jake waited. After a long minute Harley put his forehead on his knees and continued.

"But babies die and women leave." The words tumbled out quickly, as if he'd shoved them from behind. "It was my fault," he said thickly, struggling to speak. "Vicky left Mandy with me one Saturday while she went shopping. It was a hot day, so we splashed around in our aboveground pool all morning. We ate lunch and then it was Mandy's nap time. We laid down together in the hammock out back, and she fell asleep on my chest, all warm and soft. I still remember how she smelled—like baby shampoo and milk."

He paused again and said nothing for a long moment. Then he took a deep, shuddering breath and said, "I guess I slept too hard, and the hammock was so comfortable and the weather so fine. I was up late the night before and I'd had a few beers that afternoon. I always did—I mean, it was Saturday—and I guess I slept too hard. I never even knew when she got out of the hammock. She was only fourteen months old, just started walking. I didn't know she could climb the ladder to the pool."

Harley raised his head, and Jake saw the deep sorrow in his eyes.

"I just didn't know," he whispered. "I didn't know it could happen so quick and easy, so quiet. It still seems like an awful price to pay."

He dabbed his eyes with a fist, sniffed, and shifted his weight.

"Vicky blamed me for it." He snorted. "Like I wasn't doing a good enough job of blaming myself. I don't remember how it came about that she left, but she did. Everything after Mandy died is kind of hazy—me and Jackie D got to be good friends. I stayed drunk or stoned pretty much all the time—anything to get that picture out of my head. One morning I sobered up enough to notice Vicky's car was gone, her clothes too. I wasn't sure how long she'd been gone, but it didn't matter really. The space between us had got wide and empty by then.

"McDougal, my buddy from work, tried to help me over it. He came out to see me a few times, to talk, and he managed to keep the boss off my back for a while when I didn't show up for work. But about the time I started thinking I might live, I had a heart attack. A bad one. I almost died. And I had a lot of complications afterward, fluid and stuff. Stayed in the hospital three weeks, all full of tubes, couldn't talk, couldn't eat. I don't know why they didn't just let me die; I didn't have nothing left but pain anyway. Demerol was the highlight of my life.

"When I got home I started walking and gradually got my strength back, some of it anyway. I went back for a follow-up after a couple of months, and they said my heart was gonna explode. They said part of my heart was dead and sooner or later it'd swell up and pop like a bubble on a tire. I didn't care and I told them so. They said it was just a matter of time, that one day my heart would give out and I'd drop dead, end of story. They wanted to cut on me but I said no. For me, that place was nothing but a prison where they wouldn't let a man die. 'Let her blow,' I told them. 'At least it'll be quick.' "

The doctors told him he'd be dead in six months if they didn't operate. Maybe less. They said it was a fairly common procedure. The odds were—

But he didn't hear them. He didn't even stop at the desk on the way out; he just left.

He told Jake how he had pushed his rattly old truck beyond sanity, leaving the city behind, hanging over the steering wheel as if he were clinging to a surfboard, driven hard before a monstrous wave of circumstance.

Liberation first came to him in the middle lane of the expressway at eighty miles an hour, a euphoria born of the sudden realization that he had nothing left to lose. It came in waves from the top of his head, spreading downward, through his eyebrows, his eyes, his jaw. He flexed his hands, loosening his grip on the steering wheel as he sat back and shifted his feet.

The next wave came when he began to see a plan and ways to implement it. It seemed reasonable and sound and put a wide grin on his face. A few minutes later he threw back his head and laughed as he yanked the truck across two lanes of traffic, narrowly missing a Taurus and thumping across a wedge of grass to the exit ramp.

He strode into his house feeling better than he had in years. The first thing he did was jerk the trash can from under the kitchen sink and dump it out in the middle of the floor. Rummaging through the pile, scattering tea leaves, beer cans, and junk mail, he came up with two unopened envelopes, each with a large *6.9%* printed on the front, next to the word *Preapproved.* When he dumped out the contents of the recycling bin on the back porch he pulled out five more envelopes.

Within two weeks he had activated nine new credit cards, cleaned out his bank accounts, and acquired a second mortgage on the house for fourteen thousand in cash. He sold his truck, cashed out the credit cards and threw them away, then bought a late-model Harley Davidson he found advertised in the paper. He hadn't ridden a bike in ten years but figured the worst it could do was kill him, and if his heart happened to explode while he was cruising, well, a motorcycle wouldn't take out as many innocent bystanders as a Winnebago. He'd always wondered if Monument Valley looked the same in real life as it did in the John Wayne movies, and under the circumstances it seemed singularly appropriate to Johnny Alexander that he should make it the aim of his remaining life to go find out.

He throttled out of town on a nearly new Fat Boy with a uniform shirt on his back, a fist-sized roll of cash in the saddlebag, and a determination to redefine riotous living. Bruno the German shepherd lay contentedly gnawing a frozen pot roast in the front yard while the first tendrils of yellow flame licked at the windows from the bonfire in the living room. There was a short, colorful letter to Vicky in the mailbox, flag up. On the outskirts of town he stopped and called McDougal to say he might be a bit late in the morning.

He stopped once more at the cemetery out by the interstate. Leaving the motorcycle parked at the entrance, he walked across acres of grass and sat cross-legged in front of a small bronze plaque lost among a hundred other small bronze plaques. He pulled grass, rolled it between his fingers, chewed on it, tossed it in the air and looked around. He stayed for nearly an hour, fidgeting the whole time because he wanted something. He wanted *something* as desperately as he'd ever wanted anything in his life, but he didn't know what it was. Finally, as he was leaving, he turned back, ran his fingers through his hair and muttered, "Missy, I sure could use a hug."

"And then," Harley said, turning to Jake, "me and the hog and Jackie D went off to find Monument Valley."

A palpable silence hung in the wake of his words. Jake's pack held enough food to last three days, and although Harley should have been starving, he really hadn't eaten much. Jake quietly stuffed the remains back into the pack, zipped it shut, and sat staring at it.

He couldn't stop thinking about Harley's heart. The man seemed healthy enough for the moment, but if what he said was true, he could keel over at any time.

"Harley, how long ago was it when you saw the doctor?"

" 'Bout a year."

"So, according to the doctors, you should have been dead six months ago."

He shrugged. "I never been on time for anything in my life."

"You have to go down and get help; you can't stay up here indefinitely. You're going to have to deal with your heart before... before it explodes. You can't do whatever it is you're here to do if you're dead. You've got to face your problems. You haven't done anything wrong—at least not lately. And you won't be alone. I'll stand by you. Lori will stand by you. Miss Agnes will stand by you—"

"And God will stand by me. He ain't let me down yet."

Harley stood up, wiped his hands on his jeans, and walked to the edge of the cliff, or at least as close to it as the smooth curve of the rock would allow him. He stood silently with his hands in his pockets, at the naked edge of the world, looking into the abyss. Jake got up and stood close beside him.

The river had doubled in width and turned the color of peanut butter. From where they stood it looked calm except for the tumult where it cascaded over Cherub Falls. They could see the wide pools, the horseshoe bend, and the roof of the pavilion itself, though now the waters covered the entire promontory on which it stood so that the pavilion roof made a little island in the turgid river. Caught between dusty late summer and rusty early fall, the trees were tinged with a dull yellow, like broccoli on the edge of going bad. A lone hawk cruised over the bend in the river, stretching its wings in the break between showers.

Harley let out a heavy sigh, pulled his hair back away from his face, turned abruptly and started back toward the trail.

"Where are you going?" Jake shouted, gathering up the pack.

"Down," Harley said. "I'm going down. You're right—there's no use running. And if God's with me, what is there to be afraid of?" He shoved his hands in his pockets and took one last longing look around the barren rock of Joshua's Knee. "I can't stay up here forever, much as I'd like to. It ain't my job to worry about what's gonna happen to me, not anymore. I was wrong to take matters into my own hands. I should've listened and let God show me the way."

In the quiet of the Greek's cave for the last two days, fasting, talking to God, and listening, Harley had come to grips for the second time with his own inadequacy and placed himself once again at the mercy of a forgiving God.

And once again he had found grace.

Jake caught up with him at the edge of the woods. Harley had chosen a different trail from the one they had just come up. "Why this way?" Jake asked.

Harley fixed him with the patient gaze of a schoolteacher. "Well, if you go that way," he said, pointing to the precipice behind Jake, "you'll fall off the cliff."

Chapter Thirty-six

Jake followed Harley northward along the ridge, stopping often to listen. The baying of the hounds was incessant but never drew any nearer. Instead, the sound remained parallel, always between them and the road. Harley moved slowly, and for a while Jake thought he was dragging his feet on purpose, reluctant to go down and give himself up, until, after sprinting to jump over a creek, he saw that Harley couldn't catch his breath and was forced to sit on a rock and rest. Harley's sudden loss of stamina was alarming, but Jake decided not to bring it up. Nothing could be done about it until they reached the hospital.

Harley didn't go down the mountain at all but stayed above the escarpment, thereby avoiding the worst of the swollen creeks on the lower slopes. At the upper elevations the creeks were small enough so they could easily jump over them. Jake thought at first that Harley was heading for Miss Agnes's place, a thought he gave up after following Harley as he stayed high on the ridge and passed by her farm.

Finally, near the Pyramid, on the north end of Chestnut Ridge, Harley turned. A well-worn trail led down to the left and through a break in the escarpment toward the river. They sat on the rocks and rested for a few minutes, passing Jake's water bottle back and forth. Then, without a word, Harley got up and headed downhill.

Half an hour later they reached the bottom and came out of the woods onto River Road. They turned north and started walking up the shoulder toward the intersection by the river bridge not quite a mile down when they were brought up short by the bellowing of hounds in the woods just ahead. Harley froze, then glanced to his left in the direction of the river. Jake could hear the river roaring about a quarter of a mile away, and from the woods in front of them he could now hear, faintly, the voices of men.

"I don't think we want to run into them," Jake said. "They're armed and looking for an excuse. What do you say we go down and follow the river up to the bridge? Maybe we can get past them that way."

Harley hesitated but then turned without saying a word and trotted straight across the road toward the river, into the twilight under the canopy of poplars and hemlocks.

"You can go out there if you want. I'm not!" Marcus had to shout to be heard over the roar of the rapids. The middle of the swinging bridge sagged within a few feet of the swollen river, and the sight of the churning rush of water beneath the footbridge brought a knot of fear to Marcus's stomach. He white-knuckled the hand ropes.

"Chicken."

"Am not."

"Ba-GACK!" Eddy cried as he flapped his elbows.

The bridge creaked and gave a little under Marcus's weight when he took a cautious step out onto it. The middle rose a fraction of an inch to compensate. The hand ropes swayed in and out. He stepped back.

Eddy brushed him aside and stomped ostentatiously out to the very center of the bridge, turned around, and jumped up and down to make the bridge gallop from end to end. He let go the ropes and flapped his elbows again. "Ba-GACK!" he taunted, and still the river didn't swat him down.

Shamed by Eddy's performance, Marcus moved out onto the bridge. Soon both the boys were running back and forth, jumping on it. They got on opposite sides and seesawed the bridge. They discovered that if they bellied down over the middle of the river, their combined weight lowered them close enough to reach down and touch the water. This had been the challenge all along—to touch the raging river.

It was Marcus who looked up first and saw it coming: the carcass of an old oak tree, stripped clean of its branches, slithering down the current like a giant oil-skinned alligator. Its black hulk rode low in the water and appeared at first to be no threat. But it bumped against something, no more than fifty feet upstream from the bridge, and hitched a little to one side, scraping past the unseen obstruction. As it began to move again it rolled, and a great black stump of a limb raised itself dripping from the water. Near the broken end of the limb one piece of board remained nailed firmly across it. Trailing back from the board was a mass of tangled rope so fouled and blackened it took Marcus a minute to recognize it as a twisted rope ladder.

It was the carcass of their own tree come to find them.

Eddy still held a cupped hand down, letting the river snatch at it.

Marcus's eyes grew wide as he watched the limb rise like an hour hand up to twelve o'clock. "RUN!" he screamed and then took his own advice. He almost made it to the end before the bridge lurched under the blow of the log's upraised arm. His feet shot from under him, and he fell hard onto the slats. He didn't look back when the boards under him tilted and the ropes strained and groaned. Eddy's scream was strangled by water just before the ropes on the other bank parted with a rapid succession of sharp reports like rifle shots. For a moment the tangle of boards and ropes dunked Marcus under the flood, but he locked an elbow in a loop of rope and held on. When it brought him up again, he scrambled hand over hand up to the anchor post.

Hugging the post, he fisted water from his eyes and stared downriver. The limp remains of the bridge rippled on the current next to the bank like a great slatted snake. For a split second, far downstream, he saw Eddy tossed up like a bronc rider, one arm waving over his head.

Chapter Thirty-seven

Jake could see the boiling river long before he should have been able to. It was up—*way* up. It was well out of its banks and tearing through woods, surging against tree trunks, ripping mountain laurels out by the roots. Harley picked his way among the rocks and trees until he found a boulder right on the edge of the river and climbed up on top of it. Jake climbed up next to him.

"That's a definite class six," Jake shouted over the roar. "What we would have called a suicide run, back when I was kayaking."

"Wow." Harley shook his head slowly. "Awesome." After a moment he hopped down off the boulder and headed north along the bank. He went only a few yards before he stopped, sat down on a rock, and started unlacing his boots. This worried Jake.

"Harley, you're not thinking of...?" Jake motioned with his eyes toward the river.

Harley's eyebrows peaked as he glanced from Jake to the river to his stockinged feet. "You kidding? I ain't crazy, Jake!"

"Then why are you taking your boots off?"

"My feet itch." He scratched the soles of his feet vigorously, chuckling.

"I'm sorry," Jake said, running a hand through his hair. "For a minute there I thought, you know..."

"How's Lori?" Harley asked while clawing at his feet. "I'm sorry, with all this running around I forgot to ask. Miss Agnes told me she lost the baby, and I never got a chance to talk to you about it. Is she okay?"

Harley was a piece of work—sitting here with a price on his head, bloodhounds hot on his heels, nonchalantly scratching his feet and asking after the health of Jake's wife.

"She's okay, but things have gotten worse. Now the doctor's saying there's a chance she might have cancer." Jake shrugged out of his pack. "She still has dreams of having four little wild ones running around the place someday." He fiddled with the straps on his pack for a minute, collecting his thoughts, then added, "You see your future a certain way and just sort of expect it, you know? You get your hopes up and then... Now we have to change gears, forget about dreams and worry about survival."

Harley picked up one of his boots and stretched the laces. He froze, staring into the boot as if he saw something there and didn't know what to make of it, then turned a strange, quizzical expression toward Jake. "She's gonna be fine," he said. "Don't give up on your—"

He never finished the thought. His attention was torn away from Jake and focused on the river. At the same instant, from up toward the road, the hounds broke out of the brush, saw him and let loose with long keening wails that said they'd spotted their prey. Orde was in the lead, being towed along at a trot by the straining bloodhounds. Four other men were strung out through the trees behind him, running to catch up. Harley never even glanced at them. He was staring upriver toward the highway bridge.

"Look!" he shouted. "Somebody's in the river!"

Jake strained to follow Harley's stare. The river curved slightly so he could see Orde's sign on this side of the bridge, its base now submerged, its support poles throwing up huge muddy wakes in the current, but he saw nothing in the river that looked like a person. Harley clambered back up onto the boulder at the water's edge, with Jake following close behind.

"There!" Harley shouted, pointing.

Jake saw the boy then, just a head and shoulders thrown up momentarily by a vicious wave, gulping air, dragged down again mid-gulp, caught hopelessly in the current and hurtling toward them. Jake jumped down off the rock and sprinted downstream, his heart pounding, looking for something, anything, to throw out as a lifeline or a float, knowing the boy would be shooting past him in seconds. But he found nothing. He ran, hurdling rocks and downed trees while keeping an eye on the river, but the boy swept past him before he could do anything. He stopped running and bent over to catch his breath, then straightened in time to see the child bob twice more before finally disappearing from sight. Whoever the kid was, he was doomed unless he could grab a limb on the far side and pull himself out. From the looks of him, Jake didn't think he had a chance. He turned and hurried back to where he'd left Harley.

Harley was gone.

Orde Wingo stood in his place on top of the boulder, bending over with his hands on his hips, puffing and panting from the run. The bloodhounds were running loose, their leashes trailing them. They snuffled and chortled at the ground all around the boulder, and one stopped to grumble at Harley's boots. Jake climbed up onto the boulder next to Orde.

"What happened?" Jake asked, the apprehension tying a knot in his insides.

Orde hitched a breath, still gasping from the run, and pointed at the river. Jake stood on tiptoes and stared downstream, his fear suddenly confirmed.

One of the other men scrambled up onto the boulder beside them, a younger man, with dark hair and a beard. He wasn't as winded as Orde and seemed almost relaxed as he laid his shotgun across his shoulders and hung his arms from it.

"Man!" the new guy shouted. "That's the closest I ever come to ten thousand dollars. That guy must've wanted to get away something fierce if he was willing to jump into *that*!"

"He wasn't running *from*," Jake said, still looking downriver, "he was running *to*."

There was a profound confusion in Orde's eyes. He finally managed a question between gasps. "What do you mean by that?"

"You didn't see? There was a boy in the river, Orde! A child! Harley jumped in to try and help him."

Orde's face contorted, and he snarled, "Oh, come on, Jake! There wasn't any kid and you know it! Why are you making excuses for that bum?" Orde lost his footing on the wet granite and would have fallen in himself if Jake hadn't reached out to steady him. He jerked his arm away in anger. "That fool jumped in the river to save himself!" Orde screamed, his face turning an apoplectic purple with a vein throbbing visibly in his temple.

Jake was driven a half step back by Orde's vehemence. In the next second a picture of a curly blond baby girl flashed across his mind. A bemused smile crept onto his face as he turned and gazed downstream into the maelstrom. He nodded his head.

"You just might be right," he said.

Back on River Road Jake flagged down a passing car and borrowed a cell phone to alert the police and fire-rescue people. When the first police car arrived, he took the two patrolmen down to the river to show them where he'd seen the boy. While there, one of the policemen got a call from dispatch saying there had been another report on the missing child. The patrolman's face blanched when he heard that a second child had witnessed the accident and that the name of the boy lost in the river was William Edward Bonner Holcombe the Third.

Chapter Thirty-eight

In the middle of a high-powered presentation before a conference table ringed with investors, Web paused to sneak a glance at the beeper vibrating against his hip. He rolled his eyes when he saw his home number, followed by 911. They'd been over this before; he'd told her never to beep him unless it was an emergency, but he and Jenny had very different ideas about what constituted an emergency. Deftly changing gears in the middle of his presentation, he guided the prospective investors to a packet of information before them and suggested they take a minute to look it over. He then excused himself and stepped out into the hall to make what he felt sure would be a very brief call.

He never returned. He left his briefcase open on the end of the conference table next to a half-finished cup of coffee and his suit coat hanging on the back of the chair.

He pushed the silver-blue Mercedes as fast as the rain-slick roads would allow, keeping the cell phone hot, checking in with Jenny every few minutes, trying to calm her down, then calling various rescue people to update himself on what action was being taken and what could be done that wasn't currently being done. He called the Department of Natural Resources when he learned they had a helicopter equipped for mountain rescue. They told him that at the moment the inclement weather made a rescue from the air impossible. The rains had returned, the ceiling had lowered, and the winds were gusting hard again.

Less than two hours from the time he left Atlanta, Web pulled up on the circular drive in front of his house and elbowed his way through a mob of shouting, shoving reporters, only to find his house almost as crowded as his lawn. A dozen people had come to sit with Jenny, most of them from the church.

Jenny was hysterical, and Web simply didn't have the time or the patience to deal with her. There were things to be done; it would never occur to Web Holcombe to sit moaning in the house while his son was in trouble. So he grabbed a flashlight and left. On his way to the river he called a doctor friend and asked him to drive over to the house and give Jenny something to calm her down. Then he phoned the police and demanded a squad car go up to his house and clear out the press.

It was almost dark by the time Web found Sheriff Billy Thompson's search party up near the highway bridge. The search was just getting under way.

Web had learned in the course of his phone calls that Thompson was in command of the search-and-rescue effort, so he went straight to the top. He also wanted to be near the sheriff because he knew Thompson would have some way of keeping in touch with other search parties. He showed up at the river wearing a bright blue poncho he'd bought at a convenience store on the way down.

"I'm joining your search party," Web announced when he found the sheriff.

Thompson focused a little too long on the dress slacks and Italian shoes. "Not a good idea, Web. Why don't you go home and take care of your wife. We've got things under control here."

Web's expression was as dark and steady as the rain popping the hood of his poncho. "I'm coming with you," he said.

The sheriff winced. "I really think you'd be more use at home, Web. This is going to be rough. It'll be dark soon, and it's supposed to rain all night. As you can see, the river is a very dangerous place right now. The men I've got here are all either professionals or trained volunteers that we've worked with before." He squinted up into the rain. "It's going to be a long night. We don't need to baby-sit a bunch of civilians. You'd just distract my men, give them one more thing to worry about in the dark."

For Web, the point was not negotiable. He said nothing.

"Look, I'm sorry. I know it's hard. I know that helpless feeling, like you've just got to do *something*. But this is not a good idea."

Web turned around and started back up toward his car.

"Where you going?" Thompson called.

Web stopped, turned around. "Up ahead. I'll search the banks ahead of you on my own." He'd said it flatly as a simple declaration of intent, an ultimatum.

"All right," Thompson said, rubbing his face, "you can come with us. We've got enough problems without having to search for you, too. Just make sure you stay in the middle of the line, back away from the river. And if you quit, you walk out alone. Agreed?"

"I won't quit."

The sheriff shook his head. "No, I don't believe you will."

Web searched meticulously, bringing his flashlight to bear on every shadow, looking around every tree, under every overhanging rock, every bush. Ignoring the pouring rain, he scoured the ground for the smallest clue on the off chance Eddy had gotten away from the river and passed this way.

His Italian shoes chafed blisters on his heels. An hour after he joined the search his slick sole slipped on a patch of moss as he went to step up onto a boulder, and he drove his right knee hard into the rock. The next man in line heard him yelp and came over to find him sitting at the base of the rock holding his knee. Blood soaked through a fresh hole in his pants.

"You all right?" the man asked, shining his flashlight on Web's knee.

"I'm okay. Just a flesh wound." He forced himself to his feet and moved on, turning his back on the other man, but he limped noticeably the rest of the night.

His soggy pants were picked and ripped from thorns and barbwire fences he came across during the night, and the cuffs became frayed. Despite the poncho, or perhaps because of it, he was wet to the skin. The poncho kept the rain off but it had caused him to sweat, and after a long night of physical exertion, Web was almost as wet as he would have been without it. Damp and tired, the purple hour near dawn crept inside him and sent chills up and down his spine.

All through the night the ragged line of men with flashlights were obliged to stay within sight of each other so no piece of ground would be overlooked. The entire party could progress no faster than the slowest man in the roughest part of the terrain, and somebody was always bogged down in a rock pile or rhododendron hedge or blackberry thicket.

With most of the search still before them and with at least a reasonable hope of finding the boy alive, the men had shouted to each other over the rain. Web heard them passing bits of news and truncated gossip all night long. But as daybreak approached they stopped talking. They'd covered the first few miles, the most promising part of the search area, and found nothing. Even so, they pushed ahead, forging an arduous path downstream, yet they were acutely aware that every step farther down the river brought them closer to a horrible conclusion, and one by one they fell silent.

For Web, it became a very loud silence.

At first light Web tried to call home one more time, just to hear Jenny's voice, but the cell phone was dead. Morning crawled up from the ground and spread a meager palette of muted browns and grays on the soggy earth. Full daylight never arrived. The mountains hunched their patient shoulders under a monotonous downpour and waited: this, too, would pass. The search party had covered only half of the eight miles between the highway bridge and the falls. The party on the other side of the river hadn't even gotten that far.

Web stopped, arched his back, stretched and looked up toward the road. The searchers covered the slope up through the hardwood forest and the scattered outcroppings of moss-dappled rock. He had kept track of them by the pinpoints of their flashlights throughout the night. Most of them had since switched off their lights. Now, through the veil of steady rain in the gray half-light, he could spot most of their yellow raincoats. He'd secured a place in the search line down near the river where he could hear the shouted orders and snatches of conversation between Sheriff Thompson and the three men working the very edge of the water. The three were tethered together with a yellow tag line in case one of them should fall in.

When Web heard the blast of the air horn from the chrome-sided coffee wagon the searchers affectionately called the "Roach Coach," he waited. Even a shapeless, hooded yellow raincoat couldn't obscure the stoop-shouldered hulk that was Sheriff Thompson, with him laboring up the hill from the riverbank toward the coffee wagon. Web fell in step.

"Any word from the other side of the river?"

"Not yet," the sheriff replied. "Riley should be checking in shortly.

Last report, an hour ago, said they hadn't found anything." He pointed up toward the road. "You see that news van? If I were you I'd lay low. Those guys'll hound you to death if they find out who you are."

A white van with an array of dishes on top and the Channel 5 comet plastered down the side pulled up behind the Roach Coach. Two men jumped out. The one with the microphone was a neatly dressed, darkly handsome young man wearing a shirt and tie, his dress slacks tucked into a pair of rubber boots. He'd shoved an umbrella out the door ahead of himself and now stood under it while he turned on the transmitter at the back of his belt and checked his earpiece. The driver, an athletic-looking man in his early twenties wearing a nylon jogging suit and running shoes, pulled out what looked like a beach umbrella and opened it as he ran to the back of the van. A hairy giant in cutoffs and a T-shirt hopped out of the back under the protection of the huge umbrella, carrying a state-of-the-art digital video camera on his shoulder and an extra floodlight in his left hand.

Web kept his face down and blended into the little crowd lined up for coffee at the Roach Coach. The reporter caught up with the sheriff as he ducked under the awning on the side.

"Sheriff Thompson," the reporter began.

The sheriff's radio emitted a blast of static and a few garbled words. He held up a finger, signaling the reporter to hold on while he pulled his walkie-talkie out from under the raincoat. "Go ahead, Riley."

Web risked a brief glance and saw that the reporter's attention was fixed on the sheriff. He eased a little closer and turned enough so that his rain hood caught the conversation.

More static, then Riley's voice, "*... coming up on Turtle Creek.*"

The sheriff responded, "Riley, hold up at the logging road right before the Turtle. Wallace ought to be down that trail anytime now in his Jeep. He's supposed to meet y'all there with some breakfast. You found anything?"

"Nothing. You?"

"Naw, not a thread. Everybody okay?"

"Ewell turned his ankle in a hole a couple hours ago. It's swole up pretty bad. He can walk, but he probably needs to go back out with Wallace. It gets a lot steeper on the other side of the Turtle."

Sheriff Thompson sighed. "Yeah, send him out. Listen, Wallace is bringing in two rangers on loan from Chilhowee. It looks like that's it. We can't put civilian volunteers in where you're headed, and besides, there's no place to meet up and bring in fresh troops between Turtle Creek and the falls. Can you keep going?"

Web had heard about the conditions on the other side of the river. Parts of it were nearly impassable, especially with the creeks having risen up.

"We'll be all right." Riley paused, then came back on and said, *"Most of us got kids of our own. We'll push on through and come out at Sugar Hill Road. Hope we get there before dark."*

Thompson signed off and tucked his radio away. He turned back to the reporter. One of his men approached and, without a word, put a Styrofoam cup of coffee in his hand. "Now, what can I do for you?" Thompson asked the reporter.

"Sheriff Thompson, I'm Parker Stone, Channel Five Eyewitness News. Could we just do a brief interview? This won't take long, I promise."

"Most folks around here call me Billy," the sheriff drawled.

Stone winced. "Thanks, but I think I'll stick with 'Sheriff Thompson' for the interview, if you don't mind. Sounds more professional."

Jogging Suit held the small umbrella over Sheriff Thompson while Parker Stone and his cameraman faced him from under the larger one. Stone pressed his earpiece in deeper to hear something over the drumming of rain on the umbrellas, mumbled "Okay" into the mike, and turned to the sheriff.

"Sheriff Thompson, I understand you've been out here all night combing the riverbanks. Can you give us an update on the search for the Holcombe boy?" He held out the microphone.

Thompson shrugged, squinting against the lights. "We haven't found anything yet."

"Not a thing?"

"Nope." He shook his head, rubbed an eye with a knuckle.

"Will the daylight help the search?"

"Well, it'll help keep anybody else from getting hurt or falling in the river. Might let us move a little faster. But I can guarantee you we didn't miss anything where we've already looked."

"Sheriff, given the conditions and the amount of time that has passed, what do you think the chances are of finding the boy alive?"

"It's not my job to speculate, son. I'm here to search."

Stone scanned his notes, his timing thrown off by the sheriff's abruptness.

"Sheriff Thompson, it's rumored that another person, an adult, may have fallen in the river at the same time as the Holcombe boy. Can you shed any light on this?"

"We do have a report that a second person may have gone into the river, but that doesn't change anything. It just means we're looking for two people instead of one."

"Do you know the name of the second victim?"

Thompson shrugged. "If I did, I wouldn't tell you."

"Why?"

"First of all, we don't have much information on the second victim and what we do have hasn't been confirmed."

Web waited for the second reason, but it didn't come. The sheriff fidgeted uncomfortably and bought himself a few seconds by sipping his coffee. Rain pelted the umbrellas.

"And second?" the reporter finally asked.

"Second, we're not even positive there *is* another person. Like I said, we don't speculate. Besides, it don't make any difference to the search teams. I mean, if we find somebody and it turns out to be someone we didn't expect, we probably won't throw him back in."

Web had caught the sheriff's hesitation. Web knew communications, and he knew when a man was covering up.

Thompson's radio crackled again. *"Come in, Billy."* It wasn't Riley's high country twang this time but the calm drawl of Drew Milam, the anchor of his own team down by the river.

Thompson stiffened in alarm and whirled around, scanning the crowd of men milling around the coffee wagon while he fished the radio from under his raincoat. "Milam, where are you? I thought everybody came up. I knew I should have counted heads." He glared accusingly at Parker Stone. Web could see from the fire in the sheriff's eyes that he blamed the reporter for drawing his attention away from his men.

The radio sputtered, *"Still on the riverbank, boss. We need to see you down here. And bring Bergy."*

"Are you okay?" the sheriff asked.

"Yep. We're secure. Take your time," the voice said through the static.

"Be there in five." Thompson tucked the radio away.

The reporter grabbed the sheriff's arm as he started to walk away. "What's going on? Did they find something?"

"No, they didn't find anything. Bergy's our resident amateur chiropractor. Milam's probably got a crick in his neck." Billy Thompson then flashed his country-boy charm at Parker Stone and said, "I gotta go. Nice talking to you. If we find anything, you'll be the first to know."

In other words, Back off.

Thompson stopped at the rear of the Roach Coach and warmed up his coffee. Bergy was there stirring a cup. The sheriff muttered something to him, and the two of them ambled off down the trail, sipping coffee as if there was no rush. Web caught up with the two men, along with several others who trickled along behind, juggling paper-wrapped sausage biscuits and Styrofoam cups of coffee.

"What was that call *really* about?" Web asked as soon as the reporter was out of earshot.

Thompson appraised him carefully, then answered, "Milam wouldn't have called if he hadn't seen something, simple as that. He asked for Bergy because he's carrying the grappling hook under his poncho. So whatever Milam's found is *in* the river. You sure you're ready for this?"

Web swallowed. "It is what it is. All I want is the truth, sheriff."

"Yeah, well, facts can be hard sometimes."

"I'll take mine straight, thanks. And while we're at it, what was it you didn't say to that reporter a minute ago?"

"What are you talking about?"

"You said, 'First, we don't have confirmation.' Then you looked at me and decided not to say what was second. You just rephrased yourself and said, 'We're not sure there's a second person.' I know whitewash when I see it. I want to know what you were about to say but didn't."

Thompson stared into his eyes for a second. "I was about to say we haven't notified the next of kin."

Web drew a breath, then nodded firmly. "At least I know where things stand."

The sheriff found Milam standing atop a large boulder, staring down into the turgid river ten feet below. The two men tethered to him moved back up the bank where the footing was better, leaving a slack loop in the tag line but not enough for Milam to fall into the river. Sheriff Thompson scrambled up onto the rock, while Bergy hung back with the other two men. Web climbed up right behind him and stood at his shoulder.

"Get down!" the sheriff ordered. "And go back up the hill."

"No," Web answered.

The sheriff shrugged. "Fine. I tried," he said, then turned back to Milam. "So, what you got?" He had to shout to be heard above the roar of the river.

Milam pointed down to the outermost point of the eddy where the current curled around in the lee of the boulder. A tangle of floating limbs and vines had snagged in the arms of a small locust tree on the upstream side and wrapped themselves tight around the face of the rock, waving up and down under the current. Web stared at the spot, trying to bore into the muddy water with his eyes. Finally he saw something lightly colored flash for a second and then disappear. After ten or fifteen seconds he saw the flash again. Whatever it was, it rolled relatively slowly, giving the impression of weight and mass, something more substantial than a newspaper or piece of clothing. It also appeared to be the color of skin, though he couldn't be certain from a brief glimpse through churning brown water.

Thompson held his hand out toward Bergy, who instantly peeled off his poncho, heaved the heavy coil of rope off his shoulder and laid it out neatly on the ground. He found the loose end of the rope, handed it to one of the anchor men, and handed the grappling hook up to Sheriff Thompson. Rain blew through in sheets, so that by the time Bergy put his poncho back on he was drenched.

The sheriff stepped in front of Web, lowering the grappling hook and beginning its pendulum swing. Milam lifted Thompson's raincoat and clamped a hand on his belt.

The hook sailed out over the river and plunked down ten feet out, instantly jerking the line tight and ripping downstream. Thompson snatched it back, hand over hand, the large steel treble hook skipping across the waves and clanging off the side of the boulder as he hauled it in for another try. He threw it farther upstream the second time and a little closer inshore, but the current swept it by him in a flash, still too far out. He was approaching his target carefully, gauging the distance and the speed of the current with a little more accuracy on each attempt.

He spoke over his shoulder to Web, "If I get in a hurry and hang it in the snag, I might shake loose whatever's down there and lose it."

Web sensed a commotion behind him, a clot of color on the periphery of his vision, and he turned. The rest of Thompson's men had returned from the Roach Coach and now stood in a cluster a little way up the slope. Two umbrella tops stuck out above the group, most of whom had their backs to the river and seemed to be forming a wall in front of the three newsmen. Web tapped the sheriff on the shoulder and pointed to the little confrontation.

One of the ponchos stood chest to chest with the big bear of a cameraman, refusing to give an inch.

The sheriff grinned. "That's Tinker," he said. "You can tell by the shoulders. Used to be a linebacker at Michigan State."

Tinker glanced at the sheriff. Thompson shook his head, long and slow, then nodded curtly up toward the road.

Tinker turned back to the cameraman and his head tilted slightly.

Thompson chuckled. "Mr. Tinker is now explaining to the cameraman that he has never personally read the First Amendment, but he'll get to it when he has time. Then he'll assure the cameraman that he'll soon be carrying his camera back up to the van, one way or another, and that he'd probably find it far more comfortable to leave now and carry it in his *hand*."

The big cameraman sized up Tinker with a smirk. Then he surveyed the twelve other faces and concluded that, this once, discretion was indeed the better part of valor. He had a few parting words for Tinker, delivered with a pointed finger and raised eyebrows, but then he turned around and headed back up the trail with his camera. Jogging Suit kept the umbrella over him the whole way. Four of Thompson's men formed a rear guard.

"Come on, come on, come on!" Thompson implored the grappling hook as it swung in toward the boulder. His fisherman's hands cradled the line, waiting, and he hauled up on the rope when it was under his target.

It hung this time. The hook caught on something soft and came up toward him when he pulled.

Web peered down the rope as the sheriff slowly hauled in on it and saw, through four feet of water, that flash of what looked like skin. It stopped moving. Caught in the tangle of vines under the water, it refused to surface.

Keeping the rope taut, Thompson jumped off the back of the rock and worked his way around the lee side. Three of his men joined him. Together they gently increased the pressure on the rope till suddenly the object pulled free, and before the current could carry it away they dragged it up on the bank.

It was a dog, possibly a retriever. It was hard to tell with all the fur and a good portion of the skin battered off. After they pulled it up on firm ground, the body sagged like a bag of pudding, as if all the bones had been reduced to powder. Even the head had an odd shape to it. One of the men let out a low whistle.

"Like a blender full of rocks," the sheriff said. He looked out across the maelstrom. "Anything caught in *that* don't stand a chance."

Watching from the boulder, Web shuddered involuntarily, unable to tear his eyes away from the shattered remains of the dog. The sheriff's words rumbled through his mind like echoes of distant thunder.

"Anything caught in that..."

Parker Stone shoved his way through, snagged his shoe on a rock, and would have fallen face first on top of the dog's remains had not the men on either side caught him by the arms. He hung there, inches above the dog, long enough to inhale deeply before he recoiled, jerked away from the sheriff's men, ran up behind a rock and lost his breakfast.

"City boy," Thompson drawled.

Chapter Thirty-nine

Lori bolted upright in bed, jarred awake by the ringing of the phone, and snatched it up, breathless, before the second ring. She had gone to sleep worried about Jake, out in the rain searching for Harley and the Holcombe boy. The vacancy in the bed bothered her, even in her sleep, so that the phone's ringing slapped her like an alarm bell.

"I'm sorry, did I wake you?"

It took a second for the soft, fluttering voice to register. "Ruth? Ruth Wingo?"

"Yes, it's just me. Did I wake you?"

"No, I uh..." Lori's brain hadn't kicked in. A meager lightening of the room told her daylight was near. She squinted at the digital clock, which said 6:30.

"I'm so sorry," Ruth said, exasperatingly apologetic, "but I've been up all night myself and I guess I forgot some people are sleeping. I hate to bother you but I really need a favor."

Lori grunted something unintelligible, squinched her face, jammed her fingers in her tousled hair.

"Lori, the Elder is out of its banks and the upper valley's flooding. The weatherman says the water's still rising and won't peak until tomorrow around noon. There are already two families flooded out and there are bound to be more before it's over. We've been up to the church—me and some of the other women—trying to bed people down in the children's building, but it's not very comfortable. I was wondering if we could maybe borrow some cots and linens from the Women's Center?"

Lori blinked hard, concentrating. "Sure, Ruth, but wouldn't it be easier to just move the people? The Center has a fully equipped kitchen and a laundry room. Wouldn't they be more comfortable there?"

No response. Dead silence.

"Ruth?"

"I'm here." She sounded even more subdued than usual. "It's just... I didn't think I had the right—you know, after the zoning hearing." Her voice dropped to a whisper now. "Just between you and me, Lori, I begged Orde not to do that, but he's... well, he's a stubborn old goat is what he is."

This mutinous outburst, mild as it was, was so out of character for Ruth that Lori had to bite her lip to keep from laughing out loud. She took a few seconds to regain her composure.

"Really, Ruth, all I ever wanted to do was help people. That hasn't changed. Go ahead and move the people over to the Women's Center, and if anybody doesn't like it they can sue us. There's a key under the geranium pot. What are you doing about food?"

"We already put the word out that we need food and clothes. It's all coming here, or should be, in the next couple hours. Everybody's been so gracious, I don't know what to say...."

"It's okay, Ruth. Really. Listen, you're going to need some help, and you could probably use some sleep. I'll be up there as soon as I can get ready, okay?"

"Sure... yes."

"Ruth?"

"Yes?"

"Thank you."

Lori quickly showered, dressed, scratched off a note to Jake in case he came home while she was gone, and took off to the shelter. For most of the morning she drove around collecting donations of food and clothes from people afraid to leave their homes. She got a surprise when she went to Nell Prudhomme's house. For after loading a cardboard box of clothes and two sacks of groceries into the back of the Blazer she turned around to see

Miss Agnes standing behind Nell, wearing a raincoat and carrying an air-line bag.

"I reckon you'll need somebody to cook for all them folks," she said. "Get me some collards and beans and cornmeal and I'll fatten 'em up for you. Besides," she whispered, leaning close to Lori, "that old woman's about to drive me slap nuts."

Lori couldn't stifle a giggle. That "old woman" was a good ten years younger than Miss Agnes. Lori took her up on the offer. On the way to the shelter Miss Agnes asked if there had been any news of Harley. When Lori told her no, that she hadn't heard anything yet, Miss Agnes turned to the window and never said another word.

Chapter Forty

"Nothing is more enlightening than the view from the belly of the beast."

Jake Mahaffey

On his way back down to his position in the search line, Jake stepped through a break in a bank of mountain laurels and ran right into Web Holcombe. The hood of his blue poncho was thrown back and his hair was soaked.

"What are *you* doing here?" Web asked. His jaw muscles flexed.

"Same as you. I came to help look for Eddy."

Web's expression didn't soften but his words did. "I'll take all the help I can get." He turned and started to walk off.

"Are you all right?" Jake asked.

Web searched his face and saw nothing but sincerity. Some of the steel left him then and that was reflected in his tone. "I'm holding up okay. It's just—" His eyes wandered to the river. "It's just that I thought I was going to come down here and find my son and take him home. I thought it was just water, and Eddy's a strong swimmer. But that river..." He paused, and in the silence the river roared on. "It's bad. This is very, very bad." He closed his eyes and turned his face up to the rain.

"Yes," Jake said, "it's bad. All we can do is search, and we'll find him sooner or later. But whether he's alive... or not is beyond our control. His life is in God's hands."

Web didn't answer for a moment, and when he turned to Jake he wore a small and cynical smile.

"I see. You sense a moment of vulnerability and press your argument. Maybe we're not so different, you and I." He pointed at the river. "Tell me, Jake, is this your God's doing? Did He take my son? Is He holding him for ransom?"

Jake shook his head. "I don't second-guess God. But I don't envy a man in your position."

"And what position is that?"

"You don't believe in God, but you believe in the river. Right now that's got to be a little bleak."

"It is what it is." Web's face had become stone.

"Then tell me, what's your strength and cunning worth now?"

Web's eyes narrowed. "You do, don't you? You think your God did this. That's really how you think."

"No, Web. I think Eddy fell in the river. Sooner or later everybody's kid falls in the river. I know how that feels now. I know what it's like to feel small and helpless. All I'm saying is I wouldn't want to face it without God, that's all."

"I guess the weak need a crutch."

"I'd say we're all weak when the river rises. We need each other, Web. We need God. We need absolution."

"Oh, right. Absolution. Part of your Jesus myth. If you think there's such a thing as absolution, you never met my father."

"If you think there *isn't,* you've never met mine. I didn't know your father, but I'd be willing to bet you're selling him short."

"You're right—you didn't know my father. And I don't need your absolution, thanks."

He jerked his hood back up and started to leave, but Jake wasn't finished.

"That's not what I hear."

Web stopped. "What?"

"From what I hear, you could use a little cleaning up."

"What do you mean by that?"

Jake decided to lay it out and see what Web's reaction would be.

"There was a witness. Somebody who was there when the man with the ponytail set fire to Miss Agnes's farm. She knows, Web. She knows you burned her house down and put a price on Harley for it."

Web stalked back, stopping right in front of Jake, their faces inches apart. His jaw flexed. "Fairy tales, Jake! I'd like to see you prove any of it."

"It's not about proof, Web. It's the truth that matters. You know the truth, I know it, Harley knows it, Miss Agnes knows it. And what's more, God knows it! The truth doesn't care about proof."

"I don't have time for this!" Web snapped. "I've got to go look for Eddy."

He turned his back again, but before he could walk away Jake felt compelled to ask one more question.

"Tell me one thing, Web. What does your son have to do to make you love him?"

It must have struck a nerve because Web took a long time answering. Still turned half away from Jake, he splayed his hands out before him, watching the rain puddle in his palms, remembering.

"I was there when he was born," he finally said. Jake could barely hear him. "My hands were the first to touch him. He was all blue and white and slimy... and limp for the first few seconds. Then the doctor reached in, quick-like, and cleared his nose and mouth. All of a sudden that... *thing* gasped, flung his arms out and quickened, right there in my hands. My son." His arms jerked involuntarily as if a shock had run up them, and his eyes met Jake's. "My son," he repeated softly.

Jake's head tilted, and his expression softened. "He didn't have to earn that, did he?"

Web Holcombe didn't answer.

"And nothing can ever change that, can it?"

Web looked away, clinging to silence like a raft.

"So what makes you think your father was any different?"

The rain held steady as the day wore on. When the gap between the river and the road narrowed approaching the Outback Rafting Center, a third of the men from Web's search party were sent ahead to cut off the corner and search backward from the falls. Another group was sent to scour the woods on the other side of the road on the off chance Eddy had wandered across it in the night and had gotten lost on the lower slopes of the ridge.

The rafting center was a shambles, its landing dock long gone, with the main building nearest the river almost completely underwater. Only the roof showed above the brown flood running through their offices, the gift shop, and supply shed. Web gazed across the still-rising water and wondered how the building could take such a pounding. He helped look through the storage sheds and among piles of rental rafts and kayaks that had been dragged up to higher ground, but it was clear no one had been there.

The search party condensed into an even narrower space when they passed the rafting center, and within an hour they reached the highway bend above the park to find a crowd of people awaiting them. There were three news vans, all with their masts up, their dishes beaming signals to their respective stations. Ten or twelve cars were parked on the shoulders of the road, some of them family members of the searchers, some just curious onlookers. All three search parties converged on the bluff at the same time.

The park was completely submerged, the entire promontory lost under a wide sea of rushing brown. The water had risen halfway up on the cedar shakes of the pavilion roof, a hundred yards out from the little bluff where they stood. Thompson fought off the reporters and went to talk to the men who had just returned from the falls.

Web hung back, avoiding reporters and the faces of people he recognized. He already knew they hadn't found Eddy; there would have been an uproar, and the men he saw appeared tired and dejected. Defeated.

Thompson gathered everybody together on the road and took a head count to make sure he hadn't lost anybody. A bus arrived from town to pick them all up and carry them back to their cars, but there was no place for the bus to park so it sat idling in the road. Thompson trudged over to it and climbed up onto the first step, turning to face the crowd. Bathed in the lights from the camera crews, he held up his hands to hush the murmur of voices.

"I want to thank everybody," he said, raising his voice to be heard over the thundering of the falls. "I know it wasn't easy last night, and some of us are a little banged up. The crew on the far side of the river still has a mile or so to go before they reach the road, so I'm driving over to meet them, but you can all go home now and get some sleep. We'll contact you tomorrow morning and let you know where to meet to resume the search below the falls."

There was a stirring and jostling in the crowd as Web elbowed his way to the front. He threw back his hood and shoved the reporters aside, stepping in front of the lights to face Sheriff Thompson.

"You can't call off the search!" Web shouted. "My son is still out there somewhere! We can't just go home and go to bed; we've got to keep looking!"

A reporter, suddenly recognizing Web, stepped in front of him and stuck a mike in his face. "Mr. Holcombe, tell us—"

Web's left arm raked the microphone aside, and his hand smashed into the reporter's nose, sending him sprawling into the cameraman. The reporter's feet tangled with the cameraman so that they both fell backward into the crowd.

Parker Stone stepped into the breach, microphone at the ready, but before he could say a word, Web decked him with a quick, straight jab. Sheriff Thompson grabbed Web around the shoulders and hustled him into the bus. The driver closed the door behind them.

They squared off in the aisle of the bus, ignoring the throng of reporters banging on the door.

"Web, get a grip! I know how you feel but—"

"No! You don't!" Web snarled, his face dark with rage.

"All right, I don't. I have a pretty good idea how I'd feel if it was *my* kid out there, but that's beside the point. I've got a hundred men to think about. They're tired, they're hungry, some of them are hurt, and they're not thinking too clear right now. Neither are you. Listen, Web, once your boy went in the river there were only three possible outcomes. Either he's still in the river on this side of the falls, in which case there's no hope after twenty-six hours, or he's gone *over* the falls, in which case there's less than no hope, or he managed to get out of the current and drag himself up into the woods someplace."

Web breathed heavily, glaring at him.

"Web, if he was in the woods above the falls, we would have found him."

"We cannot... stop... looking!"

"Yes. We can. There comes a point when it doesn't make any sense to keep going. It'll be dark soon and these people have been on their feet for twenty-four hours. They're not thinking straight, and somebody's going to get hurt. There's no sense getting somebody else killed—"

"Somebody else killed? So we're just going to assume my Eddy's dead?"

Thompson took a deep breath. "I'm sorry, Web. We have to face facts. Cold, hard facts."

Web's face sagged, his eyes wandered.

"Go home," the sheriff said softly. "Your wife needs you. She doesn't need to hear about this on the news."

Chapter Forty-one

Web came home to a painfully quiet house. The police had chased away the reporters; the well-wishers had all gone home. He shed his ruined shoes at the back door and called out for Jenny as he passed through the kitchen. When she didn't answer he went looking and found her asleep on the sofa in the den, the television blathering mindlessly to no one. He poured himself a double scotch, turned off the TV, and sat down beside his wife near where her head rested. He raised the drink to his lips, stopped, stared at the glass of scotch for a second, and then gently placed it on a coaster next to the bottle of Valium on the marble coffee table.

He pinched his eyes, which burned from lack of sleep. He'd never felt so drained, and yet the hardest task still lay ahead. Placing a hand on Jenny's shoulder, he gave her a little shake. She moaned and stirred, then settled back into oblivion. He leaned over and whispered into her ear, "Jenny."

She didn't move.

Finally, with a sigh, he gripped her shoulders and lifted her upright. Her head lolled back against the curve of the sofa.

"Jenny," he said, a bit more firmly, cupping a hand to her jaw.

She sucked in a sharp breath, her body jerked once, and she pulled her head upright, blinking and disoriented. Seeing her husband, her mouth opened and her eyes widened. She palmed the hair back from her face.

"Web! Did you find him?" Hope and despair wrestled in the high pitch of her voice.

Shaking his head slowly, Web averted his eyes and said softly, "They've called off the search."

At first she looked as if she'd been stabbed; then the breath went out of her and her shoulders slumped. She melted into Web, weeping hysterically onto his shoulder. He held her like this for a long time, stroking her back, caressing her head. He could think of absolutely nothing to say. There was no answer, no balm for her wound—or for his. After a while her sobs weakened and she pulled away from him. She took a tissue from the coffee table to wipe her red nose, turned the wad of tissue in her fingers, and spoke to it.

"There must be something," she said in a mousy little voice. "We can't just give up. He can't be . . . oh, my poor baby—" She pressed her fingertips to her lips, and the sobs returned.

"We've done everything possible," said Web. "We searched the woods from where he fell in all the way to the falls, on both sides of the river for a mile back up the slope. He's not there, Jenny. He's just not there."

Her bloodshot eyes pleaded. "Well . . . maybe he's hurt and doesn't know what he's doing and he's walking around in the woods lost. Maybe he can't remember or he tried coming home but he's stuck wandering around on this side of the bridge. Or maybe he went over the falls and lived. Anything's possible, Web! We can't give up! He can't be . . . I know he's not . . ." She couldn't say the word, but the thought of it brought another tidal wave of grief and she collapsed against him again.

"We have to face facts, Jenny. Eddy may not be coming home." He said the words with great sympathy, but he had been there, had seen the impossible brutality of the river and taken part in the meticulous search. Thompson was right. Reason, in this case, brooked no opposition.

"NO!" she screamed, shoving him away and rising to pace the floor. She turned on him, wiping away the awful conclusion. "Eddy is not dead! My Eddy would find a way! He's a very resourceful boy. He's out there somewhere. You just haven't looked hard enough!"

Her eyes were wild, and Web sensed she had tipped across some unseen line into another place, apart from reality.

"You don't care!" she shrieked. "You never did! You don't care about your son; you only care about your little projects and your stupid airplane! EDDY! IS! NOT! DEAD!" She bent at the waist as she screamed; her fists shook, and her knees drew together with the force of each word.

He rose and moved toward her with his arms out. "Jenny, this isn't helping anything. You need to—"

"Mister Web!" Myra's surprised cry came from the doorway where she stood with a wet raincoat folded over her arm. She looked at Web, then at Jenny, and she knew. "Dear God, no," she muttered, dropping the raincoat and hurrying across the room to embrace Jenny, who crumpled with grief again at the sight of her. Myra helped her back to the sofa and sat holding her.

"Where have you been?" Web asked, noting Myra's wet clothes and the beggar-lice clinging to her ankles.

"Looking for Marcus." Her voice was tense and uncharacteristically irritable. "He took off a couple hours ago, before dark. Lord knows where he's got off to. The four-wheeler's gone. We got enough to worry about without—"

"He didn't tell you where he was going? That's not like him."

"Aw, he tried to tell me something once, but I wasn't listening. The preacher was here, and some other folks from the church, and I was fixin' coffee in the kitchen. He said something, but I didn't pay him no mind. Next thing I know, he's gone. I hope the little fool didn't go down to the river looking for Eddy. If he went anywhere near that river I'll strangle him my ownself!"

Web cocked his head at the same time he shushed Myra. When she stopped talking they both heard it, a faint sound—the unmistakable *ring-ding* of the four-wheeler's engine rounding the end of the house, slowing as it approached the garage. Myra jumped up and ran.

Web eased himself onto the sofa next to Jenny, who had quieted again and taken on a blank, lost look. In less than a minute he heard the back door slam and Myra's voice hissing and yammering at her son as she dragged him into the room by an ear, shaking her splinted finger in his face. As they came through the door she looked up and remembered herself. With a mildly embarrassed look, she released Marcus's ear.

Marcus stared at Web for a moment. He wrung some dark cloth thing in his fists and lowered his eyes. "You find Three?" he muttered without looking up.

Web hesitated. Jenny was watching closely as Marcus unrolled the baseball cap he'd been twisting. Acutely aware of Jenny's fragile state, Web was reluctant to open the wound again but felt he owed it to Marcus; he and Eddy were so close.

"No, son. I'm sorry. We looked everywhere. We couldn't find him."

Marcus stared at the baseball cap in his hands and ran his small thumb lovingly over the Roman numeral III on the green underside of the bill. When he raised his face to Web his jaw was set. His head moved slowly side to side in quiet but adamant denial.

"Ain't no can't," he whispered.

"What have you got there, Marcus?" All eyes turned to Jenny when she spoke. She sniffed, dabbed at her eyes with a tissue, and, for an instant, the merest suggestion of a brave smile came to her face.

"Three's cap," Marcus answered.

"Eddy's cap? The one he lost the other day?"

"Yes, ma'am."

"Is that where you've been? You went to look for Eddy's cap?"

"Yes, ma'am. It wasn't at the river." He glanced up at Myra as if to make sure she understood he hadn't been to the river. "It was in the woods. Took me a long time, but I found it."

"It doesn't matter where you found it," Web growled, his fuse shortened by fatigue and stress. "I think you owe your mother an apology. She was worried about you, off in the dark by yourself. It's nice you found Eddy's cap, but do you really think it was worth scaring your mother like that? It's just a cap."

Marcus straightened his back and drew his small self up before the Lord of Sutter's Cross. "No, sir, it's not just a cap." His voice was clear, and there lurked fireflies in his eyes. "It's his *lucky* cap. We got a game Tuesday night, and Three is pitching. He'll need his cap."

Web was struck speechless by the sudden collision with Marcus's profound belief, a belief so deep and so pure that Web was sure it could only be possessed by a child. But Web had felt it. He had touched the edge of it. He felt a brief but unmistakable connection with the mountainous faith he sensed in the boy's words and in the fire behind his eyes, a faith that glimpsed possibilities far beyond fact, a faith that would keep him awake for hours this night, despite unbearable fatigue.

Web broke the stare first.

Jenny rose quietly from the sofa and padded across the room, stopping in front of Marcus. She wrapped her arms about the boy and hugged him tight, then took his face in her two hands and smiled into his dark eyes. "Thank you, Marcus," she said. "Thank you so much. You hold on to that cap. Don't let it out of your hands. When you see Eddy, *Three*"—she corrected herself—"when you see Three again, you give it to him."

Chapter Forty-two

Jake and Lori dumped their filthy clothes into the hamper, showered, and collapsed into bed. Exhaustion so tangled their thoughts, they didn't speak. Then, in the dark, after a minute or two of complete silence, Lori slipped out of bed and got down on her knees. It was not her custom to pray at bedside, and Jake was puzzled until he realized what she was doing. Then he too got out of bed and knelt beside her.

After they had said a prayer for Harley and Eddy and Miss Agnes and all the people at the shelter who had lost everything, they climbed back into bed. Jake was gone as soon as his head hit the pillow.

In the middle of the night he awoke to find Lori sitting up in bed, rubbing her face with both hands. He raised up on an elbow and reached out to her.

"Sorry I woke you up," she mumbled. "What time is it?"

He tried to focus on the clock, his eyelids feeling like sandpaper. "It's 3:42. What's wrong? Are you sick?"

She sighed deeply. "No, I'm okay, I just can't sleep. There's something nagging at me."

Jake yawned. "Want to talk about it?" He was hoping she'd say no.

"There's nothing to talk about. It's just—" she jammed her fingers into her hair, yanked her head back and stared at the ceiling—"there's something we're missing. I've got the weirdest feeling there's something just... right *there.* It's right in front of our noses and we're not seeing it."

"What are you talking about? You mean Eddy and Harley?"

She nodded. "Yes. Eddy, Harley, the river. But what *is* it?"

Jake wrapped his arms about her, kissed her on the cheek and said, "You're too tired is what it is. And you've been eating barbecue. Why don't you just erase your tapes and worry about all this tomorrow?"

"I wish I could. The feeling is so strong it hurts, like a splinter in my mind. I keep picking at it and I just can't get it out." She rubbed her face and spoke through her hands, "We're missing something, Jake. I wish I could figure it out."

Long before daybreak on Sunday the rain stopped, the clouds thinned and broke up, and the remains of the tropical depression fled before a cool front. Elise had finally died. Morning found crystalline sunlight chasing ragged tendrils of mist up the east-facing slopes.

Walking out into fresh mountain air, Jake felt a cool westerly breeze on his face. An oblique morning light snapped the world into laser focus and hinted at the coming of fall. It was as if somewhere between the deep green of the recently washed mountains and the warble and trill of a mockingbird, an overwhelming, unqualified absolution had settled on the face of the world, a newness of spirit, full of bright hope and strangely incongruous with the dark knowledge that Eddy and Harley were still out there.

Somewhere.

Yet, in a far corner of his heart, Jake felt as though God were smiling on this day.

Lori joined him on the deck in her terry-cloth robe, handed him a cup of coffee, and wrapped herself around him for warmth.

"So, what are we doing this morning?" she asked. "Are we going to church, or are we going back down to the river?"

He thought for a moment, staring at the implacable mountains. "I don't feel like looking for bodies below the falls if that's what you mean. If they're dead, probably best to let the sheriff and his men find them."

She tilted her head back and looked long into his face.

"Let's stop by the church," she said. "Sharpen the saw. Then afterward you and I can go back over to the woods above the falls. They've got to be there somewhere—we just haven't found them yet."

He nodded. "I suppose."

Chapter Forty-three

"Why don't you go with me?" Jenny asked. She had been putting on her makeup when Web brought her a cup of coffee and placed it carefully on the vanity beside her makeup mirror.

"To church?"

She nodded.

He looked away, ran a hand through his hair.

"You know why," he answered. "I won't be a hypocrite. And I won't be one of those slack-jawed, unprincipled slugs who sees no God, acknowledges no higher authority until he gets neck-deep in trouble and then goes begging—making promises no God would care about, promises he'll forget when the storm blows over—just to get what he wants. It's a hard world, Jenny. The only security is in your own mind and your own two hands." There were bluish circles under his eyes and shadows of deep fatigue in the corners of the face looking back at him from the mirror.

She laid a hand on his forearm. "I know you believe that, Web. I know you, and I respect your integrity even if I can't agree with you. But these people have been so kind and so generous. They've been out there risking their own lives, a lot of them, climbing over rocks all night in the rain, just like you, looking for our Eddy. Most of them don't even know him. You won't be making any kind of statement except to say thank-you. And just this once I would really, *really* love to have you beside me. I need you there."

"People will take it the wrong way," he said, then hitched a breath, winced, and pressed two fingers into his sternum.

"Since when do you care what people think?"

He toyed with a hairbrush on the counter. Finally, he turned and left the bathroom, padded over to the closet and pulled out his best blue suit.

Chapter Forty-four

The day felt like a funeral to Jake. While wearing his finest clothes to match the blue-and-gold day, he drove slowly, an unconscious concession to the darkness in his heart. Dappled sunlight strobed through the trees on the right, striking the Blazer with light and shadow as the boiling, muddy torrent raged on in the valley to the left, heedless of the high blue sky. When they passed the place where Harley took his boots off, Jake chuckled.

"What's funny?" Lori asked.

"Ah, it's nothing. I was just thinking about Harley, remembering something Dun Thornton said yesterday afternoon down by the river. He asked me if Harley still had my pants. We were down below the park, near the falls—"

"Pull over."

"What?" Glancing at Lori, he saw that she was staring into space with her mouth open and her eyes pooled as if she'd felt a great shock. He whipped the Blazer onto the shoulder and stopped. "What's wrong?" He clutched her knee.

"Have you been to the park?" Her voice trembled.

"Well, yeah, sort of. We searched the banks around it yesterday. Not much to see, though. The whole bend is underwater—the park, everything."

She turned on him and grabbed his forearm, squeezing with an uncommon conviction. "What about the pavilion?"

"Yeah, the pavilion, too. The water was all the way up on the roof."

"How far?"

"What?"

"How *far* up on the roof?"

His brow furrowed, wondering where she was going with this. "I don't know, about halfway, I guess."

"That's *it,* Jake. That's what's been tugging at my mind."

"What's it?"

"The pavilion! Couldn't Eddy and Harley have gotten washed into the rafters of the pavilion? They could be trapped under that roof, couldn't they?"

He stared at the steering wheel for a minute.

"I guess so," he said. "It's right in the middle of the river, and the water level would have been right at the bottom of the roof when they went down the river. It's possible. But, Lori, the water has come up since last night. The flood is supposed to peak sometime around noon today. The pavilion is probably completely under by now."

"Go," she whispered.

He stared. She wiggled her fingers at the shift lever.

"GO!" she shouted.

She leaned forward, gripping the dash as the Blazer roared back down River Road, past Miss Agnes's farm, past their own home. The road rose slightly as they neared Outback Rafting Center.

Jake slammed on the brakes, and the Blazer skidded to a stop at the entrance to the rafting center, leaving a puff of blue smoke drifting over the road.

Rubber rafts were stacked like pancakes around a storage shed on the high ground near the entrance, away from the flooded cedar outpost that served as the getting-off point for rafting excursions on the river. And there, lying inverted on top of the shed, was a blue solo touring kayak.

A handwritten sign saying Closed Due to Flood hung from the chain that tied the two gateposts together, blocking the driveway. Jake jumped out and ran, yelling over his shoulder for Lori to dig the bungee cords out of the back.

"What are you doing?" she shouted after him.

"I'm stealing a kayak! Hurry!"

Jake raced the last mile to the bend in the river, pulled off onto the bluff overlooking the park, and unlashed the kayak from the roof. What was left of the bluff stuck out like a little peninsula, rising a steep thirty feet above the swollen river, right in the apex of the bend.

The pavilion was still visible, the peak of its roof standing barely three feet above the water. The trees around it were all gone, uprooted and washed over the falls, leaving the pavilion standing alone like a long, low island in the middle of the river. Butterscotch water roiled and churned from the bluff below, all the way across to the far bank where saw-toothed waves undercut the sheer wall of the ridge and dropped great glacierlike chunks of earth and whole trees into the soup as they watched. The valley, buried and leveled to the eye, seemed ten times wider than usual. The pavilion roof looked impossibly distant.

Jake shook his head. "I don't know. How am I gonna do this?"

"Carefully." Her voice quivered; she was as scared as he was.

"Maybe we should go get help."

"There's no time, Jake. Don't ask me how I know, but there's no time. We either do it now or it doesn't get done."

"You sure they're in there?"

Her fingernails bit into his arm. "They're in there, Jake. I *know* they are."

He studied the waves and eddies, the run of the current. The turbulence on the far side, the outside of the bend, was the worst, but all of it looked murderous.

He tossed off his coat and tie, shouldered the kayak, and started down the bank with it. Two steps down he lost his footing in the rain-slick clay, his feet shot out from under him, and he fell hard. The kayak got away and slid down the bank on its own. Jake lunged for it, slipped again and went belly down in the mud, fetching up against a rock. When he looked up, he saw Lori lying in the mud halfway down the bank in her Sunday dress, hugging the point of the kayak against her chest.

Together they finally wrestled the kayak down to the water's edge. Lori held it still while Jake climbed in and took the paddle. Then it hit him, and despair washed over his face.

"What am I going to do when I get there?" he said. "There's no way I can get in under there, as high as the water is now. Even if they're in there, how am I going to get them out?"

Lori puffed out a breath, hands on hips, staring across the water at the sliver of the cedar-shake roof that remained above the waterline. Her eyes searched the banks in front of her until they came to rest on a huge tangle of logs that had drifted together and jammed themselves between the bank and a massive poplar tree a few yards away. A surprised smile came to her face. "What you need is an ax." She said the words with a curious reverence.

Jake followed her stare. It took him a few seconds, but he finally saw what had caught her attention—an ax, sunk into the trunk of the biggest log in the jam. Again Lori steadied the kayak while he climbed out. He then picked his way carefully onto the pile and pried the ax out of the carcass of the old oak. He hefted the ax in his hands for a moment, turning it over, examining it. The handle was slimy and the head rusty, but it was an ax, whole and unbroken, and it had been right there just waiting for him.

" 'Preciate it," he whispered. He hurried back and stowed the ax in the kayak.

"Are you sure you can do this?" Lori asked.

He swallowed hard. "Getting there shouldn't be a problem. Getting back... I don't know. How am I going to carry a passenger?" He saw worry in her eyes and shrugged. "All I know is I have to go. Somehow I don't have a choice."

"I can't bear for you to go," she said, "but I don't want you to stay, either. What am I supposed to say?"

"A prayer."

"Done."

She kissed him, and he shoved off quickly without looking back. He had learned long ago not to give himself time to think when he was afraid. At the moment he was terrified. Almost unconsciously he uttered a prayer of his own asking God for His help.

The kayak felt foreign at first, mainly because he'd forgotten to adjust the pegs. The foot pegs had been set for longer legs than Jake's, so he had to struggle to hold pressure with his knees. But his body hadn't forgotten the moves. Great swirling eddies began to toss the stern about, when his hands remembered and instantly responded with bow strokes to compensate. Once, after swinging around to make a rush at the roof, he capsized in the trough of a wave, but with a shoulder-wrenching pull and a snap of the hips he instinctively rolled upright again, still on course. He surprised himself. In the last ten yards he doubled his stroke, leaning into the paddle and driving the kayak cleanly up onto the exposed roof, near the end, up against the chimney.

The kayak ground to a stop with its nose just beyond the peak of the roof. He wedged it against the chimney as best he could after wiggling out of it and retrieving the ax—no small feat in such a precarious position. Then, as he was turning around, something huge jarred the submerged pillars of the pavilion, knocking his feet out from under him. Landing on his chest across the crest of the roof, Jake managed to hold on to the ax but watched helplessly as the kayak bumped backward, bobbed high on the current, and spun off toward the falls.

He looked across the water at Lori, who grabbed her head. Her despair was palpable. "I guess it's up to you now," Jake muttered.

Straddling the roof, he thought hard about where might be the best place to chop a hole. Harley and Eddy could be anywhere in the hundred and fifty foot length of the pavilion. Seeing no logic, he decided that right here was as good a place as any.

He hefted the ax and soon cedar chips were flying as he raised the ax again and again, hacking at the roof. A ragged hole slowly opened up, and through it he could see dark water swirling three feet down. His feet slipped out from under him once so that he almost slid down the wet cedar into the current before catching a hand on the jagged edge of the hole and hauling himself back up. Perched on the peak, he ripped off his treacherous smooth-soled dress shoes and flung them into the river. He flung his socks after them and then scrambled up on bare feet and swung the ax again.

When he judged that the hole was big enough he sank the ax into the shingles and bellied down beside it. Sticking his head down through the hole, he twisted around to look up toward the far end where a small triangle of light still peeked through at the apex.

His heart sank. He saw no sign of Harley or Eddy.

"Jake?" The low voice, instantly recognizable, came from under the roof behind Jake. He turned around to see two white faces peering out of the darkness less than five feet downstream from the hole. Harley was leaning back on an angle with his head barely above the water, braced in the rafters with Eddy lying on his chest.

Jake reached out to them. "Give me your hand!"

Eddy reached out, but his hand fell a good two feet short. "I... I can't come to you," Eddy said. "The current's too strong."

Jake strained and squirmed, squeezing his upper body farther into the hole, the splintered roof cutting into his chest, yet he still couldn't reach Eddy. He wormed himself back out of the hole and returned a few seconds later with the ax. He held it out to Eddy, saying, "Here, grab hold of this!"

When Eddy had both hands firmly clamped above the ax head, Jake pulled, latching on to Eddy's wrist when he was close enough, then grabbing him under the arms. He had him! But as he pulled him up out of the hole, he dropped the ax.

Eddy yelped in pain as Jake rolled him out. Jake laid him across the peak and asked if he was all right.

Eddy nodded. "Yeah, but I can't stand up. My ankle's broke."

Jake grinned and said, "Best news I've heard all day."

As soon as he was sure Eddy was stable enough to lie there on his own without rolling off into the river, Jake turned back to the hole, wondering how he was going to reach Harley without the ax.

Even in the darkness he could see that Harley looked awful, his face swollen, his eyes at half-mast. He had to do something, and fast.

"Harley, I'm sorry, I dropped the ax." He was at a loss as to what to do next.

"It's okay... hang on a minute."

To Jake's horror, Harley ducked under the water. Ten seconds later he popped back up, gasping. His hand rose from the water, and Jake saw he was holding a pair of jeans. It took three tries to fling the wet jeans out to Jake, but he finally caught a leg, drew Harley to the hole and, with a strength he didn't know he possessed, rolled Harley up across his chest and out into the light.

They lay side by side, facedown across the roof next to Eddy, both of them winded. The pants were still wrapped around Harley. Jake laughed when he saw the big, apostrophe-shaped ink stain on the back pocket.

"My pants," Jake said.

Harley's eyes were closed, but he shook his head and mumbled, "I paid for 'em." He rested his forehead against the cedar shakes.

"That you did, my friend. That you did."

Harley lay very still. Jake couldn't tell if he was breathing so he leaned in close. "Harley," he whispered.

Harley pulled a long breath, groaned, and spoke without raising his head. "Sun feels nice."

Jake smiled. "It sure does." But Harley worried him. He was blue, swollen from eyes to ankles, and growing more lethargic by the minute.

Jake sat up and locked his arms around his knees as he pondered the next problem: how to get himself and two half-dead people safely across a hundred yards of brown fury to the shore. He looked across the river at Lori and spread his arms in a helpless gesture as if to say "Well, what do we do now?" She turned her back suddenly and ran out into the road, waving her arms over her head. Jake then saw what had caught her attention. The sheriff's car pulled into sight on the bluff and stopped. Lori jumped into the passenger's side.

A minute later a low pulsating thrum seemed to surge up out of the earth, growing until it was loud enough to be heard above the roar of the rapids. The big black-and-yellow helicopter of the Department of Natural Resources rose like a moon above the falls and tilted toward him, throbbing low over the middle of the river. And Jake, who lived in paradise, thought that it was the most beautiful thing he had ever seen.

Chapter Forty-five

The Sunday morning crowd at Sutter's Cross Community Church was almost as large as it had been the last time Web was there, the day of his own wedding. Jenny showed remarkable poise at first, entering the crowded sanctuary on Web's arm with her head up and a brave smile on her face despite the puffiness around her eyes. He was glad Myra and Marcus had come with them; Jenny could use the reinforcement.

They arrived well before the service was to begin, and people milled around talking, laughing, apparently congratulating each other for some reason Web couldn't fathom under the circumstances. He couldn't help noticing that the center of attention seemed to be a group of rather boisterous people in the middle of the church, most of whom wore old clothes—jeans, T-shirts, sneakers.

"People from the shelter," Jenny explained. "Most of them lost everything."

"Then why are they laughing?" Web asked.

Jenny turned away abruptly, unable to speak. Myra, who had heard the exchange, whispered an answer over Web's shoulder. "Because they're alive," she said.

As they moved down the aisle toward a seat near the front on the left side, a steady stream of people came to offer their condolences. Web watched closely. People lost their celebratory smiles and put on funeral faces when they neared Jenny. She cried on the shoulders of old friends who embraced her and said nothing more than "I'm so sorry."

One of the elders gripped Web's hand with both of his own and, with great solemnity, intoned, "What a terrible, terrible tragedy."

Web kept his thoughts to himself but stiffened progressively throughout the ordeal. He never said more than a word or two in response and was greatly relieved when he and Jenny finally made it to their seats and people left them alone.

Marcus hadn't spoken all morning. With his eyes downcast he sat next to Web, still smoothing the baseball cap he held in his hands. Very gently, Web reached over and took the cap, held it in his own lap and studied the sweat stains and the crude III marked under its brim. But he only had it for a minute before Marcus's small hand crept over hesitantly, apologetically, and tugged it back.

Chapter Forty-six

Jake clutched Harley and Eddy tightly atop the narrowing peak of the pavilion roof, waiting for the sheriff to block the road and clear a place on the bluff for the helicopter to land. They took forever to rig up a cable and harness. Harley's condition seemed to be worsening by the minute. He was conscious but slow to respond; his speech came out slurred, and he was having a hard time catching his breath.

Eddy looked to be fine, propped up on his elbows watching every move the DNR rangers made. "Do we get to ride in the helicopter?" he asked, excitement lighting his eyes.

"I doubt it. I think we're going to be swinging from the cable."

"COOL!" Mere excitement turned to unfettered joy.

As soon as the cable was rigged the helicopter lifted off from the bluff and the cable stiffened. A ranger wearing a jump suit and helmet was hoisted clear of the bluff in a swirl of damp leaves. An ambulance pulled up and stopped as the helicopter swung out over the river bearing its human pendulum. A minute later the ranger planted his feet astraddle the roof in front of Jake.

"Stay low and let me come to you!" the ranger shouted over the downwash. The helicopter pilot deftly maintained a couple feet of slack while the ranger worked his way over to Jake and knelt down with an extra harness in his hands. "Who's worse?" he yelled.

Jake pointed to Harley, who hadn't so much as raised his head. He helped the ranger as much as he could, rolling Harley's inert frame back and forth until they finally had the harness buckled securely around him. After double-checking the rigging, the ranger clipped the hook to the ring at the end of the cable over his head and twirled a finger in the air, signaling the chopper to take them up.

"Stay down! I'll be right back!" he shouted to Jake as the cable tightened and he lifted off, hugging Harley's shoulders and wrapping his legs around his waist.

The helicopter hovered over the road while paramedics unhooked Harley and hustled him out of the downwash, into the waiting ambulance. Jake was very afraid for him, for his fragile heart. He knew the paramedics must have felt a terrible sense of urgency to have let the ambulance go without Eddy. It rushed away, siren yodeling, as the helicopter roared back over the river.

Eddy was hoisted ashore next, without incident. He winced and got a little pale once when they inadvertently turned his ankle while putting the harness on him, but when he lifted off and swung at the end of the cable he let out a joyful whoop.

After Eddy was safely deposited on the bluff and the helicopter rose back up, tilting one last time toward the pavilion, Jake caught a strange movement out of the corner of his eye. Rounding the bend, riding the center of the powerful current, he saw what looked like a huge, white, rectangular raft about fifty feet long. Its great mass charged through the bend like a barge, plowed out of the current, and whumped hard against the far bank, buckling from the impact. Shuddering, it pivoted slowly, then peeled away from the bank, gaining momentum again, and drifted back into the current centering its path inexorably toward the pavilion. Jake couldn't tell what exactly it was, but he could see it was big and it was headed his way.

The pilot of the helicopter put the ranger down as precisely and softly as he had on the first two lifts, and Jake lunged for the harness.

"Slow down! Be careful!" the ranger shouted. "What's your rush?"

Jake pointed upriver. The ranger looked over his shoulder to see the great white raft bearing down on them, porpoising on the mainstream at flank speed and promising to deliver a devastating blow, and his own movements became frantic. Seconds later he clipped the hook to the cable and signaled the chopper. The cable tightened. He latched his legs around Jake in the same instant that the large white raft slammed into the pavilion. As the two men lifted off, the pavilion buckled and pivoted with a tremendous shuddering groan. Breaking up, the roof rotated slowly and one end went under, then the whole thing slid beneath the waves like a sinking ship.

While they rose higher into the air the ranger grabbed Jake's arm and pointed down, laughing. The cable twisted around and gave Jake his first clear view of the massive white object that had knocked the pavilion off its moorings. He laughed out loud when he saw the question beaming up from the river:

Where would we be without friends?

Chapter Forty-seven

The Sunday morning worship service at Sutter's Cross Community Church started pretty much the way Web remembered from when he was a boy. The orchestra played, the choir sang, the music director announced a hymn number and raised his arms, the congregation rose and mouthed three verses of a hymn they all knew by heart. To Web's surprise, he remembered the words himself, though he wasn't about to sing, ever.

After the hymn ended and the congregation sat down, Dr. Stilwell made his way to the dais. He gripped the sides of the pulpit and paused, looking down, as if studying his notes. When he looked up again he smiled sadly in the direction of Web and Jenny, then he swept the crowd with a somber gaze.

"We come here this morning with heavy hearts," Stilwell began, measuring his words. "We have all felt the weight of tragedy that has befallen our little community. Great harm has been done to lives and property this week by this terrible flood. Many have suffered great loss. The flood has claimed homes and places of business, and one home was lost in a fire. But, terrible as it may be to lose a home, nothing can compare to the sense of grief we feel when one of our own young people is lost.

"The Holcombe family is with us this morning"—he gestured in Web and Jenny's direction—"a picture of courage and faith. I feel led to offer a special prayer on their behalf. Let us pray.

"O Lord, stretch out your hand to this couple. Lift them up, hold them in your arms, and make your healing presence felt...."

Web had heard enough. He raised his eyes toward the pastor. Heads turned near him as he rose to his feet.

"O Lord, comfort and console this family in their hour of tribulation and grief—"

"Wait a minute!" Web's voice cracked the honeyed atmosphere.

Jenny tugged at his arm, pleading, but he pulled away from her. Dr. Stilwell was stunned into silence.

"No, wait... I'm sorry, pastor, but hold on."

Heads raised. There was a murmur, a rustling of movement all over the church.

Web stepped into the aisle. His first instinct, which he nearly followed, was to leave, to simply walk out, but instead he stopped to explain himself. He stood with one hand on his hip holding his coat back, the other lightly scratching his forehead as if he were addressing the Board of Examiners and trying to think of the right phrase.

"I'm sorry," he said. "I know this isn't proper, but I can't take any more condolences. See, my son is missing. That means one thing and one thing only—he hasn't been found yet. And until—" he glanced at Jenny—"forgive me, but until I see his cold, dead body with my own two eyes, as far as I'm concerned, he's not dead. He's *missing.* We can talk about condolences and our hour of grief after they dredge his corpse out of that river, and not before!" Web's eyes had sharpened to rage and leveled themselves on the pastor.

Dr. Stilwell brought out his most soothing voice. "Mr. Holcombe, I'm deeply sorry. I know how you must feel—"

"You have no *idea* how I feel!"

Dr. Stilwell froze, bewildered. Several seconds ticked by, and then two small words came from the back of the crowd to part the silence.

"I do."

Web turned, as did most of the heads in the congregation, to seek out the author of the frail voice. Miss Agnes rose to her feet near the back of the sanctuary, clutching the pew in front of her.

"I know how you feel," she repeated. Her voice trembled, but her dark eyes held Web's without wavering. She edged her way out of the pew and hobbled down the aisle.

Web braced himself. *Not now,* he thought. As she closed in on him, he gave voice to the plea. "Not now, Mrs. Dewberry. Please, not now."

She stopped in the aisle, face-to-face with Web, looked up at him and let out a surprised laugh. "Mister Web, I wish you could see the look on your face. You look like Robby did when he was thirteen and I caught him smokin' out behind the shed. You think I'm going to talk about my *house*? Why, a house ain't nothin' but rust and dust, son. Houses come and go. What I want to say to you is, I know what it feels like when your boy—" Her voice quavered, and she stared past him to the stained-glass window for a few seconds. "I know what it's like, not knowing."

It was then that Web remembered the words he'd read in the file Benny had compiled for him. They had only been words then. *Robert Dewberry, Miss Agnes's only son, missing for twenty years.* Web stood stark and alone in the grip of a powerful hush that fell across the congregation like a blanket of snow, stunned by the sudden revelation that what Miss Agnes held out to him was not condemnation but compassion. He was confronted all at once, for the first time in his life, with the pure white light of grace, and it staggered him. Unable to bear it, he turned his back on the old woman, but as he leaned on the end of the pew in front of Marcus his vision narrowed. At the end of a very short tunnel his haunted eyes saw only the cap Marcus held in his lap.

Behind him stood immutable grace; before him sat monumental faith. And for the first time these things had definition. They had faces.

His world was crumbling.

The old woman's voice pierced him. "Mister Web, I been where you're at for a long time now, and I've done asked God every way I can think of to bring my Robby home." Her voice fell to a whisper. "But God is God, and sometimes the answer is no. I reckon He must've had a powerful good reason. Blessed be the name of the Lord." She took a deep breath, squared her shoulders, and spoke on very clearly, "I know you ain't a praying man, Mister Web, and that's all right. Everything in its time. But I reckon God puts us where He puts us so we can hold one another up, and if there's one thing I know how to do, it's pray for a lost boy."

Web didn't move, didn't answer. He stared at Eddy's cap.

"If you're willing," she said softly.

"All right," he finally whispered. He nodded thickly. "All right."

Slowly, she worked her creaking body down onto one knee, then the other, right there in the aisle. She looked up at Web and reached for his hand as if to draw him down, too.

He hesitated, and her hand waited.

"It's okay," she assured him. "It don't matter what you done, child, or whether you meant to do it, my Jesus paid for it. He loves you anyway. He loved you enough to die for you, and you standing there red-handed. But I know how God is, and I don't reckon He'll do nothing for you so long as you're standing on your own two feet."

Web lowered himself slowly to his knees. Jenny eased out of the pew, knelt beside him and took his arm. When Web looked up he saw Myra and Marcus kneeling, and others followed.

Miss Agnes bowed her head. "Lord," she began, "you know me. You know I don't ask for much, and there's a whole lot of things I don't understand...."

Dun Thornton reached for his wife's hand, and she reached for the hand of the person next to her. There was a mild rustling as one by one, row by row, the entire congregation joined hands and bowed their heads.

"But I know you can change things. I've seen you reach out, just so easy, and catch me when I fall. We're asking you now, like children, like *your* children, to do this one thing. Please, Sir."

The sound of creaking hinges intruded momentarily between her words as someone entered the vestibule at the back of the church from outside.

Miss Agnes continued, "We're asking you—all of us, together—we're asking you as humble as we know how, to bring this young'un back home safe to his mama—"

For the second time that Sunday morning a prayer was interrupted when one of the double doors at the back of the sanctuary swung open. Someone gasped, Miss Agnes paused, and Web looked up to see what was happening. The woman in the doorway was a mess. Her dress was more mud than pink, and a large flap torn from the front of it hung down past her knee. Drying red clay plastered one side of her hair to her head and streaked across her face like war paint. It took a moment for Web to recognize Lori Mahaffey, even though she was staring straight at him.

"We found Eddy," said Lori. "He's alive."

Jenny fainted.

Chapter Forty-eight

At the hospital, Jake was waylaid by an incensed head nurse who shoved him into a shower, dumped his river-sludged clothes into a trash bag, slapped a set of scrubs on him, and made him put little elastic-top booties over his bare feet. Every time she got within earshot she muttered a steady diatribe about flooded hog farms and sewage treatment plants.

"... come sloshing in here, dripping a trail of crud and corruption and God knows what all ... wonder we don't have a cholera epidemic."

Harley had been taken up to Intensive Care, but by the time the head nurse pronounced Jake clean and he found the room, it was empty. Fearing the worst, he went to the nurses' station where they told him Harley was in radiology. He gave up and took a seat in the waiting room down the hall and started thumbing old issues of *Field & Stream*. An ICU nurse, wearing green scrubs identical to Jake's, found him there about the time Miss Agnes arrived.

The nurse, forty-something and exuding an air of confidence born of experience, began simply, "It's bad. The arteriogram confirmed that Mr. Alexander has a massive aneurysm. The resident cardiologist says it's inoperable—partly because of the size but mainly the location. With cardiac myopathy—"

"Cardiac what?" Miss Agnes asked. Her eyes had pooled, her mouth hung slightly open, and Jake thought he detected a slight wobble as though she might be on the verge of collapsing.

"Myopathy. His heart's enlarged," the nurse explained. "When the heart gets too big it just sort of flaps and doesn't pump very well. We monitor his output constantly, and the last reading I took said his ejection fraction was almost down to twenty percent—" She stopped midsentence and rubbed her forehead. "I'm sorry. I'm doing it again. Look, the bottom line is he's in very, very bad shape, and there's not a lot we can do about it. We're giving him Dobutrex, which helps, but I'm afraid..."

In a breaking voice Miss Agnes asked, "Is he going to die?"

Jake tightened his grip on her shoulders.

The nurse didn't answer yes or no, but her expression was grim. "I'm sorry, but I've learned the hard way not to give people false hope. Are you his mother?"

Miss Agnes drew a deep, shuddering breath. "It sure feels like it," she said.

The nurse sighed, and her eyes revealed a touch of pain. "Well, I have to tell you I've seen this before and, frankly, the only thing that could save him now is a transplant. But the chances of finding a donor before he runs out of time..." Her voice trailed off and she shook her head. "I'm sorry."

"Can we see him?" Jake asked.

"Sure. I'll take you back there."

Standing opposite Miss Agnes, with Harley's alarmingly inert body between them, Jake was torn. On the one hand, he desperately wished Lori were here. At such times he was acutely aware of her strength—he needed it, had come to depend on it—but at the same time he had no wish to impose this vision upon her, so clearly reminiscent of her mother's last days when she was no more than a scrap of translucent skin stretched tight over a skeletal frame, a broomstick barely tenting the sheet. Harley's body was more substantial but looked just as helpless, dangling as he was at the sterile mercy of technology. A clear plastic oxygen mask covered his nose and mouth, wires ran to three little round tape patches on his chest, and a tree of IV tubes culminated under a bandage just below his collarbone. A monitor beeped steadily behind an IV stand, an electronic hourglass spilling heartbeats.

Miss Agnes stroked Harley's forehead and he stirred. "It'll be all right, son," she whispered.

Harley shook his head slowly, then reached up and tugged the oxygen mask aside. Arching his neck, he struggled to speak.

"... tired, too ... tired," he said, his breath rustling like dry leaves. His fingertips pushed the mask back over his mouth.

Jake leaned close. "Don't talk, Harley. Save your strength. There are things the doctors can do these days." It was an innocent lie, told more for Miss Agnes's sake than for Harley's.

Harley shook his head. No, his lips said. The monitor beeped rapidly.

The door opened and closed very quietly, and when Jake looked up, Web Holcombe was standing on the other side of the bed. Jake stared. There was something different about Web, and it was more than fatigue, more even than the joy of finding his son alive and well, though joy was unmistakably present in the corners of his face. His eyes rested on Harley, calmly, without scanning the room, without that predatory awareness that so defined him. His hands lay gently, one on Miss Agnes's shoulder, the other on the chrome side rail of the bed. Even his posture spoke of change, for although he held himself with a certain dignity, the air of command was gone from his shoulders and the tilt of his head. Gone was the rage Jake had seen by the river. *Had it only been last night?* So much had happened.

"How is he?" Web asked.

Jake shook his head.

Web laid his hand on top of Harley's. Harley rolled his head slightly, and his eyes fluttered.

"Do you know who I am?" Web asked.

Harley gave a small nod and mouthed the words, "The boy?"

"Eddy's fine, Harley. He's going to be just fine. He's sitting up in bed next to Marcus, wearing that backwards cap, eating cheeseburgers and basking in the spotlight. His mother hasn't taken her hand off of him since she got him back. He's quite a kid."

A faint smile played at Harley's lips and he drifted.

Web leaned close. "Harley?"

His eyes opened halfway and rolled toward Web.

"Is there anything you want?"

His breath came shallow and quick. He didn't answer, but his eyes stayed on Web.

"Anything," Web repeated.

Harley nodded, finally.

"Name it," Web said, and Jake saw a flash of the old commanding presence of the Lord of Sutter's Cross.

Harley pawed clumsily at the oxygen mask until Jake moved it aside for him, to let him speak.

"Me out of here," Harley rasped.

Web blinked, stared incredulously at Jake.

"You'll *die*, Harley. Listen, I can pull strings. I can bring in the finest cardiologists, the best surgeons. I'll fly you to Mayo if you like."

Harley's head rolled from side to side. "No," he groaned, "no hospital."

Web and Jake exchanged glances.

"The ridge . . . please," Harley whispered, then closed his eyes and reached for the oxygen mask, missing badly. His hand dropped to the sheet, limp, and he moved no more. He appeared to have fallen asleep. Web replaced the mask for him. The monitor beeped a steady rhythm, the hurried beat of a child's heart.

Web motioned to Jake, and the two of them slipped out of the room, leaving Miss Agnes alone by Harley's side.

"What do you think?" Web asked.

"What—about taking him out of here?"

"Yes." Web's eyes held a depth of concern Jake hadn't seen him show for another human being, apart from his own son. "Help me, Jake. I . . . I don't know what to do." He spoke haltingly, as if he were holding a strange new thing in front of his eyes and trying to find words to fit it. "Eddy would have died if not for this man."

"He'll do for folks," Jake mused as he watched, through the window, Miss Agnes standing beside Harley's bed, holding his hand. Her eyes were closed, and she was as still as Harley, praying.

A burst of raucous laughter from the waiting room shattered the stillness.

"That would be the press," said Web, glancing toward the double doors. "I had to fight my way through that mob on my way in here. Hospital security won't let them into the ICU, but they're clamoring for you and Harley. They're calling you heroes. I'm inclined to agree. Still, I don't envy you when you walk out those doors."

"Heroes," Jake snorted, and he hesitated, pondering how he could answer such a charge. He only paused for a second, but in that second his mind's eye ran through a newsreel of the events leading to Eddy's rescue. He saw Orde, whose intentions had been anything but benevolent, forcing Harley to turn from the road, herding him down to the river where he sat down and pulled his boots off to scratch his feet at the precise moment Eddy came plunging down the rapids. He remembered the splinter in Lori's mind, the kayak, the ax they'd found waiting by the river, the sheriff who came along just when his radio was needed to summon the DNR helicopter that just happened to be in the area.

"No," he said, looking Web in the eye, "When you see the hand of God moving on the water, it doesn't take a hero to get in the boat. All it takes is a little faith."

He leaned against the door and watched Harley and Miss Agnes through the glass, her gnarled hands still clasped in hard prayer.

"A little while ago," said Web pensively, "when they were working on Eddy's leg, he told me Harley was laughing going down that river. Laughing like a kid. Eddy was finished—'toast' was his word—completely exhausted from fighting the river, when Harley came out of nowhere and grabbed him. He pulled Eddy up, laid him on his chest, pointed his feet downstream and floated, never struggled at all. He just went with the flow, laughing the whole way through the rapids. Was that faith? Is that what you're talking about?"

"Yeah," Jake said. "That's it, exactly."

Web sighed. "This is new territory for me, Jake. I don't know the rules anymore. I owe that man a terrible debt, but how do I pay it? I can get the best people in the country working on this, only is it the *right* thing to do? I don't think it's what he wants, and I… I just don't know."

"I don't know either, Web, but if Harley taught me anything, he taught me where to turn." Jake leaned his forehead against the cool glass of the door and closed his eyes for a moment. *Lord, what do we do? This man is yours; he belongs to you. What do you want us to do for him?*

The door opened, and Jake jolted upright when his forehead lost its prop. Miss Agnes stood facing him.

"We need to take him home, Jake," she said, and there was no hint of indecision in her tone. "He don't have much time, and he mortally hates hospitals. He just wants to go home."

Jake's eyes tilted upward. " 'Preciate it," he said.

"You think he's rational?" Web asked.

Jake chuckled. "He may be the most rational man I ever—"

"I'm afraid that's a moot point," a deep voice interrupted him. Billy Thompson had come up behind them and overheard part of the conversation. "He's not going anywhere."

"You mind telling me why?" Jake asked.

A shrug. "I still have a warrant for him."

Jake's mouth hung open. "You've got to be kidding. After what he's been through? You were *there*, Billy. You can't be serious about arresting him."

"It's my job, Jake. I serve the warrant, no matter what I think about it, and then I can't let him go. I'll have to post a man outside this door until he leaves... one way or the other. It's the law. There's nothing I can—"

"Billy, the man saved my son's life!" Web broke in. Jake saw in his eyes a glimmer of his old ferocity, surfacing now on Harley's behalf. "And now he's dying, and there's not a thing we can do to stop it. All he wants, all he's asking, is to be allowed the dignity to choose *where* he dies."

Web's voice lowered, and he struggled with what he said next.

"This is not about what's legal, Billy. It's about what's right."

The sheriff rubbed his face, pinched the bridge of his nose, sighed heavily and stared at the dark figure buried in a tangle of wires and tubes. "I'll tell you what, Web—it's been a long week. I'm worn out and I'm hungry, and I can't very well read Mr. Alexander his rights while he's asleep, so I'm going down to Peggy's and get some lunch before I serve the warrant. I'll be back in about forty-five minutes." He shoved his hands deep into his pockets and smiled a tired smile as he turned and ambled away.

"So what do we do now?" Web asked.

"Find out who's in charge." It was a hospital so Jake figured somebody had to sign something.

A set of green scrubs flashed past them, a nurse carrying a handful of cellophane-wrapped packs of tubing.

"Excuse me," Jake said, and she stopped. "Who's the doctor in charge of Mr. Alexander?" He pointed a thumb at Harley's room.

"Dr. Rankin is the attending," she answered, pointing to a stocky, gray-haired man studying a clipboard at the nurses' station, then sped on her way.

"Dr. Rankin?" Jake tapped the white-coated doctor on the shoulder.

He turned and surveyed Jake's scrubs with the slightly befuddled look of a man whose mind is elsewhere. "Yes?"

"We were wondering what we would have to do to remove Mr. Alexander from the ICU."

The doctor shifted his attention back to his clipboard. "Mr. Alexander is in the ICU because he needs constant monitoring. His condition is very grave."

"No, I mean, what do we have to do to get him released from the hospital?"

"Get a lawyer," the doctor shot back without taking his eyes from the clipboard. Web had already pulled a cell phone from his pocket, flipped it open, and punched in a series of numbers. When Jake glanced at him he raised an index finger, telling him to wait. In a matter of seconds the call was answered.

"Charlie? Hey, sorry to call you at home but I need a favor . . . Oh, you heard! Yeah, it's great, isn't it? A miracle . . . He's going to be fine. I'll tell you all about it Tuesday if we're still on. But listen, there's a Dr. Rankin on your staff . . ."

The good doctor pulled Harley's catheter himself, watching the monitor carefully, taking no chances that something might happen to a close personal friend of Web Holcombe's while he was still on hospital property. The nurse removed Harley's chest leads and cleaned him up, and then they hefted him onto a gurney and attached a portable oxygen bottle to his mask. The doctor told them to keep the gurney, just keep it. As they rolled Harley away, Jake overheard a nurse muttering to Dr. Rankin, "Never mess with the man whose name is on the front of the building."

Jake ran ahead to see if there was any way to get around the crowd of reporters in the lobby, but when he got there he was surprised to find the place deserted except for Sheriff Thompson, who stood waiting for an elevator.

Billy Thompson grinned over his shoulder, somewhat sheepishly, Jake thought, and said, "If you're looking for the, um, reporters, somehow they all got the idea that your friend was about to be airlifted out from the heliport on the roof. You'll need to move quick. They'll be back in a minute or two."

"Oh?"

Thompson shrugged. "There *is* no heliport on the roof."

Jake and Web were collapsing the legs of the gurney and loading it into the bed of Jake's pickup when Lori arrived. She had showered and changed into borrowed clothes at the Women's Center and, to Jake's delight, she'd even had the presence of mind to dig through a box of donated shoes to scrounge a pair of sneakers for him.

Miss Agnes's yard was still a quagmire. The deluge had washed away ash and topsoil, leaving a vast mud flat veined with little gullies and dotted with a black stubble—all that was left of her trees and bushes. An acrid woodsmoke residue hung in the air, even now, blotting out all other smells. A few scorched cinder blocks were all that remained of the house, so Jake pulled up to the barn.

As Jake and Web dropped the tailgate and started to slide the gurney out, Miss Agnes surveyed the desolation.

"Let's take him to the old home place up the hill," she said, wrinkling her nose at the smell. "Away from this."

Jake took the front end of the gurney and forged ahead, straight up the ridge. Web, being taller, took the rear yet still had to carry his end at shoulder height to keep the gurney level on the steep slope. Lori followed alongside with a hand on Harley's chest to keep him from tipping out.

It was a difficult climb, and Harley was not a small man. The morning wind had died now with the day beginning to grow warm. Jake sweated profusely but he never faltered as he picked his way up through the rugged terrain. He didn't stop until he reached the little plateau. As gently as possible he propped Harley up against the spindly chestnut sapling where Miss Agnes had played as a child so Harley could look out once more on the valley.

"I like it here," Harley said clearly enough for Jake to understand him, even muffled as he was by the oxygen mask.

Lori and Jake knelt quietly at Harley's side, opposite Miss Agnes, whereas Web shuffled his feet and looked around nervously. He finally sat down on the ground by Harley's feet, pulled a weed, and sat stripping the leaves from it to busy his hands while he spoke.

"Harley, I've been trying to think of a way to tell you what it means to me, what you did. Not just what you did for Eddy but what you've shown me. You and Marcus and Miss Agnes. I don't know how to say it. I don't understand everything that's happened, but I know I've seen something, sensed something, that I just... can't explain. Last night I had resigned myself to Eddy's death. But Marcus, somehow that boy *knew* Eddy was alive. Something, some*body* told him. He knew it."

"They was safe in the arms of God the whole time," Miss Agnes said softly.

Harley moved his head slightly and made a feeble motion with his hand to reach up to his face. Guessing his intent, Jake pulled the oxygen mask aside to let him speak.

"We *are* the arms of God," he rasped, smiling. Jake thought he even detected a weak chuckle, but it degenerated into a gasping cough. Miss Agnes quickly moved his mask back into place.

Web stared hard, and Jake saw twenty years of angst coagulate into a question in his eyes.

"But how do I get there?" Web asked.

Harley's smile faded, and his gaze fell to his hands. With tedious, painful effort his arms rose in front of him, his fingers curled into tight fists as if he were white-knuckling the handlebars of a motorcycle. Then his hands sprang open and drew back an inch or two, his fingers splayed wide. He held them there for a moment, staring, trembling, before his arms sank back to his sides.

Web's head tilted.

Lori's fingers rose to her lips and there were tears in her eyes. "Let go," she whispered.

Web stared a moment longer and then nodded faintly and turned away.

Miss Agnes pressed a wrist to Harley's forehead. "He's feverish," she said.

Web offered his handkerchief. Lori carried it to the spring and soaked it in cold water, then handed the cold cloth to Miss Agnes, who gently pressed it to Harley's head. A trickle of water ran down his forehead, tripping over his eyelashes and pooling against his eyeball.

He didn't blink.

With a sudden flutter of alarm in his own heart, Jake saw that Harley's chest had ceased its rapid rise and fall, and he wondered if maybe his friend's heart had finally exploded.

It could have, he thought. *It was that big.*

Lori must have known, too. Until that moment she had only bitten her lip; now she buried her face in Jake's shoulder and wept.

Miss Agnes called Harley's name softly, once, and when he didn't respond she pressed her ear to his chest, though Jake could see in her eyes that she already knew. She straightened herself with what he would later describe in his journal as "classic farm-woman stoicism," then brought two fingertips to Harley's eyes, ever so gently, and closed them for him. Wrapping her arms around his shoulders, Miss Agnes drew him against her and pivoted gracefully in one dignified motion that left her sitting on the ground holding his dark head in the crook of her arm. She tugged the oxygen mask over his head, tossed it aside, and began to rock as if she were holding a sleeping child. She stroked his hair and smoothed it away from his face and she began to hum, quiet and low, the melody of an old forgotten hymn, a hymn about grace and the goodness of God and seeing loved ones again one day soon.

After a while she dabbed at her eyes with the back of a wrist and looked up and found Jake. Speaking in a hushed voice, she said, "Reckon you could go down to the shed for me and get Harley's quilt off his bunk? And bring me a shovel, too, please."

She was going to bury her boy. Jake hesitated for a moment but nobody spoke up, so he rose and started down the hill.

"Bring two," Web said.

The funeral was a small, private thing, exactly what Harley would have wanted. Just four people standing tired and dirty in the diamond-edged light of a September afternoon on the ridge. Web stood motionless with his head bowed. Miss Agnes held tight to Lori's arm, borrowing strength. A gentle breeze tugged at the pages as Jake read from the old zippered Bible he had found by Harley's bed. He turned, on impulse, to the one place Harley himself had underlined, and read:

"'God hath chosen the foolish things of the world to confound the wise; and God hath chosen the weak things of the world to confound the things which are mighty; and base things of the world, and things which are despised, hath God chosen, and things which are not, to bring to nought things that are: That no flesh should glory in his presence. But of him are ye in Christ Jesus, who of God is made unto us wisdom, and righteousness, and sanctification, and redemption: That, according as it is written, he that glorieth, let him glory in the Lord.'"

Then Miss Agnes, who had wept in silence until now, steeled herself and delivered a simple, eloquent eulogy they all would remember for the rest of their lives.

"There ain't but three things worth saying about somebody that's passed on, and I can truly say all three of this good man. I loved him. I'll miss him. And I'll not be the same for knowin' him."

Faintly, out of the distance, came the cry of a rain crow.

"Amen," Jake whispered.

Chapter Forty-nine

People say it's difficult, now, to remember Web the way he was before. He cleared away his old life as quietly and efficiently as another man might clear away the dinner dishes. His first order of business that fall was to rebuild Miss Agnes's house. He offered to build her any sort of house she wanted and even brought custom plans for her to look at—designs for houses four or five times larger than the one that had burned—but in the end she told him she wanted her new home to be just like the one she had lost. She knew what she needed and what she didn't; she said a bigger house was just more to clean. She did, however, make one unusual request: she wanted to move back up the hill to where her father's house had once stood, the place where she was born.

Carpenters, plumbers, electricians, painters, and landscapers swarmed over the site, and six weeks after the fire Miss Agnes moved into a brand-new house, built on the exact spot where she had lived as a child. Amazingly, the new house, from the tin roof to the rocking chairs on the front porch, was a perfect replica of the one that had burned.

During the construction Web came by every afternoon to monitor the progress, and more often than not he would stop by Nell Prudhomme's, pick up Miss Agnes, and bring her with him. In order to haul their tools and materials up the hill, the builders had carved a winding path to the site. The switchback trail proved too tight for his Mercedes so Web hired a crew to smooth and pave it, and then he parked a golf cart in the old barn at the bottom of the slope. At first it struck him as odd that a woman of Miss Agnes's advanced years would want to live in such a remote spot, not to mention putting an arduous climb between the house and her vegetable garden. The only explanation she offered was that she wanted to return to her childhood home, but after a few weeks he began to suspect another reason. Every day, when Web drove her to the homesite, she would bring flowers with her. And every day, while Web poked around and checked the progress of his contractors, Miss Agnes planted and tended the grounds around the crooked little chestnut sapling, which was now just down the hill and in plain sight from her new home.

As soon as Miss Agnes's house was completed Web began rebuilding the pavilion. It was only a gesture, a peace offering, he said, but there was nothing halfhearted about it. He imported a team of Amish craftsmen all the way from Ohio to handpick the logs and cut and saw and plane and chisel until a new timber-frame structure, every bit as grand and perfect as its predecessor, stood on the rocky point in the crook of the Elder River.

There were some legal problems at first, mostly stemming from the burning of Miss Agnes's house and fields. Against his lawyers' strident advice, Web pled guilty. The truth, he said, did not care about proof. But his remorse was evident, and the judge read a letter from Mrs. Dewberry about her new house on the ridge. Web's sentence was reduced to probation.

A small clique of people whispered about him when he first started accompanying Jenny to church—snide remarks about how he was throwing his money around, trying to buy his way into heaven—but when these rumors came back to him he only smiled, recalling the example of Zacchaeus and quietly pointing out that his wealth was only a means of making restitution. He sought no credit or public acclaim, mending his fences as anonymously as was possible in a small town, and he would take no position of authority in the church. After a while, even Orde Wingo stopped seeing him as a threat.

Dan O'Brien kept his land. There was a closed-door meeting in Web's office, and while no one knows exactly what transpired, it is common knowledge that shortly after the meeting Dan paid off his house and added a new sawmill and drying kiln to his woodshop. Web told Gerhard Klauss to take his winery elsewhere and scrapped his plans for a country club. His vast holdings above the escarpment on Chestnut Ridge were now landlocked; there was no access, no road frontage. But Web's priorities had changed. He held on to the land and made no new plans for it. It was as if he was waiting for directions.

He continued his visits to the ridge even after Miss Agnes had settled into her new house. Sometimes he would sit and rock on the porch with her, talking, or not talking, listening to the sounds of the evening as the shadows crawled up from the valley floor, watching deer tiptoe out from among the white oaks to nuzzle the ground for acorns. As others had done before him, Web gradually adopted Miss Agnes for his own.

He would on occasion go for long walks on the ridge. There were times in the winter when a freezing rain would whisper across the foothills in the cold hour before dawn, glazing a million skeletal trees with a brittle skin of ice, and midmorning would find Web wandering the ridge watching the frozen forest break the slanting light into a shimmering sea of diamonds. In the spring, when the temperatures and the sap began to rise, Web cultivated the habit of taking Eddy and Marcus to the ridge on Friday nights. They would raise a tent beside the lake, where he had once planned to build a conference center, and spend Saturday fishing and swimming and hiking.

Sometimes the dawn would find him sitting alone with a Bible on Joshua's Knee.

It was the boys who prompted Web to build the first cabin. He went along with the plan mainly because he wanted Jenny to join them on their camping trips. She had always expressed a pronounced disdain for tents; she didn't feel safe without four solid walls and a roof. So Web hired Jake Mahaffey to build a small rustic cabin with a loft and a wood stove.

One evening that fall, about a year after the flood, Web and Jenny and Jake and Lori found themselves sitting around a campfire between the cabin and the lake, and the talk naturally turned to the Women's Center. Web had helped to get it rezoned and open. Jenny and Lori had overseen the creation of a quietly powerful ministry where women in need of help found shelter and counseling.

But there had been problems. In its first year the Sutter's Cross Women's Center had outgrown the Barfield house and women had to be turned away. Also, the house was right in the middle of town, where there were too many activities going on around it. The summer busyness of the streets proved to be distracting for some of the younger guests, and the easy accessibility of the Barfield house had made it too simple for angry husbands to cause trouble.

"I hate to admit that Orde was right about anything," said Lori, "but the Barfield house does have its drawbacks. We need to be more secluded."

"We need to be out of town," Jenny agreed. "Life would be a lot simpler if we were out in the middle of the woods someplace."

The two women looked at each other. They looked at the dark woods and the moonlit lake, they looked at the cabin, they looked at each other again, and then they turned to Web.

Without taking his eyes from the fire Web saw the exchange of glances, heard the unspoken question. He leaned forward to poke the fire with a stick, and a knowing smile crept onto his face. "Let's do it," he said.

And so Web donated the ridgetop land to the Women's Center. Miss Agnes gave them a right-of-way to use her cart path and to pave it on up through a break in the escarpment. The narrow path would be the only entrance to the ridgetop land, which, in the end, was part of its charm. Over the next few years Web would pay Jake and his crew to build seventeen cabins along the ridge. The Women's Center grew into a renowned retreat, a refuge for battered women, pregnant teens, and drug-abusing housewives. Many of the retired doctors and nurses around Sutter's Cross volunteered their time, working alongside the full-time staff Lori and Jenny hired, which included trained counselors.

Jake built a lodge beside the lake to accommodate the staff. The cabins themselves were widely scattered, connected to the main lodge only by footpaths. Outside the staff offices the Women's Center didn't allow cell phones, radios, televisions, computers, or beepers within the retreat facilities, and even though the switchback trail up from Miss Agnes's farm had been smoothed and paved, the only motorized vehicles allowed up the hill were electric golf carts. The organization paid Miss Agnes for the right-of-way and for parking space down in the flat.

The retreat on Chestnut Ridge became widely known as One Tree, a name that came about because of something else that happened, something completely unexpected.

Something miraculous.

Miss Agnes tended Harley's grave meticulously. Near his grave a stunning, diverse flower garden materialized as she transplanted cuttings from house and woods, a garden anchored by the one sickly chestnut sapling sprouting from the roots of its disease-riddled ancestor.

In the spring of the year following the flood, the sapling came back a little straighter and with three new limbs. The year after that it began to burst upward and spread. Its trunk cracked and wrinkled and changed into the bark of a maturing tree, and still it did not die. The next year it began to bear fruit; botanists came to study and to take samples. With cautious optimism, word spread that the tree had somehow overcome the fungus and was indeed growing. The optimism grew bolder with each passing year.

On a brilliant afternoon in May, three years almost to the day after Harley had shown up at the church picnic, Web stopped by to see Miss Agnes on his way up to the retreat. The lodge was complete. Most of the cabins had been finished, and the place was blossoming into something extraordinary. As busy as he was, Web still took the time to check on Miss Agnes. It was a beautiful, cool, breezy day, and when Web showed up Miss Agnes wrapped a sweater about her shoulders and asked him to take her for a walk.

"The flowers are out," she said. "I want you to meet 'em."

Miss Agnes had slowed down some. She followed the ridgeline, going neither up nor down. She gripped Web's arm often, unsure of her footing in the woods and unable to see as well as she once could. She pointed out wood sorrel, like yellow-hearted peppermints on a bed of clover that grew out of the moss. She showed him big, blazing white triangles of trillium scattered among the hardwoods and an army of chickweed asterisks all along the path. Everywhere they looked the ridge exploded with new green, decorated by a thousand kinds of wildflowers.

Web listened to her, trying very hard to pay attention. But the breeze blew crisp out of the west, and the sun hung in a polished turquoise sky. His eyes were continually drawn away from the earth and toward the clouds.

"Cranesbill," she said, stooping and plucking a small blue flower to twirl between her fingers.

"Cranesbill," he repeated while nodding. Again his attention drifted.

They came to a creek and she stopped, the bank too steep for her to attempt. Clear water chuckled over the stones. She said something to him, but he didn't catch it. He was staring out over the valley.

"Excuse me?"

"Sweet white violet," she repeated and pointed to a cluster of tiny white flowers growing in the shade of the creek bank. She watched his face turn back to the sky, and she smiled. "Mister Web, I believe I done got too old to plow."

He nodded, not really listening.

She looked down upon her farm, spread out along the flat below them. "You know," she sighed, "I couldn't even plant a vegetable garden this year on account of my arthritis. I'm startin' to feel like a old woman."

He nodded absently. She kneaded her swollen hands. He was watching the fair-weather cumulus drift and swell, with bottoms flat and gray and perfectly aligned, as though they all sat heavily on the same invisible pane of glass.

"Seems a shame for such a pretty piece of land to lie fallow," she said.

"Uh-huh."

"I was thinking, what with the house and that stand of pines out of the way, it'd be a fine place to put a airstrip."

It took a moment for her words to reach him, but then his mind returned from cloud base and he looked her in the face, forgetting to close his mouth.

"Are you serious?"

She smiled. "I reckon maybe you can pay me a little rent so I can buy groceries."

It turned out to be a beautiful airfield, a half mile of manicured bluegrass lying neat and level at the foot of the slope. The soaring club managed the place well, caring for Miss Agnes's land as if it were a sanctuary—which, in many ways, it was.

Web had sold his Discus two years before the new gliderport was built. He now owned a two-place tandem sailplane, a docile old aluminum trainer called a Blanik, and began bringing the boys with him to the gliderport. Both Eddy and Marcus soloed a glider not long after learning to drive a car, and they grew into seasoned pilots while still in high school. Web became something of a hero with his son, and he saw to it that Marcus never lacked for a father figure.

On her eightieth birthday Miss Agnes showed up at the gliderport in her Sunday best and asked Web for a ride.

"I been watching y'all fly for a long time," she said, "and wondering what it was like. I reckon I'm old enough now it don't much matter if I get killed, so let's go."

With great care and ceremony Web strapped her into the front seat of the Blanik and took her up to soar on the gentle currents where the west wind climbed the face of the ridge. She loved every minute of it. Excitement forced a steady flood of words out of her, and she chattered on like a child, mapping out all the places she knew. She was clearly astonished to recognize familiar haunts from such an unearthly vantage point.

When Web judged that she'd had enough, he bled off altitude and entered the pattern, flying a long, slow downwind leg on the river side of the field. Testing the spoilers as they passed the midfield mark, he noticed that Miss Agnes had fallen utterly silent. She was staring at the ridge. Her house lay partially hidden in the woods above, and the chestnut tree was clearly visible farther down the slope, but he knew she wasn't looking at either of those. It was the sunlit granite ledge exactly at eye level that had seized her attention.

Shortly after Harley died, Web had hired a stonecutter, with Miss Agnes's consent, and commissioned the carving of an informal epitaph into the face of the granite, in letters three feet high. The cart path up to One Tree turned sharply in front of the bold inscription so that it soon became a sort of unofficial entry point to the retreat. A thousand times Miss Agnes had walked in front of the ledge and run her fingers over the letters, thumbing through worn pictures of Harley in her mind.

But she had never seen it like this. She pressed her fingertips to the glass as her ancient eyes softened with memory, and loss, and hope. The midday sun sliced neatly across the face of the rock and raised the words in striking relief: WE ARE THE ARMS OF GOD.

Epilogue

Lori's problems eventually returned and multiplied. The number of errant cells in her blood rose to unacceptable levels, and the treatment made her sicker than the cells ever had. Her thick red hair fell out, first by strands, then clumps, then handfuls, and she suffered through endless bouts of exhaustion and nausea. But she never stopped working, never complained. Several of the guests of the retreat later confessed a seismic shift in attitude wrought solely by the daily example of the pallid woman in the floppy hat who never, ever, quit. One cynical sixteen-year-old girl with a belly like a spinnaker found Lori doubled over with nausea one summer morning, down on her knees next to the path, and stopped to see about her.

With a smirk the girl asked, "Do you still think every day is a gift?"

"Yesss," Lori wheezed, too weak even to raise her head. "Don't you?"

Sometimes, during the dark days when Lori's very life seemed always to hang from the results of the next lab test, Jake would come and sit on the garden bench in the shadow of the chestnut tree in the late afternoon. Usually he came toward sunset, after the air had cooled and the clouds had dissolved, and he would see the sailplanes ghosting home, hugging the windward slopes of the ridge until they peeled away and circled the field, settling at last on the turf. But there was one particular day he would always remember, the day he came early.

He ate lunch with Lori that day, a picnic with her and some of the staff of One Tree. He watched her in the sunlight, and it broke his heart the way she lived and laughed and kept on walking, the way she so easily adjusted her stride to compensate for the weight of fear and pain. He smiled then, for her, but the pretense drained him, so when lunch was over he stole away to the garden bench to be still for a while. His heart poured out a plea, and then he leaned back on the bench to listen for the quiet voice of God, the resonant hum of truth.

The chestnut tree rustled and swayed in a sudden gust, and moments later two sailplanes swooped in from opposite directions, banking into a fresh thermal directly overhead. Jake lay watching, mesmerized, while the two porcelain birds danced a graceful pavane, climbing the sky together as if lifted by an invisible hand, all the way up to the clouds. He lay there smiling and did not stir until after they had gone.

"'Preciate it," he whispered, and then went to check on his crew.

Reading Group Discussion Guide

Sutter's Cross

1. Sutter's Cross, the town, though beautiful, is built on a legacy of suffering and pain. Think on how the natural beauty acts as a facade for some of the problems in the town. Also discuss how others in the book (a family, a church, a business) mask their problems with a good front. Keep in mind the town is named for a cross as a monument erected in honor of the founder's son, whom he had lost.

2. Jake Mahaffey serves an interesting role in the book, partly as protagonist, but more frequently as an observer. Discuss Jake's life and what he learns through his interactions with his wife, with Web, and particularly with Harley.

3. Web Holcombe's motto for life comes from his time soaring in a glider. He defines it as, "Understand your environment and the laws of its movement, know your limitations and your strengths, command your ship and yourself, and you can soar higher, faster, farther than the next man." Explain why it's so disconcerting for Web to lose control like he does with his glider.

4. "Land," "nature," and "home" are three very important concepts in the book. Web Holcombe stands on one extreme of the spectrum while the people he is trying to buy out, including Agnes Dewberry, stand on the other. Harley accuses Web of being "wrong" in trying to buy Agnes's land. Is he? What is the "right" way to be in connection to the earth?

5. Web's story is one, particularly, of fathers and sons. Discuss his relationship with Will Holcombe as a son and his relationship with Eddy as a father. How is he making some of the same mistakes his father did? Why would a son with a moral father turn out so antagonistic both to religion and morality?

6. Discuss Harley, his conversion experience and his faith. Contrast this with the faith exhibited by Orde Wingo, for example, or others in the story. What are the similarities and differences?

7. Benny T, the ponytailed "enforcer," has a theory that if you find a person's name, you can find a person's past. And if you find a man's past, you can own that man. What in each of the characters' pasts could be used to own them? How can you not let the past own you?

8. Discuss the various signs used by the church in their marketing. Why is there such bitter humor in its message? Discuss the role the sign plays in the novel's climax and why the church bears such a burden for how it presents itself to the world. How does the sign work as a symbol in terms of motive, appearances, and the idea of communicating an accurate representation of Christ? How would you describe the link here between motive and appearance?

9. How do Marcus and Eddy differ as children? What does Marcus teach Eddy? What does Eddy teach Marcus?

10. The storm that hammers Sutter's Cross becomes a turning point for most of the characters. Why is it that the storms of life often cause so many life changes?

11. What do you think *We are the arms of God* means to each of the main characters in the book?